The Fool's Journey

A Romance

Lynn C. Miller

WINEDALE PUBLISHING

Houston

Published by Winedale Publishing Co.

Published in the United States by Winedale Publishing Co., Houston

www.winedalebooks.com

Direct quotations from Edith Wharton's work reprinted by permission
of the Edith Wharton Estate and the Watkins/Loomis Agency

This book is a work of fiction. Although some of its buildings share a
resemblance to those of a famous research university, Austin University does not
exist. All characters, departments, colleges, and events in *The Fool's Journey* are
entirely creations of the author's imagination.

Library of Congress Cataloging-in-Publication Data

Miller, Lynn C., 1951-
The fool's journey / Lynn C. Miller.— 1st ed.
p. cm.
ISBN 0-9701525-8-2 (alk. paper)
1. Women college teachers—Fiction. 2. Wharton, Edith,
1862-1937—Appreciation—Fiction. 3. English teachers—Fiction. 4.
Biographers—Fiction. 5. Tarot—Fiction. I. Title.
PS3613.I544 F66 2002
813'.6—dc21
2002010447
Manufactured in the United States of America
2 4 6 8 9 7 5 3
First Edition

Book design by Harriet Correll
Jacket Design by D.J. Stout and Julie Savasky

For Lynda, a wise fool

Acknowledgments

I am grateful to my publisher Babette Hale for her belief in this novel and her expertise in bringing it to fruition, and to early readers of the book who shared their insights and enjoyment with me, especially Claire Van Ens, Laura Furman, Christie Logan, Lee Potts and my irreverent book group (Leslie, Jean, Biruta, Helen, Mary S., Mary L., Lynda, and Stan). Linda MacNeilage and Charlotte Morrow McClure generously guided me along my own fool's journey while I was writing this book. The Dorset Colony House in Dorset, Vermont, provided me with peace and space to write in April of 1999. Thanks to Carol Bly, whose writing workshop stimulated the first incarnation of "Ivory Power." Much of the pleasure in writing this novel I owe to my partner Lynda Miller, whose faith and humor continually inspire me.

THE FOOL´S JOURNEY

0: The Fool

*How often in life do we stand at the edge of a precipice, daring ourselves
to hurtle our bodies—and lives—into the unknown? Years slip by,
passively, sleepily. Then one day, dreaming of change, we jump out of bed
and dive headfirst into the shock of the new.*

—*Daphne Arbor,* diary

"**Y**ou're good, my dear, I grant you that." Sigmund rolled over and
flopped one grizzled arm across Fiona's pillow, snagging and detach-
ing one of her earrings in the process. Those casual words and the
punctuation of this careless movement lifted a veil from Fiona's critical eye. She winced, rubbed her ear, and looked at the gray wispy
hairs scattered across his upper arm, the skin sagging along the bone.
Hadn't that arm—just last year, or the year before—been firmly mus-
cled, the arm, surely, of a much younger man?

Fiona's inner self observed her listless body lying next to
Sigmund's. The sight sent a seismic shudder down her spine. What
was she doing here, at her age? She'd been having an affair with
Sigmund Froelich, the Chair of her department, for nine years. What
had begun as a delicious escapade in her thirties, fueled by the illicit
thrill of sleeping with an older, more powerful, and decisively married man, had degenerated in her mid-forties into a boring, dead-end,

1

and derisively middle-aged routine. How had she overlooked how absolutely *tired* it all was? Fucking Sigmund seemed about as glamorous as poring over the dusty stacks in the university's special collection of Rupert Barlowe, obscure English poet and academic specialty of Sigmund Froelich.

"Sig, I need to talk to you about something." Fiona propped her back against the headboard and took in the room: the patchy, stained green carpet, the faux-rustic furnishings clumped along the walls, and the green-striped wallpaper (funny how she had never noticed before that it glossed the room in a shiny, plasticky sheen as if the entire space had been shrink-wrapped). This was Room 14 in the Manor Inn, the same room where they'd met twice a month, always on Wednesdays, for almost a decade.

She fished out her underwear from the slush pile of clothing next to the bed and balanced first on one thin leg and then the other, gingerly threading in one foot at a time. Feeling alarming twinges in her left knee and lower back, she cursed the day and encroaching mortality. She buckled a wide leather belt over her wrinkled jersey top and made a vow: she would never again set foot in this room or in this motel, and certainly not in the company of this man.

"Dearest, can't it wait?" Sigmund fumbled with his watch, pulled it within an inch of his pale blue eyes, and slapped it back down on the bedside table. "Damn. I have Executive Council in thirty minutes."

"That's what I want to talk with you about."

Sigmund groaned and hauled his six foot frame out of the bed. "Really, Fiona, I can hardly think today."

Fiona folded her arms tightly across her chest and counseled herself to be silent. It was interesting how at night Sig plotted to get her into bed with all of the concentration of a field marshal, then inevitably, the next morning, complained that his brain couldn't function. Fiona did not delude herself; this was not a compliment. Sigmund did not "lose his head" from unbridled passion. The fact was that having released his allotted portion of lust for the day (or perhaps the week,

Sig's rhythms being somewhat vague to her even after all this time), he had now moved on to the next agenda item in his life, which did not include her. Sigmund was a creature devoted to an order comprehensible only to himself.

"Sig, why is the Council convening today?"

"Oh, you know, the pesky promotions' discussion we have every Fall."

"Precisely. Is there nothing you have to tell me about this meeting?"

Sigmund looked up from knotting a red silk tie, a gift from Fiona, his face registering a blank owl-like stare. "I don't think so. It's not terribly interesting, even to me, so I can't imagine how it could be to you."

Fiona inhaled deeply. "My file is among those being considered for promotion."

Sigmund's eyes widened in disbelief. "Surely, my dear, you haven't been here long enough to be promoted, again?"

"Oh, for heavens sake, my last promotion was nine years ago!"

"Ah." Sigmund inclined his head as if that explained something of great significance. Fiona uncomfortably saw the correlation at once: she had begun sleeping with Sigmund on the eve of that promotion. She felt her face flush with the painful knowledge of time lost: her younger incarnation had obviously inspired more consideration.

Fiona sat down on the bed and forced herself to look Sigmund in the eye. "Sig. You are the chair of our department. You know perfectly well that I'm up for promotion. Of all people, you know. You have to write summaries for the file. What's going on?"

Sigmund patted her arm and then toyed with the prominent bone of her wrist. He smiled suddenly, his teeth broad and white; someone had once told him he had a disarming smile, and he used it prophylactically and often.

The smile relieved Fiona, giving her a glimpse of the old Sigmund who had first attracted her. She placed her hand over his. Only to remove it as his smile vanished and Sig spoke smoothly: "Going on?

Nothing, my dear, nothing. I'd just forgotten, that's all. You know that when I'm with you I forget that tedious other world—of departments and colleagues and budgets and you know, the deadly details of it all."

Fiona spoke softly, "Yes, but I'm part of that other world, as tedious as it may be. It's important to me."

"Of course it is," he smiled again, and thought a moment, adding, "Fiona, darling."

Minutes later, Fiona drove slowly on 26th Street, crossed the freeway, and threaded her way through the motley architecture of Austin University: the vintage red-roofed buildings with generous windows stood out cozily among newer, more severe structures.

What was Sigmund up to? Or was it just his usual benign neglect—not just of her, but of people in general? He was largely enthralled by a lifelong project: the ongoing chronicles of Sigmund. He lived for his pupils' adoration and his research, continually preoccupied with his national reputation which, however inflated, could never match his appetite for recognition. That appetite, wolfish and insatiable, sharpened with each advancing year. The rest didn't register.

Face it, Fiona, she told herself severely, you're a fool. You convinced yourself you cared for a man who can't focus on you long enough to see you. How could he see you? You stand too close. For Sigmund was a man blinded by his dream, a stunted Galileo spending his days peering anxiously at the horizon, at the beckoning constellation of his influence.

Sigmund believed himself to be A Great Man. He had a wife (Alverne, whose corporate job earned the big income needed to satisfy Sigmund's tastes for fine food, hip art, and lavish domestic accoutrements), and two children (Albert and Bob, neither bookish), a department of colleagues (thirty in all), and a host of graduate students who had laid down their lives in the service of his belief. Sigmund wore his greatness like an impenetrable skin, and his delusion protected him utterly. If he forgot something, someone pronounced that he was preoccupied by lofty thoughts; if he betrayed a confidence, well, a colleague ascribed that to a short-term sacrifice for a nobler long-term goal; if he publicly lacerated a student, another quickly excused him for his impeccable standards of perfection.

What a hoax! And to make it worse, Fiona had been a conspirator in Sigmund's Great Man Fantasy—had willingly thrown her own body on the sacrificial pyre of this feeble flame—for nine whole years. She rolled down the window of her battered and beloved MGB, and in homage to a favorite old movie, screamed into the humid autumn air: "I'm mad as hell and I'm not going to take it anymore!" She was no actress and doubted that anyone had witnessed her public rage. It didn't matter; she found it very satisfying.

When Sigmund tapped on her office door nine years ago, he had been forty-eight, with graying black hair and crisp blue eyes. His lean, mature look gave him an air both sexy and distinguished, a fatal combination for Fiona, who thought men her own age callow and ill-formed.

It was the autumn in which she had forwarded her file for tenure and Fiona was slumped over a stack of papers, stuporous. Her neck ached from her poor posture—marked by the aggressive head-jut of the computer-bound—and her patience had snapped ten minutes before when the seventh student in a row misspelled pursue as "persue." Why this small misstep should bother her, she had no idea. She discovered more egregious errors routinely—the popularity of "whatever," the proliferation of mangled clauses, the clutching for clarity. One student's succinct conclusion to an essay had become a personal favorite: "It. Was. So."

Sigmund had smiled sympathetically, "Teaching composition this semester?"

"God, yes, with a vengeance it seems. You know, it's one of those days when I can't seem to meet a paper I like."

Sigmund wore very white tennis shoes and shorts which displayed muscular, tanned legs. His eyes noted hers sweeping across his body. "Do you play?" he asked casually.

Fiona gratefully pushed away from her desk and crossed her legs. She wore her university uniform of a long skirt, short boots, and a sweater. Next to Sigmund's scantly-clothed body, she felt over-dressed and underexpressed. "Yes. I'm a little rusty but I used to play a lot. In graduate school."

Sigmund neatly removed a pile of papers from her desk and perched trim hips on its edge. He moved almost languidly, as if he had all the time in the world, a rare quality in the rushed and stressed world of academe. He folded his hands on one knee. "Tell me again where you come from—?"

Should she recite the long list of her family's many moves? An Air Force brat, Fiona was accustomed to the glazed look in her listeners' eyes when this simple question spurred a litany of dates and places. Best to keep it simple. "Pennsylvania."

Sigmund's eyes brightened. "Oh, that's right, your Ph.D. is from Penn, isn't it?"

"Penn State." Fiona watched his face carefully for a sign that such institutional distinctions mattered.

"Ah." His face was polite, unreadable. "Good school. Was Blakely still there when you were?"

"Just retired. But I took his last class. It was really something—on the last day, the back of the room and the hallway were packed. People sat on steps, stood in the aisles. And after the last lecture the ovation—it must have gone on for five minutes." Fiona smiled shyly. "I almost expected an encore. It was like he was a pop star or something."

"He was my adviser," Sigmund said simply. "A brilliant, kind man. There was no one like him. He wrote thirty books, but he was as humble as a first-year student."

"You graduated from Penn State also?" Fiona was eager to discover a shared history, a fateful rendezvous of their pasts that arced forward and created this present moment of recognition.

"No. He was at Cornell some years before." He laughed self-consciously but with an underlying confidence. "I'm afraid I'm dating myself."

Fiona was charmed. Sigmund looked years younger than his age—forty at most—his graying hair and fine lines adding a gloss of maturity to his still-youthful appearance. "Well, the years do speed by, don't they?" She looked up, abashed. "That's not what I meant—that's not how you appear. Oh, damn it, you know what I mean: the hazard of teaching is seeing those students stay the same every year while we, well, we just don't."

"Well put. We just don't. It is a profession that builds in a feeling of decrepitude, isn't it? All that unspoiled youth." Sigmund smiled, showing even white teeth. "Isn't it odd how we professors all prize youth so much? It's a kind of torture, I find. To know that eventually, no matter how well we age, all the students will dismiss us as old farts? We can't escape it." His blue eyes peered at her, dreamy and soft. "But I can't see how you'd know anything about that. You don't look a day over twenty-five yourself."

Fiona uncrossed her legs and unconsciously squared her shoulders. "Twenty-five is so long ago that I can't remember it," she said quickly. Then, she heard a voice she thought she had banished long ago, gushing, punctuated by a girlish giggle, continue: "But that's nice to hear all the same. We're all late bloomers in my family. I think it keeps us looking young, or eager, or something."

Sigmund's eyes scanned her bookshelves and then returned to her face. "You're too modest. Your record hardly reflects lateness about anything. Very impressive. You're coming up for tenure this fall, aren't you?"

Fiona experienced a momentary deflation. "Yes. God, yes. I'd forgotten it for a moment. First time in three months it hasn't been constantly on my mind."

"And then I, in my blundering way, had to ruin the moment by asking you about it." Sigmund stood up quickly and held out his hand. "Come," he said. "It's a beautiful October day. Let's go somewhere and enjoy it."

Fiona looked at the stack of papers in front of her and then at her watch. "Oh, well, thank you...Sigmund. But I have so much work..."

"Call me Sig," he said, pulling her gently up out of her seat. "I'm Chair of this department and I think one of my faculty is working much too hard." He flashed those even teeth again, a signal to adventure. "This doctor says you need a break."

Succumbing gratefully, Fiona closed the door with a flourish as they walked into the hall. "And this doctor is out."

"That's the spirit," Sig approved.

"You may have unleashed a monster," Fiona said. "Up for a set or two of tennis?"

Sigmund punched the plastic oval by the elevator. "Think I'm over the hill, do you, that I can't stay the course? Now you've let the monster out of his cage. You'll see—I'm game." He winced. "Oh, that was corny, wasn't it?"

They started to laugh as the elevator doors opened before them, discharging a lean-faced senior faculty member. "Good afternoon," Professor Lester said, his pebble gray eyes flitting across Fiona's torso before settling on Sigmund's face. He turned a precise right, heading toward the main office.

"Lester is so dour," Sigmund pronounced. "He gives faculty members a bad reputation."

Fiona watched Lester's straight, surprisingly agile figure march down the hall. "He looks like he used to be terribly handsome. Was he?"

"No, he was always homely, only now he looks like he *used* to be good-looking." Sigmund said, running one fine hand through his hair. "Sad."

"Oh." Fiona considered. "Did you say 'hideous' or 'homely'?"

"Homely. But you're right, hideous is more apt."

Fiona burst out laughing and Sigmund quickly ushered them both into the elevator and punched the 'close' button. "Get a hold of yourself, woman," he said, "you'll ruin my reputation."

The elevator lurched. Fiona braced herself against the back wall. "Which is?"

"Dour, homely, and hideous." Sigmund's blue eyes bored into her own as he slouched toward her and placed his mouth on hers. His lips were cool and fresh and a little sticky; they reminded Fiona of a favorite caramel she used to eat at the movies as a girl.

That afternoon changed Fiona's pleasant, but somewhat quiet routine as a faculty member in the Department of Literature and Rhetoric. Sigmund had been so much fun, so bright, so engaging. Then. Thinking about their protracted affair these long years later, Fiona suddenly found herself mouthing "It. Was. So."—the truncated conclusion that had so irritated her as an assistant professor. She saw why her former student had been enamored of those three words, punctuated by periods, as a finishing flourish. Three bald words that certainly signified the end.

She was back in her office in Helmsley Hall, waiting for Sigmund to come by after Executive Council. On her desk was her book manuscript, which after years of work was still only a slim hundred pages. As she stared at it, its title, in bold print, wavered in and out of focus: *Edith Wharton: A Life Apart.* In spite of her passion for Wharton's fiction, her tireless teaching of her works in seminars, her several well-received essays on the author, she had found herself blocked at the enormity of the biographer's task. Somehow, the shy, bold, brilliant, lonely, intensely private and yet very visible artist who wrote so passionately about the lives of women eluded her. Her own articulation of such a dazzling subject was flat and opaque. It just wouldn't do.

In years past, Fiona had been able to rise to the occasion of a difficult project. If she could not immediately summon eloquence, her unfailing discipline eventually created its own inspiration. But not this time. Deflated, Fiona looked out the window and noticed a female cardinal vigorously retrieving a sunflower seed from the lawn. The bird's orange beak gleamed in the sun; her swift spiral to the top of a tree signaled purpose and pleasure in movement. Fiona's head drooped forward onto the desk. Her own mouth felt hollow, empty, and hungry. If only she knew how to gather the seeds of her ideas and plant them, Fiona thought. As a scholar, as a writer, as a critic, she felt she was losing her grasp.

At 10:30, precisely two hours after she had left Sigmund at the Manor Inn, he stumbled into her office, looking unusually disheveled and sheepish.

He fingered his crimson silk tie and then loosened it. "Fiona, my dear, I'm miserably sorry but there was simply nothing I could do."

Fiona felt a terrible hot sensation in the center of her chest, a molten, stifled sob. "The committee—?" she managed just two words. She licked parched lips and reached unsteadily for the bottle of water she kept on her desk.

"They don't think you're ready for promotion to full professor. They think it's inevitable, *of course,* when the next book is done." He pronounced "of course" in a conspiratorial "it's-all-such-garbage-but-it's-the-system" tone. Seeing her stricken face, he added delicately: "That delay with your publisher—I know it wasn't your fault—hurt you considerably."

"But, the review committee told me that my file was substantial enough without it." Fiona could hear the doggedness in her voice, the futile defensiveness. It was a tone she decried in her students.

Sigmund pursed his full lips which were very red. Fiona had once found those lips sensual and promising; now she saw them as obscene. "Fiona, no file is substantial enough when the next book has been expected. Nay, when it has been promised, for what?" He scrutinized her, the judicious parent registering disapproval in his progeny, "For four years now?" He shook his head, his normally lustrous gray hair—a point of pride in his late fifties—a bit stringy around his forehead. Sigmund hadn't had time to shower this morning, as Fiona well knew.

Fiona closed her eyes briefly. Sigmund had, as somehow she knew he would, betrayed her; the Executive Council followed his lead on promotions. He hadn't argued her case strongly. For whatever reason, or perhaps for no reason, he simply didn't make the effort. "I see," she said.

Sigmund's face flushed as he sat down next to her; he patted her hand roughly. His face had lapsed into kind, patient lines. "You mustn't worry. It's not the end of the world. You're a tenured professor, Fiona. You can go up again next year and doubtless, the result will be much different." He smiled at her, an invitation. She withdrew her hand and waited a moment. She attempted to summon the strength to tell Sigmund, in her usual tactful way, to vacate her office. But tactful words eluded her. After a long silence, she heard a low, steady voice speak bluntly, coldly, and decisively: "It is the end of the world. This world anyway. I'm resigning, Sigmund."

"What?" Sigmund blinked his eyes rapidly. She could see his mind absorb his miscalculation—there would be no more Wednesdays at the Manor Inn, no more votes from Fiona out of loyalty supporting his decisions or the classes he desired to teach, no more compliments from this younger, female colleague who had viewed him as a mentor. For a moment in his uncertainty, he looked young and almost appealing. Then he retreated into briskness. "Nonsense. I reject your resignation. No one resigns over these matters. It's just politics. Why, you could be chair of the department in five years." He pursed his lips. Fiona assumed that out of kindness he omitted saying, "Unlikely, of course. But possible."

"No thanks, Professor Froelich," Fiona said. Inside, in the part of her that wanted to cry from sheer injustice and humiliation, she observed this new ruthless Fiona and wondered where she had come from. She straightened the edges of the manuscript pages in front of her and picked up a pen.

Sigmund stood up quickly. "You clearly need time to adjust. I'll leave you alone. I think the shock has addled your thinking. Of course, this setback is unfortunate. But heavens, woman. Resign?!" His usual smooth delivery cracked as he uttered that last word, a marked lapse—a steady old wagon derailed by a crack in the road. "It's inconceivable that you would leave us over such a thing. Absurd! My God, to leave this excellent position, in this superb university, not to mention all of us, your friends, your colleagues." He drew himself up, realizing he was beginning to rant. "I'll talk to you later," he said gruffly. He adjusted his tie snugly against his collar, squared his shoulders, and managed a slow dignified walk to the door.

As he was drawing the door closed behind him, Fiona called after him in a quiet voice. "Sigmund? I forgot to tell you something."

Sigmund turned, his face lapsing into a hopeful smile. "Yes, my dear?"

"You are an evil man." Fiona smiled, she hoped prettily, and turned her eyes to the pages lying on the desk, her heart pounding as if she had been onstage before a huge audience. The Department of Literature and Rhetoric, she realized at this clarifying moment, often provoked in her symptoms of stage fright. Had she only been performing the entire time she'd been working there, never comfortable to be herself? Sigmund had bullied her—no that wasn't true: she had allowed Sigmund to bully her. She would allow it no more.

It was as if years of stale air followed Sigmund out the door as he left her office. Fiona felt energized, almost euphoric. She supposed she would crash later, a mass of nerves and regret. But at the moment, the world spread out before her, as if she had finally found the key to a perpetually-locked door. Now that sealed door swung open, revealing an expanse of sky and land, inviting her into a totally new universe.

I: The Magician

Great shifts in cosmology occur sometimes very simply. In Greek
mythology all that may be required is a message from the Gods, as when
Hermes rescued Persephone from the underworld and gave her back to
her mother Demeter, the goddess of the earth. Afterward, Hades, the lord
of the underworld, kept Persephone only four months of every year. Thus
was winter born, for in those four months Demeter grieved and allowed
nothing to grow upon the earth. Each spring, her daughter rose from the
dead and returned to earth, and the land bloomed once again. A stunning
transformation may occur swiftly, but only with the aid of a catalyst: A
messenger. Or a teacher. Or a guide.

—Sigmund Froelich, introductory lecture to "Myth and Literature"

The next afternoon found Fiona in the office of her colleague
Miriam Held. Miriam, a solidly-built woman in her late fifties, had an
incisive mind—and a sharp tongue—that belied her bland, pleasant
face and lank, gray hair. Miriam was the most senior woman in the
Department of Literature and Rhetoric and its former chair; her sage
counsel was highly prized by younger faculty.

"It's a storm, Fiona," Miriam spoke bluntly but kindly. "You must
simply weather it."

"A storm?" Fiona replied numbly. "It feels like the end of the world."

"Nonsense." With surprising agility in one so stout, Miriam bent over and disappeared for a moment behind her desk, reappearing with a rock crystal glass filled with smoky, amber liquid. "Glenmorangie," she said. "Drink up. Doctor's orders."

Fiona complied, dimly thinking that her colleagues seemed to regard their doctor of philosophy as an extremely fluid degree.

"Look," Miriam spoke earnestly, her small brown eyes bright and warm. "I know you're devastated about the promotion. Believe me, I'm almost as upset about it as you are. It's a nasty business. However, it's happened before and it will happen again. You will get past this. You will get promoted." She added with asperity: "You'll just have to tough it out."

Fiona wondered if Miriam's eclectic past included a stint as head coach. "You've experienced a situation like this?" She sipped the single malt appreciatively.

Miriam laughed, a hearty sound levitating between a guffaw and a cackle. "My dear, if I'd run away from this place every time someone tried to get rid of me or failed to appreciate me I wouldn't have lasted one month. Really. When I was hired, women rarely rose above the rank of lecturer." She paused, and shook her head. "Not that we've progressed much. Females are still appreciated around here more as nubile graduate students than serious professionals."

"You give me so much hope." Fiona peered at her over her glass glumly.

Miriam half-rose and reached across the desk with a blunt-fingered hand to pat Fiona's shoulder. "I don't mean to depress you further. Things shouldn't be the way they are. But they are. No use hiding from reality. Remember, inner direction not external approval. That's the spirit to get you through these bad times." She frowned and thrummed her fingers on her desk. "Has this setback affected your work?"

"Work?" The word sounded dully on Fiona's ears. "Which aspect? Teaching? Research?" She raised her arms as if to indicate all of Helmsley Hall; her voice cracked. "My enthusiasm for being here?"

"Ah. I guess it was a stupid question. Of course everything appears altered right now." She studied Fiona with sharp eyes and a determined set of her jaw, an aging Athena surveying the battlefield's wreckage. "So," Miriam's breath lingered on the "o" as if it were a sigh. "Are you seeing anyone about this?"

"Well…I don't think I have grounds for a grievance."

"Hmmm. You should, of course, pursue that avenue if you feel so inclined. I was thinking of someone in the more personal, rather than professional, realm."

"Oh. You mean, like a therapist?"

"Yes?"

"Well, no." Fiona frowned and carefully set the glass of whiskey, now empty, on Miriam's desk. "Actually my first husband…well, my only husband…was a psychiatrist." She added hurriedly: "I just haven't had the best of luck in the therapy realm."

"I see," said Miriam. She wore no make-up, and in her pale face, her eyes—inquisitive, intelligent, a deep, polished brown—riveted Fiona's attention. "Well, I have a friend who is excellent in situations like this." She considered Fiona carefully. "She's not involved with the university. In any way. However, she's smart, she doesn't give advice, and she's not a goody two-shoes who pretends that everything will be fine. But she's very insightful. And discreet, of course."

The muscles of Fiona's upper back twanged with tension and her head throbbed. She did feel overburdened at the moment. The thought of a perceptive ear—particularly one not connected to the workplace—was seductive. "And she's not a therapist?'

Miriam folded her hands softly on her desk. "Daphne is trained, certainly. And she is a consummate practitioner in the healing arts. But her talents did not emerge from any institutional affiliation. Some would call her New Age, but that would be reductive in the case of such a unique and far-ranging perception. She possesses psychic gifts." Miriam cast a sharp glance at Fiona. "Does that bother you?"

"Bother me?" Fiona was startled. "Should it?" Like most people, she often thought of herself as unusually perceptive.

"Of course not. Some academics are...well, let's just say some academics are prejudiced against anything not easily categorized. Or, to them, rational." Unexpectedly, Miriam giggled. "As if the unconscious antagonisms we've just witnessed, from Sigmund for instance, could be called rational."

Fiona stiffened, her shoulder muscles protesting once again.

"Oh, Fiona, please don't think I'm making light of your situation." Miriam shook her head somberly, her gray hair gleaming dully under the fluorescent lights. "It just amazes me, the acts that are sanctioned under the heavy armor of reason."

Her words galvanized Fiona who suddenly had an urge to flee the building; she pictured it tilting dangerously, pulled off-kilter by its disproportion of left-brained intelligence. She extended a hand. "Why don't you give me her name and number and I'll think about it."

The building was neat and small, a small bungalow in one of Austin's oldest neighborhoods, its small wooden porch the only flourish on an otherwise square and plain structure. Modestly beige with brown trim, the place displayed no signs that a unique being dwelt within. But—Fiona's eyes swept the lavender post-it note in her hand for perhaps the tenth time—this was the place she had been instructed to find: 777 West Lynn. The door was slightly ajar. Fiona passed through and stood in the entryway, expecting at least the ominous ticking of an antique clock, the creaking of a sagging floorboard. But the office was quiet. She sat down on the edge of a plain wood captain's chair, and waited.

Her appointment was for 10:30 and at precisely 10:35 a woman appeared in the doorway. Stout and squarish, with a deeply tanned face, the woman was draped in a simple black robe. She regarded Fiona frankly. The one lavish thing about her was her hair, bright silver and spilling from her head in a tumble of curls, Medusa-like. But on closer inspection, there was nothing severe or forbidding in the keen gaze. The face was open and soft. Still, Fiona welcomed the wild hair—she was relieved to see something exotic in this plain and silent house.

"Ms. Hardison?" The voice was low but grainy, a rush of liquid over rough-cut stone.

Fiona nodded, and inclined her head almost in supplication. Even though in early middle age herself, she felt an urge to assume the role of an acolyte in the woman's stolid presence.

"I am Daphne Arbor." The woman stepped forward and grasped both of Fiona's hands in hers. She held them a moment too long, and Fiona felt a flush of heat in her fingers that leapt up her arms. She took a step back, withdrawing her hands, and hugged her arms tightly to her chest.

"Hello." Her eyes wandered over the peach-colored walls, searching for something to focus on, and then seized upon an oval creamy stone that hung at the woman's throat.

Daphne took her arm, her tone suddenly brisk and businesslike. "Come this way and sit down. Make yourself comfortable." They passed into a small room. Cave-like, it was crammed with couches and cushions. A square table stood in the center of the room. Under it was a gray and red Navajo rug. The blinds were pulled and soft light spilled from three small lamps placed on the carpet's edges.

Fiona hesitated and sat away from the light on a rust-red sofa and took off her shoes. Daphne sat next to her. Noticing that cards were laid out on the table, Fiona pointed to it. "Or should I sit there?"

"This is fine for now. Tell me why you've come."

Fiona wanted to protest, "But that's what I want you to tell me!" Instead, she thought a moment, twisting the ring on her right hand with the fingers of her left. "Well, I'm not sure. I guess I'm at a crossroads." She looked at Daphne's intelligent face, focused on her, almost in rapt attention. "It's more than that. Nothing seems to be working anymore.

The fact is, I'm resigning from my job, well, from my profession. I was forced to, really. Oh, it's a long story, sordid politics, you've probably heard it too many times before. You don't want to hear it again."

Daphne waited, and then said, "You must let me be the judge of that. However, perhaps talking is not what you want to be doing right now. Let me look at you."

Fiona flinched. Hadn't that been what the woman had been doing since she met her, looking at her, or rather, scrutinizing her? Still, she attempted to sit still and to pull her shoulders back. The muscles in her neck remained bunched and painful.

Daphne cocked her head to one side, her silver hair slithering across her shoulders, a lioness contemplating her prey. Her eyes passed slowly over Fiona's long red skirt, white blouse, and plaid vest. "You crave invisibility but you often call attention to yourself," she said softly in that voice with its touch of hoarseness, giving her words a sound of intimacy no matter what their content. "That is something torturing you now—you wish to make a difference, to be noticed, yet you want to go on as before, quietly. You are how old?" Her eyes calculated quickly. "45. Perhaps 46."

Fiona felt a sharp pang, seeing her youthful self recede in front of her very eyes. The woman had guessed right the first time; so much for Fiona's decades-old belief that she looked much younger than her age.

Daphne laughed. "You can't go on, yet you must go on. A common condition. Not to say you are in the least common. Oh, no. Let us look at this closely. Come over to the table and shuffle the cards."

Fiona looked down at her feet, nestling on the floor in a pigeon-toed huddle. They looked incapable of carrying her anywhere. Yet she picked up her shoes and padded obligingly over to the table.

The chair was straight-backed but very comfortable, its very rigidity imbuing her body with structure. Resting on the table was an oversized pack of dazzling blue and white cards. She picked them up; surprisingly heavy, they felt cold and lifeless in her hands.

"Shuffle the cards slowly. Think about yourself. Meditate on what brought you here, questions you might have. Most of all, take your time. The cards will let you know when they are ready." Daphne arranged herself carefully in a chair opposite Fiona, smoothing her gown and touching the stone at her throat almost like a talisman. She pushed the hair away from her face. Fiona noticed for the first time that her eyes were slightly different from one another, one a tawny yellow with black flecks and the other a darker brown. Both of her pupils seemed unusually large. She waited, detached and yet attentive. Sitting motionless, like a cat, she appeared effortlessly relaxed and yet complete in her focus. Fiona found herself so curious about what the woman could be thinking, she found it difficult to concentrate on herself. On what her friend Miriam called with authority her "inner voices."

"I remind you that the Tarot does not tell the future," Daphne said quietly. "Many people make that mistake. No, the cards reveal your deep emotional and psychological reality, but in the present. What is unconscious, deeply buried perhaps, comes to the surface through the cards. That is why putting yourself into a calm, meditative state is helpful. Again, I urge you to take your time."

As Fiona shuffled, at first clumsily because of the large format of the deck, the cards seemed to be warming up. Occasionally she glanced at the underside of the cards. If its face appealed to her, she carefully cut it back into the middle of the pack. She found herself reluctant to cease cutting and shuffling, as if once she did, she would somehow seal her fate. But the prolonged silence, save for the slap and scrape of the cards as she fanned them together, became uncomfortable for her and so she stopped.

Daphne narrowed her striking eyes. "Now cut them twice with your left hand."

Fiona reached out, first with her right hand, then quickly with the other and cut the cards so hastily that one pile slopped over into a heap. Daphne chose that pile and put the other two carefully aside.

Daphne's hand, creased and deeply tanned like her face, turned over the first card. "The Queen of Swords. This is the querent, you, as you are now." Fiona saw the queen sitting on a throne, her stern profile gazing resolutely into the distance as she grasped her sword in her left hand. Clouds billowed about her torso against a pale blue sky. Barren hills were sketched in behind her; a lone bird flew overhead. "She is stern, judgmental. She guards her throne, her power, from usurpers. She carries a great grief inside, but you see there is no water at her feet. She is concerned not with her feelings but with maintaining power in the world outside, with her position. She is articulate, intelligent, and she has lofty aims."

Fiona looked almost dreamily at the card. "I did have lofty aims," she said. "Once."

"That desire is still with you. It may be hidden for a time. But it's there. I see you fighting against forces around you. You are conventional to a degree, you care what those in your life think of you, and yet you are strongly individualistic. I feel your sadness. You suffer from a great disappointment." She pursed her lips. "The Queen wants vengeance."

Fiona stared at the card, feeling a wash of humiliation. The committee. Sigmund's betrayal. "If only I had some power," she said sadly.

"Oh, but you'll surprise yourself at how much you possess," Daphne said enigmatically. She lay another card on top of the first, so that its face covered about two-thirds of the Queen's surface. "This next card is the atmosphere of the matter."

The matter, Fiona repeated to herself. What wasn't the matter? Absolutely everything.

"I think of this card as the influences surrounding you." Daphne paused. "It's the eight of swords. Fear and paralysis." The card depicted a woman standing upright, bound and blindfolded, surrounded by swords, their points firmly wedged into the ground. "You are engaged in a struggle in the external world. The card signifies indecision, helplessness. Yet look at the card: the woman's feet are in a trickle of water—her intuition is there in front of her—and her bonds can be cut if she would but engage the edge of the swords to cut them." Daphne regarded Fiona sharply. "Eight is the number of regeneration. You will soon know what way to take. Perhaps you've decided already."

Fiona looked at the blindfolded woman and reached out to touch the card, tracing the figure's long dark hair. "I'm afraid the struggle is over," Fiona said. "And I lost."

Daphne waved a hand in the air dismissively. "Winning, losing, those are not the important things. They have nothing to do with the process of living. With becoming. You are letting your world be defined by others if that's where you put your attention. Look more deeply."

Fiona fell silent. Perhaps there was wisdom in what the woman was saying. Trying to advance in the academic world had never held much pleasure for her. When she saw how arbitrary the standards were, the victories she had achieved seemed hollow. Certainly she felt hollow now in her failure.

Daphne quickly slapped down another card at a ninety-degree angle to the last one. "This is the crossing card, not necessarily that which is in opposition to the atmosphere, but other forces to consider. Ah," she smiled. "It is the Ace of Wands. Wands signify fire. Each suit of the Minor Arcana cards indicates one of the four elements, hence the suit of Swords signifies air, that of Pentacles earth, and Cups, water. The Aces stand for the most creative and elemental energy of the suit. They are the number one, the number from which all others grow."

The card displayed a hand emerging from the clouds, bearing a wand with leaves growing out of it. In the background was the bare sketch of a mountain. "The Aces are all gifts," Daphne continued. "They possess tremendous energy. Wands are creative, innovative —like fire, they burst with ideas, new directions. This card, the Ace of Wands, I call the gift of creativity. A new venture is at hand."

In spite of herself, Fiona was mesmerized by Daphne's certainty. The meaning of the card corroborated her own experience. After sending Sigmund away, literally closing the door on her academic career, she had felt a sudden surge of vitality, a sense of other lives to inhabit.

"You must trust yourself, your talents, your abilities. You have vigor and health. Use these gifts. Don't look back. Be present. Look ahead. Remember the parable about the boy who could cross the narrowest bridges, no matter how wet, unstable, or dangerous. When asked how he did it, he said by not looking at his feet. He only looked ahead and so he always reached the other side."

The parable was unfamiliar to Fiona, but it didn't matter. She felt muddled by the seemingly contradictory task of both living in the present and yet always looking ahead, but she saw some wisdom in what Daphne was saying. Of course, staring at one's feet represented too much self-scrutiny. It created fear and apprehension of a misstep in the literal sense. "I'm afraid I look down far too often. No wonder I'm nervous about taking the next step." She laughed uncertainly.

"Of course. You're not alone," Daphne said briskly. "It's not that any of us can banish fear. But we have to proceed through it. Fortunately, things will always change. The best we can do is to keep flexible so that when they do change, we'll be able to move along with them. Next—the foundation of the matter."

She placed a card at the base of the three she had already drawn. It was bold and fanciful, with winged creatures hovering in clouds at each corner. In the center, a slender form, human except for its dog-like head, cradled a large disk in the curve of its back.

"The Wheel of Fortune," Daphne nodded, pleased. "This is your first Major Trump card; it belongs to the Major Arcana, the cards of which are more powerful—and significant—than those of the four suits. The Major Arcana are archetypal cards ranging from zero, The Fool, to twenty-one, The World. These mark the Fool's journey as she progresses from her awakening as an innocent seeker to a state of completion. The Wheel of Fortune is, on a blatant level, the wheel of fate. It usually stands for good fortune, but it is fortune that is seized by the seeker, not given to her. It also stands for the great cycle of life, the slow turn of man from birth to becoming toward decline and death, just as, on the wheel, we rise toward success, achieve it, lose it, and are left without it. As you are at the center of your life, with events turning around you, the center of the wheel is stable and the rim flexible, allowing fate to confront the seeker at the center. You must turn the wheel according to the dictates of your true self."

During this speech, Fiona stared at the wheel with its alchemical signs and Greek letters, its bold Sphinx staring out from the top of the rim. The card's symbols spoke of eternity just as the wheel itself had spun everlastingly through the centuries. Fiona felt humbled by the history of this card, aware of her own small struggles as a barely-discernible thread in the great tapestry of life itself.

"The next card reflects your immediate past. "Ah, the three of swords." Three swords pierced a large red heart at the center of the card. Fiona flinched and recalled Sigmund's critical words about her unfinished book, his lack of loyalty, his cavalier attitude toward their affair.

"The card signifies a broken heart on the literal level and certainly a time of emotional turbulence. Perhaps someone has disappointed you. The suit of swords indicates that the event is an external situation, not one solely inside of you. Swords represent air, mental energy. Perhaps some crisis about your work as well? You told me on the phone that you are a professor; mind is of great value to you."

Daphne paused and studied Fiona's face. Fiona simply shook her head. "Yes, there was a deep disappointment. I'm afraid I made the mistake of leaving my heart at work."

"And in the wrong hands perhaps?" Daphne inquired gently.

A deep flush began at Fiona's collar bone and rose in an angry wave across her throat and face. "Wrong hands, wrong heart," she muttered. "I made a terrible mistake. How could I have been so wrong?"

"Wrong, right, neither of these is of any consequence. I urge you again, look deeper. There are no right paths or wrong paths. There are only opportunities."

The rest of the reading passed in a blur. Daphne continued with the next card. "This crowns you," she began. Fiona vaguely heard names and images of more cards, the immediate future, the self approaching the matter, something about environment, hopes and fears. "...a path of infinite possibility ..." Daphne was saying quietly. The words "risk" and "chance" sounded at the dim reaches of Fiona's consciousness. Daphne's voice rose as she announced "the outcome" and Fiona's eyes flickered briefly on a very gray card of an old bearded man hunched upon his staff. He seemed to have nothing to do with her. All she could absorb was that her own life had come to a new turn and she had no idea how to confront it.

Her mind fixed on The Wheel of Fortune. She imagined the years of her life spinning through time, a gently revolving disk gradually speeding up, running out... She must buy a deck of cards and study the Fortune card for herself. Were the four creatures in the corners connected to myth or to astrology? There was some meaning there for her, but what?

"Don't worry," Daphne announced as Fiona finally raised her head. "I've taped the reading for you. Listen to it when you are ready. You seem very lost in contemplation of something."

"Yes," Fiona said, dazed by the rich colors, the layers of symbols and images. "Something. I'm sorry. The pictures—they're very distracting. And fascinating. I'm afraid I couldn't take it all in. But thank you. I feel on the verge of something." She laughed. "I suppose that's true of every moment of our lives. But I'm in a fog about what's next."

Daphne nodded. "I understand. You seem quite taken by the card of Fortune. It is the number ten, the number of perfection, of completion. Just as the wheel must turn, ten must yield again to one and the cycle begins again. Stability and change, the very stuff of life."

Daphne's hands made a wide circle and for a moment time slowed and caught the seer in a freeze-frame—her great head with its mass of hair poised at the top of the circle she'd drawn, a silver-haired sphinx cresting the top of the wheel. She seemed to balance there, effortlessly, peerlessly, and then the hands came down, the face became animated once more, and Daphne gestured the session was over. "Ms. Hardison, it has been a pleasure."

Fiona lifted her bag and took out her checkbook. Money seemed so banal at a time like this. She felt as though she had glimpsed the edge of the place where time slowed and space thinned and the spirit expanded. How did one set a price on the alchemy of revelation?

Daphne's rough, direct voice broke through her romantic idyll. "That will be seventy-five dollars. If you prefer, I accept all credit cards. Except Discover."

II: The High Priestess

Every artist has to have, if not a mentor, a teacher. Someone whose view of the world and whose gifts allow the student to imagine her craft differently, someone who provides her with a key to a door—and a world—formerly locked and sealed. For Edith Wharton that person was Henry James. He was not always kind or considerate, but he was always incisive and stimulating.

—*Fiona Hardison, from* Edith Wharton: A Life Apart,
unpublished manuscript

Fiona, slouched in a small coffee shop on Congress Avenue, lifted her eyes from her PowerBook and scrutinized the other patrons. Many sat alone, as she did, several tunelessly tip-tapping the keys of laptop computers; others talked quietly in groups of two or three. Monosyllables, rattling and rolling like carelessly-thrown dice, struck her ear from those clustered at tables: "...Turk?...he's so *bad*...no!!....yes?... truth?....liar!!...hey, don't, don't ever go there..."

Fiona irritably finished her now chill cappuccino. The cafe wasn't an escape from campus at all; she might as well be in class with her undergraduates, so familiar were the phrases—"not conversation, but punctuation," as Sigmund in an insightful moment had characterized the talk of the young.

Fiona longed for real conversation, for the sparkling interchange of like minds, for an era of engagement such as the one she was chronicling in her manuscript. Its new title beckoned her from the screen: "The Age of Inconsequence." The interchange with Sigmund, his betrayal and her response, had given Fiona a prism to hold up to the Gilded Age and the early decades of an uncertain century. Edith Wharton would have been discouraged to learn that so many years later, the old practices—the strictures of Old New York, the creaking hierarchy of social conventions that choked lives—had simply assumed new guises. Old New York was not dead: Fiona now saw it as a gateway to her own era. The past always provided a mirror for the present, however cracked or constricted its vista. It refracted the present moment somewhere on its surface, a revealing shimmer on the glass, a sly wink scuttling across the slick glaze of time.

She pitched her focus back to 1906, to an England high on the Edwardian Age where Edith Wharton made the rounds seeing her new, but already fast, friends. Fiona recreated a slender Edith in her middle forties, surrounded by admiring and intellectual (and largely, but not openly, gay) men at Lamb House, Henry James' residence in Rye, or Queen's Acre, the home of Howard Sturgis in Windsor. Visualizing the retinue of ninety years ago, Fiona ignored the mumbling around her and resumed editing:

The lone female, Edith Wharton perched among them, basking in their admiration (of each other as well as her), partaking of their sheer pleasure in the superiority of their own company. At first she sat in their midst hesitantly, uncertain of her place in this constellation of stars. Younger, in her twenties and thirties, she had lacked confidence in her intellectual and artistic identity. In fact, she had met James twice before the turn of the century, each time dressing in her newest, most becoming clothing to attract his attention, yet each time the master simply didn't notice her.

As time went on, Edith assumed her seat in the entourage, and her part of the repartee, with greater assurance. Publication in 1905 of the novel which would bring her international success, The House of Mirth, *emboldened her. Indeed, her acquaintance with James had blossomed shortly before; following the publication of her Italian novel,* The Valley of Decision, *she truly began the epistolary conversation with the peerless friend whom she would later address as* Cher Maître. *Even James' criticisms of her she found fascinating and artful.*

Fiona stopped and thought of those two lions, Henry James and Edith Wharton, subtly dissecting each other's work and personalities. The two friends had shared a love of the life of the mind, and dined often on delicious details of gossip. But they could be cutting in their criticism of each other's writerly shortcomings. Fiona paged through Edith's autobiography to find a passage where Edith had decried Henry's lack of environmental detail in his later novels. When she asked him why he had suspended *The Golden Bowl's* four main characters "in the void," he had replied: "My dear—I didn't know I had!" He was stung, not just by her criticism, but by his envy of the younger novelist's popular and financial success. He still smarted from the failure of his New York Edition to engage the public. Economic rewards eluded him throughout his career. Once when Edith told him she had purchased her latest automobile from the royalties of her novel *The Fruit of the Tree*, he had responded that with his royalties from *The Wings of the Dove* he had purchased a handcart to carry his guests' luggage.

Early in her career, James had admonished Edith about the insubstantial development of some of the men in her fiction. And, on one occasion, James had teased Wharton, in public, about writing a story for publication in French, a language which she spoke well, but did not inhabit fully as she did her native English. Fiona doubted that anyone could have done it more incisively than Henry James, nineteen years Wharton's senior, at the peak of his fame and personality:

James' visit glided along for some days, until a newcomer to their party blurted out what Edith had hoped to keep secret. Beaming, licking his lips in that ingra-

*tiating way young men did around the great man, he said, "Mr. James. Did you
see that Mrs. Wharton has written a story in French—in* French—*for the*
Revue?"

*James smiled indulgently at his young, hopeful, and, there was no doubt about
it, handsome face. There were so many appealing young men around him now
who wished to solicit his opinions. They sat so close, as if his words spilled out in
a private stream that they could drink, if only their lips were close enough to his.
It was quite overwhelming. Quite lovely.*

*James put down his teacup, a bone china cup with pale yellow flowers twin-
ing around its curves, so delicate it fairly whispered when it grazed its saucer.
Edith could see the skin around his mouth shift slightly, a tiny ripple which
nonetheless telegraphed to her that he anticipated enjoying himself hugely. He
scanned the room, made sure each pair of eyes was upon him, especially Edith's,
those bright eyes in that squarish, almost masculine face (how he wished it had
been he who had called her "a self-made man" but she had thought of that herself
and announced it, daringly, already).*

*He shifted his bulk in his armchair, and began in his slow, thoughtful, almost
halting speech: "Of course I've seen the story. Remarkable—most remarkable! An
altogether astonishing feat." For a moment he paused and patted his waistcoat,
which fit ever so snugly over his burgeoning stomach. His eyes turned toward
Edith, those eyes that could be so grave, yet which contained the merest twinkle if
you knew where to look for it: "I do congratulate you, my dear. I applaud you on
the way in which you've picked up every old worn-out literary phrase that's been
lying about the streets of Paris for the last twenty years, and managed to pack
them all into those few pages."*

*Edith sat back, chagrined. Yet, his words were amusing, and true, if she could
just put ego aside for a moment and admit it. She had used clichés, or perhaps she
could call them shortcuts, that she would never dream of employing in English.
The room erupted in a shout of laughter, Edith's well-modulated, musical voice
joining in with the rest. Yes, laughing, even at herself, was the easiest path to take.*

Fiona paused. Hadn't women always smiled away their discomfort?
She thought disagreeably of faculty meetings in her department, of

times when she had smiled to hide her confusion, her smile a mask behind which she could retreat, recover, or disappear.

When Edith had first ventured to England, younger, less established, but determined to make her place in the world of letters, she had been much more smitten, less aware of the conversational dynamics and stakes. Eager for stimulation, she succumbed easily to the heady atmosphere of Henry James' circle.

Next to them, her neurasthenic husband, Teddy Wharton, uninterested in culture and learning, drawn only to sports and hunting and his own pleasures, must have seemed poor company indeed. Teddy Wharton, going slowly mad from an inherited nervous condition, was not sleek or witty or learned. He was simply Edith Wharton's disappointing husband, and that knowledge did its part to drive him ever deeper into the labyrinth of his disintegrating personality.

Fiona lifted her eyes from the screen. And yet how could anyone pity Teddy, when he brought no emotional or sexual pleasure to one of the finest writers of the twentieth century, when he dampened a spirit so wistful and desirous of love, so generous with her friendship and her genius? Fiona recalled herself in the early days with Sigmund, surrounded by his handsome, brainy, male friends and their slender, sexy, oh-so-bright girlfriends, feeling a little less clever, a bit less experienced, and a lot less hip. Sigmund's friends would pass her a joint conspiratorially, but it would only make her cough, rather than confide the "deep thoughts" they cherished. They were junkies for confession as well as stimulation. Or Sigmund would insist they try a concoction—the most expensive marijuana flavored with a touch of mescaline—guaranteed to be an aphrodisiac, and Fiona would lose consciousness before she could take off her clothes.

But thoughts of Sigmund were bad for concentration. She bent to her task:

—

While the Whartons seemed grossly incompatible by any measure, the woman who had married Teddy Wharton in 1885 was transformed so completely that it isn't surprising their marriage couldn't survive her metamorphosis. The young person of twenty-three who accepted Wharton's marriage proposal was naive, insecure, desperate to leave the home of her socialite mother, Lucretia Jones. Her beloved father had died when she was twenty, leaving her, the youngest child, with a cold woman interested only in clothes, fortune, and reputation.

On the eve of her wedding, Edith Jones was completely ignorant of the demands of married life, so unprepared and ignorant about sexual relations that she turned to her mother, perhaps the most unsympathetic person she knew, for information about the intimate duties of her coming union. Her mother dismissed her with, "You've seen enough pictures and statues in your life. Haven't you noticed that men are...made differently... from women?" At Edith's assent, Lucretia, having discharged her responsibility with this obvious visual aid, chastised her daughter for pretending ignorance, "Then for heaven's sake don't ask me any more silly questions. You can't be as stupid as you pretend!"

Fiona paused again. With a pang of sympathy, she thought of Edith Wharton, alone in an overdecorated room in her mother's brownstone on West 23rd St. in New York City. She could clearly imagine the young woman, pale, sickly and thin-lipped, looking anxiously out a second or third story window, wondering what her life was to be like beyond the walls of her mother's proscribed existence. For the young Edith was often ill, tormented by nightmares and by her feverish imagination. She began in her youth what was to become a pattern for her adult life: fevered periods of activity followed by breakdowns of health and will, long stretches where she could do little but convalesce. Her nerves were a torture, particularly the first half of her life. No wonder she had little patience with her husband's neurasthenia, his disintegrating health, his helplessness. No, Fiona thought, it wasn't impatience, it was fear, utter terror of the invalidism that had once threatened her own life and her artistry.

———

It is difficult for anyone at the beginning of the twenty-first century to imagine the insulated existence of a well brought up, upper class young female in the 1870's and 1880's. In the realm of intimacy, Edith Newbold Jones had lived a life in quarantine. Late in her life, Wharton had written in A Backward Glance: *"From a childhood and youth of complete intellectual isolation—so complete that it accustomed me never to be lonely except in company—I passed, in my early thirties, into an atmosphere of the rarest understanding, the richest and most varied mental comradeship."*

Decades of success and the esteem of others had armored Wharton by the time she wrote these words, yet she still hid from the emotional deprivation of her childhood, couching her loneliness only in intellectual terms. The simple words revealed how hollow the young novelist's life had truly been; she had been so devoid of love she couldn't even bring herself to mention it. No wonder she had married a man incompatible with her inner life: she'd had no acquaintanceship with that part of her self at all.

Almost twenty years after she had married, she gained the courage to look back as a writer on her New York childhood. She produced the dazzling novel The House of Mirth, *creating a heroine who could not survive the ruthless pursuit of New York society. Lily Bart, the gossamer butterfly whom everyone collected—brilliant, beautiful, socially adept—was one of the crowning inventions of Wharton's novelistic life. Lily craved all that wealth could bring, but she yearned for a life of the mind and spirit as well. She was unable to resign herself to a gilded cage, unwilling to sell herself to the highest bidder in the marriage market. Like her creator, she was proud. But unlike Edith Newbold Jones, Lily Bart was not a survivor.*

Edith poured much of her memory and her passion into the incomparable Miss Bart, even giving her the name, Lily, that had been one of her own nicknames as a girl. But the inclination to write about her own milieu came from a friend, a dear friend old enough to be her father and unquestionably successful as her father had never been. Uncannily intuitive, aware of the ideal direction of her gifts as a novelist, it was Henry James who urged her after her Italian novel to "tether herself to her native pastures" and "DO NEW YORK!" He knew that

Wharton was the natural chronicler of the society they both had known as children.

Without James' encouragement at this key stage of her writing life, we can't know if she would have found the fortitude to write about the world of her youth, and to expose the tastes and mores of women like her mother, Lucretia Jones. Surely Lucretia had been the model for the elderly aunt, Mrs. Peniston, who dangles her inheritance before Lily Bart. And snatches it away when Lily is most desperate. The Mrs. Penistons held the keys to the fortress that was Old New York. It was a fortress Edith Wharton never cared to occupy, or to hide behind. And most of all, she didn't want to be trapped behind its stolid walls, which could neither let in the fresh air of new ideas nor allow the stale air of tradition to escape.

Fiona slowly nodded approval at what she had written, and then added a flourish to underscore Henry James' role in her subject's development:

But Wharton's talents, like those of any artist, needed nurturing. They required guidance from a man who, before her, had built a house of fiction with an architectural brilliance no one could match. That guiding intelligence, that fount of intuition, was for her Henry James. His was the androgynous intelligence that inspired her. Friend, travel companion, counselor, Henry James was more than a mentor to Edith Wharton. He was her muse.

Satisfied, Fiona snapped shut her laptop. She looked round the café—at all the young faces and bodies, the copious hair flopping carelessly into eyes, the scuffed boots resting on chair legs, the carefully-calculated stubble on the men's chins, the vivid tattoos on the women's firm upper arms. She needed to talk to someone her own age. Better yet, she needed to see a friend.

III: The Empress

*My God, but I envy women. Women with big breasts and big buttocks
and thick thighs like glorious Grecian goddesses. How I want to bury my
head between their breasts, drink in the light from their soft,
understanding eyes, run my hands over their silky, moist skin. I worship
them. On second thought, the hell with worship. I just want to be them.*

*—Dennis Reagan, conversation in the elevator after watching Bettina
Graf step out on the second floor*

Bettina Graf lived in an old bungalow a half mile north and east of
Helmsley Hall in Hyde Park, hailed as Austin's first suburb many decades earlier. Like many of Austin's prime central neighborhoods,
Hyde Park sported spreading live oak and pecan trees and a healthy
mix of bourgeois bohemians, eccentrics, and dogs.

A colleague of Fiona's, Bettina taught seminars in contemporary
British literature. She specialized in two figures from the Bloomsbury
Group, Virginia Woolf and Lytton Strachey.

"I get so tired of these wrangles about classification," Bettina had
told Fiona recently after the usual lengthy Friday afternoon meeting
of the British Lit faculty. "The fact is no one on my faculty wants to
teach anything after 1850. Anything the slightest bit innovative, or

written by a female, nonwhite or gay person, gets labelled 'contemporary'."

Fiona frowned. "So that's why Virginia Woolf is contemporary? Because she was lesbian and female?"

"That's one possibility. It could mean that she's contemporary because she's not enslaved to the fogy-ish notion of what constitutes 'traditional'."

"But that's so convoluted," Fiona complained. "Contemporary simply means anti-traditional?"

Her friend impatiently brushed shaggy red hair away from her face. "I wish you'd stop questioning *me*, for heaven's sake. I'm as baffled as you are. I just know that when Sigmund doesn't understand something, it's immediately classified as post-modern."

This day, Bettina was serving them Darjeeling tea in huge ceramic mugs half-filled with milk. The two women discarded their shoes in the kitchen and went into Bettina's thickly-carpeted study, plopped on the couch, hefted their bare feet onto the coffee table, and began to devour Bettina's daughter's fabulous chocolate chip cookies.

"These are wickedly good. How's Clare's business going?"

"Well, she's determined that her business plan will be a success if everyone in Austin gains three pounds from her desserts by December 31."

"Can those of us who've gained more than three pounds donate their excess to those irritating perpetual skinnies?"

Bettina threw her a sharp look. "Sort of like the sick-leave pool at work? Ha. Well, that just doesn't work. And how can you even think about it, when you're one of those perpetual skinnies we all hate?" Bettina grabbed another cookie. "I feel I have to eat these in self-defense when I'm around you."

Fiona munched a cookie. "Why?"

"So that when you notice that I've gained weight, you'll think this is the reason. When the truth of it is I put on pounds just from thinking I might leaf through the pages of a new cookbook."

Bettina stretched out a plump and shapely hand and pushed the plate of cookies out of her reach. She turned to her friend with a worried look. "So tell me, are you really resigning at the end of spring semester?"

"Sigmund hasn't accepted my resignation, but I did write him a letter stating that I'm resigning as of May 15, yes." Fiona's stomach lurched in a newly-familiar way at the thought of being jobless. Or was it a residue of anger at Sigmund?

"What courage you have."

"It didn't take courage particularly. I just opened my big mouth and that's what came out." Fiona reached for another cookie, feeling consoled as peanut butter and chocolate melted around the pecan chunks and swirled deliciously over her tongue. "I'm too terrified to feel courageous." She considered. "The only thing I feel good about is taking action. I can't tell you how devastated I was when Sigmund told me—so easily, so nonchalantly—that the department didn't want to promote me. I was flattened and…what is that expression Dennis likes to use?"

Dennis Reagan was their friend from the Drama department, addicted to crisis but unaccountably reliable in bad situations all the same. "Gut-shot?" Bettina offered, and looked carefully at the greyish smudges under Fiona's brown eyes. She wondered if she should be worrying about her friend. Fiona appeared relatively unfazed by recent events, but perhaps she was severely upset, or even depressed. Bettina resolved to call Dennis the moment Fiona left.

"Gut-shot. Exactly. Bleeding from every pore. And then felt humiliated that I was bleeding. I didn't know what else to do but decamp."

"Well, I know it's not that easy. I admire you. Don't get me wrong, I think you're fabulous. But I don't know how I can stay in that place without you. It's bad enough with you there." Bettina looked down at her feet glumly. "Really, Fiona, you can't leave me alone with those vultures."

"Why don't you quit, too? We'll celebrate our unemployment to-gether."

"Be serious. Who do you think is keeping all of the entrepreneurs in this household afloat? Clare still needs subsidizing—especially with this new catering business—and Carl starts college next fall. And Marvin—as you well know since I bring it up practically every time we talk—has brilliant strategies for marketing his hybrid roses and his native plants and whatever else he's growing around here. But so far the only green I'm seeing is the seedlings in the greenhouse."

Marvin was Bettina's husband of twenty-five years. After two de-cades in the Botany Department, he'd quit to start his own nursery. In the mid-80's, when Austin real estate went begging on the auction block, Marvin had possessed the foresight to buy an adjacent lot which he now called his "pasture."

"My father laughs and laughs," Marvin had said one evening as the three of them had drinks on the Graf's back deck. "Our family farm in Wisconsin was only a section—a mere 640 acres. He always wanted more land. So when I showed him my treasured eighth of an acre he said, 'Pasture? Huh. More like an overgrown patio. Marvin, this yard isn't big enough to grow vegetables to feed a family of four, even one that doesn't eat very much.'"

Marvin had sighed wistfully. "Dad can't imagine how a man can be a success if he can't support his family with the fruits of his own hard labor. I had never made anything with my hands until I started our garden. It thrills me every time we eat a tomato." Marvin's eyes wid-ened to almost perfect circles of blue and for a moment he looked sub-limely happy.

Fiona delighted in Marvin's experiments and was glad to take the "failures" off his hands, vegetables or flowers that he found too warped or imperfect to show Bettina. Marvin adored his wife—Fiona couldn't help but notice, with a slight ping of envy, how his gaze rested contentedly on his wife's large, beautiful face and ample body whenever she was near—and thought her too sublime to present with flawed offerings. He was like a child who, in a roomful of people, has eyes only for his mother. Except Marvin did not love his wife only for her considerable maternal qualities. As he had told Fiona the first time they met, while Bettina was pouring the wine in the kitchen, "After five minutes with her I thought she was the sexiest, sweetest thing I'd ever seen. Now, that's an unbeatable combination."

Marvin was right, at least from Fiona's own experience in the realm of romance. The sweet men she knew were not at all sexy, and the sexy ones, well, their very sexiness seemed to revolve around their sultry, serious attitude toward seduction. Absent were the humor and endearing qualities that suggested sweetness to her. Fiona realized gloomily that this was somehow her own fault. She was obviously attracted to men who were incomplete and that meant she was lacking herself. Sigmund was a perfect example. He had once been sexy but never sweet, and now he was neither. In fact, Fiona imagined that the very concept of "sweet" was foreign to him; he probably reserved it as a descriptor only for certain activities—like a perfect golf swing or an unexpected toss in bed with a graduate student.

Bettina's combination of Eros and tenderness created an environment in which the entire Graf household flourished. Two more healthy and apple-cheeked offspring than Clare and her brother Carl did not grace the city of Austin. The food served on the Graf table was opulent and delicious—gleaming platters of roasted poultry and crisp-skinned duck, mounds of thick, creamy potatoes infused with just the right amount of garlic and herbs, architecturally-challenging towers of chocolate parfaits—and the house itself, while never perfectly clean (a calculated messiness was a badge of distinction among most of the academics Fiona knew), seemed to have a patina of warmth and care about it. And, in spite of her grumbles, Bettina's career appeared charmed as well. She was the rare academic blessed by effortless promotions; she had even escaped the tortuous system of building a file for tenure. Austin University had simply offered it to her when they wooed her away from the University of Wisconsin.

Fiona smiled fondly at her friend, whose hand snaked through her curly red hair as she processed some thought or other. And yet Bettina deserved it all, the loving husband, the lovely children, the apparently effortlessly run household. She was a generous friend and colleague, who lavishly gave advice, lecture notes, books, free meals, and impulsive hugs to a wide circle of people. Bettina Graf's largesse was legendary, and Fiona had not yet met the person who desired to be on the outside of her dispensations for long. How could Bettina be the victim of turf wars when her warmth and presence constituted the very turf that made life pleasurable for so many? No, where people were concerned, Bettina possessed a green thumb. And perhaps that ability to cultivate and soothe even the prickliest of personalities ultimately attracted the botanist in Marvin, the consummate grower and nurturer of living things. Marvin tended plants to produce the choicest fruit; Bettina harvested the best in people.

"I don't suppose I'll ever be able to retire," Bettina announced glumly.

"What?" Absorbed in a vision of Marvin and Bettina presiding over the flora and fauna of the earth, Fiona had lost her way in the conversational flow.

"Retire. You know, not work, at least not for money or in this job. You've heard of a little detail called a job, haven't you, Fiona? You still have one, you can't be this far removed."

"Oh, God, I guess I am removed. Not absent-minded, perhaps, but lost in my 'little gray cells' as the great Poirot calls them."

"Hmm." Bettina thought Agatha Christie—and most mystery writers—to be overrated and overpaid. But she chose not to pursue that well-worn argument. "So, how's your book?"

An expression of pure pleasure crossed Fiona's face. "Oh, I'm loving it. You know how blocked I've been for years—amassing huge amounts of research on Edith but not being able to convert it into a book? Well, amazingly, as soon as I told Sigmund I was resigning, the words just started pouring out of me. I can't make it out."

"Well, that doesn't take a neo-Freudian to figure out, just a couch potato analyst like me. Let's see, you had a miserable relationship, with Sigmund—have you ever realized that he shares a given name with Freud by the way?—and a job (mostly because of Sigmund, again) that made you insecure. Those two things recede, and *voilà!* you're able to write. Hmmm. Can't imagine why."

Fiona leaned across the table and snared another cookie. "Good grief, B., you make me sound like such a simpleton."

"That's not what I meant. It's wonderful that you're happier. I'm your friend. I'm thrilled that you've unloaded some of the dead weight you've been carrying around." She glared at the clutter of books and papers, the tangled cords snaking across the floor from computer equipment and fax machine, the stacks of floppy discs and unanswered correspondence. "We should all be so lucky."

Chewing, and dusting the crumbs from her lips, Fiona mumbled, "How'mIgonnalibIwonder."

Bettina smiled. "How will you live? With ingenuity, my darling, as you always have."

Fiona thought, how Carl and Clare must have hated to grow up, to relinquish their mother's expression of pure benevolence surrounding them when they burbled in pain after falling down the stairs or when, in clogged voices, they confided their inner distress. How they must have loathed giving up the certainty that their incoherence would be perfectly understood, by this one person at least.

The air conditioning cut off abruptly, leaving the two women in silence. Outside, the September day looked perfect and inviting, sunny and bright, with long shadows creeping over the lush lawn and turning it a darker green. Unfortunately, temperatures still averaged in the high nineties, and the beautiful day turned oppressive as soon as one stepped out into it. Fiona noticed Marvin's familiar blocky body moving briskly, hefting bags of mulch from a wheel barrow onto a flower bed in the side yard.

"I don't know how he can work outside in this heat," she said.

Bettina didn't even look. "He has different blood than the rest of us. Midwestern, hardy, indestructible blood—it adapts to anything. I sweat if I look out the window. Now, tell me more about the book."

"It's dreamy really, writing about Edith Wharton and Henry James. It's the most satisfying writing I've ever done as an academic. You know, everyone talks about James as so intellectual and removed, so much the Great Man. But I see him, in relation to Edith, as rather feminine."

"Well, he was a classic closet case, wasn't he? And, my God, the microanalysis of human interaction in his books—few women could have been more perceptive to the shadings of feeling or behavior than he was. Clearly an intelligence that wasn't limited by anything as rigid as gender. It's not surprising."

"No," Fiona thought a moment. "It's not surprising but very unusual—the way their friendship played out. I don't think either of them was quite the same with anyone else." At Bettina's arched brows, Fiona held up her hands. "Oh, don't get started. Of course any two people's friendship is unique. That's not what I mean."

"So, what do you mean? Go on, I'm interested." Bettina's wide, intelligent face was receptive and utterly still, a calm pool that reflected what she was hearing. Fiona smiled, thinking of how many students and colleagues had slipped into that pool and fallen in love with Bettina; like Narcissus, they fell madly in love with this flattering mirror of themselves.

"I'm trying to capture how he shaped her, as a person and a writer, how he revealed her to her inner self."

"Hmm. Henry James as oracle." Bettina's wide mouth stretched in a delighted smile. "Yes, The High Priestess of Lamb House. Oh, very good, Fiona!"

Fiona flushed, suddenly embarrassed. "I have to be careful. I don't want this to be another book about a great woman writer that is really about men. Most of the book is about her life. James is not the major figure, but I see him as instrumental in the development of her writerly self."

"The man behind the Great Woman. It's a bit of a role reversal."

They both laughed. Bettina continued, "Except James was not quiet or silent or retiring. And as for greatness, Wharton felt annoyed her whole career by how critics compared her to him, didn't she?" Bettina leaned over and softly brushed away a lone cookie crumb clinging to Fiona's lip. "By the way, what is this book? A biography? A critical reading of Wharton?"

"Good question. It began as a critical study of the fiction, with the life interwoven into readings of the stories and novels." Fiona paused and thoughtfully pushed the hair back from her forehead. "But now it's changed course—and even titles. I'm now calling it *The Age of Inconsequence*." Fiona pronounced the new title hesitantly, releasing it, like a timid fledgling, into public space for the first time. "The book is much more of a biography now, one with a life of its own. Sometimes it veers off into fiction."

"Oh well. These hybrid genres are quite popular now." Bettina lifted her eyebrows dramatically. "And I love the title. 'Inconsequence.' Isn't that what we're all trapped in, pathetic little gerbils spinning on the proverbial wheel? Don't be shy—pass some of it by me when you're ready."

"Thanks, I will. How is your writing going?" Fiona, grateful, reflected back a pale imitation of her friend's solicitude.

Bettina's aura of grace disappeared. "Oh, Christ, I don't want to talk about it. Not only has my book on Woolf been totally scooped by Hermione Lee—and so brilliantly—but I can't get any funding from the Tower to finish the damn thing." The Tower was shorthand for the University's main administrative building which did indeed soar in phallic remove over the entire campus.

"God," Fiona said. "Have you ever actually tried to go to the Tower, by the way? It's a rabbit-warren over there."

Bettina looked doubtful. "I have ventured into Main a few times. All I remember are wide staircases."

"Yes, well," Fiona continued, "that part of the building is only four stories high. The Tower connected to it has twenty-some stories. But here's the thing. All the elevators on those first four floors are labeled: 'No Tower access.' I actually had a meeting on the fourteenth floor. I ran up and down those four stories twice and asked directions three times before I found the obscure passageway that led to an elevator that actually took me up there."

"What actually happens in the Tower?" Bettina asked. "It was the main library at one time, I've heard. Odd that a library, even a former library, should be so difficult to find. This is an institution of higher learning presumably."

The two women lapsed into silence, mulling over the mystery of bureaucracy that was Austin University.

Fiona stirred first. "But about funding for your research: you're due, aren't you?"

"Yes, well, it's not like pregnancy, where you know the reward is definitely coming and in good time too. I think I'm overdue but the research leave fund is temporarily depressed this year, they tell me."

"That's a tired excuse. Beyond tired, in fact. Hmm." Fiona thought a minute, licking the last smudge of chocolate from her fingers. "What might that be—fatigued? exhausted? lassitudinous? Is that a word?"

She and Bettina often played word games together, but this mention of the dearth of research funds had put Bettina into a rare irritable mood. "Oh, who cares. It just means that I'm not getting any."

Fiona laughed. "You sound like an assistant professor who hasn't been laid in three months."

"Oh?" Bettina's green eyes were hooded at half-mast. "Well, that's another tired story."

Suppressing more giggles, Fiona said, "Oh, for heaven's sake, things aren't that bad surely?"

"You've never been married for twenty-five years, darlin'. So just don't even talk about it."

Fascinated, Fiona prodded. "Really? You and Marvin are having problems?"

Bettina tossed her red hair and finally managed a wink. "Honey, who said anything about problems? I think I just used the word 'tired.' After twenty-five years, some things just get tired, that's all."

"You don't mean worn out?"

"No," Bettina snapped back. "I'm sure rejuvenation is possible at any time." She folded her arms. "Let's talk about something else."

Fiona looked at her watch. Five o'clock. "Oh God, it's late. I'm sorry, B. I've taken up your whole afternoon and now I've put you in a bad mood. I've got to go. Lunch next week?"

Bettina nodded and stood up, pushing back the sleeves of her silk sweater, which stretched tightly across her breasts and hips. "Of course. Mother's Cafe okay with you?"

"I've had it with tofu. I need meat these days." Fiona flexed her thin arms above her head. "I have to keep my fighting weight to deal with Sigmund and the department."

"Sigmund? Why do you even have to talk to him?"

Before Fiona could answer, Marvin stuck his head in the door. "Honey, it's Sigmund Froelich on the phone."

"Well, that's easy, Marv. Just tell him I'm not here."

"Sorry, but he says it's an emergency." Marvin shrugged his big shoulders. "The guy's a bulldozer. Too bad I can't use his attitude to dig fence posts."

"Oh, for Christ's sake." Bettina walked to her desk, waved a hand at Fiona to stay, and picked up the extension. "Hello?...very well, and you?...good...hmmm?...no, this isn't a good time...what?...you're not serious...Sigmund, if this is supposed to be a joke, it isn't funny…Now, I mean it, stop fooling—what? WHAT??…Oh, all right. I'll see you at nine tomorrow."

Bettina slammed down the phone and turned around. Her normally-robust complexion had paled to a sickly, paste color. She turned and looked at Fiona and then at Marvin, her eyes huge and glistening.

Marvin quickly went to her side and put an arm around her, guiding her back to the sofa. She collapsed into its cushions, while her husband and best friend hovered over her, as anxious as two mother geese flapping and cooing over a sick gosling.

"That was Sigmund," Bettina said unnecessarily.

"Yes?" Fiona prompted. "And?"

Bettina chewed on her lower lip, hard. Fiona noticed flecks of blood appear on the reddening flesh.

"Bettina, talk to us," Marvin pleaded.

His wife sighed. The release of breath seemed to diminish her. She looked almost frail huddled below them. "You won't believe this, but I'm being sued."

"Sued?" Fiona's and Marvin's voices struck a single discordant note.

"Sued. For inappropriate conduct." Bettina tried to laugh, but her voice came out a soft, strangled groan. "An undergraduate honors' student is suing me."

"Who?" Once again, Fiona and Marvin croaked together.

"Kyle Cramer."

"Kyle Cramer," Fiona repeated woodenly. The name meant nothing to her. "And what do you mean, 'inappropriate conduct'?"

"Sex, that's what I mean. Kyle is suing me for sexual harassment."

"Sexual—?…Good Lord," Marvin finally managed, and then blurted: "It's impossible…well, isn't it? Honey? I mean, he doesn't have any cause, does he?"

There was a silence. Bettina's usually placid, round face tightened into a pinched grimace of despair. "Kyle is a she."

IV: The Emperor

Virginia Woolf wrote that the woman writer had to kill the "angel in the house"—the spectre of the good, self-sacrificing mother—before she could find her art. But many women artists born in the nineteenth century were in thrall to powerful fathers or father-figures. The shadow of these men—whether cast by the power of a penetrating intellect, great wealth, a towering personality, or a critical eye—cast a pall upon their daughters. The fact is—and this hasn't changed in our age—those who succeeded walked boldly through the looking glass, avoiding the gaze of the patriarchal elder entirely.

—Bettina Graf, *from* Virginia Woolf: A Life,
unpublished manuscript

The next morning, Fiona drove Bettina to Helmsley Hall for her appointment with Sigmund. It was frightfully hot, even at 8:45 in the morning. Beads of moisture trickled between Fiona's breasts and stalled in a puddle at the bottom of her bra; she turned up the car's air conditioning to maximum. Beside her, Bettina, wearing a long-sleeved cotton sweater and full skirt, shivered. Fiona decided to forego her usual lame jokes about hot flashes in light of her friend's acute distress.

"I just don't understand it," Bettina began for perhaps the fourth time. "Kyle was always so *friendly*, so eager to see me, have coffee, talk, and so on."

Fiona bit her lip. Dare she ask what the "and so on" referred to? Instead, she said: "But, doesn't that make sense? Maybe she's a stalker or something. Aren't they always friendly, at least at first? Don't they always lead one on? I mean, you remember MonicaGate..."

"Oh, please!" Bettina looked at her with pure rage. "Don't even bring that shit up. Isn't it enough that we had to endure months of wretched television coverage? Must Monica Lewinsky become the chief metaphor for our sexually-infantilized country? My God, it's enough to make me want to move abroad. All these people who can't get it up, who never got it up, who have absolutely no idea what sexual intimacy is..."

Fiona interrupted this rant, one she had heard before. "I'm sorry. Bad reference. But you know what I'm saying. Of course Kyle was friendly and eager. Students on the make always are."

"Kyle Cramer was never on the make." Bettina, breathing heavily, spoke in a grim monotone. "This simply has to be a mistake."

"All right, I'll shut up. I obviously don't know what's going on here."

"Are you insinuating there is any truth to these utterly stupid and cretinous charges? My God, Fiona, wise up. This could happen to you, too. Let me tell you what happened: we met for coffee, we discussed English literature, I gave her a copy of *To The Lighthouse*—heretofore not a crime in this state—and, once, I drove her home when her car was broken down. I did not go into her apartment. That's all. Period, the end."

"Well, that's good. You should have nothing to worry about then." Fiona turned up the radio gratefully. "I'm sure there's some explanation for all this."

They drove for some time, not talking, their nerves semi-soothed by the high, pure notes of a female vocalist interpreting Celtic songs. Hesitantly, Fiona asked: "Is Kyle gay?"

"You mean, is she a *lesbian*? I assume she is if she's making these accusations. On the other hand, she could be rabidly heterosexual as compensation for closeted lesbian feelings....oh, Christ, how should I know?"

By this time, Bettina's arms were clutched across her chest in a vise-grip. "The world has gone crazy."

"That's the truth." Fiona reached over and patted her friend's shoulder. "And none of this is probably your doing. I mean, it's not your fault that you're so earthy and sexy that everyone falls in love with you."

Bettina heard nothing but the "probably." "Fiona, you are my best friend. But even you know better. Of course I had something to do with this! She's accusing me and it's never happened before so I must have somehow encouraged her."

"Not necessarily. The fact that it's never happened before means everything. To me it means it has nothing to do with you."

Bettina groaned. "Sort of a chaos theory of sexual relations? Somewhere, someone thought a sexual thought which took an aberrant path and eventually collided in the universe of one Bettina Graf, age forty-eight, a sexually frustrated female decidedly peri-menopausal and probably crazy anyway? God, spare me."

Fiona fiddled with the radio knob and then twisted it to its "off" position. She asked quietly, "Are you serious? Are you sexually frustrated?"

"Aren't you? Isn't everybody?"

"Bettina, be serious. Is something wrong with your marriage? Is Marvin—"

"I don't think anything is particularly wrong with my marriage. We're just in one of those slack times. It's the loneliness of the long-distance runner. Sometimes, after *decades*, for God's sake, you have to take a breather. Sex can't stay at the top of the agenda all of the time." Bettina drew in a ragged breath. "Usually it doesn't bother me."

"And sometimes?"

"Sometimes it does. And sometimes when it does I have a fling. But not for very long and not seriously." Bettina's green eyes glinted and she attempted a wicked smile, but Fiona could tell her heart wasn't in it. Her lips turned down, and for a moment, the skin under her jaw puckered. Fiona was reminded that her friend was indeed middle-aged and not impervious to time. "I'm very discreet. I don't want to hurt Marvin."

"Oh." Fiona didn't know what to say.

"It's okay, really. I'm not going to break. I love Marvin. You of all people know that. But we all have our addictions, and I'm afraid sex is mine. It absolutely drives me crazy when our sex life dribbles off."

Fiona winced at the word "dribbles." For Bettina, immersion in the great river of life was everything. Small quantities—dribs and drabs of leftovers, half glasses of wine, even tiny boxes of clothes detergent—offended her. Poor Marvin. "What does this have to do with Kyle?"

"I suppose something. She's a beautiful young woman and she was very flirtatious with me. I'm sure I was flirtatious right back. It was fun and I supposed, wrongly, harmless."

"What do you mean by 'flirted'?" Fiona asked carefully.

"Don't interrogate me, Professor Hardison. I'm not in the mood. I'm saving my explanations—and contrition—for Herr Meister Froelich."

"Sorry, dear. You know I trust you."

"After what I just told you? Have you wondered about your judgment lately?"

Now it was Fiona's turn to be exasperated. "Just because you like sex doesn't make you untrustworthy. Besides, you're not cheating on me."

"'Cheating'? Interesting word. A bit old-fashioned. I'm surprised at you."

"I am old-fashioned. You know that perfectly well."

"I suppose people who have never been married can afford to be old-fashioned—and romantic—about marriage."

"You forget I was married for five years."

"Five years. A mere blink of the eye as far as I'm concerned." Bettina's expression softened. "Not that I don't take your experience seriously. I'm just feeling old right now. Like an old married lady. And I guess I don't like it much."

Fiona giggled. "Honey, I know what an 'old married lady' looks like—my mother has about fourteen friends that fit that description—and none of them looks like you."

Bettina's cheeks flushed and then she laughed, an open, joyful sound that gave Fiona a glimpse of what the teenage Bettina might have been like. "When I was a little girl my grandmother had a friend named Margaret Hawke. A classic of the genre. She always wore black flat-heeled slippers when my grandmother invited her to tea—of course, she just lived upstairs—but I still remember those shoes, dangling at the ends of the puniest legs you'd ever seen. They looked like little rubber chicken legs. You know, because of the support hose."

Fiona nodded eagerly. "My grandmother had a friend like her, Miss Lister. The support hose were rolled below her knees, yes?"

"The same. And she wore belted housedresses, all with flowers."

Fiona snickered. "Huge flowers with bright colors. Oh, and now I'm really being evil, but Miss Lister's teeth protruded every time she poured the tea—she always reminded me of a flabby bunny rabbit."

"Yes! I never met her but I can just see it, the teeth in the crepey face. Imagine how young people are looking at us now, just like this—cruel, cruel. But the housedresses! There was always, *always*, a long thread hanging from the hem. I wondered if I tugged on it if the whole garment would unravel. I so yearned to find out. I had to practically sit on my hands to keep from snagging that thread."

Laughing hard now, Fiona pulled the car into a convenient driveway on Whitis Street. Tears tickled her eyes. "Miss Lister had a way of cocking her head and peering at me, with pursed lips. Oh, God, I was fascinated by the wrinkles around her mouth. I'd never seen that many wrinkles on a living person."

"I suppose we'll have to get used to it, if we live long enough." Bettina's eyes were bright and red-rimmed, and as she looked impishly at Fiona, the two of them collapsed into more choked laughter.

"I don't know why this is so funny," Fiona muttered. swabbing her eyes.

"Because we're still young enough, and smug enough, to believe it can never happen to us—the wrinkles, the incredibly saggy breasts, the trembly thighs—the whole depressing old lady thing."

"Oh, but I think it is happening to me. I see the signs everywhere."

"It's true! They say the first sign is when you look at your profile in a mirror and what sticks out isn't your tits but your gut." Bettina sucked in her stomach, arched her back, and peered down at her substantial bosom. "I'm still ahead in that department. However..." She pinched a bit of flesh under her chin and waggled it.

Fiona felt the skin of her own throat in apprehensive sympathy. It seemed to have slackened further overnight. Her startled eyes collided with Bettina's animated ones and the two women sagged forward, snarking with laughter.

Ten minutes later, they walked into the basement of Helmsley Hall and ran into Dennis Reagan waiting for the elevator.

"What's happened to you two?" His lean face creased with alarm. "Were you in an accident?"

"You might say that." Fiona turned to Bettina, who was adjusting her clothing: "That's it! Aging is exactly like a car wreck!!"

Bettina giggled. "Yes, yes. And it's not preventable—there we all are, negotiating the curves and bumps of life, cautious at first, but then, as time speeds up, we do too. We punch the pedal to the floor, trying to get the most out of life, and soon we're out of control, careening down a slippery slope right into a tree. It's preordained: you see that tree, you pump the brake, but you keep heading straight for it. There's no way to turn. Oh God, I have to pee."

Dennis looked bewildered. "Are you sure you're all right?"

"No," they chorused. Bettina staggered into the women's room at the end of the corridor.

"Good grief." Dennis watched her lurch through the doorway. "You two women are dangerous. Speaking of danger, I heard an impossible rumor about Bettina this morning."

"It's true. She's ten minutes late for a showdown with Sigmund."

Dennis leaned one slim hip against the wall. "Are you sure he didn't manufacture this whole thing? I mean, *sexual harassment?* Bettina has been hit on so many times, she should be suing the university for use fees."

Fiona shook her head and pushed her hair impatiently away from her face. "I'm afraid it doesn't work that way. For some reason, she has to go through this."

"It's all bullshit. I know Kyle Cramer."

"And?"

"And, I don't get it. She's a faghag—she's had crushes on every gay man in the Drama Department."

"On you too?"

"Oh, please." Dennis looked flattered. "She likes boys, my dear." He smiled. "Can't say I blame her." He ran his fingers through his short blond hair. "Just kidding. Carter would slap me if he heard that."

Fiona took Dennis' arm. "No, he wouldn't. He has a sense of humor. He knows you adore him. And no one, even twenty years his junior, is nearly as handsome as he is."

"Lucky bastard. I keep searching for that hideous picture he must keep in a closet somewhere."

"Ummm," Fiona glanced toward the women's room. "Look, let's leave Bettina to get herself together. I told her we'd see her later, after the meeting, if she needed to talk. I volunteered your services, too. I hope you don't mind."

The elevator arrived and opened its doors with a faint whine and a shudder. Fiona hesitated. Dennis eyed its bleak gun-metal gray interior and then walked warily inside. Fiona followed him. "Oh, and Dennis."

"Hmm?"

"Do you know if Darryl Hansen is involved in Kyle's complaint?"

"The Dean? Well...," Dennis considered. And then decided Fiona was safe to confide in. "I guess he is, since he's the one who called me this morning and told me about it."

Darryl Hansen, the Dean of Liberal Studies, was truly liberal in his appreciation of scholarship and intellectual pursuits. He'd even spearheaded a reconsideration of the meaning of "publication" in promotion and tenure cases, maintaining that the present bias toward printed texts discriminated against half of his faculty. Hansen had famously urged the University to take the twenty-first century into account by at least acknowledging the twentieth, dominated for decades by images, sound, performance, and other non-print media. The Provost had not yet acted on his recommendation, but Darryl's sally against the text-bound Tower lent him the aura of a brave knight among the faculty just as much as if he had actually stormed Main with a lance.

"Well then, why did you call it a rumor? That's about as substantiated a claim you can get if the Dean told you himself."

Dennis grinned. "Just protecting my sources. Until I found out how much you knew. But he's strictly conservative on the moral front, you know," Dennis added primly.

"Yet he can still be friends with you?" Fiona shook her head in mock-amazement.

"What do you mean?"

"Oh, please." The elevator arrived on the seventh floor, lurched, and then stalled slightly below the floor level. They stepped up and out together, quickly, before the arbitrary device could change its mind and take them somewhere else.

"Look," Fiona continued. "Darryl Hansen is one of the fairest men on this campus. I respect him. And he's a great admirer of Bettina's work. I'm glad he's involved, because that can only help her. I don't trust Sigmund's motives on this one."

Dennis stabbed at the elevator button again. "I didn't mean to get off here," he said crossly. "Christ, it's going back down to two."

"Don't you have anything to say?"

"About what?" He was fixated on the floor indicator light above his head.

"Dennis, about what I just said!"

Dennis turned to her. Under the fluorescent lights of the hallway, his eyes were deeply shadowed, surrounded by fine lines. "Honey, I've already told you this Kyle Cramer grievance is a crock. And you know I agree with you about Darryl. He's not a fool, unlike the chair of your department." Dennis craned his neck and scanned the hallway. It appeared empty, but he lowered his voice anyway. "Sigmund's going to run with this because he's under so much pressure himself."

"Oh? What kind of pressure?"

"There's talk of removing him as chair."

Fiona blinked rapidly. Her lips moved silently, as if she were calculating an impossible string of numbers. "I don't believe it. This news is floating around the Drama Department? No one's said a word here in Literature and Rhetoric." She made a note to call and ask Darryl to have lunch with her. A former chair of her department, the Dean was canny about negotiating the labyrinth of psychological corridors. As if he possessed a secret map, he knew the dangerous pathways where spite and rancor lurked thinly underground and where it was safe to tread. Besides, Darryl was charming, handsome, and an excellent gossip.

The elevator arrived with a twang, this time a step above floor level and Dennis hurriedly hopped inside. "There is no rumor. Darryl told me." As the doors closed, he put a finger to his lips. "Don't tell anyone."

———

After a brief stop in the mailroom, Fiona walked quickly down the corridor to her office, slipped in, and shut the door. She flipped through the memos and book catalogues, found nothing that couldn't wait, and dumped the pile on her desk. With only the steady drone of the air conditioner as accompaniment, she sat down at the computer and opened the file "EW. Inconsequence."

She re-read what she had already written about Wharton's difficulties conforming to the life demanded of a young married woman of her class. Except for the stolen pleasures of reading, Wharton's dreams of becoming a writer faded amidst the pleasures of fashionable society. She idled away her days in the company of other young couples, dogs, and horses, at her mother's estate, Pencraig.

Fiona thought back on her morning. The tension between her and Bettina had evaporated in the face of their hysterical laughter in the car. No difficult situation could change without a catalyst, she thought firmly. Thinking of the events that turned Wharton toward a life of authorship, Fiona began to re-work a passage that previously had suffered from disorganization and muddled thinking.

Restless, Edith sought stimulation in travel, and fortunately, Teddy was a compliant companion. In the early years, they spent February until June traveling in Europe. While the couple may have faltered in the sexual intimacies of marriage, they traveled together ardently. And for a time, the excitement of new terrain and undiscovered worlds satiated her appetites.

One turning point of her life was a long cruise on a chartered yacht to the Mediterranean. On these three glorious months she and Teddy spent their combined incomes for an entire year. It was a reckless move, and according to both of their families, outrageous and sinful. But Edith was vindicated. Not only did the voyage nourish her fascination with Italy and the Aegean, laying down the sensory imprints for her later travel writings, but during their trip her cousin Joshua died, leaving her $120,000 outright, an enormous sum in the late 1880's. The trip inspired her first, though unpublished, manuscript on travel, "The Cruise of the Vanadis." More significantly, it encouraged her for the first time *in her life to take risks. From this point on, when something truly compelling beckoned, she would not let it pass her by because worldly conditions weren't ideal.*

Fiona admired her subject's ability to take risks, to defy her milieu and her family, especially their expectations of a socially-appropriate life. Writing as an occupation had not come easily for Wharton; it demanded courage to bare her mind and spirit in the face of ruthless criticism. Fiona pictured her Austin University colleagues on the Executive Council considering the value of her essays as they weighed Fiona's request for promotion, their eyebrows arched in judgmental salute. Even in Fiona's time, a woman wielding a pen was over-scrutinized, her intentions—and femininity—suspect. But at least Fiona's peers had the benefit of several generations of female models. Wharton's mentors had all been men, stimulating yet demanding.

Yet the man who required the most of Edith's emotional life until she was fifty-one years old was not a Great Man, but her intellectually undistinguished and sporting husband, Teddy. Gripped in his fifties by depression and neurasthenia, like his father before him, Teddy Wharton alternately raged at and clung pathetically to his wife. His bouts of anger and selfishness—culminating in the misuse of his wife's money while he flagrantly kept a mistress and another household at her expense—were complicated by his passivity and helplessness.

Fiona paused, absently fingering the keys with the barest pressure; the soft clacking sound externalized her mental churning. How could a woman of such discernment make such a poor choice in selecting a mate? Of course, her father's death left Edith prey to the pressures of her socially rapacious mother. Lucretia was most likely alarmed by her daughter's advanced age—twenty-three—and fearful of the prospect of a dependent, spinster daughter. In the absence of her father, lacking any evidence that her writing would bear fruit, Edith had little guidance. The constant in her life was the obstinate pressure from her mother to marry. Enter the socially appropriate, genial, and, at thirteen years her senior, somewhat fatherly Teddy Wharton.

Teddy Wharton was handsome, placid, and steady, a safe contrast to her own more anxious, emotional outlook. Yet the two of them had almost nothing in common, save for a privileged background. Fiona wondered what the honeymoon of the young, inexperienced Edith and the older, more worldly bachelor who had become her husband must have been like.

Fiona remembered reading in R.W.B. Lewis' biography of Wharton that the marriage had not been consummated for three weeks. For Fiona, the couple's sexual dysfunction held at least a partial key to the creative paralysis that also afflicted the novelist at this time in her life. She opened a new computer file, labelled it "speculations," and attempted to place herself within the rigid nineteenth century world that enclosed the inexperienced and hyper-sensitive young woman. Fiona pictured Teddy and Edith both in long white muslin night-clothes easing in to their respective sides of the bed:

… The young bride looks at her husband with misgivings and yet with confidence that he will know what to do. She has watched him with horses, and knows him to be a gentle man. For his part, Teddy waits for a look or a touch, some demonstration of his wife's ardor. But the young woman beside him appears wooden and disinterested. In reality, she is terrified, frozen in her utter unpreparedness.

"My dear?" Teddy asks. She doesn't answer him. She doesn't know what to say. Tentatively, he kisses her lips. They are stiff and cold. He pauses, wondering what Edith expects of their first night together. He realizes uncomfortably that he has never had sexual intercourse with a virgin before. Perhaps he should wait until she is more comfortable?

"My dear?" he asks again. Edith waits, her breath held tightly. She wants her husband to gently lead her into…into what? She can't speak, so limited is her vocabulary about the body, especially her own.

She says nothing. With another sigh, Teddy kisses her lightly on her fore-

head, pats her shoulder, and turns over on his side. "Good night, dear," he says softly...

Fiona shifted in her chair. Had the Whartons' failure been an utter collapse of communication? Had both partners—Edith, sorely disappointed in her husband's lack of imagination and skill, and Teddy, mystified by his wife's lack of interest—simply done nothing by default? Or, had things progressed even more predictably...

Edith lies beside her husband, her heart clamoring in her chest. Her mouth is dry, her limbs cold, her stomach lurches so precipitously she is afraid she is going to be sick. She feels wounded, a wingless creature caught in the web of her ignorance. How can she have married without knowing more than she does about the physical aspect of marriage? She opens her mouth to ask her husband a question, "Should we—" she begins and then freezes.

Teddy turns and throws his arms around her. "Yes, dear," he says. His large-boned body wraps itself around her thin frame. She cannot move. Before she can even think—and truly her head is beginning to pound dangerously, she suspects a migraine is coming on—hands rush under her nightclothes, range over her breasts, her stomach, her most private parts. Teddy is on top of her now, so heavy, so demanding, she fears she might suffocate. His flesh stabs painfully at her lower regions. "No!" she begins to scream...

Fiona drew a deep breath. Perhaps not. She drummed her fingers once again, her thoughts tumbling on the gerbil wheel constructed of too little first-hand knowledge. Perhaps things didn't go predictably at all...

Edith and Teddy lie together for the first time in the bedroom on the second floor that had once been her parents'. She doesn't know what is expected of her. Her nerves are stretched tight, so tight she imagines them shrieking like a swarm of tiny birds, an unpleasant, no, an unendurable sound. She turns to Teddy: "Please, help me."

"Edith? What is it?" Teddy's cheeks blush scarlet. "Are you unwell?"

"My head is pounding, I feel..." Edith touches her husband's face in mute appeal. She feels if he doesn't make love to her she will die. Her body feels numb and strange and yet restless and excited at the same time. She knows she wants him to touch her. After that, she doesn't know. But she feels so alone, so afraid, if only he will just stroke her softly, hold and comfort her.

"What is it?" he repeats. His wife looks to be in pain, lying there so stiffly. And they haven't even begun. Perhaps something serious is wrong—? Her hand crawls across his face, cold, faintly moist. He begins to feel seriously alarmed, and revolted.

"Oh, I don't know," she moans. "Please, love me."

"Of course I love you," he says quickly. Her hand rests on his chest now; it stabs at him. What has he done, marrying this young woman who seems so terrified, so unhappy? If he isn't careful, she will drag him down with her, into the terrible miasma of her despair.

"Let me get you some valerian tea," he says, removing her hand from his chest and leaping from the bed. He pulls on his robe and makes for the door. He will call one of the servants, the nice young one with the brunette hair. He can't remember her name but she will know just how to proceed. And then he will go to sleep in another room. Surely, at least for tonight, that will be best.

This last scenario appealed to Fiona. Given the history, it made sense to her that both Edith and Teddy had experienced terror in the conjugal bed. The biographer in her itched for documentation. A loud knock sounded at her office door, cutting short her speculation. She hastily selected "save" and called out in a distracted voice: "Yes?"

The door opened and Sigmund stood before her, his cream linen suit rumpled and baggy. Beads of moisture stood out on his forehead, even though the building's air conditioners chilled the air to a frosty sixty-five degrees. Fiona wondered if he were developing high blood pressure.

"I need to talk to you," he said, his imperious tone undercut by a hoarse cough. Allergies. Fall elm, most likely. "In the office. Right now. If you please."

Fiona peered at Sigmund, her eyes narrowed as if she couldn't quite assemble the parts of his body into a coherent whole. "But I thought you were meeting with Bettina..."

"Of course that's just what I'm doing. And we need to talk to you. Please." Sigmund actually clapped his hands as he began to walk down the hall, as if to hasten her to follow him.

Fiona stared at him, strutting down the corridor, his elbows angled away from his torso like tightly-furled wings. Once a proud cock of the Helmsley Hall corridors, Sigmund now was just another hallway crank, croaking his crisis du jour to anyone who would listen. She imagined his pale flesh against the white sheets in their rented room at the Manor Inn. Her mind immediately hit the "delete" button, and with a regretful glance at her computer, she closed her door.

After two steps she returned, re-entered the office. What was she doing following Sigmund anywhere? He was acting unconsciously, and therefore was unpredictable, even dangerous. Seeing Sigmund reminded her of her conversation with Dennis earlier in the day and of her resolve to check in with Darryl Hansen about campus rumors. She picked up the telephone.

"May I speak to Dean Hansen?" she asked the pleasant female voice that greeted her.

Moments later, Darryl came on the line. "Darryl? How are you?...I was wondering if you had time for lunch tomorrow....Today? In forty minutes?...Excellent!....I'll be there."

This time Fiona locked the door, and with a jaunty step, made for the main office.

V: The Hierophant

The God Chiron wanted to die because he was in great pain and his wounds would not heal. He sacrificed his immortality in exchange for Prometheus' mortality, thus sparing Prometheus the terrible cruelty of his punishment for giving the secret of fire to man (Prometheus was chained to a rock and each day, the birds pecked at his flesh). Though Chiron gave up the ability to live forever, he gained in knowledge of Life's Mysteries. His sacrifice imbued him with vast wisdom in the healing arts. His greatest lesson, taught by other extraordinary spiritual teachers—Christ in the New Testament, Lao-tzu in Taoist philosophy, The Hierophant in the Tarot—is that all knowledge resides within us.

—Sigmund Froelich, class notes for "Myth and Literature"

Seated around the large conference room table adjacent to the mail room were Bettina, Sigmund, a young woman Fiona didn't know (presumably Kyle Cramer), and Miriam Held. As Fiona took a seat at one end of the table, Miriam frowned and nodded at her rather grimly. Sigmund occupied the other end of the blocky table, its faux-oak surface gleaming dully.

"Fiona, I don't believe you know Kyle Cramer," Sigmund announced stiffly, indicating the person at the center of the table. "Kyle, this is Professor Hardison."

61

Kyle stared at Fiona almost to the point of rudeness and then said: "Hello, I've heard of you, of course."

Fiona resisted the impulse to reply, "And I've certainly been hearing about you." Instead, she said simply, "Hello" and attempted to keep her face neutral and unrevealing. For Fiona found herself startled by Kyle's appearance. Impossibly young and pale and freckled, Kyle was tiny (surely no more than eighty pounds), with full, curly red hair that cascaded down her back, giving her a Pre-Raphaelite quality.

Distracted, Fiona struggled to pay attention to the proceedings around her. Kyle looked like a child—she stared at Kyle's lips which were as bright and startling as her hair—albeit a very sexual child. Without thinking, Fiona looked disapprovingly at Bettina, who was sitting next to Sigmund.

Bettina took in her friend's critical glance, her eyes widening with alarm. Her hand came off the table, as if to ask "what is it?" Fiona shook her head and turned to Sigmund.

"So where are we?" she asked bluntly.

"Where are we," he repeated slowly. "Where you might expect. Kyle has repeated her charges and Bettina has refuted them."

"Well, not exactly where you would expect," Miriam broke in, her broad face slightly pink, as if the skin was under pressure from the exertion of keeping her temper in a particularly annoying situation. "I for one did not expect to be in this situation, sitting in judgment of one of my colleagues," she said in a cool voice. She patted her forehead with a white linen handkerchief, its creases as crisp as her tone.

"Ladies, please," Sigmund said. "No one is sitting in judgment of anyone. This is an informal hearing. We're simply here to see, to ascertain, where this complaint…ah…grievance…stands."

"Law suit," said Kyle Cramer.

"What?" Sigmund's chin jutted aggressively toward the young woman.

"Law suit," the young woman repeated. "I intend to sue unless Bettina Graf is removed from her position on the faculty."

Bettina's pale face blanched further. "I—" she began.

"Ridiculous," Miriam pronounced. Among her other roles, Miriam carried the mantle of institutional memory in departmental disputes. She waved a hand dismissively. "We're not in the practice of removing our faculty. For anyone. Go ahead and sue. From what I've heard, you'll spend a lot of your money, and waste all of our time, for nothing. But, if you have nothing better to do, go right ahead." Miriam scooped together the scattered papers in front of her into a file folder. Her preparations for departure announced clearly that she had wasted sufficient time already.

"I resent your attitude," Kyle Cramer said with surprising pluck.

Fiona had been having trouble taking anyone who looked as young as she did—no more than twelve, she decided—seriously. Now she turned her full attention to Ms. Cramer.

"This woman," Kyle continued, gesturing at Bettina, "this professor, my *mentor*, whom I had total trust in, took advantage of me."

Captivated by the dramatic flourish of Kyle's words, Fiona shook her head in wonder. No one, least of all a student, should have total trust in anyone, least of all a human being belonging to the flawed genus of professor.

"...after taking me home," Kyle's eyes filled with tears, "and I turned to thank her, she *kissed* me, a very long kiss, on the lips."

The room was silent. Then, Bettina spoke tightly, as from between clenched teeth, "This is absurd."

Miriam held up one hand. "Let her finish."

"But we've heard this before," Bettina said, her voice measured. Fiona knew from experience that her friend was getting very, very angry.

"Is that all?" Miriam inclined her head at Kyle.

Kyle had the grace to blush. "*All?*! Isn't that quite enough?"

"Did you kiss this woman?" Miriam demanded of Bettina.

"I gave her a hug," Bettina replied. "I did not kiss her. We had just had a very long talk, she had told me about some things that were upsetting her—confidences I shall not break to repeat to you all here. Unless I am forced to, of course." Here she stared at Kyle defiantly. "And to reassure her as I left, I gave her a *hug*. I hug many of my students."

"Perhaps that is unwise," said Sigmund.

Miriam picked up her file, straightened her long, full—and very rumpled—black skirt, and stood. "I believe Bettina." She turned to Kyle. "You are sullying the name of a kind and generous teacher. You should be ashamed of yourself."

She tapped the file accusingly on the table. Kyle looked at her expressionlessly. Miriam continued, more forcefully: "I for one would be happy if Professor Graf gave me a hug when I was upset. Even a kiss. I would count myself fortunate to receive her affection." Miriam strode to the door.

Sigmund threw up his hands. "That is irrelevant, Dr. Held! Whether or not you want to be kissed or hugged by Professor Graf has absolutely nothing to do with anything!"

Miriam swiveled to face him. "I think it does. Except in your case, and a few others, I've seen Dr. Graf hold and kiss, at different times, the entire faculty of our department. She is an affectionate person, that's all. We're lucky to have her. That's just how she *is*. It doesn't prove her to be a sexual predator but rather a compassionate person."

Sigmund groaned. "Fiona, surely you have something pertinent to offer to this discussion."

"Perhaps we could hear a fuller accounting of the incident from Professor Graf," Fiona offered.

"Oh, we've gone over that already. That was of no help whatsoever. Please leave, all three of you. I need to talk to Miss Cramer alone."

Miriam opened the door and paused, stalwart and stout in the doorway. "I'll bet you do. Bettina, you should leave. But, Fiona, per-

haps you had better stay or we may have two lawsuits on our hands."
With that, she exited.

Bettina stood up quickly and followed her.

Fiona rose also. "I have an appointment. Ms. Cramer, I urge you to
think very carefully about what you're about to do. It's true that reputations are at stake. Your own as well as that of other people. And try
to remember we teachers are just human beings. Sometimes we make
mistakes and trust those we shouldn't." She stared at her with significance, and then she said pointedly to Sigmund: "I think it's wise to
leave the door open."

Outside in the mail room, Bettina was shaking with rage. "Oh, did
you see him look at her, that carnivore of young flesh, that user,
that—"

Miriam was stroking Bettina's right shoulder, as if the younger
woman were an irritable child. "My dear, this will all blow over."

"No, it won't. Can't you see Sigmund wants to get her in his debt?
He'll support her in this outrageous accusation! It's an excellent way
to get back at me and get a grateful undergraduate in his bed at the
same time."

Fiona winced. "Has he done this before?"

"Get real," Miriam and Bettina said in unison.

Miriam moved away from Bettina and put her arm around Fiona.
"My dear, I know what you think, or used to think of Sigmund, but I'm
afraid he's rather too fond of undergraduates."

"Oh, God." Fiona looked at Bettina. "I'm so sorry that you have to
go through this."

"Actually, I'm feeling better. It's my word against hers. I have an excellent reputation. I didn't kiss her, I never kissed her, and I can't
imagine how she can prove that I did."

"It could be very unpleasant and very damaging, Bettina dear,
though, if she actually brings this to court." Miriam said.

"She won't." Bettina shrugged. "Or maybe she will. There's nothing

I can do about it. But, Sigmund. There's something we can do about him."

"What do you mean?" Fiona asked.

"Never mind," Bettina said. "But, believe me, if he has an affair with Kyle, it won't be a secret."

"How will you know?" Fiona stared at her friend.

"I'll know." And Bettina marched out of the mailroom, leaving Miriam and Fiona gazing in mystification at her retreating form.

Fiona arrived in Dean Hansen's office huffing, five minutes late after a sprint across campus. Hastily, she combed her fingers through her ash-blond hair, hoping she didn't look too bedraggled. She'd had a tough time extricating herself from Miriam. It wasn't like the older woman to be so motherly, and Fiona wondered why she was being quite so solicitous in this case. Perhaps she saw Bettina and herself as in need of her protection, both bruised and battered respectively at the hands of an insensitive student and an even more insensitive colleague.

Cheryl, the Dean's executive assistant, looked up cheerfully. "Have a seat. You're not late. Or rather, we operate on Dean's Time here." She typed into her computer, checked her watch, and then thought. "At this point in the semester that's about twenty minutes behind schedule."

"Oh, good," Fiona said, welcoming a few minutes to clear her head. A pen and a copy of *The Gazette of Higher Education* lay on a table. She picked them both up, tapping the pen absently as she began to scan the newspaper's front page. Concentration eluded her, though, as her mind kept cycling back to the meeting she had just left.

"I like it. Higher education needs some livening up," a voice close to her ear said after what seemed mere seconds later. Fiona looked up to see Darryl Hansen's tanned and craggy face smiling down at her.

"Oh," Fiona regarded the elaborate doodle she had unthinkingly scrawled all over *The Gazette's* front page. She folded the paper and tucked it neatly under another newspaper. "The atmosphere in your office must be inspiring."

Hansen motioned for her to precede him and they walked out of his office together. "No one's ever accused us of that before."

They took the stairs from his fourth floor office. "The elevator's been more than usually perverse this week," he said. "I think it's going to go out again. We don't want to be on it when it does." His low voice rose an half-octave as he said with pleasure: "Dennis was trapped for forty minutes last time."

"What did he do?"

"Well, you might know he's claustrophobic. So he said the only way he remained sane was to recite over and over again Marc Antony's funeral oration for Caesar."

"Good grief. Why that?"

"It's the only thing he could remember in a panic."

As they walked out of the building into the intense sunlight, Fiona laughed at the thought of Dennis declaiming Shakespeare into the void of the elevator shaft.

"September is the cruelest month," Hansen said, squinting in the brightness.

"In central Texas, yes." Fiona stood still for a moment, gauging the weather. "But you know, I think the temperature's beginning to drop. I don't think it'll get over ninety today."

"How could I have forgotten—it's practically autumn," Hansen said. "Where do you want to go for lunch?"

"Not the Faculty Club. Everyone will want to stop by and talk to you. I need your undivided attention."

Darryl lifted one eyebrow, a small pleased smile playing over his face. He cleared his throat. "Let's clear out of here then. How about downtown? I'll drive."

They retraced their steps back into the second floor of their building, to the small parking garage that held only a select few parking spaces. The Dean opened the passenger door of his white BMW for

Fiona. "The only real privilege of being Dean," he said, indicating the parking space with his name on it.

They ended up at the restaurant at the Four Seasons Hotel. After they'd each consumed two martinis and a leisurely lunch, Fiona announced: "I feel absolutely sinful drinking in the middle of the day and—" She looked at her watch, "—It's two o'clock! We've been here two hours already."

Their waiter cleared the table, poured more coffee, and left. Darryl leaned back in his chair and focused lazy blue eyes on Fiona. "Thank you for playing hooky with me. I do it so seldom anymore." He sighed. "I think a sure sign of taking oneself too seriously is spending too much time in the office, fearful that if you're not available you might miss something."

"That doesn't sound like your style at all."

"I've let myself be conned into believing my presence means something. Cheryl fosters this impression. Most likely because she handles everything, really. She probably doesn't want me to know how irrelevant I really am." He smiled at Fiona. "So tell me, what's going on in the dread Literature and Rhetoric? Nothing you can't handle, I don't imagine."

Relieved that Darryl had brought up the subject of campus politics himself, Fiona plunged in: "I know you're aware of the proposed law suit by Kyle Cramer against Bettina Graf—" When Darryl looked at her sharply, she said: "It's all right. Dennis told me."

Darryl relaxed again. "That's okay then. I was afraid someone was starting a rumor."

Fiona was perplexed, wondering what exactly the difference was between the truth and a rumor in this case. She decided to ignore the distinction: "Is there a chance this could really go somewhere? I mean, I was just at a meeting where Kyle Cramer demanded Bettina's removal from the faculty."

"Really? On what grounds?"

Fiona suspected he knew already but she dutifully replied: "She said Bettina kissed her on the lips."

Hansen smiled uncomfortably and shifted in his seat. His eyes stared fixedly over her head. Fiona was startled. The body language was unmistakable. Bettina must have had an affair with Darryl Hansen. But when? Fiona remembered hearing that he and his wife had planned to split up at least two years ago. She calculated rapidly. Had he and Bettina gotten together that recently or while he was married? Bettina, that sly dog, would have to fess up and soon.

"Really?" he said, one hand rubbing his jaw reflectively. "And Bettina, I imagine, denies it. Kissing her on the lips, I mean. She may have kissed her on the cheek. You know Bettina." Fiona thought she detected a slight flush on his high Danish cheekbones.

"Yes, I know Bettina. In a way, I'm amazed this has never happened before. You know, students fall in love with her right and left...and she's so affectionate, so occasionally flirtatious all in the name of good fun..." Fiona stopped, embarrassed. Hansen's eyes were once again locked on a spot on the opposite wall.

"Well, no matter," Fiona said, stopping to swallow a mouthful of almost cold coffee. "I believe her when she says she did nothing but give Ms. Cramer a comforting hug."

Darryl seemed to have regained his composure. He'd loosened his tie and removed his jacket. He rolled his shirtsleeves halfway to his elbow. The shirt was pale yellow in a cotton fabric so soft it draped his arm like silk. The color showed his tanned, thick forearms to advantage. Irrelevantly, Fiona said: "Some Scandinavians tan very well, don't they? I always imagine them to be so fair."

"Some of us are quite dark and not particularly sensitive to the sun," he said, looking thoughtfully at her. He swept his graying brown hair away from his forehead with a careless hand. "It's none of my business, but are you and Sigmund still—"

"No," Fiona said crisply. "We're not."

"Ah," he said and looked at her. His eyes were a very dark blue, set rather closely together, but resting deeply in their sockets, making their gaze very intense. And attractive.

"Well," he said more briskly. "About this Cramer business. Just between us, she has registered a formal complaint with my office. And I've heard from her father. He's in the Texas House of Representatives." He rolled his eyes. "So there's that complication. However, I don't know if you're aware that Kyle Cramer has initiated other grievances. Four that I know of in her three years here."

"Oh? No, I didn't know. How extraordinary. And did any of them stick?"

"Just one. Do you remember Tim O'Neal in Folklore?"

Fiona thought, took another gulp of the tepid coffee, and shook her head. "Don't think so."

"Well, he did resign. Of course, one of his Ph.D. advisees also filed a complaint against him at the same time, and apparently he was actually having an affair with him and delaying his dissertation defense so that he wouldn't leave."

"Him?"

"Yes. Another reason why there didn't seem to be much veracity to Ms. Cramer's accusation."

"Just out of curiosity, who else did she accuse?"

"Well, me, for one."

"You?!"

"And Dennis Reagan."

"Good grief. Well, she certainly has eclectic tastes."

Hansen laughed. "She registered a grievance against me after her accusation of sexual harassment against Dennis didn't go anywhere."

Fiona sighed. "I hate to see a young woman behave this way. It gives us all a bad name."

"I don't think that's true. Why should it be surprising to find the occasionally sex-obsessed young woman? She clearly needs to believe that everyone desires her. We see it in men all the time; it just manifests itself a little differently."

Fiona frowned, realizing Kyle Cramer disturbed her a great deal and she wasn't sure why. "It just seems pathetic in a way. That she needs attention that badly. She's certainly attractive, if you like the dramatic, nervy type." Fiona peered at Darryl for a sign that he did but he seemed merely eager to explore a subject other than Bettina. "It doesn't make sense."

Darryl signaled to the waiter for more coffee. "Now you're being stereotypical again. And perhaps a little misogynistic. Just because a woman is attractive doesn't mean she can't have fantasies that everyone is after her, does it? Why should such desperation be more believable in an unattractive woman?"

Fiona accepted more coffee and added cream to her cup. She watched the butterfat spread and settle through the dark liquid. "I don't know." Was she really saying that she had separate, more stringent, standards for desirable women? And had she even brought up the subject of attractiveness or had Darryl? "This is confusing," she mumbled. The whole subject oddly excited her and yet filled her with shame at the same time.

Hansen leaned forward and touched Fiona's hand lightly where it curved around her coffee cup. "Enough about Kyle and Bettina and all the rest. Let's talk about you."

An hour later, Fiona parked her car in her driveway. She felt sleepy and disoriented. She never drank during the day, what had she been thinking of? Thank God she had no classes today; her brain was positively fuzzy.

Of course, she'd had a terrific time with Darryl, both of them telling each other the carefully edited and calculatedly amusing stories of their lives. While Darryl hadn't confessed to the affair with Bettina, he did reveal details about his break-up from his ex-wife Janice, who still taught in Modern Languages. Fiona had glossed over the demise of her affair with Sigmund. It was too raw and recent to be a story to dine out on, she had discovered.

Her calico cat brushed against her legs as she fitted her key into the back door. "Hungry, Dynamo?" She picked up the long, lean, warm body. Dynamo purred and allowed Fiona to carry her into the kitchen where she skittered to the floor and clamored for Pounce treats.

Fiona ignored the blinking answering machine on the kitchen counter and went straight to her office and the computer. She collected email. Twenty new messages. Most were from students and colleagues; she couldn't face those yet. She opened one from Daphne Arbor announcing her new web site: www.selfdiscover.com. She didn't check on the new site but consulted her calendar and emailed Daphne back, requesting another consultation for next week.

Fiona recalled the tape Daphne had given her of the Tarot reading. As soon as she realized she had no memory of where she had put it, the tape beckoned tantalizingly in her mind, an electronic Rosetta stone, the key to all of life's nagging questions. She began rummaging about her office in search of it. She hadn't listened to the recording since she'd gone to see Daphne, nearly three weeks ago. After scattering the contents of various mole-hills of paper on her desk, she found the tape in her briefcase.

She inserted the cassette into a battered portable tape player. Daphne's warm but rough voice spilled into the room in spite of the poor and crackling quality of the player. As she listened, Fiona catalogued the cards at the beginning of the reading: she remembered the vengeful Queen of Swords and the tortured woman surrounded by swords. And the crossing card, the Ace of Wands, the signal of a new venture. She thought of how well her book on Edith Wharton was progressing and felt a rush of pleasure. The rush deepened into a full-body flush as she recalled her delightful lunch with Darryl. Wands were spiritual energy, could they be sexual as well? The foundation card of the Wheel of Fortune still fascinated her. The turn of the wheel, the random, measured spin of fate. She wasn't sure what that corresponded to in the moment. But the card of the immediate past, the Three of Swords, emotional turbulance, that was all too obvious; she hit fast forward.

The crowning card she had no memory of, so overwhelmed had she been by the possibilities of the tantalizing Wheel of Fortune. She punched the tape player into reverse, then hit play, and listened again to Daphne's seductive voice: "This card crowns you. A major trump card, it's the Devil, the number 15 on the Fool's journey. The crowning card signifies the best that can happen. Although it is a coming action, it may already have begun to manifest itself. The Devil is a complicated card, indicative of revelry and unbridled sensual appetite as symbolized by the Greek God Pan. Some readers see evil in this card but it reflects merely our instinctive nature, our natural impulses, which with the dawn of Christianity became interpreted as evil. You see the chains on the man and woman at the Devil's feet: these are the chains we forge ourselves, the chains of our own unconsidered habits.

"Reflect on those behaviors you perform because you've always performed them; you have the power to break the bonds of habits which are unconscious and bring them into the light of consciousness. But most of all, the card signals that we must accept our Shadow side, our dark side, in order to feel whole. Embrace your sexual instinctive nature, your natural desires, and they will no longer control you. As you accept these forces in yourself, you will be able to feel compassion for others."

Fiona paused the tape. Was she judgmental of others' sexuality —Bettina's generous sexual impulses, Kyle Cramer's desperate desire to be wanted, Dennis' passion for men—because she did not accept her own? All those years she had lusted after Sigmund, reveling in his touch, in the secretive nature of the relationship. Or, at any rate, she had thought it was secretive. Conversations with her colleagues today had shown her that her liaison was common knowledge. And this afternoon, she had certainly felt desire for Darryl Hansen.

She resumed play and listened to the card of the immediate future:

the Nine of Swords. She heard her voice inquire of Daphne: "So many swords. What does that mean?"

"Swords indicate strife and represent air, the mind. Your tensions exist in the world of ideas and perception—you can use your mind incisively like a sword to ascertain the truth. Much of your conflict is bound up in the academy, an edifice supposedly built on ideas but powered by emotion—the quest for recognition, greed for accolades, the envy of others' success.

"The Nine shows us a woman sitting up in bed, her head in her hands as if awakened from a nightmare. Above her hang the nine swords. The card depicts one who is distressed, who is deeply worried and afraid. But, remember, the swords do not touch her. They appear threatening but may not be. You can dismantle them at will: the card tells us to face a threatening situation head on and its threat will dissipate. Bring the conflict into the light of day and resolve it and your nightmares will cease."

Fiona shut off the tape. She did feel storm clouds looming but she had thought they were affecting those around her, Bettina particularly. She was apprehensive about her resignation, certainly, and come May would need to find other employment. But this knowledge was plain to her. Was she repressing other fears?

Fiona felt more restless than afraid. She walked down the corridor to her bedroom in the back of the house. A room shaded by a stand of live oaks in the back yard, it was cooler than the rest of the house. She needed to review a film for her Literature and Media class the next day. She popped a tape into the VCR, propped herself against pillows on her bed, and leaned back to watch "Don't Look Now," adapted from a Daphne Du Maurier short story. As the opening credits rolled, Dynamo slid in beside her, turned around twice, and fell asleep.

Onscreen, the labyrinth of Venice's canals provided the perfect setting for a thriller which blended the landscapes of the conscious and unconscious minds. As she had on previous viewings, Fiona felt encroaching dread as the images unfolded: a flood of red flowing over a slide of a stained glass window, a child drowning in a red jacket, a murderer fleeing over a bridge in a red coat. Her psyche, along with those of the characters, twisted along the trail of blood and water, loss, redemption, and death. Absently, Fiona reached down to touch Dynamo's warm body as if it were a talisman.

She pressed "pause" on the VCR. Fiona thought again of the card Daphne had described of the woman sitting up in bed amidst the swords of nightmare. Dread. So easy to inspire, so difficult to dismiss once it had taken shape in the mind. Like Venice, so much of life seemed full of passageways that appeared clearly marked, but upon entrance they curved back on themselves or led to blind alleys. Fiona looked around her bedroom as if the key to negotiating the next passage in her life was somewhere in plain view—as in an Alfred Hitchcock movie—if only she knew how to see it.

VI: The Lovers

What we often forget in thinking of the tales of great love affairs is that romantic love may confer great joy but it also exacts a substantial price. Repercussions and consequences always follow the choice to love wholly. In Romeo and Juliet, for example, one price of the two lovers' actions is a severance from their families. Another, more serious, is that their love is so consuming and isolating that when Romeo thinks Juliet has committed suicide, he unhesitatingly joins her in death. When she awakes from her drugged sleep, it is not to her lover's kiss but to find her Prince Charming dead. She then kills herself. I don't mean to say that intense love must result in death, but only that it is always a very complicated affair.

—Miriam Held, office discussion with a student about the "C" grade on his paper entitled "Romantic Romeo"

At home in her office the next morning, Fiona sorted through index cards and computer files as she prepared to tackle the romance that had transformed Edith Wharton at forty-five. She read a card, filed it, went back to it and read it again. For herself, too, a love affair (in her case the end of one with Sigmund), as well as a professional crisis, marked that time in her life. The middle forties offered up treacherous shoals for most of the women she knew. Fiona imagined a job description for turning forty-five: Woman in prime of life required; undaunted by perimenopausal hell; capable of juggling a squeeze play of duties to generations on either side without complaint; ability to cook, program electronic devices and leap tall buildings useful; intrepid travelers only need apply.

In 1907, Edith Wharton entered an intrepid period of her life. She wrote her dear friend Sally Norton that she had met the journalist Morton Fullerton in Paris. The meeting was to prove momentous:

Fullerton, a protégé of Henry James, was then forty-two, a small and dapper man of great charm and seductive appeal. Irresistible to men and women alike, a veteran of many amours with older, wealthier women, Fullerton also frequented the circle of Oscar Wilde in London. It is not known the extent of his involvement with Henry James, only that James addressed him warmly as Dear Boy and "Cher Enfant" and followed his amorous adventures with vicarious pleasure.

Edith at this time was approaching the height of her energy and artistic powers, and after twenty-two years of marriage to Teddy, restless. Teddy's mental health was failing and he was increasingly difficult and dependent. She found Morton Fullerton "mysterious" and interesting, yet if it were not for James' intervention she might not have entered the trajectory of Fullerton's seduction.

In the Fall of 1907 Fullerton arrived in Massachusetts, carrying a letter from Henry James urging him to let Edith Wharton know of his presence so that she could invite him to The Mount, her summer home in Lenox, in the Berkshires. During Fullerton's stay at The Mount that October, he and Edith developed a deepening friendship, sparked by much intellectual discussion and a growing physical awareness. His thank you note to her after his visit included a sprig of witch hazel they had found one day in the snow. The shrub blooms in the autumn when other plants are dying and it was sometimes referred to as "the old woman's flower." Enclosed in Fullerton's note, the witch hazel was a tantalizing reminder of the warmth the middle-aged Edith had felt in Fullerton's presence. For Edith, the plant held the promise that love could bloom in the autumn of life as readily as in the spring.

A gradually escalating correspondence ensued, and soon afterwards Edith began a private journal entitled "The Life Apart." This journal, which she did not yet share with him, was addressed to Fullerton in the second person and kept separate from her regular diary.

Fullerton, as many of his friends and mentors often noted, was full of promise. Intelligent, articulate, sensual, a wonderful conversationalist, he made a fascinating companion. He was a specialist in mirroring his lovers' concealed yearnings for tenderness and understanding. He had, put simply, a gift for intimacy. This gift, plus his intelligence, made him naturally attractive to a woman like Edith Wharton. From their earliest time together at The Mount, she sensed in him a rare empathy and appreciation. For a woman who had experienced little intimacy from her husband and who had had no lovers since her marriage, to encounter Morton Fullerton was to encounter the vitality of life itself.

Wharton's nature was a deeply passionate one. Her writing expressed her love for sensuous surfaces, her appreciation for beauty in people as well as landscapes, her nuanced awareness of love and desire. In 1883 in Bar Harbor, Maine, when she first met Walter Berry, who would later become one of her dearest friends, she had briefly glimpsed the possibility of a physical and spiritual merger of like minds. But for various reasons, the two young people missed the moment, and Berry departed her life. Two years later she was engaged to Teddy Wharton, and her resulting marriage sealed off her hopes for a more complete union. While she had close friends—and she was thought a generous and loving friend—a deeper ardor had been compressed inside her for forty-five years, waiting for the one man she could share it with on every level.

While Fullerton promised much, he often didn't deliver. His intellectual gifts never matured into the great writing that James thought he was capable of. Lover after lover discovered the limits of his constancy. When he first met Edith, he was entangled with an older mistress of some duration, Henrietta Mirecourt, as well as his fiancée Katherine Fullerton, his first cousin who had been raised in his household as his sister. Edith knew nothing of these complications. Fullerton was a master at concealment, compartmentalizing his life as it suited his pursuit of pleasure. His entrepreneurial attitude toward love, his passion for seduction, and his inventiveness were essential tools to enable him to penetrate the cultivated order of Edith Wharton's life.

On the surface, Edith Wharton was enormously self-possessed, intellectually formidable, in charge of her existence. It took a man of huge self-confidence to seduce her. It was the kind of challenge that Morton Fullerton relished, not that his affair with Edith was calculated. Just as much as she, he was fascinated. His ardor was genuine, for a time.

By February, 1908, Fullerton had cleared up his other entanglements sufficiently to pay court to Edith. In Paris, before they had consummated their physical union, Edith's fear and inexperience showed themselves. Spending a quiet evening reading together on the rue de Varennes, Fullerton spontaneously said something—did something?—that disturbed Edith's idea of the perfect companionship of the mind. In a note, she asked Fullerton why he had destroyed their rare and exquisite communion. She accused him of shattering their intimacy—that "frailest of glass cups"—because she mentally had less to offer than he.

In reality, the painstakingly self-educated Wharton, the world-traveler fluent in four languages and conversant with the classics of literature, architecture, opera, and the visual arts, was more than a match for the Harvard-educated MF. Yet, newly in love in her middle age, Edith was as shy and uncertain as a young adolescent. She didn't know how to conduct a love affair. Acutely conscious of her married state and opposed to divorce, she was horrified that people, even the servants in her household, might talk about her growing liaison with Fullerton. She wished to shield her love even from her beloved housekeeper, Gross. It was all excruciating to the private and proper Edith. And tremendously exciting.

At some point in 1908, between March and May, with Teddy away in America seeking medical attention, her emotional connection with Morton assumed a physical dimension. This turn unleashed a storm of sensuality in Edith Wharton, who had believed at the age of forty-five that she would never experience for a single hour what the most ordinary woman might enjoy often in her life: sexual happiness.

Fiona took a break from writing and paced her small office, stopping to stare out the window. Outside, the sun shone relentlessly. She checked the calendar: October 1. In two weeks, at least according to accepted wisdom, the interminable central Texas summer would give over to Fall. She made her way to the kitchen and brewed her third cup of tea that morning. Listlessly, she plopped a bag of Zen green tea into a cup of boiling water. If only she could find a more complete accounting of Wharton's affair with Fullerton. Oh yes, there were the letters, and journal entries, Wharton's poems, and the biographical treatments, but even when romantic, they were all so literary, not quite the down and dirty documentary accounts Fiona wanted.

Reviewing Edith's letters to Morton once more, Fiona realized that the heart of the affair beat strongest in the silences. And while her contemporary mind, used to the explicit revelations of the early twenty-first century, craved physical detail, her literary self understood clearly that Edith Wharton's journey as a person and artist took place in the emotional awakening that the affair provided. As liberating as sexual intimacy was to Edith, the nurturance of her deep, repressed self proved even more transformative. Above all, as she immersed herself in the correspondence, Fiona found herself aware of the disappointment and pain Wharton suffered at the hands of her inconstant lover. Fullerton's pattern was to communicate with great regularity, inciting Edith's passion, then lapse into protracted silences.

Writing of one such occasion, Edith wrote: "I re-read your letters the other day, & I will not believe that the man who wrote them did not feel them…. What has brought about such a change? Oh, no matter what it is—*only tell me!*"

Yet, Edith's passion lit up her life in spite of her lover's limitations. Fiona dug in the pile of notes beside her and retrieved a fragment from a letter where Edith addressed her fears that Fullerton might smile at the "shining treasures" of her expressed passion: "And if you do? It's *your* loss after all! And if you can't come into the room without my feeling all over me a ripple of flame, & if, wherever you touch me, a heart beats under your touch, & if, when you hold me, & I don't speak, it's because all the words in me seem to have become throbbing pulses…"

Fiona put down the paper. Edith's verbal outpouring showed more of her inner reality than any graphic sexual account ever could. The physical act of love had many variations but it always came down to the same thing, really. It was impossible to characterize the unique nature of two people together just by imagining their coupling. No matter how creative, it was finite in its possibilities.

In the kitchen, she heard the phone ringing. She had removed the extension from her office so she wouldn't be disturbed writing, but now she made a mad dash into the other room to answer it.

"Fiona?" a resonant male voice inquired.

"Yes—? Is it—"

"It's Darryl," he replied before she could hazard a guess.

"Oh, Darryl. Hi."

"I've been thinking about you. Just thought I'd call and see what you're up to."

Should she tell him she was trying to conjure up the details of what a sexual encounter between Edith Wharton and Morton Fullerton might have been like? And detail for him her struggle to avoid the Gothic, the pornographic, and the simply prurient? "Oh, just working," she said. "Well, I don't mean 'just,' well, you know what I mean."

Amused, he said, "Well, it is Thursday morning at eleven o'clock. I guess we're in the middle of what they call working hours."

"You're not at work?" she asked.

"Oh, I am, yes."

There was a long silence. Fiona thought she heard the sound of a printer whining in the background, and several muffled voices.

"Well," she said.

"Well," he said and cleared his throat.

His voice sounded a bit raspy. Fiona hoped he wasn't allergic to fall elm too, just like Sigmund.

"Fiona."

"Yes, Darryl."

"Would you be interested in dinner some night?"

"Sure," she said quickly. Best not to think too much.

"How about tonight?"

"Tomorrow would be better," she said, not consulting her calendar, but feeling unprepared for a date so soon. Plus, she recalled something on with Bettina and Marvin.

"Tomorrow it is," he said. "Seven?"

"Shall we have a drink here first?"

"Excellent," he said. "Your house is in Travis Heights, isn't it?"

Fiona wondered how he knew her south Austin address—and then realized it was printed in the campus directory along with her phone number. "On Alameda, across from the school."

"Got it," he said cheerfully. "See you tomorrow."

Fiona hung up, and stood in the kitchen, absently tapping her fingers on the counter. She wasn't surprised Darryl had called, not after their protracted lunch, but she hadn't expected him to contact her so soon. She found it hard to believe there was no one in his life. She hoped Bettina would be a source of information, as always, and not begrudging of details. She recollected Darryl's reticence the other day about Bettina and resolved to ferret out that secret history.

She wandered back to her office and hovered distractedly in front of the desk chair. The mystery of Edith Wharton's sexuality faded a bit in the face of her own. Darryl's overtures raised complications. Like Sigmund, he was another man who shared her workplace, another man with a complicated sexual history. Hadn't the experience with Sig been harrowing enough? But then, she recalled the appealing tenor of Darryl's voice, the glint of the light on his bare forearms at lunch, the deep-set, interested eyes…Fiona sighed, shoved this conundrum to another room in her brain, and firmly shut the door.

She turned her attention back to the Wharton-Fullerton affair, now all the more alluring because of its remove, its twists and turns a matter of record, however ill-advised. The story of any two people's romantic life together was a buried treasure virtually impossible to excavate. There were guideposts, of course—the discovery, in the 1980s, of Fullerton's letters filled some of the gaps of Edith's one great sexual passion. But, still, the real life of it remained behind the locked door of the past. Even if that door miraculously opened wide, we lacked the sensibility, the intimate knowledge of "the custom of the country," to read it as familiars.

But as Fiona planted her rear in her chair once more, and the words began to flow from her fingertips, she experienced little difficulty bridging the gap of years. The language of love, after all, was always present tense.

The affair between Edith and MF lasted roughly three years, about average for Fullerton's entanglements. But she had given all of herself to the younger man, innocently, trustingly. And, after the first flush of sexual excitement, when the inevitable silences began that characterized Fullerton's flagging response—the unanswered letters, the absences, the ignored entreaties—she was devastated.

Perhaps her greatest mistake was letting him read her private diary, "The Life Apart," a document that revealed the wild flights of her passion, the subjugation of her personality to her lover. It didn't show the slightly removed, impenetrable Great Woman who had been so enticing to seduce, to bring down from her exalted perch. To a man like Fullerton, with his constant need for new stimulation, knowing that she was so much his was bound to dull the sharp appetite of his interest, even while the signs that he might take her for granted, just a bit, didn't appear for some time.

When she returned to America, she received a letter with each steamer from the still-attentive Fullerton. But, when he was back in Paris, in the autumn of 1908, Katherine Fullerton arrived for a year's sabbatical from her post at Bryn Mawr. Attracted as always by immediate gratification, Morton Fullerton slipped back into that attachment and was seen daily in his cousin's presence. The letters to America began to arrive with less regularity.

In the Spring of 1909, with Edith back in Paris and Teddy gone, the two had a resurgence; some of her most concentrated writing during that time took the form of another series of poems for MF. Although their sexual congress was as satisfying as before, Edith grew ever more clear that Fullerton did not share the nuances of her emotional experience. One of her poems, "Colophon," poignantly addresses this lack of complete communion. Fullerton had the grace to recognize the truth of their lack of shared vision, writing a note in the handwritten version Edith gave him: "I saw not what she saw, and that's the tragedy of it."

In the waning months, Edith was to be sobered by two sets of revelations. First, she became aware of Morton's long-standing and often sordid relationship with Madame Mirecourt. Then, in 1909 Teddy confessed to her his own tale of adultery and mismanagement of her funds, having taken a mistress in Boston while he embezzled fifty thousand dollars from one of Edith's trusts. As he neared sixty, Teddy's mental instability was reaching a crisis. Still, the fact that her husband's infidelity coincided with her own affair with Morton Fullerton must have given Edith cause to wonder at the complex symbiosis between her own greater independence and success and her husband's dissolution.

Her disappointment in both her husband and her lover left Edith Wharton in 1910 more than ever clear-eyed and unsentimental about the workings of the human heart. At forty-eight, Edith knew intimately the huge pleasures, the considerable costs, and the impermanence of romantic happiness. She was truly a woman of the world.

Fiona's burst of writing left her feeling drained and a little wistful. If anything, delving into her subject's emotional turmoil had only heightened her own. Thoughts of Darryl lurked around the edges of her narrative. What if he, like Fullerton, was just another attractive but inaccessible male, dazzling but disappointing? Fiona took a deep breath and exhaled slowly. She realized it was already too late—she'd made her choice. The lure of a new attachment inevitably left one with one foot dangling over the edge of a cliff; still, despite the danger of falling, the possibility of flying was simply too delicious to resist.

Fiona's memory had been correct—she did have a date to get together that evening with Bettina and Marvin, and at 5:30 she drove north on the interstate, got off at 45th Street and wound her way west to Avenue F. As she pulled into the drive, Marvin emerged from his greenhouse and waved cheerfully. His face was smudged with dirt and he wore filthy gloves.

"Hey, girl," he said.

"How are you, Marvin?"

"Digging in the dirt and happy to be there."

Bettina was in the kitchen, opening a bottle of chilled white wine. "Hi, darlin'," she hugged Fiona warmly. "There's two glasses in the freezer, take them out, will you?"

"Marvin joining us?"

"Not 'til 7. This is his favorite time to work. He says he likes to transplant things now when the sun is fading so that the plants can rest until morning."

"Right." Fiona recovered the glasses and followed Bettina onto the porch. The porch faced tree-lined streets and lush, flower-filled front yards.

"Can you believe it?" Bettina said. "October first and it's cool enough to sit out here in the evening. A good omen."

"For what?"

Her friend shrugged as they sat down in heavy cast-iron chairs. "Thanks for being such a rock on Tuesday. Sigmund turns everything into an ordeal. Was making love with him that onerous too? You're a braver woman than I. Well, thank God for you and Miriam."

Fiona winced at the reference to sex with Sigmund. "I didn't do anything." She waved a hand, dismissing Sigmund and the past as well as Bettina's insinuations, and took a sip of the wine. "Delicious. What is it?"

"Rodney Strong Chardonnay. You did too do something. You made me laugh for one thing before that wretched meeting."

"You made *me* laugh!"

"Whatever." Bettina paused and brushed an unruly reddish curl out of her face. She looked at Fiona appraisingly. "What did you think of Kyle?"

"Oh, well," Fiona said. "Quite an operator. And interesting looking—a kind of miniature femme fatale."

"So that's why you gave me that disapproving look. She's cute enough, but so young. Please don't insult me by assuming I would ever be tempted by...children."

"Well, now that you mention it," Fiona said, returning her friend's measured look, "it occurs to me that she looks like you might have looked at the verge of puberty—just smaller and thinner perhaps—and I'll bet plenty of people were tempted by you."

"I was never anorexic," Bettina said curtly, but she looked pleased just the same.

"You know Kyle has made other complaints against her professors in the past?"

Bettina frowned. "Yes, she has. But never against a woman faculty member before."

"That is interesting, isn't it? Especially to choose a clearly heterosexual woman."

"And what does 'clearly heterosexual' mean versus just 'plain heterosexual' might I ask?" Bettina fingered the large amber stone hanging at her throat. She looked genuinely curious.

"Oh, I guess that's a dumb distinction to make. But it's just that you're married and there's no history of you being with women. And, look at you..."

"Fiona, my dear, if I didn't know better, I'd think you were interested in women yourself sexually. You're obsessed lately with how every female in the place looks. And now you're being so stereotypical about homosexuality. Miriam Held would not be pleased to hear you talk this way."

Fiona picked up her wine glass again. Was Bettina teasing her? "I've never said I'm uninterested in women. With the right person I don't doubt it could be a possibility." A flush crept over her cheekbones as she blurted this last sentence out. She had never said that aloud before—the idea that the 'right person' could be female. Had she even said it to herself?

Bettina sat quietly, just smiling at Fiona.

Fiona continued, somewhat doggedly: "As for Miriam, I don't think she looks stereotypically gay either. For heaven's sake, since when have you become so p.c.?"

"Don't be defensive."

"It's hard not to be, with everyone being defensive around me." Fiona studied the yard for a moment. "Is that a new peach tree out by the garage?"

Bettina followed her friend's gaze. "One of three new arrivals."

"Umm." She quickly added: "I'm writing about Edith Wharton's love affair with Morton Fullerton."

"And?" Bettina inquired, as if references to peach trees always led to unusual disclosures.

"Nothing. I've just noticed since I've been researching and writing about it that everyone around me seems preoccupied by sex."

"Including you?"

Fiona said nothing for a moment. "Bettina, do you mind if I ask you something?"

"Hmmm?" Bettina slid a footrest under her feet and settled back with her wine.

"To your knowledge, is Darryl Hansen seeing anyone?"

Bettina studied the liquid in her glass, drank, and then set the wine on a nearby table. "How should I know? Why?"

"Well, he called and asked me out today. And I'd like to know if he's attached."

"Why not ask Dennis? They're bosom buddies these days."

"Because I'm asking you."

Bettina removed her feet from the footrest. "Fiona, out with it."

"What do you mean?"

"Whatever it is, just ask me."

Fiona looked around to make sure Marvin was nowhere near and lowered her voice. "Did you have an affair with Darryl?"

Bettina pursed her lips, and then gnawed on her bottom lip. "Did he say that?"

"No, he didn't. But when I mentioned you the other day—we had lunch—he had you know, *that* look."

"I see."

In the silence, Fiona felt the uncomfortable sense—very rare in her experience with Bettina—that she was intruding. "We don't have to talk about this if you don't want to," she said softly.

Bettina sighed. "It's very complicated." She laughed. "Of course. Isn't sex always complicated? It's kind of like reaching your hand inside the box of caramel corn and getting the booby prize instead of the real prize. You know, we're attracted to someone, they're attracted to us. The candy looks good, smells good, it seems we should just be able to reach into the box and have a handful. It seems so simple." She sighed again, heavily. "But it never is."

Fiona didn't know what to say. She began to wish Marvin would join them. She looked down at the porch floor and then glanced discreetly at her watch: it was only 6:15. No rescue would come from that quarter.

"It's none of my business," Fiona said. "I'm sorry."

Bettina's wide face turned to Fiona with a look of calm understanding. Fiona received her friend's glance gratefully. For a moment, she felt bathed in forgiveness, even though she wasn't aware of having done anything wrong.

"It's all right," Bettina said. "It's not like I like to keep secrets. But you're close to Marvin. It doesn't seem right."

"You're absolutely right. We shouldn't talk about this."

"But," Bettina stuck resolutely to the topic. "You say Darryl's asked you out?"

Fiona nodded. "And I accepted."

Bettina's pale eyebrows rose a fraction. "He's a very attractive man."

Irritatingly, Fiona felt her face redden.

"He's also married," Bettina said calmly, watching the color deepen on her friend's face.

Fiona stared at her feet for a breathless moment. "I was under the impression that he and his wife had split up," she said, her voice unsteady.

Bettina raised her wineglass to her lips and drained the contents in one swallow. Lights bloomed on the deck in the dusk, gracing the creamy skin on Bettina's throat with a glaze of gold. "True. They're not together anymore." Her green eyes appraised Fiona. "But they're not divorced either."

VII: The Chariot

"Sometimes, woman, you just have to act: get on your horse and ride into
battle! Stop thinking and waiting around for someone else to rescue you.
Of course you'll feel unsure one minute, and wildly justified the next. But
fight, for God's sakes! What other choice do you have?"

—*Blake Burnois, advice to Fiona at a coffee shop in Greenwich Village,*
at the news her advisor was plagiarizing her Master's thesis, 1978

On Friday night Darryl arrived punctually at 7:05. Fiona met him at
the door in an oversized, deep blue silk shirt and a short, and tight,
black skirt.

"How does a martini sound?" she asked him, watching with interest
as he removed his sport coat. The thin knit polo shirt he wore underneath the jacket revealed the developed chest and arms of someone
who worked out or did heavy lifting.

"Great. I like a woman who isn't afraid of hard liquor."

Fiona reached into the pantry for a shaker, vodka and vermouth.
The thought occurred to her—unwelcome—that his comment was
something Sigmund would say. Perhaps it was generational; Darryl
was in his fifties also. This equation of women with "soft" drinks like
sodas or even wine rather than Scotch or bourbon seemed dated.

"I drink vodka; would you prefer gin?" She pulled out of the freezer two trays of tiny ice cubes shaped like the state of Texas. Bettina and Marvin had given them to her as a joke but their small size made them perfect for martinis—Fiona followed Marvin's recipe religiously, allowing the vodka and vermouth to "cook" on the ice for exactly ten minutes before straining.

"Vodka is fine. And olives, spicy ones if you have them."

When Fiona came into the living room with the drinks, Darryl was sitting on the sofa facing the fireplace and leafing through a pile of New Yorker magazines on the coffee table. "I can't keep up," she said. "Not with that and the newspapers too." She handed him a glass and sat in a rocker adjacent to the sofa Darryl occupied.

"I don't even try." He accepted a frosted martini glass. He raised his drink, "To Autumn," he said, and took a generous swallow. "Excellent," he pronounced.

"Thank you. I use Marvin Graf's recipe; it works every time."

"Which is?"

"Can't reveal his secret. He made me promise."

Darryl laughed, a trifle uneasily. Was it the mention of the name Graf?

"What's Marvin up to? I heard he retired." He sat back and put his arms behind his neck.

Fiona tugged at her skirt and squirmed in her chair, remembering why she seldom wore snug-fitting clothing. She crossed her legs, feeling that anything else would be unsafe. "His dream. His own greenhouse."

"Hmmm. He's not very old; I doubt as old as I am." Darryl unconsciously sucked in his stomach. "I applaud him that he can swing it financially."

"Well, he's good with money. And, of course, it helps that Bettina has a regular job."

"Yes, a spouse with a regular job is always a help." Darryl smiled at her, the skin around his blue eyes creasing sharply almost to his hairline.

Fiona studied his left hand, which, as she recollected from their recent lunch, held no wedding ring. "Darryl, was your marriage to Janice your first, if you don't mind my asking?"

His smile didn't fade. "Second. For both of us."

"Has she remarried?'

"Not that I know of. I have a hunch that both of us will be shy of tying the knot a third time."

Fiona winced at the expression "tying the knot." It implied such entrapment. In any case, Darryl was acting about as unattached as anyone could. Fiona wondered if Bettina was playing tricks on her, telling her Darryl was married.

"I know what you mean. I was only married once, as I told you, but it left a lasting impression."

Darryl helped himself to a plate of mixed salted nuts. His hands were large, the fingers long and supple, and he plucked three almonds from the dish with dexterity. "You said your ex-husband was a psychologist?"

"A psychiatrist."

"Ah. Was he compulsive about being a shrink at home, too?"

"An occupational hazard, I suppose. But he left private practice while we were still married. Tim specialized in organizations. He developed a niche working in wellness for high-tech companies. Very cutting edge." Fiona sighed, taking note of how academics with her specialty lurked at the very opposite end of the demand curve as far as jobs went. "That's one of the reasons he was happy to move to Austin when I got this job. He had five job offers before I'd even called the moving company."

There was a short silence. Darryl broke it with: "Why are we sitting here talking about old marriages? There are few things as depressing."

"And limiting, I suppose," Fiona added. "Just speaking for myself, failed marriages—well, failure of any kind, actually—depresses me."

"I couldn't agree more." Darryl looked at his watch. "Our dinner reservations are for eight o'clock. Perhaps we should think about going?"

Fiona drank the rest of her martini in one gulp and felt the reassuring throat-burn and head-spin of high-octane alcohol. "I'm ready if you are," she said.

Darryl had selected one of the few established Austin restaurants that had survived the mid-'80s when oil prices and the Texas economy cratered in concert. The predictable and yet excellent food and wine no doubt explained in part the eatery's resilience in those uncertain times. As if cued by their surrounds, their conversation avoided controversial territory. Kyle Cramer's grievance came up just once, for a bare five minutes. Fiona surprised herself by inserting in that brief discussion: "Bettina is my best friend, you know."

Darryl's fork, loaded with duck and orange sauce, paused mid-way to his mouth. He put the bite back on his plate carefully. "I understand that's why this whole thing is so upsetting to you. Try not to worry about it." He smiled across the table almost tenderly and Fiona's heart lurched while a warning signal went off in her brain.

After dinner, Darryl walked her to her door and waited, small-talking long enough that Fiona knew he hoped she would ask him in for a drink. He stood very close to her, with one hand leaning against the door frame, so that his chest arced toward hers. He was only about an inch taller than she—about five ten, she guessed—and their eyes met straight-on. Finally, she said: "I've got an early morning, Darryl, so I'd better turn in. I had a lovely time."

"Busy weekend? Well, that's too bad—I, well..." He stopped talking, kissed Fiona abruptly, and turned to go.

Fiona liked the kiss—firm, a trifle exploratory, but not too insistent. She wouldn't have minded another taste and almost reversed her decision about the nightcap. But in spite of herself, she held firm.

"Goodnight, Darryl," she called, watching him stride towards his car.

From the end of the walk, he pivoted and raised his hand in a half-salute. "Goodnight, Fiona. See you soon, I hope."

Fiona opened the door, stepped inside, and picked up the furry little body that collided with her legs. Holding Dynamo, she leaned against the door. "Well, that was a close call, kitten." The cat snuggled her head into the curve of Fiona's neck and purred her assent.

She gave Dynamo a dab of the wet food she liked as a special treat and pressed the button on the answering machine.

"...hi sweetie...just wondering how your big date went tonight...Talk to you tomorrow." It was Bettina, calling at 10 p.m. Surely she didn't think Fiona would answer if she and Darryl were here together, and so why call? Fiona made a wry face: Big Sister checking up on the usurping younger sibling, perhaps?

There was a second message: "Hey, Fiona. It's Blake...I know I've been a rat for not keeping in closer touch, but you know me, I hate email and I hate the phone...anyway, call me tonight, even if it's late....I have a favor to ask you...one you might like to grant me...bye, babe."

Fiona smiled. Blake Burnois had gone to graduate school with her at Columbia. He stayed there for his Ph.D. while she went on to Penn. State. Recently, he'd been made a senior editor at *The Gazette of Higher Education*, an appointment that gave the two friends no end of chuckles. Fiona and Blake had spent most of their graduate education decrying academia and now they'd become the establishment, one a tenured professor, the other a chief arbiter of academic viewpoints and news. An old story, even a "tired" one, as Bettina would no doubt point out: young rebels sell out and become the bastions of institutional life. However, she and Blake still nursed their anarchistic impulses.

Fiona checked the clock, 11:15; after midnight Blake's time, in Washington D.C. But she knew Blake still kept graduate student hours, so she punched the buttons quickly, curious about her friend's summons.

He answered on the second ring. "I knew you'd call," he said, sounding not a bit sleepy. "How's my girl?"

"Things are dicey here, Blake, decidedly. I think you should come for a visit in the next month or so."

"Oh? Let's have it."

"Do you want the short version or the long?"

His voice was gleeful in anticipation of gossip. "Need you ask? Long, longer, longest, please!"

She filled him in on the rupture with Sigmund (including an editorial on how stupid she'd been and for how long), her resignation (still unacknowledged by Sigmund), Bettina's mysterious behavior and sexual harassment charge, and the murky atmosphere surrounding Darryl's overtures.

"My God," Blake said, his baritone voice positively vibrating, "High drama in Austin, Texas. You've got it all: broken hearts, deception and betrayal, and sex, sex, sex. No wonder the music down there is so damned good."

Fiona felt a bit let-down. "Blake, maybe this sounds like entertainment to you but it's my life we're talking about. I'm not having too much fun."

"Sorry, dearest. Really. I know it must be tough."

She could hear the overlay of concern barely covering the still-simmering mirth. "Liar. You just want to dish and you don't care at whose expense. I'm really not doing well at all."

Blake sounded almost contrite. "Fiona, darling, I am sorry. I will come down, I promise. I'd like to see Dennis again too. Are he and Carter still together?"

"Yes." On Blake's last visit to Austin, he and Dennis had become fast friends. Fiona wasn't sure how fast.

"Too bad. Oh well, I'll come anyway."

"Wonderful, just give me three days' notice."

Blake assented. There was a preoccupied pause and Fiona said: "Isn't there something semi-urgent you wanted to talk to me about?"

"Lord, you got me so excited about intrigue in LoneStarville I almost forgot. Yes, there is. You know the inside back cover of *The Gazette* where we always have an essay, a viewpoint, or something?"

"Yes. Although I have to tell you, lately that journal of yours just puts me to sleep...in fact—"

"Fiona, listen. I don't care about your sex life or lack thereof." Over Fiona's muffled protests, he continued: "Okay. I had this sweet essay on demolishing liberal education all lined up...I know it sounds crazy but it wasn't anti-intellectual in the least...and the writer blew me off, well not actually, darling, you know what I mean...anyway, I have this beautiful empty page all primed and waiting for YOU."

"Me?" Fiona couldn't decide if she was flattered or terrified.

"I know you. You always have little gems stashed away in your desk that you haven't bothered to send out for publication. Hmm? And, now that we've had our little talk," Blake's energy level escalated a decibel, "I'm betting that since you were denied your promotion and signed off with Sigmund—what, a month ago?—that by now you've written something about it, something dark and derelict, probably fictional but blatantly autobiographical, something delicious. Am I right?"

Fiona counted to five. "Yes."

"Hah! I knew it. What's it called?"

"'Ivory Power.'"

"And does it make Sigmund look horrible?"

"Well, it makes the promotion process in general and the chair of a department of English at the Texas Institute of Technology in particular look horrible. Well, actually, all of the senior members look pretty bad."

"Fiona, I'm swooning! A thinly-disguised Austin University—that'll get people talking—mired in petty academic politics no doubt, all the more vicious because so petty. Oh, it's too good. Fax it right up to me, will you? I'll bill it as a fable for our times."

"Blake, slow down," Fiona cautioned, growing alarmed. "Better read it first. It's pretty much of a parody. Not serious or scholarly."

"Well, yes, that's what the doctor is ordering. You don't name names or anything do you? Or give revealing descriptions our readers would recognize?"

"Of course not. I'm just not sure...well, I wrote it for myself, as an act of vengeance you might say. I never considered publishing it."

"Bullshit. No writer I know doesn't positively salivate at the thought of every drooling syllable of his or her brilliant prose at some point appearing in print. Truth?"

Fiona sighed, hating the perspicacity of this wretched but dear friend. "Truth. But you might really find this pure drool, since you mentioned it."

"Can't imagine it. Send it tonight." Blake lowered his voice conspiratorially. "By the way, I hear there's a rumor Sigmund might be deposed?"

Why did everyone's voice drop when they were talking about Sigmund Froelich? "You've heard that?! You must be wired into some deity." Fiona was astonished at Blake's network; she had barely heard this news herself.

Blake sounded almost sheepish. "Naw, I ain't that intuitive. Or that good a reporter. Dennis passed that on. We've had several late night conversations lately—"

"Blake, listen. I don't care about your sex life or lack thereof, to quote a dear friend. But, it is time for Sigmund to stand down as chair. He's become inept, and entirely self-obsessed—"

"Isn't it funny, darling, that when *one* stops sleeping with *one's* lover that person seems completely self-obsessed whereas always before he appeared fascinating and insightful, during that idyllic time when *one* thought he was obsessed with *oneself*, I mean."

Fiona giggled in spite of herself.

"But, back to Sigmund. It's time the king falls out of his tower, I agree. So, fax me your goodies. You'll feel better, I promise. Revenge is almost as good as sex."

"Okay, you asked for it."

"Fabulous. But before you ring off, Fi, dear. You said you've re-signed. What will you do come spring?"

"I don't know. I'm not letting myself think about it for two months. I had to promise myself to keep from wholesale panic."

Blake sighed. "We were idealists when we were chicks, weren't we? Thought it could never happen to us—we'd never get caught in the academic cage and be plucked and trussed for dinner like all the other poor scratchers. So," his voice dropped to almost a whisper, "you're worried to pieces in spite of your promise?"

"Yes," Fiona whispered back, feeling a familiar lurch of dread. She repressed an urge to ask Blake for a job on the spot.

"Honey, you'll come through." His familiar cheer unexpectedly returned. "You're the best and the brightest. Look, I'm not going to be one of those cloying creeps who tells you that one door closes and another opens, but I have a good feeling about this. There's a whole world out there. Trust Uncle Blakey."

Fiona smiled at the thought. "Remind me—when has your advice been good?"

"Exactly. I don't even follow it. But you should. This time."

"I have to get off the phone. If you want your essay. Bye. And, Blake, thanks."

"You may be cursing me before long."

"I'm not talking about the story, you goof. Thanks for being so funny and...sweet."

"Kisses to you, my dearest Fiona. I'll be getting back to you very soon."

Fiona took her computer off sleep mode, and clicked on a folder enti-tled "manuscripts." A quick scroll, and a double-click brought up:

IVORY POWER
by Fiona Hardison

The English Department Budget Council at the Texas Institute of Technology (a department undergraduates cannily referred to as Lit TIT), was about to convene. On today's agenda was the case of Dr. Lawrence Benson.

Professor Birdwell, the department Chair, opened the meeting promptly at 3:30 on Friday afternoon. "Let's begin the meeting, if everyone is here." He looked at his watch; he had a 4:30 tennis date, and he fully expected to make it with at least ten minutes to spare. He looked at the five people gathered around the table, their faces registering a varied expressive spectrum ranging from exhaustion to boredom.

"Everyone's not here," snapped Professor Lindstrom, a man marked by a thin frame and quick judgments. He glanced systematically around the room and blinked his eyes, which were small and bright, almost as if he were recording events around him with a point-and-shoot camera.

"Oh?" said Dr. Ernest White, the oldest member of the Council, looking up from an elaborate sketch he was making on a light blue legal pad. "I don't see who isn't here," he said in a slightly hoarse, vaguely east coast, and clearly annoyed voice.

"It is difficult to see who is not here," agreed Professor Janquist, the only woman on the committee. Janquist was in her late forties, slightly overweight, and carefully dressed in a gray wool skirt and dark green sweater. A green and turquoise silk scarf jauntily encircled her neck.

Dr. Birdwell sighed and shifted his thickening, yet still markedly muscular, body in his chair. Getting this group of people to focus was always the most difficult part of negotiating their frequent meetings. He smiled, brushed his longish brown hair away from his forehead, and assumed a tolerant air: "I believe everyone is here except John."

"John," Dr. White spoke the name musingly, as if recalling a long-buried detail from the deepest recesses of his capacious memory. "Ah, you must mean Maxwell." He breathed audibly and returned to his drawing.

"We do have a John Maxwell on the faculty." Dr. Lindstrom looked up from a stack of student papers he was grading with alarming alacrity. He paused a moment, pencil in hand, and then readjusted his glasses in readiness for an impetuous raid on the contents of the next manuscript.

"Indeed we do," Dr. Janquist said calmly. "But he isn't here, is he? I propose we begin."

Birdwell sighed again and tried to peer at his watch: 3:40. Good God, if he didn't hurry these people on, he'd never make his match. It was doubles too, with the luscious Irene Mason. He couldn't miss that. He paused a moment, picturing her floating across the tennis court, her full breasts, encased in a purple sports bra, bobbling toward him. A simply stunning woman. And a woman of such courage—she had once been married to Lindstrom, who had maneuvered not only to walk cleanly away from their divorce, but also to take the bulk of their assets, including ten acres of prime lakefront property, with him. Birdwell passed a hand over his face, as if to clear his vision, and then looked around the room solemnly. "Yes, let's begin. I assume everyone's looked through the file?"

"What file?" Professor Canning raised his head like a turtle cautiously peeping from its shell to sense the turn in the weather, and judge it fair or foul. Canning's eyes resembled those in a Doonesbury cartoon drawing, heavily shadowed and perpetually half-mast.

"Larry Benson," Birdwell explained patiently. "He's asked us to consider his file for promotion to full professor."

"Oh, heavens, again?" complained Professor Lindstrom. "Didn't we just look at this two years ago?"

"Well, yes, but he is entitled to a review every year," Jane Janquist said, her voice catching on the word "entitled." She smoothed the wrinkles out of her scarf and looked hopefully at Birdwell.

"Is he?" Canning glared around the room, his sleepy eyes struggling to focus.

"Well, yes, it is policy," Dr. Dent said quietly from the other end of the table, his small, neat head nodding slightly for emphasis. All heads swiveled to look at him. Dent only spoke three or four times a semester, usually on matters of policy.

"Well, let's get on with it then," urged Lindstrom, tossing the pile of graded student papers in his briefcase with relief, as if emptying a basket of noxious trash into a leak-proof bag.

"Indeed," Canning agreed. "I have a good deal of work to do, unlike some of you. But get on with what exactly?"

"Here's the file," Birdwell said tightly, pushing the bulging manila folder toward Canning. It was 3:50. He loosened his tie. All the professors except Lindstrom and Janquist made a mad scramble for the file. Canning snatched it and held it to his chest protectively. "I simply must review one or two points," he said.

Birdwell exchanged a sober look with Janquist. She continued to look to him, as if for guidance, even after he had turned away. Damn it, the woman expected too much from him. Of course he was her friend, well, even considerably more than a friend. But he couldn't be expected to hold this committee to her high standards; the members simply weren't controllable. He wasn't God after all. He glanced at her again, at her soft brown, appealing eyes. But of course he had to try. He drew himself up straighter in his chair and sucked in his stomach: "As we discussed two years ago with Benson, we expect him to complete the book he began after his last promotion and..."

"When was his last promotion?" White's eyes remained on his doodling, which Birdwell couldn't help but notice had increased in frequency and complexity of late.

"1984," Lindstrom calculated quickly. The fingers of one hand tap-danced jerkily on top of his closed briefcase.

"Good Lord, that's sixteen years ago," White said, pulling himself away from his notepad where he had been carefully shading what looked to be a cartoon of a bloated rabbit. "What *has* the man been doing?"

Canning opened the folder, and scanned the first few sheets of paper. "Here we are: Benson, *curriculum vitae...*" His head hovered over one page, wobbling slightly as he traced a column of closely-packed print with a rigid forefinger. "Well, he hasn't finished that book, I can say that with authority. He has written six essays."

"In Class I journals?" Dent, amazingly, spoke up again.

"Oh, I wouldn't call them that," White said, seizing the file from Canning and staring at it with a look of amazement, as if he had never seen it before. "Regional, at best." He paged through the file gingerly, touching only the outermost edges of each page as if in fear of bruising the paper, or perhaps his own pale skin. Then, having translated the entire career of Lawrence Benson into a few key vital statistics in less than one minute, he set the file aside and went back to sketching.

"In all fairness," Professor Janquist said quietly, "we did ask him to publish those six articles."

"Really?" Canning stared at Janquist as if she were exhibiting signs of acute nervous disorder. He stretched a hand toward her—for a moment Birdwell thought he might check her pulse—but then he withdrew his hand and scratched one ear instead.

Birdwell checked his watch. It was now 4:05 and the file had only made its way to Dent, who would most likely never, ever relinquish it until he retired. "Yes, I believe we did."

The committee members looked at each other silently for some time. White's pencil scratched steadily. Dent closed the file and pushed it to Janquist, who passed it to Lindstrom, who irritably placed his eyeglasses on top of it. "Well," Lindstrom said, staring at Birdwell, who surreptitiously noted the time at 4:12.

Janquist took a deep breath, braced her arms on the table, and spoke in her most controlled voice: "Larry has told me, and all of us actually when we went through this two years ago, that he simply wants to know what we want for his promotion and then he'll know how to proceed."

"The book, of course," Canning pointed out.

"He has the manuscript completed." Janquist held firm. She carefully looked at each professor around the table. "It's being reviewed, I believe, right now, or will soon be sent out for review. And of course, he has produced the six essays we asked for."

"That's true..." said Birdwell, beginning to sweat. He was unable to sense the tenor of the entire committee's mood and it was already 4:15. Four pairs of eyes focused on him expectantly.

White looked up, his sparse gray hair glinting in the

overhead fluorescent lighting. He finished his drawing with a proud flourish, raising his hand off the page like a conductor cueing an orchestra. "Well, that settles it then." His voice was calm and confident, a voice accustomed to decades of captive audiences.

Lindstrom snapped his head around to stare at White. "Oh?"

"Indeed," White intoned. He caught Dent's eye for a moment and a strong, but silent, signal seemed to pass between the two men.

Birdwell was captivated by this exchange. He had seen this odd mediation occur between the two senior members of the department before, but he wasn't sure what it was that they did; neither man seemed to move a muscle, yet inevitably, some tacit—and mutually satisfying—contract was agreed upon.

Apparently gratified by this transaction, White shifted his eyes from Dent and scanned the room. He spoke slowly and painstakingly as if lecturing to a roomful of obtuse undergraduates: "Benson's petition must be denied. We as a committee simply can't be treated this way—promotion, as we all know only too well, is a very complex issue. We can't merely spell out for Benson what is required of him to be promoted. In the first place, he should know that for himself. The man purports to be a scholar, doesn't he? And secondly, and I must add, most importantly,"—here White paused gravely for emphasis—"we can't just tell Benson exactly what he needs to do, because then he'll assume that if he completes that work, that we'll absolutely have to promote him. This committee has never been held hostage to its recommendations. It's outrageous."

"I agree." Canning's eyes glowered out from their shadows like the fierce orbs of a nocturnal creature deep in its cave. "It's absolutely unconscionable. This is a university, not a public utility."

"Quite so." Dent bowed his head firmly and folded his hands on the table in front of him, as if bestowing a blessing.

Lindstrom considered, his quick eyes flashing at the committee members in a lightning tally, and then he nodded slowly. Janquist looked baffled, the skin of her forehead contracting. She opened her mouth to speak, looked round the table, perhaps to note that the others were vacantly staring—out the window with its view of campus rooftops, at each other, at any rate anywhere but at her—and then closed it again.

Pleased with himself, White began to gather his papers. He passed on the rabbit drawing to Dr. Janquist, who accepted it with a tenuous smile.

Birdwell breathed out with relief. It was only 4:23. He had plenty of time after all. "All right, we're agreed then. Excellent meeting. I'll see you next Friday when we meet to recommend merit pay increases for this committee. There's not much money available this year, but in light of the heavy work load you've all had to assume with promotion and tenure cases, I think we can work out something that's quite adequate."

Professor White smiled and shook his large head serenely. "It has been a very difficult year. So many requests, so few resources."

Birdwell, stuffing Benson's file into his briefcase, smiled uncertainly. What was it the old bastard was muttering about? He'd gotten his way, as usual, did he have to have the last word too?

Aloud, Birdwell murmured, "Ah, yes, well put," and then made a dash for the door. Janquist and then Lindstrom closely followed him, taking deep gulps of air. He could almost feel their breath on the back of his neck; it reminded him of the eager panting of children released for recess.

As the younger people fled the room, Dent and Canning leisurely assembled their papers and books, their various writing instruments. They inclined their heads approvingly to White, and then judiciously filed out.

———

Fiona read over the story, copied the file into a fax document and was typing in Blake's number when she paused. Should she so rashly send this to him? Something nagged at her, a snippet of a dream or a conversation, something about being clear about her own motives and staying out of the web of others' entanglements. She felt vaguely uneasy. But "Ivory Power" was simply a parody, containing no deeper meaning. Nothing about its machinations would surprise anyone remotely knowledgeable about higher education. Fiona considered. It contained no revelations, stepped on no one's toes. She was sure that the story couldn't be more harmless. "Ivory Power" was too slight to harbor any consequence. At least that's what she told herself. She punched "send" and the modem dialed and connected, sending the fax on its way.

So successful was she in convincing herself that her motives were innocent—she had none, only to help an old friend in a tight place, in fact—that she fell into bed and slept the heavy, thick, and insensate sleep of a teenager.

VIII: Strength

So many academics operate unconsciously, acting out of primitive cravings for authority. Many possess fine intellects, yet emotionally remain stunted, enfants terribles grasping for recognition and control. They just don't get it, as the saying goes, that subtlety and imagination will triumph over brute displays of power.

Darryl Hansen, notes for In the Service of Narcissism, *his secret history of the Department of Literature and Rhetoric*

The next morning, Fiona woke early, remarkably refreshed, and charged into the day. Fortified by the act of sending "Ivory Power" out into the world, and armed with the day's first cup of tea, she tackled her manuscript. She admired her subject's capacity to use turmoil in her daily life as a generative source for her writing and resolved to do the same herself. She plunged in, fingers flying over the keyboard.

Edith Wharton's ability to transform the limitations and anxieties of her life into great art saved her emotional and creative selves. From roughly 1891, when she published her first story in Scribner's Magazine, *until her first volume of fiction came out in 1899, she suffered from episodes of illness and sporadic fits and starts of creativity. In the middle of the decade, she suffered a series of breakdowns. Her ill health punctuated a traumatic identity crisis over whether she would live her life as a socially-appropriate wife and daughter (as Lucretia Jones' daughter properly would), or as a woman of letters.*

One of the worst crises was precipitated when her publisher, Burlingame, expressed his excitement about a book-length collection of stories; his enthusiasm was met with silence from Edith for sixteen months. Her neurasthenia took the form of nausea, depression, complete exhaustion, and insomnia. Yet once the first volume, The Greater Inclination, *appeared in 1899, to favorable reviews, Wharton's health improved. And as she began to write and publish more steadily, her siege of debilitating emotional illness receded firmly into the past. While the state of her health would always reflect the state of her emotions, she had gained sufficient mental control over her base fears so that she could almost always function and write. Such was her dedication to her craft that the woman who produced her first book of fiction at 37 would go on to publish fifty-two volumes during her lifetime of 75 years. Not surprisingly, the chief ailment of her mature life took the form of exhaustion.*

Fiona believed that The Mount, Wharton's mansion completed in the Massachusetts Berkshires in 1902, signaled her coming of age. She designed the house herself, with architect Ogden Codman, and supervised the details down to the profusion of flowerbeds that spilled down from the Italianate terrace. Moving into the house after she turned forty, she wrote a great deal of *The House of Mirth* there, generating from this new habitation her first major success. The Mount served as a symbol of Edith's arrival as a mature, formidable woman—internationally famous author, hostess extraordinaire, and designer of an architectural landmark of beauty and innovative design.

The massive construction on 113 acres of prime Berkshires property also showed the integration of her personality: For one thing, its blend of Italian, French, and English styles—informed by her particular Americanness—stood as a symbol of her cosmopolitan personality. For another, it graced a location, rural and wooded, that she deeply loved. The house was an almost perfect blend of Wharton's equal needs for community and privacy, with its large public rooms on the first floor and Edith's fiefdom of privacy, her suite, on the second. The property also proudly proclaimed a connection to her family, as she named it after the home of her great grandfather Ebenezer Stevens, an ancestor of energy and courage whom she particularly admired.

Fiona didn't think it a coincidence that Wharton set one of her greatest fictions, *Ethan Frome*, in the countryside around The Mount. The location gave her the security she needed to unravel her role in the triangle made up of herself, Morton Fullerton, and Teddy Wharton. Just as Ethan did in her novel, Edith occupied the center.

Wharton often switched genders in her fiction. Newland Archer, for example, in The Age of Innocence, *clearly shares his author's attitudes toward books and culture, and the stifling limitations of Old New York society. It is interesting that "old man" was a nickname Teddy used for her in the early days of their marriage, and that she referred to herself and to her neighbor in her youth, Teddy Roosevelt, as "self-made men." Part of her identification with masculinity was quite obvious: like her contemporary Gertrude Stein, she did not have female models who were artists or intellectuals. More unconscious, perhaps, was the imbedded voice of Lucretia Jones and her definitions of femininity; for her mother, women were fashionable, not intelligent, thus creating the doubt for Edith that in some basic way she was not feminine. In her memoir, she makes her incompatibility with her environment a point of humor: "I was a failure in Boston because I was thought too fashionable to be intelligent and a failure in New York because I was too intelligent to be fashionable." The failure of the sexual aspect of her marriage, and her childlessness, could have only added to this insecurity about her female identity. One of Morton Fullerton's many gifts to her was to assuage her insecurities about her womanliness and attractiveness.*

Fiona wondered if Edith's involvement with the bisexual Fullerton might have awakened her own androgynous nature, expressed through her transmogrification of Edith into Ethan. Certainly the

James-Fullerton-Wharton ménage seemed a testament to the ambisexual nature of all three parties. As Fiona was beginning to see even more clearly, writing provided a fantasy field to embody the other gender. For as she occupied the consciousness of a James or a Fullerton, Fiona found herself viewing the feminine aspects of Edith, or herself, from an intriguing remove.

Ethan Frome, published in 1911, provided Wharton such an avenue, allowing her to transform a time of duress—the deterioration of her marriage and her affair with MF—into disciplined writing. Fiona imagined Edith scribbling furiously in bed, as was her morning routine whether in Paris or at The Mount. Exorcising her feelings of dread about her marriage, she transmogrified her lush, summer Berkshire environs into the bare and frigid winterscape of the fictional Starkfield:

Ethan Frome *tells the story of a man trapped in a tortuous marriage who falls headlong in love with a young woman, his wife's cousin, Mattie Silver. Like Edith, Ethan (the names are similar) is married to an incompatible spouse considerably older, while Mattie (like Morton) is close to his own age and sensibility. Continuing the parallel to her own situation, the wife, Zenobia, like Teddy Wharton, suffers from depression and chronic illness. The marriage is joyless and sterile. Mattie brings life into the house and the light of new possibility for Ethan.*

But the lovers are doomed—Ethan can never abandon Zeena to solitary destitution—and when his wife sends Mattie away, Ethan and Mattie plot to commit suicide together by sledding down a steep and dangerous hill. They hit a tree, and instead of dying, live on, crippled. Mattie's injuries are so severe they deform her personality as well, and she becomes even more whining and querulous than Zeena. At the end of the novel, Ethan, Mattie, and Zeena continue to live together in a hideous no-exit household. The novel's last sentence, spoken by a neighbor of the Fromes to the narrator, encapsulates their misery: "...the way they are now, I don't see there's much difference between the Fromes up at the farm and the Fromes down in the graveyard; 'cept that down there they're all quiet, and the women have got to hold their tongues."

This Gothic rendering of Edith's situation shows her debt to Hawthorne and even Poe. While the novel's end is gruesome and hopeless, Edith writes of how happy crafting the work made her, that it was the first time she felt fully in command of her art. Written from the rue de Varennes, at a remove from its American location, the novel benefited from a synergy between her given American heritage and her chosen Parisian life. A catharsis fueled by her past and present, the crafting of Ethan Frome *served as a grand release for the novelist and a way to tenderly describe, in the closeness between Mattie and Ethan, the love and understanding she had felt with Morton Fullerton.*

A few days earlier, discussing the novel in her undergraduate Literature and Film class, Fiona's students had balked at the barrenness of the book. To these young people, Starkfield in the nineteenth century appeared as a symbol of deprivation, almost inconceivable in a twenty-first century Austin awash in technology dollars and the lure of unlimited opportunity.

"Why doesn't he just leave?" complained one young man, squirming in his seat as if the very notion of Starkfield spurred his limbs to revolt against confinement. "He could just take Mattie and run. Save himself. What could his wife do?" Several other voices chorused agreement at this seemingly sensible suggestion.

"Try to imagine a person in the nineteenth century, with no money, no prospects, no education," Fiona said. "His wife isn't the only thing restraining Ethan, although marriage in his time was a sacred obligation. Poverty and lack of choice have circumscribed his life. It's hard for us to envision in this beautiful setting—" she gestured outside to the sunlight sparkling on green lawns—"but Starkfield is an inner landscape as well as a physical place. Ethan's world is bleak and inhospitable."

Another student raised his hand. "It's hard to picture. Now someone would just move to another town and start over."

"You have to have resources to do that," said another. "Ethan does-n't have money or the habit of thinking he's free. He's as trapped as if he lived in a prison."

Fiona saw her students, with their lives beckoning richly before them, shrink from this spectacle of hopelessness. They didn't want to imagine that such a dead end existence could ever happen to them. But Edith Wharton had known the feeling of imprisonment well, after twenty-five years of a confining marriage. Like Ethan, Edith must have felt her youth stolen from her.

"Let's look at how trapped Edith Wharton felt in her life to under-stand the generative impulse behind *Ethan Frome*," Fiona told her class. "Devoting one's life to literature was not an easy choice for a young woman who had grown up in an almost total absence of literary culture—she remarked in her memoir, *A Backward Glance*, that, in her family, authorship was regarded as something between a black art and a form of manual labor. While the mature writer could acknowledge such derision with grace and humor, the young Edith, struggling to find her voice and vocation as an author, suffered paralysis."

Fiona selected a book from her desk. "One of Wharton's earliest published short stories, 'The Fullness of Life,' provides a clue to the fate she saw for women brought up as she was: "'I have sometimes thought that a woman's nature is like a great house full of rooms: there is the hall, through which everyone passes in going in and out; the drawing room, where one receives formal visits; the sitting room, where the members of the family come and go as they list; but beyond that, far beyond, are other rooms, the handles of whose doors are never turned; no one knows the way to them, no one knows whither they lead; and in the innermost room, the holy of holies, the soul sits alone and waits for a footstep that never comes.'"

Back at home, after class, Fiona summarized the significance of The Mount as a marker of Edith's sense of self:

———

Wharton's Berkshire home testified to an open and optimistic view of existence, compared to the lonely, trapped woman in the ironically-titled "The Fullness of Life." In just ten years, Edith Wharton had transformed herself. The distance traveled by the newly-married, vocationless woman who lived in the humble Pencraig Cottage on her mother's estate to become the mistress of a remarkable mansion on an estate of her own was very great indeed.

Fiona surveyed her own humble house fondly. It wasn't grand, like The Mount, but it was of her own making, the first house she had ever bought on her own. After a childhood spent moving from one Air Force base to another, and years of graduate school gypsyhood, she felt anchored at last. A refuge and a comfort, the house pleased her and contained her life quite nicely. Dynamo, her face naturally masked in patches of black and caramel-colored fur, appeared on the windowsill from behind a curtain and squeaked.

"Well, girl, do you think we should have some lunch?"

The cat padded agreeably behind her into the kitchen. She put out some tuna bits in a dish and watched Dynamo first sniff and gingerly paw it, then attack the food greedily. Animals expressed their natural appetites; they didn't worry about funneling them into another mode of expression.

Fiona often thought there was a parallel between writing and psychotherapy. But to her, writing channeled a different kind of process than therapy, where an active listener intervened. As a writer, Fiona often had little conscious awareness about what deeply rooted experiences of her own were projected into her work. But she knew that whatever captivated her attention also had deep hooks in her hidden mind and emotions: the writing served to dredge this undersea world as if for buried treasure.

She wondered what unknown corridors of her psyche were being traveled in her excavation of Edith Wharton's world. Fiona's middle-class, peripatetic upbringing, largely in the midwest, couldn't have been more distinct from Wharton's upper class childhood, rooted firmly in Old New York. Yet Edith Wharton, a woman who had built an important and meaningful emotional and intellectual life painfully from the void of an empty world dominated by money and "society," resonated strongly with her. Even though bolstered by wealth, Wharton had fashioned herself, without models or encouragement, into a professional writer. And yet, for all her success and discipline to her craft, Wharton was criticized brutally during her life and after, for being too social, too wealthy, too "successful," too popular, too prolific, too formidable, too cold. Like women in every era who broke the mold, Wharton was simply derided as being "too much." As nothing else did, that disapprobation, to use a Wharton word, forged a bond of sympathy and empathy for Fiona.

More than Edith the adult, though, it was Edith the child who tugged at Fiona. The little girl, plagued by nightmares, writing alone in her room, ignored by older, male siblings and distant parents, moved Fiona in a way that the wealthy, successful Wharton never could. The formidable adult self housed the lonely child whose imagination both terrified and inspired her. Fiona knew all about escaping into a fantasy life. For while her family's frequent moves forced her to develop a facade of competence, able to greet new situations and people with apparent ease, she had often felt detached and left out from the tightly-knit lives of friends rooted in one place. As her subject had, she had played make-believe, building worlds that she could control and in which she became the central figure. Fiona had created elaborate plays and acted out all the roles in the privacy of her room. And like Edith, she had been an only daughter, not the recipient of her parents' expectations. Except in the universes of her own creation, she had stood outside, alone, looking in.

Hunger cut her ruminations short. Fiona was about to step out the door to forage for food when the phone rang.

She listened to the machine and when she heard Blake's voice, picked up.

"Fiona?...the story is delicious."

"I'm here. You really like it—it isn't impossible fluff?"

"Oh, indeed, no."

"Well...thanks." Fiona said shyly. "...um, do you mind telling me what you like about it?"

"Well, I confess I love how it kicks ass."

"You mean to academia in general?"

"Yes, sure, and to dirtbags like Sigmund Froelich in general."

Sigmund...why should Blake care? "It's sweet of you to be outraged on my behalf, but—"

Blake's quick mind appeared to have streaked on to the next thing. "Gotta go, doll. Barring any complications, it should come out in the issue after next."

A mere two weeks away... Fiona had never had anything published that quickly. For a moment, she was giddy. But the question of Sigmund still puzzled her. "Ah, Blake?"

"Hmm?"

"I know I've talked a lot about him...but did you know Sigmund before?"

"Ho...you mean Herr Doktor Professor Froelich? How could you forget? I taught with him at Indiana twenty years ago. My first job. He was something of a wunderkind—already a full professor at thirty-five. I was a lecturer, of composition, along with thirty other lowly cattle. He had us all fired, so the department could save money by hiring graduate students. You really don't remember?"

"God," Fiona said, a dull burning sensation spreading through her stomach. "I don't know how I could have forgotten."

Blake grunted. "That's because you've always been at least a horse on the academic farm, darling, never just another pair of bovine hooves on the feedlot. It isn't fun."

"Funny," she said. "The other night when we talked, I thought you only knew of him through me. Well, everyone here, really."

"Fiona, you charm me. The world is so much smaller than you think. I really do have to go. *Ciao.*"

"Bye." Fiona replaced the receiver. She'd also forgotten how Blake never let go of a grudge. He resembled Dynamo in that regard—once he identified his prey, he always pounced.

IX: The Hermit

Why does Beauty get locked away in a castle with the Beast? Well, in every hero's journey, there comes a time when she has to be removed from outside events so that she can concentrate on unworldly things. Beauty had to learn that what's inside is far more important than external appearance. She came to love the Beast for what was inside him, not how he looked. This lesson gave her a gift of spiritual wisdom.

—Bertram Hardison, reading to his daughter the story of "Beauty and the Beast," 1960.

Outside, the October sky shone clear and sunny. The temperature hovered at a pleasant eighty degrees, but Fiona didn't notice. She trudged six blocks to a neighborhood cafe in a sober mood. She had grown weary of academic politics: they felt like high school endlessly recycled. The boys that nobody wanted to dance with became bullies and full professors, the girls endlessly tried to be pleasant and smart, but not too smart to fit in. Consequently they were rarely taken seriously, or in academic parlance, promoted. And they never were allowed into the locker room—the executive councils—where all the strategizing took place.

She selected a table and ordered the enchilada special, spinach and zucchini, a favorite. Although she smiled and joked with the waitress, her gloom steadily gathered. Higher education had deteriorated into a playground for immature, spiritually bereft people. Filled with loathing, partly for herself, she swallowed a large quantity of iced tea as if to flush her system of acrid tastes and thoughts.

After lunch, she strolled down Congress Avenue. On this south side of the river that divided the city in half, the broad avenue sported bright little shops featuring cool junk, hip clothes, and funky jewelry. A large cut-out cartoon dinosaur leered down onto passersby. Fiona stared straight ahead, planting her feet one in front of the other; no spring lightened her step.

She stopped, squinted up at the sky, and sniffed the breezeless air. A change of scene, that's what she needed. She checked her watch: 1:30. She could be down on the Gulf Coast by 5PM. She calculated quickly: it was Sunday. She taught on Tuesday but her T.A. could take her undergraduate class, which meant she wouldn't have to return until Thursday to meet her graduate class and the next meeting of the undergraduate Lit. and Film course. Breaking into a jog, she cut east on Monroe and over toward the park near her house. She was home in five minutes.

A phone call secured her a reservation on Port Aransas, at a worn but homey condominium complex Dennis had introduced her to. In a few more minutes, she'd thrown together shorts, t-shirts, a bottle of wine, a few spices and canned items. She'd buy fresh seafood from stands at the beach and broil it once she got there. Scooping up Dynamo on the way out, she bounded down her back steps to the garage. She tossed Dynamo into the car; the cat immediately leapt into the back window, her ears perked. Trained to accompany Fiona on drives since kittenhood, she loved the car. Fiona ran back into the house for her notebook computer—just in case she got an urge to work—several books on Wharton, and a couple of Ruth Rendell mysteries.

Fiona left a voicemail message for her T.A. and pondered whether or not to change her phone message to say she would be out of town.

Opting to step off the information trail, she locked the back door, and was off.

The drive down Highway 183 was not a swooping Whartonian motor-flight through the countryside, but familiar and soothing just the same: the habitual stop for barbecue in the small burg of Lockhart, then the winding through more small towns, none too prosperous, before hitting the flatlands of south Texas. Port Aransas was on Mustang Island, home to far more feathered creatures than two-footed ones. A lack of direct motor access preserved the island's charm; a staid ferry provided the only way across from the mainland. Dynamo glowered at the pelicans but retained her window seat with dignity.

Once ensconced in her third floor condominium, Fiona opened all of the windows and doors on the seaside and let the ocean roar in. She put Dynamo's sheepskin bed in a glassed-in corner so that she could keep track of the pigeons. Then Fiona headed for the beach.

The Texas coast wasn't the cleanest: cars were allowed to drive on the beach, and the ghosts of old oil spills lurked in the sand. But Fiona loved prowling the dunes in the salt air. Each winter a nearby wildlife refuge housed the largest colony of whooping cranes in North America, and the shore boasted abundant bird life. As Fiona walked the beach, egrets, terns, and gulls soared overhead, dipping down to pluck snacks from the water, and sandpipers scattered before her.

After about three-quarters of a mile, Fiona angled toward a large dune and huddled against the high, broad mound which shielded her from the wind. Tufts of grass bloomed out of the sand. The air felt different here—the humidity caressed her skin even while the salt tang tickled her throat. She took slow, deep breaths and felt the tension leak out of her. She leaned back and let her mind go blank.

As she watched the water cresting and breaking on the shore, Fiona noticed a great blue heron slowly glide down the beach and come to roost only about three yards from her, on top of the dune she rested against. The bird hunkered down and scanned the beach along with Fiona. She stole a look behind and above her at the blue and gray feathered creature, its craggy profile sharp and interested in the world below. As he hunched there, his long neck folded into his wings, his thick breast plumage spilled down from his beak like a long, gray beard. The bird's presence reassured Fiona; it had been here before, often, she assumed. The creature possessed an air of belonging to this coast that few could claim. The bird had a natural air of sagacity and calm, an old soul surveying its domain.

Fiona sat with the heron for hours, until hunger and sleepiness drove her indoors. When she walked away, it spread its majestic wings and soared off. Fiona felt blessed.

Inside her apartment, she filled Dynamo's bowl with Eukanuba pellets and fed her a few Pounces. Fiona made a tuna fish sandwich—dispensing to Dynamo the juice, which the cat lapped up daintily—and then settled in an armchair to read.

She opened a curious volume she had found in an outer pocket of her duffel bag, something she must have bought on impulse on a trip and forgotten about; she wasn't sure how it had come to be there. Oversized, with a worn blue leather cover, the book had been handled so much its surface was smooth and—(was it an illusion?)—warm to the touch. Even the tiny cracks on the cover, sanded down from heavy handling, felt soft to her fingertips. It reminded her of a book her father used to read aloud to her when she was a child. Hefty and chock-full of promise, it invited her to open it.

When she did, she found it contained a series of fables, all illustrated with elaborate, fine ink drawings. The longer she studied the illustrations, the older they appeared—the thin pages whispered under the caress of her fingertips, the pastel inks faded and bled into the fine paper—until she realized that the worn volume in her hand might be quite rare. She paged forward, her eyes arrested by a picture of a man, very stooped and old, dressed in gray. She thought a moment; it reminded her of a picture of Father Time, Kronos, who in Greek myth had been Zeus' father. The lone figure peered soberly downward from his vantage point on a snow-covered mountain. A gentle yellow light infused his lantern, complemented by the warm yellow of his staff.

Fiona stared at the image for a long while. It spoke to her of calm and patience. She thought of the great blue heron she had seen earlier on the beach, surveying the scurrying people and creatures beneath its calm perch. The day faded around Fiona as she immersed herself into the lives of an aging king caught in the myth of his own power, and the strong queen who led him to find strength in the diminishments of growing old...

Fiona started in her chair and woke up as if from a deep sleep. When her head cleared, she found in her lap not the worn volume of fables but the paperback mystery she had brought along on the trip. She groped near the chair and underneath it with no success. She searched everywhere, but the book with the cracked blue cover had disappeared. After rifling through the apartment, Fiona could reach no other conclusion but that she had dreamed both the book and the story into existence. The sense of loss she felt reminded her of a time her younger brother, then only three, had eaten one of her favorite stories, "The Snow Queen." Then, as now, she had experienced an intense visceral longing to feel the particular texture of the vanished book.

The story, and the steady pounding of the waves against land, calmed her, however. The host of problems back in Austin receded: she stopped wondering if Darryl would call or if she should call him, whether she could trust him, or Bettina either. Sigmund's antics and Kyle Cramer's lawsuit seemed merely tiresome and unimportant: the idle posturings of people focused only on the external trappings of power. Even the publication of "Ivory Power" faded into the realm of a non-event. None of it had anything to do with the business of life, it seemed to her.

She remembered reading Gertrude Stein's remarks about why American artists began to live in Paris: "The reason why all of us naturally began to live in France is because France has scientific methods, machines and electricity, but does not really believe that these things have anything to do with the real business of living. Life is tradition and human nature." Fiona found it true that much of her own life, with its frantic juggling of appointments, email, and voicemail, along with the whole accompanying dance of bureaucracy and intrigue, certainly missed the point of the process of living.

She found a small library in Rockport and checked out a few books on Greek myths and various volumes of ancient stories and fables, none of which was the enticing volume she had read at her beach apartment. As she read, however, she came to see the crises of the human life cycle repeated in the stories of peoples in all eras and cultures. Innocence, love, betrayal, war, marriage, separation or exile, maturation, decline, death: the forms of their portrayal varied, but the outline of events and the lessons frequently were the same.

Reconnecting with the timeless world of myth made Fiona miss her father more than usual. His voice, quiet and soft-spoken but compelling, had introduced her to the stories of gods and goddesses, forest creatures, and witches. She called her mother, Janet, in East Grand Forks, Minnesota, on Monday even though she had just spoken with her the day before (she and her mother had a standing phone date every other Sunday).

"Fiona, what a surprise!...is anything the matter?" Fiona's mother usually found breaks from routine alarming.

"Oh, no. I'm just taking a little vacation, in fact, not scheduled..."

"And you're sure nothing is wrong?" The words "not scheduled" had set off further alarm bells.

"No," Fiona laughed. "Can't I just pick up the phone and call, Mother?"

"Well, yes, of course. I love hearing from you, you know that. Where are you?"

"The Texas coast."

"Oh." Fiona detected a slight tone of disappointment. Her mother possessed the disdain certain northern Midwesterners reserved for what they saw as uneducational and "empty" sunbelt destinations.

"How's Dad, Mom?" Fiona asked wistfully. Her father had suffered a stroke the year before and had not regained the power of speech. Fiona found this affliction particularly tragic for her father, whose voice was so melodic, and who so loved singing and conversation.

"The same, dear. But you mustn't feel too badly. He makes the best of it, and you must try to, also. Bert is very alert. And he reads a lot and likes me to read to him."

"I know. He's very brave. And so are you. It's just..."

"Honey, don't even say it. What is, is. You know that. And there's no use wishing for something else."

Fiona sighed. Her parents had a very philosophical attitude toward aging and death. Fiona hoped she still had time to cultivate one for herself.

"And how are you, Mom? It's not all too much for you, is it?"

"Oh, no," her mother said brightly. "Only, there is one thing..."

"Yes? What is it?"

"Well, I do so love that fudge you sent me from that health food store you have down there. Your father loves it too."

"Right. Well, I'll send some up right away, as soon as I get back."

"That would be lovely, dear. Everything all right at work?"

Fiona bit her lip. Although her mother's sympathy always cheered her, the intricacies—and arrogance and prevarications—of her department seemed somehow inauthentic next to what Janet Hardison dealt with on a day-to-day basis. She couldn't bear to bring any of it up. "Terrific," she said. And, before she could stop herself—sometimes her mother made her feel like an adolescent again—she added: "I've started dating someone new."

"Oh, that's wonderful. I want to hear all about it." Fiona heard coughing and scraping sounds in the background. "Oh dear, we'll have to talk Sunday as planned. I'll call you. Nothing to worry about—I'm afraid your father is choking on his lunch again."

They hurriedly rung off. Without a doubt, her mother's life centered around "the real business of living."

X: The Wheel of Fortune

*In the great cycle of life, the seeker slowly rises from birth to becoming
and falls toward decline and death, just as the Wheel of Fortune
symbolizes the rise toward success and the falling away from it. Fate
doesn't find you: you turn to meet your fate. You must turn the wheel
according to the dictates of your true self.*

—*Daphne Arbor, consultation with Fiona Hardison*

The phone rang shrilly as Fiona fumbled through the back door with
her bag, a pile of books, and Dynamo's fleece bed precariously stacked
in her arms. Dynamo streaked in front of her and Fiona, stumbling,
dropped everything in a heap as the machine picked up. A distinctive
male voice said: "Fiona?...Where are you?...Are you there?..."

Fiona dove for the phone. "Darryl...hi. Uh huh, I've been down to
the coast....yes, trying to find some peace to write...now?...uh, okay.
Come on over."

She hung up and gently plonked herself on the head with the phone
receiver. What could she be thinking of? Salty and sweaty from a last
walk on the beach and then a mad dash home, Fiona, as well as her
hair and clothes, begged for immediate attention. And—one glance
confirmed this—the house was similarly in a shambles. She ignored

the pile of bags on the floor, including a plastic sack of fresh shrimp, and headed for the shower.

When she resurfaced, a towel over her head and wearing nothing else—she'd left the air conditioning off in her house while she was away, and the atmosphere hovered in the humid ranges—Dynamo greeted her, contentedly munching shrimp. Several crustacean tails protruded from a kitty-sized hole in the bag.

"Ugh." Fiona scooped up several squiggly lines of entrails from the floor, resacked the shrimp, and stuffed it into the packed freezer. On second thought, she pulled them out again, deveined and beheaded the shrimp, and tossed them into a pan on the stove. A quick boil, a brief sojourn in the freezer, and a dash of cocktail sauce would solve her problem of hors d'oeuvres. The wall clock showed 5:30. Darryl said he'd be over around 6. Fiona selected a dry Italian white wine, placed it and two glasses in the freezer, and sprinted off to get dressed. On her way to her bedroom, she put Dynamo out in the yard, remembering the shrimp detritus in the sink.

Forty minutes later, she and Darryl sat on the back deck clinking frosty glasses of wine. "Salud," he said. He scanned her arms and legs critically: "You managed to get some sun along with your writing."

"Are you fishing?"

"Not at all. I've sure your work habits aren't as eccentric as some."

Fiona laughed. "I wish they were eccentric, just a bit. There's no mystery. I went down to the coast. Autumn fever, I guess."

"Was it crowded?"

"Heavens, no. Texans like their beaches 98 plus in the shade. Too cool now for the natives."

They exchanged the conspiratorial smiles of northerners living in the strange state of Texas. Had there been native Texans present, those Texans would have traded similar glances, this time over the baffling cool-weather obsessions of Yankee transplants.

"I came back a day early," Fiona volunteered.

"Hmm?"

"This is Wednesday, isn't it?"

Darryl checked his watch. "Yes, but what does that have to do with anything?"

"Apropos of nothing, I thought I was going to stay down there until Thursday, but I guess you wouldn't know that. I debated whether or not to put it on my machine, but it seems I didn't."

"No, you didn't. I've been calling since Sunday." Darryl stretched out his legs and slumped in his wrought-iron rocker.

Nice legs, Fiona noticed. Did she dare ask if he played tennis? But no, it was all too reminiscent of the beginnings of her affair with Sigmund.

"Do you play tennis by any chance?" he asked.

She regarded him suspiciously. "You don't do fortunes as well, do you?"

"Oh, dear, am I mind-reading again? My wife—Janice—used to accuse me of that regularly. But, just thought I'd ask. I'm fresh out of partners."

"Me too," Fiona said reluctantly. "I haven't played, though, for about two years. I'm probably too rusty for you."

"Well, I'll give a call next time I get a chance at doubles," he said lightly. "And we'll see. No pressure." He reached for a shrimp. "What are you thinking?"

"Honest?"

He nodded.

Fiona sighed. "I don't know, I guess I'm superstitious. Every man I've gone out with seriously over the past twenty years has played tennis. And it's not as if those relationships have worked out so well, so..."

Darryl swallowed and took a long drink of wine. His deep blue eyes narrowed as he smiled. "And you blame tennis?"

"No, of course not. But, you know, now that I think of it, every one of those relationships—well, there were really only three—was intensely competitive. About everything. There was an element of game-playing in all three that I don't have the stomach for anymore."

She looked at Darryl seriously. "I've been thinking of changing my life. No, let me rephrase that. My life is changing whether I think about it or not. And I'm certain that I don't want competition to be a dominant chord in the next relationship I have, not if I can help it."

"I think I understand. You know, I'm not sure men think about competition in the same way women do. Oh, you're frowning, you're thinking, 'Oh not another generalization about how women think'."

Fiona refilled their glasses. "Not entirely. I'm listening. Of course, listening critically."

Darryl grinned. "Well, let's see how I can get myself out of this." He filled his broad chest with air and slowly exhaled. "All I wanted to say, and I should've just said it, was that I never thought of competition that way—that I had any choice about engaging in it. It's been so ingrained into my life, first with sports and games in school and then with the jobs I've had, I've never questioned it. Not seriously anyway. And perhaps it's time I did." He paused. "It was a problem in both my marriages. Particularly the last one."

Fiona also took a deep breath. "Okay. Cards on the table?"

Darryl put his arms out straight and turned palms up to the sky. "No hidden coins or rabbits here."

"Are you and Janice divorced or still married?"

His face went blank and he looked at her narrowly. "I've told you the marriage is over."

Fiona waited.

"Fiona..." he hesitated. "Does this have to do with something someone told you?"

"I'd rather not say."

"Well, I don't want to make it a mystery, any more than you did your whereabouts the past few days. It's just damned awkward. The divorce is in process, but not final yet."

Fiona made a puzzled face. "That didn't seem so hard."

"What?"

"Why didn't you just say so?"

Darryl crossed his legs and scanned the yard. When his eyes returned to Fiona's face, he looked uncomfortable. "It's rather a longer story than that."

Fiona pushed back her chair and rose. "Shall I get some more wine? Start making dinner? Do we need additional fuel to make it through?"

Darryl stood also and lightly captured her wrist. He drew her toward him and kissed her. "How about we hear it later?"

Fiona gently pushed him back. "Oh no. I think this is one I need to hear before we go any further."

"Then let's make dinner while we talk. Is there something we can fix? Or, I can make a run to the store."

Fiona led him inside. "Well, there's eggs. We can make omelettes. And I still have some serviceable salad makings."

"Fine. I like chopping. It helps me think."

On their way into the kitchen, their hips lightly touched in the doorway. Darryl stopped, and as he twisted to let her pass, she turned also, toward him. His chest brushed her breasts, and their bodies, in the slow natural rhythm of plants seeking sunlight, drew together. Fiona laid a hand on his shoulder and raised her head. "Oh," she began. Darryl's eyes were soft, openly staring into her own. She found she couldn't look away.

Two hours later, they lay back in the bed, their legs tangled in the sheets. Fiona shifted, and looked down to see Darryl's tanned hand resting on her pale stomach. She felt a momentary dislocation. Hadn't she promised herself she would stay away from married men? A snippet of the movie *Indiscreet* flashed into her head, the moment when the outraged Ingrid Bergman discovers that her handsome married lover (Cary Grant, of course) *isn't* married. Don't flatter yourself Fiona, she told herself. This man's marriage won't just disappear.

"Another glass of wine would be very nice about now," Darryl said, tracing a finger along Fiona's arm from the shoulder to the wrist. "You have such lovely, long bones."

She kissed his finger. "It's in the fridge. I'll get it."

"No, allow me." He slid out of bed and disappeared through the door. Fiona liked how unselfconscious he appeared to be about his body. Of course, it was a perfectly nice body. But not a flawless one: broad-shouldered and stocky, thick-muscled arms and legs, with a small roll of extra flesh at the waist that Fiona rather liked. Men with perfect bodies too often expected women to have them too, and while Fiona had a slender, athletic body, it bore the incipient sags and droops of middle-age. She was very aware that unless she had the inclination to spend three hours at the gym every day, which she didn't, she would never see "ideal" in the mirror.

Darryl appeared at the door with the wine on a tray and two glasses. "You know, now I really do have to think about some food," he said.

Fiona laughed. "You mean telling your story took every calorie in your body?"

"Every one."

Fiona took Darryl's hand. "I'm not quite sure how this happened. Part of my brain was listening to what you were saying, and another was telling myself to 'go slow.' So how did we end up here?"

Darryl shook his head. "I don't know. I guess it's what everyone says, great minds think alike. And compatible bodies get compatible." He raised his eyebrows at Fiona. "I forgot to tell you, corny comments are my worst feature."

"It's one I'm used to. My whole family are cornballs. There are worse sins."

"Oh, yes," Darryl said enigmatically.

They punched the pillows behind their shoulders and propped themselves up to sample the wine. They sipped companionably for a bit and then Fiona said: "Some of what you told me has just had a chance to sink in. I'm stunned that Bettina was considering such major changes and breathed not a word of it. I had no idea she was such an actress. To think she came close to leaving Marvin over a year ago, and getting a divorce...well, I'm astounded."

Darryl spoke thoughtfully, "I don't think she wanted to deceive anyone, especially you. But it was complicated: we both had to get divorces to be together. And we thought if our spouses didn't know we were involved with someone else, it would all be less painful. Then, when we were both free, we planned to tell everyone."

"And so you started divorce proceedings and she didn't?" Fiona couldn't help but think that seemed too simple. She wondered about Bettina's version of these events; she had never known her friend not to keep agreements.

As she worried over Bettina's motives, like Dynamo attacking a rag toy, she drifted off from Darryl. "—in the end, she just couldn't break up her family," he was saying, his eyes soft, and intensely dark blue. "She's an amazing woman."

"She is," Fiona agreed quickly, hoping she hadn't missed anything significant. "I don't blame anyone for falling in love with her."

Darryl leaned back against the pillows. "You two are very close."

Fiona studied his face, wary of subterranean meanings. "We are," she said cautiously, "although this news has shaken me a bit."

"You said you couldn't blame anyone for falling in love with Bettina. Does that include you?"

Darryl sounded merely curious, but Fiona felt the sure awareness that they were getting into a territory of strange loyalties discussing her feelings for Bettina. She considered saying "no comment;" instead, she said lightly, "Well, I've always been in love with her. But if you mean, did we ever have a lesbian relationship, the answer is no. It just didn't happen." Fiona tilted her glass and caught the reflection of one distorted eye. "It came up once, when we were traveling together in California one summer."

"What happened?"

Fiona raised her shoulders and let them drop. "Nothing. We just talked. And I said if I ever lost her as a friend, I couldn't bear it. She agreed and that was that."

"You could have still been friends."

Fiona shook her head. "Becoming lovers changes things. And you never know how in advance." She glanced briefly at Darryl, who was frowning. "I think you know that."

He closed his eyes for a moment, and then looked away. "When Janice found out about Bettina, it ruined our friendship. Permanently. She'll never forgive me for being so secretive. Not to mention disloyal."

Fiona's mind immediately seized on other adjectives: Dishonest. Untrustworthy. Deceitful. "How did she find out?"

"I was completely distraught when Bettina refused to leave Marvin. The way I acted—depressed, well, whacked out in general—she knew something had happened. It didn't take long for me to tell her everything." Darryl shook his head. "I'm not proud of that. Spilling my guts to the one person who couldn't stand to hear it. Just to ease my own pain. Pathetic."

"And so, now, Janice is dragging on the divorce proceedings?"

"Let's say she's making it as difficult, and as expensive, as possible. But I hardly blame her. God knows what I'd do in her place."

"Do you want the marriage to be over?"

Darryl put his glass down and folded his arms across his chest. "All the trust is destroyed now. And knowing it's my fault makes it worse. This is terrible to say, but it makes it hard to look Janice in the face. I've let her down. I broke our contract. I feel like a horrible person around her and that makes me not want to be near her."

"Guilt doesn't usually make much of a bonding agent," Fiona said simply.

Darryl stared into Fiona's eyes. "What about you? How do you feel after sleeping with a man who's just told you he's betrayed his wife with your best friend, and that he's still technically married?"

———

The word betrayal echoed in Fiona's mind the next morning as she contemplated her manuscript. Although a word tossed around easily in conversation, its meanings and ramifications were far from simple. Sigmund's lack of support of her promotion certainly earned the use of the word. And, had Fiona not tendered her resignation, she would have felt that she had betrayed her own principles. Yet, as one of her graduate students had pointed out, to resign in the face of departmental adversity could be seen as an expression of cowardice. The student had urged Fiona not to betray her students by leaving, but to "stay and fight rather than let the creeps win." But in an atmosphere where Fiona now had so little trust, what did fighting even mean? How could she win in such a situation?

Bettina's affair with Darryl, for another example, constituted on the one hand a betrayal of her marriage. Yet, she had stayed with Marvin and so didn't pursue what could be considered the larger betrayal of divorce, perhaps leaving Darryl feeling betrayed by her retreat from him. The fact was that given the multiple facets of such a situation, demonstrating good faith to one person could manifest itself as a deep disloyalty to another. Her head muddled by the relativity of it all, Fiona immersed herself into the betrayals and counter-betrayals in the marriage of Edith and Teddy Wharton.

For years, since Edith's initial literary success, Teddy had prided himself upon his management of her trusts, income, and real estate, as well as the running of The Mount. But following his embezzlement of her funds, and his speculating with her money to buy a house in Boston for his mistress, Edith removed her husband as her financial director, in essence depriving him of his only occupation in the world. Desperate, Teddy repeatedly begged to return to his former position of responsibility, repaying her the $50,000 he had stolen from her trust funds.

Edith adamantly refused. Even as she was sympathetic to his need for responsible employment, Teddy's erratic behavior frightened her. Her friends—and her husband's doctors—agreed that his condition could not be trusted. Hoping to prevent future unpleasant scenes, Edith wrote Teddy in advance that when re-united they could not talk about money or initiate further discussions of his re-instatement as financial overseer. Fearing her husband's reaction to her letter, she dreaded their coming reunion.

In July of 1911 Teddy returned from a fishing trip to join Edith at The Mount. The reunion initiated the first scene of what James later told Edith was "the storm and sorrow of the last act of your personal drama." Before Teddy's arrival, Henry James, Gaillard Lapsley, and John Hugh Smith already were ensconced at The Mount, enjoying Edith's and each others' company. Earlier talk of selling the property, and the superb state of the weather and grounds put Edith into a sentimental mood about her home. The Mount had never appeared more resplendent.

By the time her husband made his appearance, only Henry James remained. Struck by Teddy's robust physical aspect, Henry was doubly appalled at his psychological dis-ease. Teddy wavered between outraged outbursts at Edith and tearful, piteous appeals for forgiveness. Alarmed for Edith's well-being, James planned to depart The Mount as scheduled only with the greatest reluctance.

Fiona speculated about Edith and Henry's last conversation before James' departure on July 14. In an era that blanketed mental illness under benign terms like "nerves" and "exhaustion," had they been able to speak frankly about Teddy's condition?

The two friends sat in the library over a last cup of coffee the morning of Henry's departure, July 14. Henry leaned forward in his armchair. "My dear," he began, his face a mask of worry. "I can't possibly leave you with the man. He's taken his childish outbursts to new levels of irrationality. This is not a mere tempest in a teapot, a brief flurry of rapids in an otherwise calm crossing. You could be in danger."

"Please. You are thoughtful and kind, Henry, to think of me, and I am deeply grateful. I—"

"A sanitarium, my dear. That is what you must consider."

Edith shook her head vigorously. "Out of the question."

"Edith, please. Even if it would make him happier, more comfortable?"

"His family is completely against it. And I cannot abandon him now, not when he is so ill and so confused. He would not do so to me, surely. In truth, I could not forgive myself. Perhaps when he is better..."

James' head swung slowly from side to side. "When he is better you will simply forgive him again, give him another chance, and another. What about your life? Your peace of mind and spirit? And let us not forget your health."

Neither of them thought it necessary to mention the painful truth that Teddy's father William Wharton had committed suicide after years in a sanitarium. And neither cared, or perhaps dared, to speculate where Teddy's manic-depression might finally lead him.

The two friends stared at each other, Edith's eyes hooded as if staving off the bright light of scrutiny, Henry's wide open and penetrating.

Edith's hand toyed with her pearl necklace. "But perhaps Teddy is right. Perhaps I am being stubborn and untrusting. If I would allow him back as manager, give him the responsibility of the trusts, he will right himself again."

For a moment there was a silence, and then James thundered: "It's bad enough that he has robbed you of your happiness and comfort! Must you let him literally plunder your security as well? Damn it, Edith, don't sacrifice the bounty that fortune has granted you. You will only tempt fate to turn its wheel the other way and drag you down with him."

Fiona pondered James' immersion in his friends' difficulties and *amours*, a sure complement to the Jamesian absorption in the plight of his fictional characters. Rarely had a friend existed who experienced more acutely the distress, and the pleasure, of those in his orbit. The Watcher of Lamb House, Henry James endlessly dispensed advice and concern to those afflicted, and wrote voluminously of the perils of his intimates to mutual friends. Like Edith, he wore the mantle of friendship seriously, throwing the weight of his intellect and insight behind his ministrations. Edith, Fiona thought, was fortunate to have had such a champion.

———

In the days after HJ's departure, relations between Teddy and Edith broke down further. He strenuously pushed for the restoration of her confidence in his financial stewardship, disregarding her instructions that she could no longer discuss the matter with him. One evening, Teddy came to her bedroom to make amends.

"Edith, I beg you to accept my apologies for my conduct over the past ten days." Teddy's head, with its few lank strands of gray hair, hung down, and the flesh sagged away from his jaw. "I have been unreasonable."

Edith, seated in an armchair, beckoned for him to sit across from her on the settee near the fireplace, the hearth cool and silent amidst the summer heat. She hesitated, fearing that if she accepted his apology he would accuse her of passing judgment on his behavior. Yet, if she didn't acknowledge his regrets, he might retort that she was impossible to please.

"Please, my dear. I know I have caused you distress." He frowned. "Henry barely looked me in the face. He has washed his hands of me. As have all your friends." His tone remained abject, but a glint came into his eyes when he mentioned her friends. He had raved the day before that they had all turned Edith against him.

"Teddy, thank you. All of this, as you know for yourself, has been upsetting." She put her book aside and earnestly addressed him. "I would like to think things will one day be better between us once again."

"Yes, yes. I feel the same," he said eagerly. His eyes, she noticed, were deeply shadowed, the skin under them creased and worn. "I am aware that certain...certain things have transpired"—he looked keenly at her—"for both of us that are hard for either of us to forgive." He held up a hand. "Please. Hear me out. I come not to reopen painful wounds. But to ignore them is scarcely possible."

Mollified, Edith nodded. He was right, of course. How could each of them forget quickly their recent infidelities? Her anger at his betrayal rose in her, but as quickly the shame of her own culpability. She shut her eyes on the slumped figure of her sixty-one year old husband.

Teddy was talking again. "—we both know what we have risked..."

What did he refer to? Edith pushed Fullerton's cool yet sensuous face out of her mind.

"But we have too much together to let it go easily," he continued. He looked up,

his eyes glistening. "Dearest Edith, please allow me back into your confidence again."

Edith bristled. "Teddy, please, I've begged you about this. I cannot talk about money with you, not tonight, not tomorrow—"

"Of course. I was just going to say you have been most generous, allowing me to direct the affairs of The Mount. Your offer of a household account to that purpose...most generous. I accept your terms."

"Oh," she breathed, her distress alleviated by his unexpected words. Then, she hesitated, threading her way through the most treacherous thicket of all: "And do you also agree to resign as co-trustee? I know how difficult this is for you, dear. It's just that, right now, with things as they are—your moods—" She hesitated again.

Teddy's face closed around his inner distress; it was stiff, unrevealing, like a good soldier taking his medicine. "Yes, it is very hard, Edith. It is something I was always so proud of. But, in view of...of my condition, I understand. I will resign." He cleared his throat. "Give me just a fortnight and I will sign the papers." His chin came up. "I do believe I will regain your confidence and you will wish me back in my former position before long. That will be my solace."

Edith looked at him gravely and said nothing.

He cleared his throat again. "I am delighted you still want me to manage The Mount. You won't be disappointed. I'll see the place is put back to rights again. We've let a few things slide." He gestured at her fireplace. "The chimney to this fireplace, and the roof around it, for example. Things need attending to."

"That would be wonderful. No one runs the estate as you do," she added warmly, seizing upon a point of mutual agreement.

"We agree on that, then. Good." Teddy's mouth, beneath is moustache, broke into a delighted smile. He looked years younger. "I so want to earn your good thoughts again, my dear. I am certain you will find me able and deserving."

"So we are agreed that I will stay on with you here for another few weeks, and then I will go first and open the Paris apartment?"

"Absolutely. The best thing. I shall stay here and manage things. Get the gardens in shape for the fall and winter. Oversee the renovation to the stables. Yes, yes, excellent."

"You do so enjoy the shooting in the autumn," she said.

"It pleases me no end. My favorite time of the year."

"It is lovely here then," Edith said wistfully. "I'm glad one of us will be here to see it again. Teddy," she said impulsively. "You did absolutely the right thing to turn down the contract of sale we received in Paris. It is the very best thing to keep our home here."

Teddy's face opened up. "I'm so glad you approve. It didn't feel right. And the offer, insufficient anyway, don't you think?"

She nodded. "Outrageous, really. It reminds me of all the proposals and counter proposals we suffered through when we built this house. You remember how unreasonable Codman could be..."

Ogden Codman, an inspired but not always efficient architect, had not only designed The Mount with Edith, but co-authored her first published book as well, The Decoration of Houses. *To complete construction on the Lenox property, she'd had to replace him with another architect.*

Teddy laughed. "Too taken with himself as a great architect, yes? Obsessed with design but neglecting its reasonable execution? Yes. But you set him straight, Edith. You were fine."

She smiled back at him. But the memory of the building of The Mount stabbed at her. What optimism, what excitement, what hope for the future the two of them had shared then. Tears pricked at her eyes; she blinked them rapidly away. "So you will join me in March at the rue de Varennes?"

"Capital." He stood then and stepped toward her. For a moment, she thought he would extend his hand. Instead, he bent stiffly and kissed her on the cheek. "'Til tomorrow, then, my dear."

He left the room. Flooded with relief at the outcome of their conversation, Edith immediately copied down the details of their agreement. In a letter addressed to Teddy's brother Billy, she summarized what had transpired, and reviewed the history of their past six months of discussions. Of late, Billy had criticized her handling of Teddy, insinuating, she thought, that her treatment of Teddy might be at the heart of his difficulties.

Edith drafted the letter carefully. She was horrified that her husband's family thought her abusive of Teddy. Nannie Wharton, Teddy's sister, meddled terri-

bly when her brother had stayed with her, gushing to Edith that Teddy was per-
fectly well, and hiding the details of his true condition from her. Billy and
Nannie condemned her, and not their brother, Edith well knew.

She finished the letter but did not seal it. By nine thirty she had bathed and
retired to her bed, where she lay propped up on pillows reading. Her clock chimed
the hour of ten just as a knock sounded on the door and Teddy once again stepped
into her room.

"My dear?" Edith started. "I thought you had already retired."

"Couldn't sleep," he said.

"Is something wrong?" she asked, tightening her peignoir around her throat.

"Oh no, nothing." He smiled. "I thought I might bring you a cup of tea."

Edith rarely drank any stimulants after dinner, a fact her husband doubtless
knew. "Thank you, but no. I find I'm rather tired."

Teddy paced the room. "So sorry to disturb you. I'll leave you then."

Edith's eyes fell on the unsealed letter, which rested on a small table next to the
bed. She indicated it with one hand. "I was just writing your brother. In fact, I
would like you to read the letter before I send it to him, and make a note that you
agree with my account—I've written down the terms of our agreement."

"Of course." Teddy picked up the thick envelope and sat down on the settee as
before. He withdrew the letter and read quickly, his eyes darting erratically
across each page. His hands began to tremble.

"This is not what we discussed," he said, his face masklike.

Edith spoke carefully and softly, " Why, Teddy, yes it is. It's what we agreed
upon less than two hours ago."

"You must think me a dolt. A puppet whose strings you can jerk. Well, I'm not.
I didn't agree to resign as trustee," he said obdurately.

"Ah," she said. "You said it was difficult for you but you would do it. You
would still be in total control of The Mount."

Teddy leaped to his feet, the foolscap falling around him like dead leaves.
"Keep control! Yes, with you depositing $500 in my account every month. By any
stretch, that is not control. It puts me in the position of an old retainer, and not a
very trusted one."

"That isn't what I meant," Edith replied firmly. "You will run the estate. As you see fit. The money is simply earmarked for that purpose."

"Nothing is simple here, Edith. You mean to strip me of everything. My brother is right—you're trying to buy me off with a pittance. After the way in which I guided your fortune all of these years."

Edith sat still, stunned. What had happened to this man in two hours? His face was white, his eyes wild. Who was he?

"I won't resign as trustee!! I have managed your affairs for over twenty-five years. And your wealth has greatly increased, not mine. I've given you every-thing. And you betrayed me. With a younger man, a sycophant, a man not worthy of—"

"Stop it!" Edith covered her ears with her hands. "Leave at once. We will dis-cuss this when you're calm."

"Calm!" Teddy's voice cracked. "How can I ever be calm again? The moment my back is turned, you'll sell The Mount—and leave me with no home at all! I'm being disenfranchised."

His anger died suddenly. Falling to his knees, he began to sob. "I would rather die than steal from you." He entreated her, using an old family nickname: "Puss, please. Don't ask this of me. Don't humiliate me. I must retain the trusteeship." Through his tears, he began to mutter.

Then, just as abruptly, he raised his voice again and cursed her. She watched him numbly, too shocked to speak. He stood unsteadily and staggered around the room, hitting the walls with his fists. Edith began to feel really frightened. She must act and quickly. Rising from the bed, she clapped her hands loudly, shouting "No!" as if she were warning off a growling dog.

She hurried to him and thrust her face to within two inches of his. "Teddy, listen to me. Get out of my room. Right now." She grasped his arm and squeezed it as hard as she could. "I shall start screaming if you don't leave now."

Teddy's arm stiffened and he jerked away from her grip. He strode to the door and opened it. "Yes, I'll leave. But you won't be quit of me this easily. I am your husband. Don't forget that, Edith. I am not some pretty, smarmy scribbler, a jour-nalist for the love of God—"

Edith shut the door on his ravings. Rage fueled her. Her husband was mad.

Yes, she would leave Teddy. For her own sanity. Her own dignity. She would never allow him to talk to her like that again.

For several days, letters flew back and forth between the spouses. Edith wrote to Billy further, adding another letter to the original one she had shown to Teddy, telling him that she had tried, unsuccessfully, to live with her husband. She believed they must separate. To Teddy, she reiterated she would deposit the $500 for the running of The Mount each month, and that she hoped he would re-gain a "normal view of life."

Edith left Lenox. Her experiment at reuniting with her husband a failure, she retreated to Paris, to her friends, and a way of life that salvaged her self-respect. By November, The Mount had been sold through Teddy's efforts. In selling it, he dispatched his only reasonable occupation, caretaker of the property. But he had also asserted himself, legally, as Edith had left the decision up to him. In spite of her sense of betrayal at the sale, and her husband's increasingly erratic behavior, Edith had abandoned the idea of separation.

Edith's about-face puzzled Fiona, just as it had those who knew her at the time. It seemed inconceivable that she would leave her prized possession, The Mount, in the hands of a deranged and untrustworthy husband. Fiona suspected that Edith wavered between her own certainty that she must leave Teddy, and her fear of what she would face as a divorced woman. Perhaps she had sacrificed The Mount in order to keep the bald truth at bay: that she had given herself and much of her adult life to a man she no longer loved nor even respected. Fiona could only imagine her subject's reluctance to admit such a truth after more than twenty-five years of commitment. Yet she knew from her time with Sigmund the powerful drive to maintain the status quo. Once one has abandoned the familiar, uncertainty and the necessity of change remain.

It was not surprising to Fiona that the last months of the marriage exacted a toll on Edith's health. She suffered from anxiety and vertigo. While she managed—remarkably—to finish her novel *The Reef*, she also abruptly broke off her career-long relationship with Charles Scribner and sold the novel to Appleton.

Contemplating her draft, Fiona was struck by the climactic nature of the Whartons' break-up. Even the world stage mirrored Wharton's personal drama as The Titanic sank with over fifteen hundred lives lost. Most divorces occurred after the marriage simply ran out of energy, coming to a halt like a watch whose battery loses juice. In the end, neither party has the energy to continue the struggle. Fiona considered her own marriage a rote example in that regard. She and her husband Tim fought and reconciled and fought and reconciled until one day they fought and gave up.

In spite of more spectacular evidence, Edith was finally pushed into the divorce court by simple infidelity. She found out that Teddy, on his return to America, was living a dissipated (and expensive) life in Boston. He boasted of driving his new automobile at speeds of one hundred miles per hour; frequently, he was seen in the company of young women. Worse, Edith discovered that since 1908 her husband had been traveling in the company of women in Europe, registering as "Mr. and Mrs. Wharton" in hotels. This final humiliation proved to be too much. The end coincided with a letter from one of her brothers who not only sided with Teddy, but claimed that Edith had abused her husband. Fiona imagined how Wharton must have felt at this precipitous time of her life.

Edith walked outside onto the balcony. She could hear the noon bells chiming from her nearby church, Sainte Clotilde. Paris spread out around her. She would initiate divorce proceedings at once. Teddy's flagrant infidelities were easily proven and her lawyers assured her he would be found at fault.

On all sides, the contracts that had sustained her life lay broken. Her parents were both dead and her two brothers estranged from her. Her marriage was over. Her original publisher considered her a traitor.

She breathed in the fragrant spring air, with its promise of full-blown summer. In January, she had celebrated her fifty-first birthday. The dawning of her second half-century promised a new beginning. She had her city, her work, and her friends. And, finally, without encumbrance, she had her own life. It lay before her, as rich and varied as the city spreading around her. She intended to consume it to the fullest.

Fiona lifted her fingers from the keyboard, satisfied. The divorce was a major key to Edith Wharton's life. She had abhorred the necessity for it, but by initiating it she finally threw off the shackles of Old New York. It represented a bridge to a new, less charted phase of her existence. For the first time in her life, the author could assume full agency in directing her life.

Unbidden, the face and body of Darryl appeared in Fiona's mind. A rising anticipation accompanied the bloom of pleasure. She and he stood at the border of an unknown territory. A new relationship altered the balance of possibilities as profoundly as one that had ended. But as Fiona knew only too well, the two were not comparable: the beginning of an affair blossomed with the allure of infinite potential, while the end of a marriage shriveled with the pain of unrealized expectations.

Outside her study window, Fiona could see a pair of squirrels playing tag in a hackberry tree. They swung easily up through the branches, unfettered, it seemed, by gravity. Fiona pondered, as she watched them, on the ties and obligations that kept human beings anchored to a particular path. Naturally, she wondered at the form the keys to her own freedom would take. Her eyes shifted back to the screen. Writing this book, for example, had the potential to alter the course of her life. Every action led to a sequence of events: some doors opened as a result, and others would close. Fiona's mind looped from Edith on her balcony in Paris to herself in a small room in Austin, Texas. All lives had mileposts, all actions had consequences, and the life one saved could be one's own.

XI: Justice

Acting is largely a matter of achieving equilibrium. If a character behaves extremely in one way, let's say has a ferocious temper, look for where in her life she might express tenderness. Review the motives behind an individual action: it might result from a chain of events seemingly far away or in the past. Weigh your role as impartially as you can, and then decide how to play it.

—Dennis Reagan, studio class in Acting I

Three days later, Fiona picked up the phone to the blitz of electricity that was Blake Burnois. "My dear. Good news: I'm coming for a visit on Friday. How about a dinner party? Invite Dennis and Carter, of course—I've already talked to Dennis, naturally, and they're free that night. And Bettina and Marvin, if you want. And, of course, your new beau."

"Beau? Blake, who have you been talking to—"

Blake's laughter cascaded from the top of his baritone register. "I knew it. Darling, it's simple. You've broken up with Sigmund—thank God—and quite some time ago, well, more than four weeks. Hence, you must have a new man by now."

"Oh?"

"O! Fiona, you can't fool little Blakey. Outside you're all midwest-

144

ern, pressed and proper, but inside you're as horny as an eager chorus boy. Admit it, you're just not the abstaining type."

Before Fiona could even protest, Blake continued: "Wait. That's redundant. All chorus boys are horny. So, what's his name?"

"You make me sound utterly predictable," Fiona said, somewhat offended.

"Oh, not at all. I admire you immensely. I have nothing against sex, as you know. It's the best part of a relationship. After a while, the rest just ends up as Sturm und Snore." Blake stopped—Fiona heard the clink of ice cubes—and then he went on with renewed energy: "And your taste is usually impeccable—I'll forgive you your egregious lapse with Sig. It must have been the water after those ghastly floods back in 1990."

"There weren't any floods in '90, I don't think," Fiona said impatiently.

"No? Then it's just passing strange. I suppose most people's fancies are. You remember Edward, whom we met at Columbia back in '76—"

Blake's characteristic whirl from subject to subject began to have the familiar effect, and Fiona's circuits signaled overload. "Look," she broke in, "you're welcome to stay here, of course. I'd love it, but you really want a party? Next Friday?" Fiona's fingers flew through her calendar: the coming Friday showed nothing after three in the afternoon.

"Honey, it's six days away. That's tons of time. I'll help."

Fiona's eyes lifted heavenward. "Don't tell me: Buffalo canapés? Kiwi daiquiris? Or—?"

Blake sounded hurt: "Well, then, I won't help. But I will bring you a present. Your personal copy of the next *Gazette*. Others won't get them for days."

Fiona sat absolutely still, her nerve endings jangling. "Oh, God. I'd almost forgotten."

"Forgotten? This will be your triumph, dear girl! Your colleagues haven't published anything that anyone might actually enjoy reading in a decade. Well, except for Miriam Held. That's one cookie with both brain and brawn. Why not invite her on Friday?"

Fiona felt baffled. "What are you talking about? Miriam is not heavy, she's—"

"Oh, stop. I meant she's a real heavyweight, intellectually and politically, you dimwit. Or are you just putting me on?"

Fiona felt a deep twinge near her neck and sensed the dawning of a headache. "How could I? You've ambushed me. I just got out of the bathtub. I *was* all sleepy and relaxed. And from the sounds of it, you've had a steady diet of caffeine for days."

"Ah. I forgot about your low blood pressure, darling. Hot water is a sure downer: best not to answer the phone at those times, hmmm? Well, have a toddy and go nod off. I can't wait to see you, dearest, and to meet—what's his hunkness' name?"

"Blake, really." Fiona choked back a laugh in spite of herself. "It's Darryl. And for God's sake, he's the Dean of our College."

Blake clucked his tongue. "Good Lord. You simply must wean yourself from powerful men. I know they're attractive, but it's not safe. First you ditch the Chairman, bully for you I say, but now you've taken up with the *Dean?* In the out-on-a-limb department doesn't this put you on course for a crash landing? Have you thought about Al-Anon?"

"Blake, you're foaming at the mouth. What's wrong?"

There was a silence. And then a sigh. "Oh, nothing. Just pining, I think. Your friend Dennis is such a doll. But he's married. Everybody's married."

Fiona was touched at the sudden melancholy in his voice. "Oh, honey, someone will come along. Just when you least expect it—"

"Darling, I always expect it—"

"Let me finish! You'll find someone. You're quite a catch, you know."

"A catch! Fiona, you do cheer me up. My mother used to say that to me every week about the girl next door. Rachel, that was her name. Nice girl, but never mind. Well, I'm flattered that you think so. Can't you arrange to have Dennis' friend sent to the Pacific or something?"

Fiona ignored this last. "E-mail me your flight information. I'll be there to pick you up."

Fiona hung up, light-headed at the prospect of Blake and the new edition of the *Gazette* charging into her life in less than a week.

The next morning she called Bettina. "B., it's me. Can you come over?"

Bettina yawned. "Sorry. God, Clare came over with her helpers from the new catering business last night. Brought champagne. It seems they broke into the black last month for the first time. Well, I don't know if they ever left. But I woke up in my own bed, so perhaps I had some sense after all."

"Mmm. Well, good news about Clare's company."

"Oh, yes. Terrific. So what's up?"

"I haven't talked to you for over a week."

"True. How was the coast, by the by?"

"Fine, fine." Fiona felt suddenly desperate. "I really must talk to you."

"Well, why didn't you say so? I'll be over in a half hour. Do you have food?"

Fiona looked at the clock. It was eleven. "Do you mean for breakfast or lunch?"

"Whatever," Bettina said.

Bettina arrived, an hour or so later, delightfully disheveled in a tank top, long skirt, and alligator cowboy boots. She sank gratefully into a rocker on the back deck. "Lord, I just can't drink anymore," she said.

Fiona handed her a large glass of orange juice. "No, it's one of the first things that goes."

Her friend lowered her sunglasses and looked at Fiona sharply. "Well, hardly the first."

Fiona's nerves still pinged from her conversation with Blake. She sat in a spring chair across from her friend, her back ladder-straight with tension. How to begin? "Oh, Bettina," she began, and then stalled, a revved-up engine caught in neutral.

Bettina's mouth curved from a wry pucker to a puzzled smile. "What is it, sweetie?"

Fiona's voice sounded little to her own ears. "I'm afraid I've been horribly rash."

"Yes?"

Fiona nodded miserably.

"Well, it can't be that bad, surely?" Bettina's voice, calm as a still pond, invited comfort and confidence.

"It is. First, I sent Blake Burnois a story I wrote in a rage after the promotion debacle. And he's publishing it in *The Gazette!*"

"Well, good for you. How terrible can that be? It's a publication, and a national one at that."

"It's silly, really. It's called 'Ivory Power' and it's a parody of the promotion process, at a disguised Texas university. One that just happens to be right here in Austin."

Bettina's face crinkled appreciatively. "Sounds grand to me. Look, Fiona, you're not the first to lampoon the arcane creakings of the academic bureaucracy. Look at Carolyn Heilbrun with her Amanda Cross series, for one. And there's a long history of the genre from Mary McCarthy's *Groves of Academe*—and remember that delightful take-off by someone else, *Graves of Academe*—to that marvelous novel I just read, what is it? Oh, *Cold and Pure and Very Dead*. I could go on and on."

"Please don't."

"What?" While Bettina thought mystery writers overcompensated, she read their books, her mind-candy, with the same voracious abandon as others surfed the net.

"I just don't trust Blake. It turns out he abhors Sigmund. And the Chairman in my story is suspiciously like him, about five years ago, before his hair turned gray."

Bettina waved a languid hand. "Oh, so what. Half the chairs of English departments in the country are womanizing dolts. It means nothing."

"I just have a bad feeling about how Blake will frame it. He's very vindictive sometimes. And it's utterly transparent—how many research universities are there in the state of Texas with a Sigmund-like Chair of the English Department? Only one, I'm afraid."

"I don't see why that's a problem. The clowns in the Tower won't care, they'll just think it's good—and free—national publicity. Poor sods. Besides, your character is hardly unique: he's vain, he plays tennis, he encourages students, and female faculty, to dote on him—need I go on? He's positively generic. Fiona, you'll weather it. My own situation is a case in point."

Fiona slumped in her chair. She hadn't even asked Bettina how she was managing as the Kyle Cramer dispute ground on. "Oh, I'm sorry. I know your situation is horrible. I've been so—"

"Don't worry about it. You look terrible. Something else is going on, something I suspect much more troubling," Bettina said shrewdly. "Out with it."

"It's Darryl."

"Uh-huh." Bettina removed her sunglasses and locked her green eyes onto Fiona's brown ones. "What have you gotten yourself into?"

"Nothing, yet."

The eyes, as ruthlessly revealing as a spotlight trained on a fleeing suspect, swept over Fiona. "But you've slept with him, haven't you?"

Fiona felt ridiculously guilty. "Yes. Once."

Bettina rocked back in her chair, crossed one booted leg over the other, and adjusted the folds of her skirt. "For heaven's sake, don't look like that, like I'm going to slap your wrists or something. I don't give a shit if you've screwed his brains out."

"You don't?"

"No. You're welcome to him."

Fiona rubbed her moist hands on her jeans. "But the other night, at your house, you said it was all so complicated and difficult—"

"Well, it was. But that was a year ago. And, the night you and I talked—or rather didn't talk—Marvin might have popped in at any minute. It didn't seem the time to discuss it."

"A year ago? Well, thank goodness. I've been so uncomfortable..."

"But not uncomfortable enough to stay away from Darryl?" Bettina laughed. "Oh, don't worry. I understand perfectly. Sometimes one just makes the leap. Or the slide."

"Oh, B., I was afraid I had really messed things up. Between us. And after how serious the two of you were. The thought of you divorcing Marvin—"

"Divorcing Marvin? Whoa, girl. That was never on the table." Bettina brought both feet flat onto the deck with a thump. For the first time that morning, she appeared fully awake.

Fiona turned a stricken face on her friend. Bettina was right when she'd said sex was always complicated. And an affair reinterpreted to an outsider—Darryl's summary of his relationship with Bettina a case in point—often swamped the facts in a mire of assumptions. She took a shallow breath. "You never told Darryl you would leave Marvin, get a divorce, and marry him?"

Bettina, for the one and only time in Fiona's experience, looked dumbstruck. Her mouth actually opened and then closed without so much as a mumble or a curse.

"I guess not," Fiona said.

"Is that what he told you? Let me get this straight. What I thought was an affair between consenting and safely married adults has now been turned into a soap opera of Wagnerian proportions? Well, Lordy be, as my mother always said."

Fiona mused, "My warning signals went up as he was recounting this. But he seemed utterly sincere. He said your affair caused the breakup of his marriage."

"Oh, now it makes sense—and for heavens sakes have your early warning system checked as soon as possible. My sweet gullible friend," Bettina's face assumed a patient expression, "don't you see, he wanted to impress you with the tragic story of his divorce. In reality, that marriage was over when I got involved with him. And, let me tell you, I doubt I was the only woman he was sleeping with besides Janice at the time."

"But he told me you were the love of his life."

"For seven minutes three times a week maybe. Ha. Sorry to be crass. Dearest Fiona, that's very flattering but it's not true. The man falls in love easily and often. And has a very wide range. He had a fling with Kyle Cramer, for pete's sake."

"Kyle Cramer! But he told me she brought a grievance against him for sexual harassment."

"She did. The grievance died for lack of proof. But that doesn't mean her accusation wasn't true."

"But how can you know that it *is* true? It doesn't seem in character...well, Kyle is just so young..."

Bettina tugged at her skirt impatiently. "Does it really matter?"

Fiona's head was once again reeling. "You know what, Bettina? I'm out of my league here."

Bettina inched her chair closer and picked up Fiona's hand. "Honey, Darryl's not a bad guy. He's a darling man, really. He just likes to fool around and he thinks, rightly, that most women don't approve. His telling you that I was the love of his life is a measure of how much he thinks of you."

"What?"

Bettina's soft fingers gently massaged Fiona's hand. "He assumes that by representing the breakup of his marriage as a grand passion, you'll be more sympathetic to him," she explained patiently. "Think about it: if you think he's a philanderer, that gives him no points, but if he strayed out of mad, passionate love, well you won't blame him for that, surely."

"But, don't you see, it all seems so calculated," Fiona protested.

"Oh, but I don't think it is. I doubt this is a conscious strategy. I'm interpreting his behavior for you. It's just me, Bettina, your couch-potato analyst talking."

"But you have thought about it a great deal," Fiona said, wishing she could just launch herself into Bettina's lap and huddle there until everything confusing passed away from her.

"Absolutely. My head was more than a little turned by Dr. Hansen."

"Do you mean you considered divorcing Marvin?"

"I actually did, for about five seconds, after Darryl told me the same story he told you: that his marriage with Janice was over because of a prior affair. And you guessed it: she was the absolute love of his life. Until I appeared in his life, of course. I was what was missing in his life but I wasn't breaking up his marriage. He wasn't divorced yet because Janice was punishing him by delaying and blah blah."

"Who was he in love with this time?"

Bettina sighed and shook her head gently. "I don't think I should say."

"And you wouldn't have talked about this with me if I hadn't brought it up, would you?" Fiona couldn't decide whether to feel betrayed or pleased that her friend kept confidences so well.

"No, I wouldn't. I have a lot to lose by being indiscreet."

"Even with me?"

"Honey, especially with you. You're Marvin's friend as well as mine. I would never put your loyalties in the wringer that way. I told you that before."

Fiona thought a moment. "You did the right thing. I admire you for being able to keep all of this inside." And handle it like an adult, Fiona told herself, which seemed more than she could manage at the moment.

Bettina smiled wanly. "Well, if I can't keep my hands to myself, or my skirt on, it's the least I can do to keep my mouth zippered. I owe that much to Marvin."

"To yourself too," Fiona said automatically.

"Oh, Fiona, I'm not proud of my behavior," Bettina said.

Fiona was struck by her words, almost the exact replicas of ones Darryl Hansen had spoken—and uttered with the same tone—three days before.

"Bettina, thank you for talking to me and being so frank."

Bettina leaned forward and kissed her on the lips, a soft, lingering kiss. "You're sweet, Fiona," she said.

Fiona's mouth, fully awake, tingled. She ran her tongue over her lips delicately, as if tasting the kiss again. Was this how Bettina had kissed Kyle Cramer? Lord help us, she thought.

XII: The Hanged Man

It's the damnedest thing—sometimes I'll put something in the ground and it'll just freeze. You know, look stricken and pitiful. Sometimes the plant even loses all of its leaves. You're certain it's not going to make it. But you have to have faith to garden in this godawful climate. The thing's growing on the inside all the same. You just wait, and if you're lucky, out of this half-dead little stump can come the most beautiful foliage and flowers.

—Marvin Graf, conversation at Barton Springs Nursery

In the days before Blake arrived, Fiona drifted in a sea of indecision. Darryl called and came over, twice. They made love and went out for dinner. Both evenings, as before, passed very pleasantly. No mention passed between them of Bettina or Janice or commitments or campus politics. They simply spent time together in a blissful unconsciousness. As they lay on the bed, Fiona imagined that they floated together on a raft equidistant from the mainland and an unreachable island, marooned in a limbo between the pragmatics of their lives and the fantasy of a life unmoored from responsibility and consequences. She knew it couldn't last but inhabited the bubble anyway, grateful for the respite from what lay outside its glistening and delicate walls.

Her classes provided solid ground in the midst of flux. The graduate class, American Moderns, scampered along the twisting trail from modernism to postmodernism and beyond. In the undergraduate class, a screening of the recent film version of *Ethan Frome* had fueled more intense wrangling about Puritan bleakness.

"How could a woman as brilliant and privileged as Mrs. Wharton be obsessed with such futility?" asked Anne, one of Fiona's most vocal students. "Unless it's therapy. Put all your disappointment in a book, send it out into the world, and move on."

"This goes beyond, way beyond, seeing the glass half-empty," someone grumbled.

"A waste of a beautiful face," lamented another, referring to Liam Neeson's tortured visage in the film.

"What if we look at this differently, less literally," Fiona said. "As a fairy tale, for example. Ethan Frome is the *doppelgänger*, the deprived little creature living inside the novelist's brain. On the outside she is wealthy, striking, her life a whirl of publishing, literary parties, and opulence. Writing this story is therapy of a sort, a way of projecting out the little girl inside her who was trapped and starved for affection by the wicked mother, Lucretia. It's one way of reconciling the fears of the past with the potential of the present. She tells a ghost story—you recall Edith Wharton shared an affection for dark tales with her friend Henry James—and exorcises the demons until the next time they rear up in her consciousness."

"Okay," Anne broke in. "Call it a ghost story, gothic story, cautionary tale, whatever." She grinned. "It's really Edith, as Ethan, staging an exorcism. Cool."

Whenever she scrounged time away from classes, meetings, and dissertation advising, Fiona continued to forge ahead on *The Age of Inconsequence*. However, Wharton's path, after the divorce, followed a continental drift of its own:

In the fifteen months following the dissolution of her marriage to Teddy Wharton, Edith, her spirit stunned and exhausted, marked time by incessant travel. Several small dogs in tow, she roved throughout Italy, Germany, and England in 1913. While exotic adventures and perpetual motion soothed her nerves, inside, in the calm center of her grief, she stood still while the world whirled around her.

James observed her burning energy, and as always, feared its consummatory powers. He marveled that Edith could still produce art from such a whirl-a-gig existence, when he required such a point of stillness for his imagination to take flight.

But write Edith did, delivering the book five years in the making on time for Scribner's in October of 1913. The Custom of the Country *found success both commercially and critically and produced one of Wharton's most audacious heroines, Undine Spragg. Edith, late in her life, proclaimed this novel one of her five favorites. Yet the avaricious and utterly ruthless Undine, a woman dedicated purely to her social and financial ambitions, proved a rarity among Wharton's creations. Most amazingly, Undine Spragg manipulated the institution of marriage to obtain her ends, marrying four times during the course of the novel, with a fifth hinted at by the book's close.*

In creating the rapacious Undine, Wharton devised a woman who triumphed by bending to her will the very structure that nearly destroyed her creator. Was Wharton, through her fiction, seeking the only revenge she could muster against the institution of marriage? Or, always the lover of a good joke, did the author devise Undine to amuse herself, a conquering hero who defies the strictures of society and triumphs over its dictates? Undine Spragg, unlike Edith, curbed any humanitarian impulses and lacked the fetters of moral scruples. Yet, like Wharton herself, Undine indefatigably kept moving forward.

Throughout this period, Edith's dependence on Walter Berry grew; he replaced Teddy as trustee of her estate. In December of 1913 she and Walter visited New York, her first trip back to her native city since her divorce. She stayed only briefly, finding the speculation of relatives and friends about her relationship with Walter too much to bear. Back in Paris, she sequestered herself at 53 rue de Varennes, writing and reading, and recovering from the brutalizing experience of facing New York as a divorced woman. She passed her fifty-second birthday reclusively, hiding from the biting January cold. It proved to be a discomfiting time as the heaters gave way and then chimney fires left her house without heat. The frigid atmosphere of New York engulfed Edith even as she retreated across the ocean.

Fiona shivered as a blast of air conditioned air hit the back of her neck. Irritably, she checked the thermostat. The electrical worker who had serviced her cooling system had left the system at sixty-five degrees. She intensely sympathized with an Edith Wharton tortured by the impoverished standards of a Parisian heating system circa 1914. No wonder she took flight in travel as a way of achieving equilibrium.

Fiona took a break to forage for food in the kitchen, and was eating day-old linguini when the phone rang.

"Oh, thank God you're being social for once in your life," Blake rasped.

Fiona yawned. "Not social, stuck."

"Ah, the manuscript. The opus of the moment. Tell me again, it's called—?"

"*The Age of Inconsequence.*"

"Aren't they all?" Blake replied. He paused, and Fiona heard the sound of scratching. "Tell me, why that title?"

"Well, you know, it's a play on Wharton's novel, *The Age of Innocence.* Which describes the Old New York of her childhood."

"Yessss, I know it's a great book and all that, but what's the significance of 'inconsequence'?"

Why did Blake even care? But Fiona replied, like the good little student she had always been: "Wharton was fascinated by the fate of Old New York. It had seemed indomitable, stretching back nearly three centuries before her birth. But in just fifty years she saw it sink from view. She said it vanished like the ancient city of Atlantis. She found Old New York trivial and life-destroying, but far from simple which is why her use of 'innocence' in her book's title is so ironic. That intrigued me. I saw a parallel in the academia of our own time. Now

I'm not sure if that comparison needs to be actually a part of the book, which at the moment is unfolding as more of a creative biography, but it's certainly in my mind as I write. The two cultures are incredibly similar—"

"Uh-huh, I get it." Fiona could almost hear Blake's mind shifting into a higher gear. "Academe's traditions are ancient and doddering, like those of Old New York, its institutions just as arcane and baffling to an outsider." A note of glee infused Blake's voice. "Oh, and better: people in the university fight tooth and nail but over minutia and miniscule rewards. In Old New York, the social codes governed every tiny bit of behavior. Appearance was everything. In both cases, the system often seems utterly meaningless, unless you know the code. Good, very good. It certainly works for me."

Fiona heard more scratching. "What are you doing?"

"Just making notes. Dennis sent me this fabulous fountain pen. I feel like a real, old fashioned editor, inky fingers and all."

Alarmed, Fiona put down the banana she'd begun to peel. "Notes?"

"Not to worry, O paranoid one." Blake said absently. "I'm just working on a lead-in to your story, so of course I want to mention that you're a Wharton scholar, what you're currently writing, and yakkety yak."

"Blake, leave all of that out. Please. It has nothing to do with 'Ivory Power.' Can't you just let the story speak for itself?"

"But, dearest, 'Ivory Power' is the *Age of Inconsequence* personified! Of course they have everything to do with each other. What could be more arcane, murky, and coded than the promotion process? It's so divine that your research parallels the story which parallels your experience which...well, I told you it's a fable for our time."

"Blake...why..." Fiona found herself mentally stuttering and couldn't articulate a rebuttal.

"Darling, stop worrying. Get out of the house and do something physical. You sound terrible. Thank goodness I'm coming to see you. I'll feed you soup by hand and nurse you back to health, poorest one."

"I'm, fine, just fine," Fiona sputtered. "Honestly, you are so try-ing—"

"I am trying to help you, yes, that's right. Look, I'll see you in just a few days. Ta ta."

Dazed by Blake's staccato rhythms, Fiona put down the phone and slid into a chair. What had Blake said several phone calls ago about the academic feed lot? Lately, everything she said turned into fodder, for jaws bigger than her own. Fiona began to see new meaning in Jane Smiley's use of "Moo" as the title for her novel of academic life.

Friday night brought sultry, humid weather, the air thick with the menace of thunderstorms. Arriving the day of her dinner party, Blake's flight had landed on time, in advance of bad weather. Always sleep deprived, he immediately cranked down the air conditioning and burrowed under the comforter in the back bedroom with Dy-namo. As Fiona readied the house for company, the two were both fast asleep. Normally loyal only to Fiona, Dynamo responded to the first whiff of Blake Burnois as if he were the rarest catnip. Her little tor-toiseshell body immediately super-glued itself to his pants leg, or shoulder, or any available patch of skin.

Fiona stood in the kitchen, flanked by a hefty cookbook and a clus-ter of bowls and pans. How had she allowed Blake to talk her into making dinner for eight people? Fiona had intended to prepare some-thing new and elaborate, but after a brief tour through the book of rec-ipes (traditional French) given to her by her mother (a fabulous cook), Fiona had shelved it. What Janet Hardison considered elementary in the kitchen presented a conundrum of Holmesian proportions to her daughter. Fiona opted for her fail-safe spinach lasagna. Two decades of preparing it for graduate students enabled her to design it for any number.

The first pitcher of martinis had barely begun to chill when the doorbell rang at 7:05. Darryl arrived, and on his heels were Dennis and his partner Carter. As if on cue, Blake emerged from the bedroom looking impossibly sleek and dapper in perfectly pressed khakis and a fine cotton v-necked sweater (pale blue to match his own baby blues).

"Dennis...you darling dog you...Of course I remember Carter, what's to forget...Derrick? Oh, *Darryl*, excuse me, of course..."

As Blake took over as host, Fiona retreated to the kitchen. Darryl appeared behind her and planted a kiss on her neck. "Don't think you can leave me with the guys in the living room. I know where the real action is."

Fiona handed him a knife and a cutting board. "Isn't that a bit of a reversal? Don't you want to be in the living room and talk football or something?"

"Very funny. I think those three have progressed as far as Armani at the moment." He picked up a knife. "And I'd love to help with the salad."

"Just because they like clothes doesn't make them any less fun."

Darryl put the tips of his fingers together as if to pray. He bowed his head. "Real men love Armani too. Of course, master."

"Oh, stop. Would you answer the door?"

Darryl bowed his head again and left. The voices of Bettina and Marvin filtered in from the hall.

Bettina gave a little shriek when she saw Blake, or was it Blake's shriek? Fiona couldn't be sure. Their voices blended together in a harmonious cry of: "You look *marvelous!*"

Fiona emerged with the pitcher of martinis to find Blake sitting cozily on a sofa with Dennis on one side and Bettina on the other. Darryl and Marvin were nowhere to be seen.

Carter, across the room in a reclining leather chair, looked up from a magazine and said, "On the deck." He smiled and cocked his head toward the threesome on the sofa. "Getting some oxygen, I imagine."

Fiona joined him. She leaned over and gave him a hug. "You don't mind?"

Carter's face, deeply but beautifully lined, looked tanned and relaxed against an open-collared white shirt. "You mean about the drama queens? Heavens no. Let them rave on together, I say. I mean, look at them. They're so happy."

Fiona looked. Dennis, Blake, and Bettina were intertwined in an animated knot, voices overlapping, heads bobbing and weaving, arms gesticulating, all in happy synchrony. "It's a love fest," she agreed.

The bell rang again and Fiona ushered in Miriam, wearing an ankle-length, loose sheath and sandals, an outfit at odds with her squarish, black leather handbag.

"You look cool," she said, bending to greet Miriam.

"Thank you. Daphne bought me this. She told me it was time I stopped dressing like a middle-aged, dowdy academic. But I told her that I am a middle-aged and dowdy academic." Miriam sighed. "She didn't listen." Miriam advanced on Blake, brandishing her purse. "Dr. Burnois!"

Fiona left them and went outside. Marvin and Darryl sat contentedly, each holding a sweating bottle of Shiner Bock. "Nice night," Darryl said. "Have a seat."

"I can't. It's so quiet out here, if I sit down, I'll never go back in there."

"Blake can handle it," Marvin said. "Relax, have a beer."

"I left a martini somewhere."

"I'll get it," Darryl said. He took Fiona's hand and squeezed it as he went past her.

Marvin rocked back in his chair, his broad face appraising Fiona. "How long has that been going on?"

"Darryl?"

"Who else?"

"Oh, not long. A couple of weeks really."

Marvin nodded. "Nice guy. Too nice probably."

"What do you mean?"

"Likes too many people. Can talk to anybody." Marvin grinned. "My father always told me to beware of men like that. Too charming, too agreeable. Dad didn't like people who kept their meanness out of view. 'Can't trust a man who always smiles and never loses his temper,' he'd say, 'when you least expect it, he'll bite you in the back'."

"Well, you're pretty affable yourself," Fiona replied.

"I know. My dad never trusted me either." Marvin scratched his buzz cut blond hair as if he had just been bitten.

"You? But you're the salt of the earth. And you were a Marine. How could he not trust you?"

"Well, that's why I went into the Marines in the first place, I imagine. Trying to impress my dad. Trouble was, both of my brothers had already been in the Corps. So it was no big deal." Marvin sighed and finished his beer. "It looks like Darryl got way-laid. Should we brave the mob and get you a drink?"

When they rejoined the others, the configuration had shifted. Dennis and Blake, knees lightly touching, now huddled on the piano bench at the far end of the living room. Bettina and Darryl occupied the couch, absorbed in discussion. Fiona satisfied herself that even though their bodies leaned in toward each other, there was room for another person between them. She turned away reluctantly, thinking: Only, of course, if the person weighed fourteen pounds.

She found Miriam and Carter occupied in the kitchen, Carter mixing another round of martinis, and Miriam cutting radishes into precision slices. Fiona checked her watch: it was only 8:30 and already she felt exhausted. Thank goodness these two people had pragmatic instincts. And where had Marvin disappeared to? She poured herself a hefty martini and checked the oven.

The party's decibel level rose over dinner. Fiona, supplying the table with Merlot at regular intervals, somehow muddled through. In fact, by 10:30 she thought she might make it, when Blake chimed his spoon against his wine glass.

"My friends," he said, standing in an elegant posture of attention. Fiona noticed that his pants still maintained their perfect crease and wondered, in a tired haze, how he managed that. Blake's slender frame weaved a bit as he raised his wineglass. "I have a toast to our hostess.

And a congratulations." He reached behind his chair and brandished a large format newspaper in the air. "Here's to Fiona, who has a featured—and very important—publication in *The Gazette of Higher Education!*" He rattled the copy of *The Gazette.* "And here it is, my dears, hot, hotter, hottest right off the press!"

Fiona groaned. "Blake, could you put that away—"

"Wait! Let me just read you the lead-in: 'Fiona Hardison, noted Edith Wharton scholar...'"

"Hear, hear!" Dennis chimed in.

"... has found a contemporary manifestation of Wharton's Old New York in university life at the dawn of the twenty-first century. As archaic as the minutely-layered social world of the 1870's, which Wharton ironically labeled 'The Age of Innocence,' the academic world presents its counterpart in, as Hardison finely puts it, 'The Age of Inconsequence.' She hastens to add that scholarship itself is not inconsequential—she refers rather to current *institutions* of so-called higher learning. A vivid example follows in Hardison's eloquent parody, 'Ivory Power.'"

Miriam turned to Fiona: "Fiona, you sly thing, you've not said a word about this!"

Before Fiona could reply, the others joined in with cheers "To Fiona" and the issue was passed from hand to hand. Fiona shrugged helplessly and wandered out to the back deck as Blake's acerbic voice announced: "Wait, let me read you just this little bit about a fictional tennis-playing, womanizing chairman, a bit past his prime. You'll absolutely die..."

She sat outside, dully staring at the overcast night sky. A smudge of moon shone through the thick layers of clouds, its light so shrouded it couldn't illuminate much of anything. Fiona, feeling cast over and near-sighted, recognized a kinship with it. The world appeared murky and impenetrable to her at the moment.

A comforting hand gripped her shoulder as Marvin joined her. "You'll survive," he said.

"I sincerely doubt it."

"Hey," he said, "these are your friends."

"Oh, Marvin, that's what worries me. If I feel this uncomfortable with them reading the story, what will happen when the whole department sees it?"

He dropped heavily into a chair. "Oh, people in your department don't really read *The Gazette*—or much of anything current—do they? I wouldn't worry too much."

"It's just that... Well, it's really Blake's production, isn't it?"

"What do you mean?"

"You heard him. He wrote that introduction. It's his old vendetta against academia. And Sigmund, of course. You'll see, if you read it."

"But you must feel some of his cynicism yourself. You wrote the story."

Fiona briefly tried to think of a way around that fact. She said defensively: "You've been in the university. You know it's impossible not to feel cynical at times. That's true in any organization, probably. The key is to let those low moments pass by and not to react. I wrote that story to amuse myself. And exorcise some demons. I shouldn't have sent it to Blake."

Marvin thought a moment, his heavy shoulders slouched forward. "Well, let's think of it another way. It's okay to poke fun at institutions. They are restrictive, and ridiculous at times in their workings, especially to outsiders. That's just the nature of bureaucracy. Why not let everyone in on the joke?"

"That's all very fine. But it's a bit too personal, don't you see? I wasn't brought up for promotion, a lot of people probably know that."

"Oh, so you're feeling embarrassed. You maybe revealed that rejection got to you more than you wanted to? You showed your bruised ego?"

"And then struck back at the 'big boys'—I'm afraid it's going to look spiteful."

"Hmmm. But I like your comparison of academe to Old New York.

The place is the ultimate insider's club. It's like the military. A few people devise a protocol. It's complicated. Littered with conditions. People follow it but after a while lose track of what the hell inspired it in the first place. That way those on the inside are accountable to no one but themselves. Eventually, they're the only ones who know—or understand—the rules. It's like the old Four Hundred —wasn't that what it was called?"

Fiona nodded. "Very good. Yes, Edith's family was part of it. It began because that's how many people could fit into Mrs. Astor's ballroom. Those families thought themselves the cream of society. Old lineage, old money. They all came from the same Dutch and British stock, descended from the original settlers of New York in the seventeenth century. They took themselves very seriously."

"That fits with your metaphor exactly. Think how seriously people like Sigmund and old Lester in your department take themselves."

Fiona sighed. "Too true."

A slow smile of pleasure moved across Marvin's face. "But there is one hazard of guarding your secrets too closely."

"What's that?"

"There are always barbarians at the gate. Old New York society went by the wayside, didn't it? In time, too few people knew the code. Or cared."

Marvin settled his big frame more comfortably in his chair, while Fiona considered his words. The two friends sat comfortably together, in silence, letting the gentle humid breeze caress their faces. After a while, Bettina joined them.

"Hi, honey," Marvin said.

She leaned over and gave him a kiss. "Hi back."

"What's going on in there?" Fiona asked.

"At your party? Oh, Blake's holding forth. And holding Dennis' hand by now."

"What's Carter doing?"

"Nothing. Sitting back. Ignoring them. Talking to Miriam and Darryl."

"Do you think Carter doesn't care what Dennis does or is he just being socially correct?" Fiona asked her.

"I don't really know. Carter is very inscrutable sometimes. It's part of his considerable appeal."

Marvin harrumphed and folded his arms across his chest. "It might be the only way to live with Dennis. He's so childlike in his antics. What does someone with any common sense do? Your choices are to be parental or to be Sphinx-like, I suppose."

"There's another," Bettina said, her skin pale and polished in the faint moonlight. "You can always leave."

Fiona and Marvin nodded. And the three of them sat back in the near-blackness, their chairs huddled together. The night air settled around them, heavy and quiet, occasionally disrupted by a harsh noise from the vacant lot across the street. A few minutes later, Fiona pointed to the corner of her backyard. Rising from the birdbath, its wings and breast an eerie incandescent pearly white, a screech owl hovered for a moment, its staring eyes upon them, and flew away.

"Incredible," Bettina said breathlessly.

Marvin whispered: "I've never seen one before."

A small "Oh..." escaped from Fiona's mouth.

For a moment, an imprint of the bird gliding phoenix-like into the air lingered in Fiona's vision, an echo of grace etched in space. Fiona reached out for her friends' hands, and they strained together as one body, longing to hear the sound of the whirring wings descend upon them again.

XIII: Death

Honey, don't worry. Sleeping Beauty isn't going to die. In fairy tales, the hero appears to die or ventures into the underworld to undergo a great change. Something is stripped away to allow for something new to take its place. Beauty might lose her faith or her innocence, but she'll gain, well, love and maturity. It's the way of the world—nothing stays the same.

—*Bertram Hardison, reading* Grimm's Fairy Tales
to his daughter, 1961

On Monday morning, Fiona stepped off the elevator on the seventh floor of Helmsley Hall to find "Ivory Power" displayed on the department bulletin board. She lowered her head, put her sunglasses back on, slunk down the corridor to her office, and gratefully disappeared inside. She shuddered at the stacks of memos, the piles of manuscripts stacked around the desk. The space begged for a filing squad to set it to rights. Fiona shoved the books and papers aside, creating new and even less coherent piles, and called Bettina at home. There was no answer, so she punched in Bettina's office number, just two doors away.

"Hello?" Fiona whispered as the phone was picked up.

"Hi, Fiona. Why are you whispering?"

"The bulletin board—someone posted 'Ivory Power'," Fiona croaked.

"Oh, that. Didn't see it. Wait'll you see what came in the mail for me. Come on down."

"You better come here." Fiona examined her office as if someone might be lurking in the corners.

"Oh, Lord. All right."

A moment later, Bettina tapped lightly on the door and stepped inside. Fiona rushed to shut and lock the door behind her.

"Fiona, relax. No one reads the bulletin boards. Except Sigmund and Richard Lester."

"Exactly," Fiona said.

Bettina stepped gingerly around the assorted stacks of paper and planted herself in front of her friend, hands on hips, looking alert and authoritative in a heather-gray suit of light wool. "Time for a reality check, dear. Aren't we taking ourselves a wee bit too seriously?"

Observing her friend's vitality, Fiona's confidence flagged further. At this moment, she felt kinship with Henry James as he struggled to keep up with the formidable Edith Wharton. Surely he must have said, and often: "You are too much for me. You consume the fruits of the world in huge mouthfuls, you ravage my serenity with your excitement and your imagination, you traverse the globe as easily as if it were a mere city block and leave me far behind, doddering with half-steps and outstretched arms."

"Fiona?" Bettina waved a hand in front of her friend's face. "Are you with us?"

Fiona took off her sunglasses and collapsed into her desk chair. "Oh, sit down. I've just got the jitters."

Bettina sat at the edge of a plain wooden chair. "Fiona, you're a tenured professor. You haven't done anything. No one is going to fire you. Plus, you've already resigned."

"Sigmund is holding the letter," Fiona said blankly. "Although not for long after he sees this." She gestured vaguely in the direction of the bulletin board.

"Well, if you want to pull the letter, pull the letter. If not, it'll go to the Dean. Darryl will wait to talk to you first before he sends it on."

Fiona leaned her head on one hand. She felt drained.

"Brace up. Now, turn your attention to something that's really serious."

Bettina thrust a piece of thick white paper at her. The letterhead read: Thompson & Riley, Attorneys at Law. Fiona skimmed the page. She read aloud slowly one glaring sentence: "Our client demands the immediate removal of Bettina Sedon Graf, Professor in the Department of Literature and Rhetoric." She blinked at Bettina. "This seems extreme."

"I'll say. After years of in-house grievances—none of which came to anything—Kyle Cramer has finally gone outside for redress. Unlucky me. I do, however, have a few ideas why she's chosen this incident for a crusade."

"Will you have to get an attorney?"

"I'm working on that right now. Miriam has referred me to someone. I imagine the University will handle it for now. I'm meeting with Darryl this afternoon."

Fiona felt a stab of jealousy and then internally berated herself. "You've already discussed it with Sigmund?"

Bettina's green eyes opened wide. "This is the only good news. Sigmund is supporting Kyle's lawsuit."

"Good?" Fiona sputtered.

"Hear me out. He and Kyle are sleeping together, and conspiring together. And I have proof!"

Fiona shook her head sadly. "B., you know how hard that is to prove."

Bettina shook her head, hair glowing red-gold under the fluorescent lights. Fiona imagined she saw sparks flying. "I mean *proof.* Photos, records of phone calls, the works." She drew back her shoulders and thrust out her chin, a sergeant at arms, battle-ready. "I hired a private detective. Best money I ever spent."

"I'm impressed. So you're going to argue..."

"I'm confident this suit will be dismissed when it comes out that Sigmund encouraged—or shall we say *enticed*—Kyle to go outside to private attorneys and said he would support her—"

Fiona leaned forward. "You have evidence of that too?"

"—tape recorded and documented—and when Kyle heard that, she agreed to go to bed with him. It's sleazy, and it's slimy, and it's Sigmund Froelich at his toadiest. Wait here."

Bettina reappeared with a videotape which she popped into the player crammed into a corner of Fiona's office. They rearranged their chairs to face it. "Check this out," Bettina stabbed the remote control. "I hope you didn't eat very much for breakfast."

And, indeed, Fiona choked at the first frame: the hotel room was unmistakably at the Manor Inn, and it looked identical to Room 14, which she and Sigmund had occupied for their bimonthly meetings for nine years. In the queen-size bed a young woman lounged, naked, alone. She extended her long thin arms out into space.

"Si-i-i-g!" she called. "Aren't you coming?"

"Here I come, sweet girl," a sugary, throaty male voice announced. Sigmund appeared on the screen, fresh out of the shower, his hair gleaming and tousled. He held his chest out and his stomach in, a towel draped carelessly around his hips. Fiona had to admit he looked ten years younger than when she'd last seen him—fresh conquests appearing to enliven him as fresh blood did a vampire—but still old next to the twenty-one-year-old in the bed.

"I don't know whether to laugh or throw up," Fiona said.

"It gets better."

In a parody of a strip-tease, Sigmund slowly unwound the towel. Then, at the last moment, he dropped it and dove under the covers. Fiona caught a flash of red bikini underwear. Kyle Cramer looked at Sig with hooded, bored eyes. "Aren't you going to take these off?" She reached under the bedclothes and appeared to snap the elastic on Sig's briefs.

"Oooh," he giggled uneasily, "that stings."

Gingerly, he removed the shorts. A pale hand appeared outside of the sheets and dropped the garment on the floor. Fiona noticed black stripes threading through the red fabric. A present?

"I've been waiting for this a long, long time," Sigmund said, his voice descending to a throatier level.

Kyle smiled. "Let's go slow," she said. Sigmund brought his face up to hers and began to nibble at her lips. She pushed him away playfully. "Tell me again what you're going to do to Professor Graf. It turns me on."

"Yes...let's turn on...Professor Who?" Sigmund squirmed closer to nibble on Kyle's earlobe.

"Bettina Graf," Kyle tried for patience. "You said you'd write a letter..."

"Hmmm?" Sigmund's lips left a trail of moisture down Kyle's neck. "Yes...a letter...ah, you taste so sweet..."

"To the attorneys...."

"Oh, yes..."

"Saying Graf has done this before..."

"Absolutely....again and again..." Sigmund shuddered, his lips reaching Kyle's tiny breasts.

Kyle held him away. "You won't forget?"

"I'll never forget you...just relax now..."

"No, Sigmund." Kyle's voice sharpened. "The letter, you won't forget the letter?"

Fiona heard a sucking sound. "What?...oh, oh, that...in my jacket pocket."

Kyle sighed. "Good." She grabbed Sigmund's face so that his cheeks pooched out and his lips turned fish-like. "Come here, you dirty old man you."

Sigmund grinned wolfishly and snuggled closer. Kyle's head disappeared under the covers.

"Shut it off," Fiona said, pressing her fingertips to her eyes. "Please."

Bettina clicked off the tape and the set. "Are you feeling nostalgic, my dear?"

"Unfair," Fiona said irritably. "God, what an oaf. And he's gotten so prissy."

"He's always been prissy," Bettina said carelessly. "But, he was certainly more attractive in the old days. Fiona, don't flagellate yourself. You're not the first woman who was misled by a prick." Bettina laughed at her own joke and then added primly: "We all make mistakes."

"But some of us make bigger ones than others? And have worse taste?" Fiona groaned softly. "But, B., you've certainly got the goods. Now what are you going to do?"

"Pending my talk with Darryl, I'll either counter sue or the University will instigate proceedings against Sigmund."

"You think it'll go that far?"

Bettina studied her nails critically. "*I* may go that far. This goes beyond harassment. It's exploitation, extortion of sex by promising political favors, sexual blackmail, whatever the hell you want to call it. It's immoral. We're a public university. It can't be legal."

Fiona studied her friend's determined face. "And Henry James called Edith Wharton 'The Angel of Devastation,'" she said admiringly. "He'd never met you."

"Fiona, this is my livelihood we're talking about. And my professional standing." Bettina flared at her. "This isn't just a 'cool move.' That man and that woman are trying to destroy me."

"I'm sorry. I didn't mean to make light of this. I'm just very, very impressed." Fiona said softly.

To Fiona's relief, the Furie before her abruptly transformed into a friend once again, and Bettina replied quietly: "Oh, I know, honey.

But, I'm telling you, stand back. Sigmund's days are numbered." Bettina tucked the videotape under her arm. She picked up the letter from Thompson & Riley and considered it thoughtfully. "You might consider a lawsuit yourself. About the way Sig handled your promotion. He's vulnerable."

Fiona said uncomfortably: "I'd have to make it public that we were sleeping together. I don't know if I can do that."

"Sigmund used you. He was in the position of greater responsibility, not you. And Fiona, you did not commit adultery, he did."

"But I should take responsibility. He didn't force me to have an affair."

"No, but he led you to think he was your ally and your advocate. He misled you. And he misused his power as Chairman."

Fiona opened her mouth. "But—"

"Think about it," Bettina said crisply.

After Bettina swept out of her office, Fiona sat dully and stared at the floor. How had things come to this—the pursuit of lawsuits instead of the fervor for learning and sharing ideas? She had earned her Ph.D. because she loved the savor of research, the hunt for the explanation, background, context of a thought. For her, teaching had been a privilege, not a way to a student's bedroom. She felt thoroughly ashamed of her place in the scope of the current machinations. Worse, her excitement about the life of the mind, the community of scholars, had withered away in the trite atmosphere of gossip and mistrust.

Later, at home, Fiona escaped into work. After the clandestine battles in Helmsley Hall, she welcomed the open confrontation that marked 1914. Edith Wharton described the beginning of the Great War as "strange, ominous and unreal, like the yellow glare which precedes a storm." The conflict soon took over her life, transforming her from a writer engrossed in a fictional realm into an activist who tackled head-on the plight of the displaced, abandoned, sick, and aged.

———

She launched humanitarian efforts on a variety of fronts, founding the American Hostels for Refugees, sanitoria for tubercular patients, and homes for displaced children. Soliciting money from the same wealthy New York and Newport society she had so often satirized, by 1917 her combined charities occupied twenty-one houses in Paris and its environs. She had raised more than any other private citizen in France for the war effort. Her remarkable contribution garnered her the highest recognition for a civilian in France: she became a Chevalier of the French Legion of Honor. The award, a tremendous honor and even rarer for an American citizen, occasioned a flood of telegrams from friends from many countries. The Great War had made Edith Wharton truly a citizen of the world.

In addition to her burgeoning humanitarian work, she began to visit the front lines as a correspondent. Her articles on the war were published by Scribner's Magazine and eventually collected in her book, Fighting France, *in 1915. The first American woman writer to describe the front, Edith wanted to raise American consciousness about the crippling effects of war. She and Henry James felt deeply distressed at America's neutrality in the global conflict. In an act of bitter (and to Edith, shocking) protest against his native land's inaction, James eventually renounced his American citizenship to become an English citizen. The reality of the war surrounded Edith, from the wounded and displaced to the terror and atrocities of the front itself.*

Fiona noted how thoroughly the exigencies of war turned Edith away from the worlds of her imagination to the practical needs of the real people in her care. By giving freely of herself, Edith, childless—and now husbandless—had found a way to imprint children's lives. Yet while her days revolved around the saving of lives, the Land of Death, which she witnessed at the Somme, extended to her personal circle as well. During the War, Edith Wharton lost many who were close to her, including her dear friend Egerton Winthrop, her former governess and secretary Anna Bahlmann. But the most shattering loss was Henry James, her Cher Maître. Mentor and fellow traveller, his was the friendship that was "the pride and honour" of her life.

———

After hearing of James' death, Edith wrote his secretary: "We who knew him well know how great he would have been if he had never written a line." But the fact that the two friends had shared the world of letters had cemented their close-ness further. Edith had lost her partner in, as she had put it, "the real marriage of true minds."

Fiona sat back, listening for the voices of the past. How she wished she could capture their sounds and rhythms in a room and visit it when-ever the urge came. Of all the things lost in the sweep of decades, it pained her most to lose the humor, the wisdom, the intimacy of their murmuring. For with Edith and Henry, surely, to preserve their talk would be to capture their magic.

At five o'clock, Fiona checked her email to find an urgent message from Sigmund. He asked her to appear in his office the next day at eleven. She discovered a similar demand on her phone machine. She thought about not responding, and simply ignoring his summons, but then decided to get it over with. She left a message saying she would come and see him at one o'clock. Best not to hearken to his call too readily, lest he imagine her as still compliant.

XIV: Temperance

The little girl fell off the cliff and she went down, down, down to the
bottom of a lake. It was very dark and she was afraid. She thought she
might die. But after a long time, she opened her eyes and saw a light far
away. She swam toward it. She found she could breathe under water.
She swam and swam and came to a little cave. Inside was air and food
and a flute. She sat down and ate and played the flute. She was going to
be all right, she thought. And tomorrow she'd find her way home.

—*Fiona Hardison, third grade story, 1961*

The next morning the bleat of the telephone burst into her consciousness at 6:45. Fiona reached over Darryl's sleeping form to grope
for it. Darryl mumbled and turned over as her arm grazed his hair.

An impossibly chipper voice assailed her ear: "Fiona...dearest one,
how are you?"

"Blake, it's very early."

"Ah...have some company, sly thing? Good for you. Say, I'm at the
airport..."

"Coming or going?"

"Ha ha. I don't suppose you wondered what happened to me on
Friday night?"

Fiona rubbed one eye cautiously. "I did think of you. And wished you had stayed to see me through the bombshell of your 'special delivery.' But then I supposed you flew back to Washington."

"Oh, please." Blake adroitly ignored the mention of his calling "Ivory Power" to everyone's attention. "And not say goodbye? Not like me...'only connect' is my watchword, remember?"

Fiona winced. "Blake, I have a very busy morning—"

"I'll bet you do. So I'll keep it short. I liked Derrick, by the by."

"Darryl."

"Right. Look, never mind. Since you're such a crabass today, I won't let you in on my adventures." Blake's stiff delivery screamed his hurt feelings.

"I hope they don't involve Dennis." Fiona snapped back.

"Who else? Since when have you become such a prude? We spent a few days at the coast. Not exactly California, but if you shut your eyes, the surf *sounds* romantic."

Fiona counted to twelve. How could Dennis get himself entangled this way and with the most feckless man in the universe? "You should be ashamed. I hope you gave him a grand time because you've probably wrecked his life."

"Fi, Fi, Fiona. Carter was with us."

"What?"

Blake yawned. "Do you think your beloved Dennis wants to lose Mr. Handsome? Who just happens to also be Mr. Rich I found out. No doubt that's the real secret of his appeal. But, the three of us had a very nice, very chaste time. Well, I can't speak for the two of them. I didn't sleep in their bed...unfortunately."

Relieved, Fiona summoned up the half-ounce of kindness she felt Blake deserved: "I'm sorry if you were disappointed—"

"Oh no, the hunt goes on." Blake sounded positively cheerful. "You think I give up this easily? As everyone knows, even you my dear, anyone can be had. Dennis will come around, I promise you."

"What do you mean as even I know? Oh, never mind." Fiona pushed the hair out of her face. "I really have to go."

"Fiona, wait." Blake dropped the banter and spoke earnestly. "Honey, don't be mad at me. I know you think I'm a trouble-maker and a lout, but you'll see. This *Gazette* piece will transform your life. In some very nice—and unexpected—ways. In the meantime, I love you madly. And I really am sorry I ate and ran. I'm afraid my gonads were calling. To no avail, alas. And now I must go and soothe them, the poor things are shriveled with dejection..."

Fiona giggled; try as she might, she could not stay angry with Blake. His bad-boy act delighted the part of her that adored anarchism in almost any form. "All right. Stay out of the men's room."

Blake brightened immediately. "Where do you think I'm calling you from?" He paused and then whispered, "Oh-oh, you can't imagine the hunk of heaven who just walked in. Gotta go, doll."

Fiona replaced the receiver quietly. Darryl playfully grabbed her arm as she lay back. "Who was *that*? And are you laughing or crying?"

Fiona wiped a tear from her eye. "Blake. He's awful, I know. But he makes me laugh." She sniffed, reached for a kleenex and blew her nose loudly. "I didn't want to wake you, so I held it all in."

"Oooh, don't hold anything in." Darryl crooned, kissing her. "It's terrible for your health. And mine." He gestured at the phone. "Your friend's quite the actor."

"Blake? He's brilliant, really. Reads everything, can talk about all manner of things. He just gets bored easily." She looked slyly at Darryl. "He'd make a good dean, actually. Didn't I just pretty much list the perfect attributes?"

"Well, yes. But I don't know if the 'brilliant' is absolutely necessary. Say, do you mind a little pillow talk? Bettina showed me her videotape of Sigmund." He whistled. "I'm afraid his nine lives have run out."

"Really? I can't imagine he won't wiggle out of it somehow." Fiona kissed Darryl quickly and then slid out of bed. She headed for the shower. "I have an appointment with him later today."

"Take notes," Darryl called after her.

She popped her head back through the doorway. "Seriously?"

Darryl leaned on his elbow and studied her appreciatively. "The administration isn't happy with Sigmund. He used to be a strong chair, but lately—" He shook his head. "Bettina told me how he handled your promotion, by the way." Before Fiona could interrupt, he added: "I might be able to do something about that, if you'd like."

"Good Lord. Is that a bribe?" Fiona smiled uneasily. "This is sounding a little like Sigmund's promises to Kyle."

Darryl's eyes widened. Fiona burst out laughing. "Just kidding. I think."

Fiona met her undergraduate class at ten and handed back papers, an analysis of a novel adapted into film. Amid the rustle of pages turning, Fiona asked if anyone had discovered anything surprising as they completed the assignment.

One student said: "I'd noticed that making movies out of Stephen King's stories was an industry, but I was surprised to find that's true of Henry James's novels, too."

Fiona thought a moment. "You're right. Aside from Jane Austen, he might be the classic novelist with the most adaptations in video stores. Ideas why that might be?"

"He writes about people and relationships," a woman in the back said promptly. "We're always interested in that." She shrugged. "Besides, really, people haven't changed that much."

"That's very good," Fiona nodded vigorously. "You know James was always troubled by how little money he made from his fiction and how poorly his work sold. He envied Edith Wharton her best sellers." She paused and thought. "He would have been immensely pleased to know that in this electronic age, his painstaking recording of human nature would still have currency." Fiona surveyed her class, pleased herself by evidence that words still mattered and that the intricacies of human communication remained consequential in spite of the blinding pace and often impersonal tenor of modern life.

The remainder of the class continued in this satisfying vein. Afterwards, invigorated by the exchange with her students, she walked the six blocks to Miriam Held's house for lunch. After the party Friday night, Miriam had expressed a desire to talk with Fiona. "Nothing urgent," she'd added, "but overdue just the same." Miriam took her position as senior woman faculty member seriously, and collie-like, herded each of her charges to her Hemphill Park door at predictable intervals.

Fiona appreciated her colleague's ministrations but always felt a keen sense of apprehension at these visits. To keep up with Miriam, one had to look sharp and not lollygag about. *The Prime of Miss Jean Brodie* was a favorite novel of Miriam's, and indeed the older woman, albeit shorter and packaged in a German edition, did share some of the characteristics of the sharp-minded, fictional schoolteacher. The sight of Miriam's front door roused in Fiona an old schoolgirl desire to measure up, to qualify again as the "crème de la crème."

Miriam's partner, Vivian, answered the door. Very thin and tall, with a large elegant nose and prominent eyes, Vivian resembled a contemporary Edith Sitwell, albeit with a New Jersey accent. "I guess I missed quite a time at your dinner party," Vivian said, leading Fiona into the kitchen.

"It was something," Fiona said.

"That's what Miriam said, too. Hey, I'll leave you two. I have a deadline this afternoon and still have ten pages to write." With a fluttering of long fingers, Vivian disappeared up the stairs.

"Fiona!" Miriam turned from the oven and advanced on Fiona with arms outstretched. Her face glistened with moisture, even though the late-October day was cool. Fiona smiled. With her hair wisping around her broad face and an apron stretched across her stocky torso, she resembled nothing so much as a prototype of a German grandmother.

Miriam swiped a towel across her brow. "This kitchen makes me boil. It's too small. Poor ventilation also. Come into the dining room and sit. Would you like a glass of wine?"

"Better not. I have meetings this afternoon."

Miriam passed her a shrewd look. "You might need a little spirit, but suit yourself. Coffee? Good." She bustled off to prepare it.

Fiona took in the cranberry flowered wallpaper and heavy walnut table. Everything about Miriam's house reflected its owner: furnishings and appointments of good quality, sturdy construction, and maximum utility. With the exception of the wallpaper and a few fragile figurines, Miriam's surroundings proclaimed a no-nonsense, no-frills mode of life.

Instead of sitting, she wandered into the living room while Miriam went back to the kitchen. A solid wall of built-in bookcases showcased the part of Miriam, and Vivian too, that reflected imagination and discernment. A quick glance at titles revealed that Miriam read voraciously, from the Enlightenment (Fiona noticed a well-thumbed copy of *Candide*) to contemporary classics like *Beloved*.

Miriam joined her with a French press and two heavy mugs on a tray. "So, tell me about your new book. Did you ever finish the study on Jewett, by the way?"

Fiona's book on Sarah Orne Jewett, listed as unpublished in her fall promotion package, had been—according to Sigmund—the reason her file hadn't gone forward. "Yes, I did. But I've shelved it. There's something, well, vacant about the thinking in it. Or at least that's how I see it now."

Miriam poured a hefty portion of cream into her coffee. "Yes? Well, you didn't get discouraged with it because of the fall promotion meeting, did you?"

"I certainly felt discouraged by that meeting. But, no, I'm just not happy with the book."

"That happens sometimes." Miriam hoisted her short legs up on an upholstered footstool, and settled back into the cushions of her chair. "I read 'Ivory Power.'"

"Oh, Lord. You mean you weren't sufficiently put off by Blake's excerpts the other night?"

"Most intriguing. You did make the poor lone female on the board look very bad, though. Surely, she wasn't based on me or Bettina?"

"God, no." Fiona scalded the top of her mouth with an injudicious quantity of coffee. She lowered her cup. "Although, on second thought, she's kind of a composite of all of women in the department. Earnest, eager to please, diligent, and outfoxed every time."

Miriam spooned sugar into her heavily-creamed coffee. "Well, not every time. 'Janquist,' isn't that the name you gave this composite? Her Scandinavian name and Midwestern manners reminded me of you, of course, and the extra poundage unfortunately made me wonder if you had been thinking of me." She laughed. "But then given your character's obvious sexual history with the chair...with Birdwell, was it?...that definitely let me out."

"I never thought of you or Bettina when I wrote it, only myself. I was thinking of all of the times I had depended on Sigmund in those situations, only to be outmaneuvered. I understand why you wondered—you and Bettina are the only female full professors in the whole department and so the only women who could be there. But I take full responsibility for poor Janquist."

"Well, I hope it shakes up a few members of our esteemed department. Or at least makes them see how ridiculous and pompous they are. Lester, for instance. Surely, he was Dent or White?"

Fiona smiled. "It's fiction, dear Miriam, remember?" She sat back and cautiously sampled the coffee again.

"Well, back to the new book. Bettina told me you are writing on Edith Wharton, is that true?"

Fiona nodded and Miriam continued: "A puzzling choice. The jaded aristocracy of Old New York is very far from your middle-class upbringing in a series of military outposts. You would seem to have nothing in common with Edith Wharton, who grew up in a hermetically-sealed brownstone, and as a child never was even allowed to go to school." The older woman scrutinized Fiona as if she wished to paint her portrait and found the light wanting.

"She fascinates me," Fiona said simply. "Since I was a girl. I suppose I empathized with her girlish ambitions to write, the lack of support in her family, her penchant for nightmares. Oh, there are so many things."

Miriam frowned. "You know, of course, that she was anti-Semitic and homophobic. Completely elitist and snobbish. And entirely wrapped up in a privileged world you and I can only half-imagine."

"She did give herself over to unfortunate people during the First World War," Fiona objected mildly.

"Yes, but you said the correct word—Wharton would have seen the poor and homeless as 'unfortunate,' as creatures decidedly far below her own station in life. There is a condescension there, I think."

Fiona stirred herself defensively. "I disagree. Look at the two Berkshires novels, *Summer* and *Ethan Frome*. She feels more in step with Charity Royall or Ethan, I think, than the spoiled, insipid May Welland in *The Age of Innocence*."

Miriam peered critically at her companion once again. Under her watchful eye, Fiona resisted the urge to straighten her own clothing or smooth down fly-away hairs. Miriam asked point-blank: "You think she was a good person?"

"That's rather beside the point. She certainly produced very fine writing and that's what I'm most interested in. But yes, I do."

"Come with me." Miriam abruptly hoisted herself out of her chair and led Fiona down a short corridor and into a small study, where she gestured at a wall of books. "Come," she repeated. She walked up to the middle bookcase and pointed to a long row of books: Fiona counted nine Edith Wharton novels, and three biographies of the artist.

Miriam smiled broadly. "I adore her work. I was just checking to see if you saw your subject's shortcomings as well as her strengths."

"You've read them all?" Fiona asked.

"Oh, yes, some of them several times. I just read, for the first time, her unusual novel *The Reef.* I thought it flawed but quite splendid."

"You know Henry James thought it perhaps her best work." Fiona pulled the book from the shelf and opened it. "Not surprisingly—the novel is the most Jamesian of her oeuvre!"

"I'm in good company then," Miriam said with satisfaction. "The architecture of the book interests me, the interlocking fates of the four main characters, meeting in the disembodied chateau."

Fiona replaced the novel with the others. "I think it's her first attempt to write convincingly about sex. The characters are familiar. A woman, Anna Leath, confined by the sexual prudery of Old New York, drawn to a much more worldly man, George Darrow."

"Yes, Darrow—facile, attractive, and sensitive—is another shadow of Morton Fullerton. Without him, Edith's life would have been similarly stilted and empty, just as Anna's was before she met Darrow."

Fiona nodded. "But the tight cocoon that they inhabit reminds me of James. He delighted in showing his characters caught like tiny insects in an elaborate, enveloping web."

"He just can't resist turning the screw so to speak," Miriam said happily. "And in *The Reef,* Wharton manages that effect very well."

"Yes, well, she loved complex psychological situations and could dramatize them just as well as he could. And you know they both were aficionados of the ghost story." Fiona turned to Miriam. "Just because he was older, more established—and dare we say it?—male, he gets proclaimed as her influence. That comparison dogged her—and galled her—her entire professional life, as fond as she was of the man himself."

The two women looked at each other agreeably, content in the way book lovers often are when they've found an author or a subject in common.

They returned to their seats and their coffee. "Now, we can talk brass tacks," Miriam said. "Even though your upbringing was so very different, there are some incredible similarities between you and Edith Wharton."

"Please, go on," Fiona said, flattered that Miriam had put so much thought into the matter.

"First, as you intimated minutes ago, you most likely came from a family that did not encourage women to excel in a profession."

"That's true," Fiona acknowledged. "My parents wanted me to marry and have children. And perhaps do something traditional, possibly become a nurse. Certainly they didn't encourage me to be a writer. My father has an artistic temperament and read to me often as a child, but like Edith's—you see, in our imaginary conversations, she allows me to call her Edith—my father was quiet and introspective. Compared to my pragmatic and very vocal mother, that is."

"Oh, dear, I hope at least she is kinder to you than Lucretia was to Edith."

"Considerably."

"That settled, let me continue. I suspect you consider yourself a late-bloomer. Even though you earned a Ph.D. at a fairly young age. Something tells me you have only recently discovered your true work."

Fiona squirmed. "Unfair. I think you've been talking to Daphne."

"Be that as it may," Miriam replied, not in the least flustered. "A good scholar leaves no source untapped."

"Go on," Fiona said.

"Yes, I shall. A correspondence most fascinating to me lies in your relationships with men." Miriam held both hands like a caution signal. "Don't worry. I haven't interviewed your lovers. This is pure observation. As a woman who hasn't lived with men for twenty years, how other women negotiate their relationships with them interests me very much." She thought a moment. "You are forty-five years old. You have just started a relationship with a charming man who is known to be very attractive to women and who finds them hard to resist. Does this sound familiar?"

"Well, yes, I am seeing Darryl; I suppose he could be described that way." Fiona flushed slightly and seized her coffee cup as if for ballast.

"No, no. I mean does this suggest anything to you as a scholar of Edith Wharton, my dear? She was forty-five when she met Morton Fullerton, a philanderer in the Darryl Hansen mode. I hope I don't offend you."

Fiona started, the coffee she held lapping dangerously close to the edge of her cup. "I don't think Darryl's bisexual."

Miriam shrugged. "He's very close to Dennis. But that means nothing. Perhaps. No, what is very strange is Darryl's involvement with Bettina, who is like a sister to you. Morton Fullerton, you will recall, was involved with Katherine Fullerton, who grew up as his sister."

Fiona set down her cup. "Miriam, I am very uncomfortable with all of this. Is there something you wish to tell me about Darryl?"

"Not at all. I just thought the coincidences very great indeed. Please, I really do not mean to offend you." Miriam sighed, and dabbed her forehead with her napkin. "Vivian tells me that I mortify people with my observations. I forget that people might mistake my intellectual curiosity for rudeness, or prying. I assure you I am very fond of you. And I do not mean to hurt you."

Fiona sat very still, trying to gauge her feelings. "It's all right," she finally said. "I think I can take this in the spirit in which you give it. So you're saying that unconsciously I must feel a deep kinship with this woman I'm writing about? So much so that I've attracted a Morton Fullerton into my life? That's rather frightening."

"Oh, no, that's not why you've attracted Darryl. Look at your relationship with Sigmund. That started long before you began writing about Edith Wharton. Now, that I have from a most reliable authority—you," Miriam said, a small smile twitching at one corner of her mouth. "It is just the coincidence that seems striking—your age, the similarities of Darryl and Morton Fullerton. But, in general, you find intellectual, powerful men very appealing."

Fiona groaned. "That's what Blake told me."

"Oh, Blake." This time Miriam smiled outright.

"You're not going to tell me that my friendship with him resembles Edith's with Henry James in some way, are you? After all, he's gay and brilliant. And voyeuristic about his friends' affairs."

Miriam frowned and wagged a finger at Fiona. "Now I am offended. I had rather hoped to claim that part for myself." She stood up and put her hands on her aproned hips. "Here you are, starving to death, and I'm raving on like an amateur Dr. Freud. I'll serve us something to eat." She walked toward the kitchen in her determined way. Fiona imagined she taught the way she walked: utterly fearlessly and with great economy.

Fiona called after her. "You'll have to get in line behind Bettina for the James' role. I believe she fancies herself The Master of my life."

By the time she made her way back to Helmsley Hall at one o'clock, Fiona rather wished she'd accepted Miriam's offer of a glass of wine. Their protracted, strangely intimate talk had drained her completely. The comments about Morton Fullerton particularly unhinged her. All the while writing her book, Fiona had puzzled over Edith's choice of Fullerton, had wondered how such an intelligent, perceptive woman could have fallen for his manipulations and infidelities. And now she saw how easily it occurred. No matter how insightful or penetrating one's intuition about other people's behavior, one's vision about one's own life tends toward myopia. Especially in mid-life, Fiona conceded.

But, she reflected, Miriam had extended her observations after lunch. Embracing Fiona in a decidedly motherly way, she'd held her at arm's length and said: "Think of this: Morton Fullerton may not have made an ideal partner for Wharton, but after her affair with him, she did her very best writing. Perhaps such a renaissance is in store for you as well." But Fiona felt very far from a renaissance, indeed would have described herself as lost in a long, shadowy tunnel peering anxiously for a way out.

The bright light of day did nothing to dispel her lost-in-a-fog sensibility. Skirting the group of people at the elevator, she trudged up the stairs—another dim corridor—to the seventh floor and presented herself to Anna, Sigmund's secretary, in the main office.

"Head on in," Anna said, her nose buried in a thick file of book orders for spring semester.

Fiona stood tall and entered Sigmund's office. She had decided she would stand during their interview, to take the high ground in all respects.

"Sit down," Sigmund said peremptorily, his back to her. He coughed and Fiona heard the squeeze of a spray bottle. Nasal spray? He turned around, his eyes red-rimmed and swollen. "Damn mold," he said. "It doesn't matter what season of the year it is, I'm allergic." He looked up at her irritably. "Why are you standing there?"

Fiona sat. Perhaps a casual approach might be best. "Sig, anything on your mind?"

Sigmund stared at her and then sneezed. "Plenty," he said thickly, his nasal quality coming out "plendy." The poor man did appear to be under the weather.

Fiona waited, appreciating Sig's expansive view of the campus, which differed from hers. She could see the Tower rising above the red roofs in one corner of his window.

"Your story in *The Gazette* is ridiculous," Sigmund snapped. "Fortunately, so much so that no serious-minded person will give it a moment's notice. Fiona, such a pathetic attempt to discredit me and to cast aspersions on this department is beneath you."

"I wasn't writing about you," Fiona said. "You flatter yourself."

"Nonsense. It's patently obvious. You're denied promotion, your pathetic stand-in, what was his name, Lawrence something, is denied promotion. You imply a vast conspiracy, whereas it's simply a case of standards..."

Fiona got to her feet. "I assumed we were going to have a collegial discussion. This is pointless." She checked her watch. "I have work to do."

Sigmund's jaw clicked shut. Fiona thought she heard the sound of teeth grinding. "Of course, and none of the rest of us do? You assume rather too much today."

"Sigmund, I know you're under some stress. Let's talk about that if you like. But attacking me will get you nowhere."

Rising quickly and shutting the door, Sigmund pulled up a chair next to hers, and changed his demeanor completely. He took her hand and sat, pulling her down to resume her seat. Confidentially, he asked, "Fiona, do you know anything about a videotape?"

"A videotape?" she repeated. Had Sigmund seen it already?

"Look, my friend," he smiled. "You and I have been through a lot together. We mustn't quarrel. Dr. Graf's lawsuit I'm afraid is unhinging her judgment. She's panicking. And most absurd," Sigmund hazarded a glance at the door and lowered his voice, "she's accusing me of discrediting her. It's idiotic. But you know university politics, all very disagreeable." He looked at Fiona hopefully.

"Sig, this situation is beyond me. I'm staying out of this. I counsel you to do the same. If you're involved in Kyle Cramer's case, extricate yourself. It's a very volatile situation."

Sigmund's back sagged a bit. "I'm afraid I am involved already."

"Then uninvolve yourself. Brace up." Fiona took particular pleasure in urging Sigmund so blithely to do what he had so often suggested to her.

"It's not that s-s-simple," he stammered, his face turning white.

"Yes, it is. Tell the attorneys you have no information about Bettina's interactions with Kyle. Stay out of it."

"It's too late," he said miserably.

Fiona disengaged her hand and stood up again. She took two steps toward the door. "I have to go. I don't understand you. Do you intend to throw away your career on undergraduate dalliances? Have you told your wife?"

"I need your help," he said.

"I'm the last person you need."

"A word to the Dean right about now could do wonders." He had the grace to look away.

Fiona didn't answer him. The utter nerve of the man rooted her to the floor.

"Fiona, please. I'm appealing to you as a friend, as someone who was once more than a friend..."

This last released her muscles and Fiona reached the door. She turned and asked, genuinely curious: "Sigmund, what do you want?"

His face flushed a dark red. "Respect. Affection. I've worked in this department for eighteen years. And after all that time, no one, I repeat no one, is offering to support me in this. I'm deeply offended."

Fiona studied her former lover. His cream-colored linen suit, well-cut, bagged on his large frame. His chest seemed to have collapsed into his belly. Was it possible that this was the first time he had been treated in the callous way he had treated everyone else in the department for the past six years? And was it plausible that he didn't see any correlation between his behavior and how others treated him now? Obviously crushed, Sigmund stared at the floor.

She opened her mouth. Phrases crowded into her mind: as ye sow, so shall ye reap; join the club; it's a cruel world; put up or shut up... Instead, Fiona said: "If you try, if you're really sincere, if you fess up to all the bullshit you've heaped on your colleagues' heads for the last few years, it might not be too late to earn that respect back, Sigmund. But then again, it might be."

He looked at her bleakly. Fiona slipped out of his office and closed the door. It didn't matter that Sigmund had the ethics of a scorpion. She hadn't let him goad her into a mean-spirited shouting match; she hadn't succumbed to his appeals to her vanity ("I need your help..." "I'm appealing to you as a friend..."); and most of all she had stayed out of his intrigue. As she strode down the hall, she raised her head and straightened her spine. She imagined that she could balance a book on top of her head and walk without it falling off. For the first time, she really felt like the "crème de la crème."

XV: The Devil

Live! Indulge yourself! Take your pleasures while you can. And baby, take it from me, flattery feels almost as good as sex... What do you mean, it's all an illusion? It looks real to me, at least in the mirror I use... Bad habits? I don't have those... What's bondage to you is obviously nirvana to me. I'll worry about paying the piper later. If there is such a thing—plus, if he can be paid off, why worry?

—Blake Burnois, telephone conversation with Dennis Reagan

Fiona returned to her office to pick up her briefcase and sunglasses. When the phone rang, she answered it crossly, certain that Sigmund had recovered his wits enough to launch a parting salvo at her.

A cool, male, and unSigmundlike voice energetically assailed her ear: "Dr. Hardison?...I'm Stanley Cross, with the *Los Angeles Times*. We're doing a special story on higher education and your essay crossed my desk."

"Which essay?" Fiona found it hard to believe that the *L.A. Times* would be panting after snippets from the lives of Sarah Orne Jewett or Edith Wharton.

"Um...drat, my screen just went blank...here we go, that's it—it slipped my mind for a moment—'Ivory Power.' Great read, by the way."

Fiona cleared her throat. "Oh, yes. Of course, that piece is a *short story*, not an essay."

"Fine. My editor was quite taken with it. And, so am I, of course. But let me get to the point."

Fiona lifted the phone away from her head and inspected it for signs of tampering. Was this for real? She replaced the receiver to her ear. "...think that institutional life...gone south..." he was saying.

"I'm terribly sorry. We must have a bad connection," Fiona said. "Would you please repeat the question?"

"Certainly. I asked you if you thought that institutional life in the United States has reached some kind of nadir. Or do you think the kind of malaise you describe is limited to academia?"

"I do think there's a crisis in institutional life in general in this country," Fiona began. "Academia is no longer a 'kinder, gentler' world separate from corporate America," Fiona warmed to the question, prepped by endless discussions with Bettina and Marvin on the issue. "Bureaucracies, particularly publicly-funded ones, seem to have lost their flexibility, and with that their ability to promote and reward creativity..."

"You've found that to be your experience?" Stanley interrupted.

Fiona considered a moment, not wanting to sound like a whiner. "At times, yes. I think people of my generation, who were raised to follow their dreams professionally, are somewhat horrified to find that the bottom line has replaced inspiration as the measure of what is worthwhile."

"Hmm." Stanley chuckled. "I'm afraid it's been like that in the whole ten years I've been working. But I hear ya—I'm afraid 'process' sold out to 'product' a long time ago. So you're saying there's a glass ceiling in corporate America that's not just about gender."

"I didn't use that phrase. To me, 'glass ceiling' implies someone's looking up and paying attention to what they see. My story is really about the lack of vision, a myopia of the spirit if you will."

Stanley chuckled. "Good sound-bite, 'myopia of the spirit.' You could say that about journalism any day of the week. Okay, let's see. Let me get just a little bit more here. You live in Texas. Do you think universities are more, well, constipated, in the southern part of the country?"

"No, I think this malady is an epidemic across regions."

"Ho. You're a very quotable lady. I'll take that one on, too."

Fiona waited. Was that a compliment? Nice midwestern girls always said thank you at the slightest provocation, as Janet Hardison had pointed out tirelessly when Fiona was growing up. But Fiona had read and heard too many butchered attributions in her time. She mentally apologized to her mother about her manners.

"I think I've got it," Stanley said in a moment. Fiona heard the muted whirring of fleet fingers on a keyboard. "Nice to talk to you Professor Hardison. Good luck to you. Maybe you'll be president of that university someday and change everything around."

God forbid, Fiona thought as she hung up the telephone. Mr. Cross most likely was more of an idealist than he imagined.

On impulse, she swiveled her chair over to her computer and checked her email. Out of fifteen messages, two stood out: one from someone at the *Wall Street Journal* and another from *The Dallas Morning News*. Fiona felt a strange excitement. After years slogging away in the academic trenches, where the average journal article had perhaps twenty serious readers, the feeling—even the illusion—of being noticed rather thrilled her.

Her phone rang again. This time, Darryl's voice greeted her. "How's my most famous professor?"

"What do you mean?" Fiona asked.

"I just got a call from someone at the *Houston Chronicle* asking me what I thought of 'Ivory Power.' And did I think, like the 'insightful Professor Hardison on your faculty,' that at Austin University, only mediocrity was rewarded?"

"Oh, dear," Fiona said, secretly pleased.

"He was very polite. He assured me that he wasn't referring to 'cutting-edge thinkers' like myself."

Fiona heard a chuckle amid the crackling of paper on Darryl's end. "And, check out your favorite campus newspaper," he continued. More rustling. "Let me just read you the headline of a story on the first page: 'Ivory Power' Maligns Tower.'"

"Too much. Why do I get the feeling that this story won't gain me friends in high places?" Fiona tugged at her hair. "Oooh. I didn't say that."

"Hey you're entitled to a few bad jokes. It's amazing this is being picked up. *The Gazette of Higher Education* doesn't exactly have a hip reputation. Until you gave it one. So, are you agog with happiness?" Darryl asked.

"Have you been talking to Blake?" Fiona replied suspiciously.

A warm laugh greeted her. "Well, yes, how'd you guess? He called to crow about the attention your story was getting. His conversational style is kind of contagious, isn't it? But hey, as he'd say, take it in, girl."

Fiona smiled, feeling her skin heat up. "I am enjoying it, just a bit."

"I should hope so."

Shyly, she asked, "You don't mind?"

"Mind? Think of it this way—the national newspapers could be calling me over Kyle Cramer's sexual harassment suit or a certain over-the-top videotape we've both seen. Which would you rather talk about?"

"Um, do I have to choose now?" Fiona said, smothering an unfeminine cackle. "I just had an image of the Texas Speaker of the House reading 'Ivory Power'."

Darryl groaned. "There would go our careful argument about needing increased funding to be competitive as a research institution. And I can see the illustration—some newspaper cartoonist's rendition of your Professor White's bloated rabbit doodle. Because bloated is what The Lege thinks of our reduced teaching loads and spending on buildings and equipment."

"If they think of us at all," Fiona said. "I imagine we get lost somewhere between Big Oil and the Silicon Hills."

"Don't even get me started. Look, Fiona, how about some champagne later tonight? Let's celebrate now, because who knows what tomorrow will bring about all this."

"You're on. My house or yours?"

"Let's do mine. Rocky is craving your company." Rocky, Darryl's long-suffering Golden Retriever, liked to get Darryl and Fiona to himself, without the demanding Dynamo's interference.

Hoping to find grounding in a day played out on an emotional high-wire, Fiona took refuge in work. She turned back the clock to a less-frenetic time. But while she shut off the phone, and ignored the whine of an incoming fax on her computer, she found it harder to dismiss Miriam's astute comparison of Darryl to Morton Fullerton. At first, her mind churned in irritation. Well, of course it wasn't surprising that she gravitated toward a charming, intellectual, good-looking and sensitive man, even though he might be easily distracted. After Sigmund, she didn't want to get too attached herself. And, it wasn't as if there were so many available—and wildly appealing—men around to choose from. Really, Miriam had no idea how difficult was the plight of a single woman in Austin, Texas. Remembering her friend's kind, interested face, Fiona admitted Miriam hadn't really judged her. Yet, somehow, after their conversation, Fiona judged herself. Was she having yet another lapse in judgment about men? Was it simply that she liked Darryl? She certainly enjoyed sleeping with him. Wasn't that okay and was that enough?

She began to shuffle furiously through her book notes, much as a runner sped around a track, hoping that the speed of movement might quiet her racing thoughts. Edith Wharton had embedded romantic turmoil into her fiction, developing her most resonant work. Fiona resolved to follow her example. Before her was a chapter on Wharton's 1912 novel, *The Reef,* begun at the height of the author's fascination with Morton Fullerton and her preoccupation with her failing marriage. Not surprisingly, the book heralded a surprising new focus on the erotic. From *The Reef* on, Wharton began to explore the nature of female sexual responsiveness with a new daring and depth.

Wharton's affair with Morton Fullerton awakened her in three ways: First, it re-connected her with the vital, physical passion that was a part of her nature. Second, through her gradual awareness of Fullerton's prolific liaisons, it opened her understanding to the difference and range of sexual natures. And third, as she divined Fullerton's infidelities, the relationship cultivated in her an ability to forgive rather than to simply condemn a moral sense different from her own.

In The Reef, *Anna Leath must confront her lover's infidelity, but she cannot rid herself of her horror of it. And she cannot imagine herself capable of the impulsive passion that George Darrow tries to describe to her, even though she desires him. She finds herself unable to leave her Old New York training behind—she lacks access to her uncensored sensual self. She judges readily, but cannot yield easily. By novel's end, Anna discovers she must marry Darrow anyway, because she cannot live without him, yet she and he are trapped by her condemnation into a tortuous cycle of blame, guilt, and forgiveness.*

Wharton's first-hand experience of the War further expanded her reservoir of empathy. By the time she began to write Summer, *in 1916, she described much more freely a young woman's passionate feelings. She called the novel "the hot Ethan Frome." Unlike Ethan and Mattie, who never consummate their love, Charity Royall passionately makes love to the architect Lucius Harney and becomes pregnant with his child. Interestingly, Charity is a poor, rural girl. Treated roughly by life, she has neither family nor position to bolster her. Thus, she represents a "natural," "primitive" sexuality; the fetters of society have not molded her every thought and feeling. When she releases her lover to marry someone else, Charity goes back to the man who had been her patron, the much-older lawyer, Royall, whose proposal of marriage she had earlier rejected. Mr. Royall once again takes her in. He marries her and agrees to raise her child as his own. By the novel's end, Charity has accepted her fate and lawyer Royall's goodness; she finds a security and satisfaction in her new life. Like the season of summer that gives the novel its background and title, Charity has matured and ripened.*

While Ethan Frome *ends in loveless misery, this other Berkshire novel, its companion, allows for both sexual pleasure and security, for romance outside of marriage and the comforts of home and husband. Published just six years apart and set in the same New England countryside, the two novels occupy different worlds of feeling. Charity survives the world of adolescence and uncertainty. She makes choices, and while she can't possess all that she wants, she achieves a satisfactory adult life.* Summer, *balanced and lyrical, is a powerful, satisfying work. In it, Edith Wharton's art reflects the integration she has found as a person and an artist.*

Fiona pondered Wharton's continuing attraction to the primitive, represented in *Summer* by Charity's strong physicality. After a journey to Morocco with Walter Berry at the end of the War, where Wharton witnessed an unfettered sexuality, she wrote a travel book called *On Morocco.* Later, perhaps triggered by her startled observances of the frequency of incest in that country, she composed an outline for a story based loosely on a sixteenth century woman, Beatrice Cenci, who had an incestuous relationship with her father. Writing the outline in 1919, Wharton renamed the character Beatrice Palmato.

Discovered after her death, the outline includes a fully-dramatized scene called "unpublishable fragment of Beatrice Palmato." The fragment describes in striking sensual detail sexual foreplay and intercourse between Beatrice and her father. To evoke a sense of an "other," exotic culture, Wharton specifies that the father is half-Levantine. In the outline for the never-written story, Beatrice Palmato later kills herself when her husband expresses affection to their daughter, terrified that his attentions are a precursor to the perversion she experienced as a girl. The narrative rendered the powerful seductiveness of incest as well as its destructive force. Was the story inspired by Wharton's travels and readings, or by something more?

Fiona scanned her bookcase for a copy of the R.W.B. Lewis biography of Wharton. Locating it, she turned to Appendix C and read again the actual passages of Wharton's text of Beatrice Palmato. The fragment quickly progressed from Mr. Palmato's initial tender caresses to its inevitable conclusion.

As she finished the brief document, Fiona paced about her small office, as if propelled by the energy in the prose. "Beatrice Palmato" really was something. Even today, the scene still shocked. Its sexual detail and vividness...well, Fiona found herself amazed, almost shaken. This writer—explicit, lushly erotic—this too was Edith Wharton. Fiona picked up her phone and punched in Miriam's home number.

"Hallo," Miriam answered. "Held and Winter residence."

Fiona paused a moment, utterly stimulated by what she had been reading and writing, her mind flying unbidden into a speculation of what Miriam and Vivian's intimate life was like.

"Hallo?" Miriam said again.

"Miriam," Fiona finally managed rather breathlessly, "I'm so glad you're there. I have...I have a Wharton question for you."

Miriam laughed. "Oh, Fiona, it's you. For a minute I thought it was a crank call. Another one. I was just interviewed by *The Chicago Tribune.*"

"Not about—"

"Oh yes, 'Ivory Power.' The reporter did his research; he knew I'd graduated from the University of Chicago and he asked me if your story could be as true of the 'top private universities'—his words—or just to 'the random public factories.'"

"Good grief. What did you say?"

"I said I'd never worked in a 'random public factory' but that in my opinion, 'the top private universities' were the worst and most inconsequential of offenders," Miriam recounted dryly.

"Miriam, you didn't!"

"I did. Then he asked me the tiresome question, that as a full professor in your department, did I see myself as the lone woman on that committee?"

"Ugh. The Janquist question."

"Well, I told him naturally that as a German Jew and a lesbian, no, I did not."

"And then?"

"And then he thanked me and hastily hung up."

The two women shared a hearty, conspiratorial laugh. "That's what he gets for goading a Chicago Ph.D.," Fiona managed.

"So, I'd be very happy to talk to you about our Edith instead," Miriam said pleasantly.

Fiona smiled at this reference. Henry James often referred to Edith in his letters to mutual friends as "our Edith." "Okay. I'm writing about EW's focus on sexuality, particularly during and after the Great War."

"Eros and thanatos, hardly unusual," Miriam pointed out. Miriam had a way of inserting her incisive comments neatly in between the speaker's thoughts. In a threatened moment, Sigmund had once referred to her as "the bloodless stiletto."

"What? Oh, yes, good point. Images of death evoke images of fruition. I hadn't made that connection."

"Of all people you should. Why do you think your postwar generation is so huge?" Miriam sighed. "You baby-boomers. Your scant knowledge of history makes me tear my hair."

"But younger generations are much worse, "Fiona protested lamely.

"That is an excuse?" Fiona could envision Miriam shaking her head eloquently, her fine gray hair flying about her face. "God save us from the young."

Fiona laughed. "Miriam, you're only twelve years older than I am, at most fifteen." Miriam's exact age was unknown to her colleagues.

"Hmm," Miriam did not enlighten her. "It makes no difference. I shudder to think what will happen to the country when all of my generation dies out."

Nudging her friend away from this uncharacteristically morbid note, Fiona offered: "To quote a dear friend of mine, Miriam Held, one shouldn't obsess about problems that don't concern one."

After a brief silence, Miriam said: "What were you saying about Edith Wharton?"

"After the reticence of her earlier books, the language of her novel *Summer* is so at ease with the erotic world. And then, soon after, we find the exotic, steamy sexuality of the Beatrice Palmato fragment."

"Yes. That is all documented. Of course, these works follow the affair with Fullerton— he himself said that Edith Wharton in love displayed the reckless passion of a George Sand."

"Even so. The Palmato scene is so vivid, so full of the pleasures of the forbidden, very realistically portrayed. Do you think Wharton was recounting a personal experience with incest?" Fiona asked.

"We'll never know that, will we?"

Fiona heard footsteps and then pages rustling in the background.

"You've read Cynthia Griffin Wolff's discussion of the subject, haven't you?" Miriam registered Fiona's assent and then continued: "She thinks Wharton may have had some feelings for her father, but nothing out of the ordinary. But she sees the Palmato fragment as a key to Wharton's being able to reclaim the positive aspects of her New York childhood."

"I think that's stretching it. Why incest? I think Wolff sees Wharton's sexual inhibitions as greater, and perhaps more pathological and destructive, than they were."

"Really? You think it's normal for a woman to accept a marriage for twenty-eight years that was asexual? Let's say she was virtually celibate for twenty-two years until she met Fullerton. That implies some very great repression indeed."

Fiona thought aloud: "Most people of my generation would barely be able to imagine that kind of abstinence."

"About sex, perhaps," Miriam said, as usual a full ten steps ahead of her. "But about other things, I imagine not. For example, the denial of aging is a huge example of repression in your generation. Or how about the pain of loss of the natural world?"

"Miriam, please, I need you to stay on this subject with me. We can talk about my entire generation's failings—and no doubt they are legion—another time. I just wish we knew the secrets of the Whartons' marriage."

"But we don't. Clearly, the coldness of the mother, the utter shame she evoked in the young Edith whenever she brought up any question of sexuality, laid a disturbing groundwork. Add to that the weak father figure, the much older brothers whom she barely saw. There is no evidence, by the way, that there was any incestuous relations with the brothers or the father."

Fiona broke in: "What she saw in Morocco, apparently the very common occurrence of incest...perhaps Wolff is right that it made her rethink the need of the extreme repression of her upbringing."

"Yes, if incest is such a pleasure and so available, a temptation coiled within the heart of every family like the proverbial serpent," Miriam said with some excitement, "then it's not so shocking that her reflection about it brought her to a new understanding of why strict codes for sexual behavior existed in Old New York. That culture wished for a genuine 'age of innocence' even though it wasn't really possible."

"It makes sense. And then there were the rumors of Lucretia's having had a lover and Edith's being the product of that affair, which Benstock explores so thoroughly. Perhaps Lucretia's own sexuality was shameful to her, so much so that she could not bring herself to speak of it to her daughter."

Miriam's voice was wry. "Or perhaps Lucretia simply hated being a woman. And despised the straitjacket she had to occupy. But the rumors of Edith's parentage have been pretty much been laid to rest. She resembles her father's side of the family."

"True. Well, once again, we just don't know."

"Even if we knew the facts, we wouldn't be able to decipher the exact nature of Wharton's feelings—the layers of feeling and memory, the complications of desire, the nuances of her motives—no, it's the great secret at the heart of every life."

Fiona had to acknowledge that her friend's words rang true. Before she could think of anything to add, Miriam broke in. "Plus, there's the other problem."

"What's that?" Fiona said, her mind still on Wharton's family mysteries.

"So-called facts are based on what is recorded. By human beings. And as we have found out only too well in the past decade, there's nothing people lie about more than sex."

Later that day, Fiona drove to Daphne Arbor's house to keep an appointment she'd rescheduled several times. In front of Daphne's house, brilliantly-blooming pansies paraded down the sides of the walk leading to the porch.

Inside, the late afternoon sun gave the rooms a golden quality. Fiona sat down on a stack of pillows in the corner of the entryway and rested her head against the wall. She breathed in and out slowly, and as her mind emptied, she slid into the shadowy border between consciousness and sleep.

"Fiona," a low voice called gently. It appeared to be coming from a strange forest with a great stand of clubs instead of trees. The clubs merged into a gleaming mass of thick, waving fibers...

Fiona focused on Daphne's dramatic silver hair and then the disconcerting, dissimilarly-colored eyes. She sat up straight, feeling curiously refreshed. "Oh, hello."

Daphne helped her to her feet with a firm hand and they went, as before, to the room with the Navajo rug. Daphne's midnight blue, ankle-length dress flowed rather than billowed around her as she walked.

Without preamble, Daphne gestured for Fiona to take a seat at the table, in the precise center of which was a pack of cards. "So," Daphne said, studying Fiona with a knowing smile, "the broken heart is better?"

"Yes." Fiona smiled.

"When you canceled our appointment several weeks back, I thought as much."

"Oh, but really, I just couldn't make it then. Some things came up at school..." Fiona began earnestly.

"Please don't apologize. I just know that when my clients postpone or cancel seeing me, their lives usually have taken a turn for the better. Now, what are we concentrating on today?"

Fiona filled Daphne in on the confluence of events in her personal and professional lives, although she had a feeling that Miriam probably had already regaled her friend with the juicier details.

Daphne consulted a blue folder which rested on the table in front of her. "From your last reading, I'm not surprised that your life has heated up, so to speak. Have you a specific question?"

Fiona considered. "I'm confused about two issues and I'm not sure which to ask the cards: one is my uncertainty about Darryl."

Daphne regarded her shrewdly, and Fiona felt herself rendered completely transparent. "You wonder perhaps if he is sincere, if you can trust him?"

Fiona nodded.

"I see. And what is the second thing?"

"It's the publication of the story I told you about. It appears to be stirring some things up, making kind of a fuss—calls from the press, that sort of thing." Fiona laughed self-consciously. "I'm not used to that kind of attention."

Daphne handed Fiona the Tarot cards. "Begin shuffling," she said. "What is your fondest wish? Quickly, answer me, without thinking."

"That I have freedom." The words slipped out of Fiona's mouth as easily as an eel glides through water.

"Ah. We shall start, then, with a question reading and see what it reveals. Let us ask the cards how you can attain freedom."

Fiona shuffled and then cut the cards. She sat back, and as Daphne picked up the stack to the right, Fiona felt comforted that for the moment, she could be less vigilant. Her life nestled in Daphne's capable hands.

"Our first card is the 'what' of the reading," Daphne stated, turning over The Devil. "Unfettered sexuality, Dionysian revelry. You have had this card before." Daphne stared at the man and woman chained together in the center of the card. "But this time I think it means something less obvious. This isn't about sex, as surrounded as you seem to be by its manifestations, but rather about freedom, about your question. The chains can be slipped off at will, but the will to do it has to be there. It is as Joseph Campbell pointed out, only the person inside the cage can open its doors and free himself. Something keeps you chained to circumstances in your life, those very circumstances that make you dream of liberation."

"That sounds so circular," Fiona protested.

"Of course. Old habits of mind or action put us on the gerbil wheel. We go around and around and wonder why nothing changes."

Fiona well recognized the gerbil wheel of obsession. "But how," she mused, "just how does one pass through that door?" She looked at Daphne. "I want to open it, if only I could find the key."

Daphne's face remained calm, unmoved. "Just remember, you must loosen the bonds before you can step out. Let us see what the other cards tell us."

Daphne flipped over the next card. "This addresses the 'why' of the question. The four of swords."

In the card, a woman lay on a pyre or a bier, her hands folded across her breast. Three swords mounted on the wall pointed downward menacingly. The fourth sword rested horizontally on the bier, parallel to the resting figure.

"The why is that you have been asleep in your life for some time.

Resting perhaps from a great struggle or illness. But the resting has renewed you and at any time you can awaken. I think, Fiona, you are ready to arise and move your life forward. The swords suggest that your mind will illuminate a new path. Or, perhaps the fruits of your mind."

"My writing," Fiona murmured.

"You are now ready to use your gifts in a more deliberate way." Daphne smiled shrewdly. "Of course, first you must arise from your bed—be jarred from the inertia of your hibernation—and that requires a catalyst. But be assured, life always provides us a push when we need it."

Fiona smiled wanly back. Her life seemed to be full of pushes enough at present. She cast her eyes longingly at the resting figure, envying the sleeper her blissful dormancy.

Daphne revealed the third card. "Let us now look at 'how.'" The card of Justice emerged on the table. Fiona imagined she saw the scales tipping back and forth very gently.

"Justice will be done," Daphne stated baldly.

"To me?"

Daphne's eyes—hooded, half-closed—regarded the card. "You are not exempt from the scope of Justice. And neither are others around you. It is the law of karma. Remember that karma comes from the root word that means work. We earn Justice and we work to dispense it. Something important lies in the balance of the scales, of course. Reputations, reparations, rewards, we shall see."

Fiona's neck and spine tingled briefly. A sudden notion possessed her to snatch the card and place it back into the deck. "I'm not sure I'm ready for that," she said quietly.

Daphne opened her eyes wide. "We rarely are. For all that is written in the Bible and all of our idle, and angry, talk, we seldom seek Justice. We crave it, we feel we deserve it. Perhaps. But to seek it is to release something into the universe, something that could affect us in ways we're not prepared for. That force may be potentially damaging even while it may be apt."

"What do you mean?"

Daphne straightened her broad shoulders. "It is like opening Pandora's box. Tipping the first domino, if you like. Others will fall down as a result."

Fiona heard this oblique reply and hesitated to question her further. Yet, she could not help but ask, "Do you see a danger?"

Daphne's face closed down, Sphinxlike, as if Fiona pressed too far. "Justice is very powerful. Take care that you are compassionate in all of your dealings and that will keep you the most safe."

Another card turned face up, a large yellow moon hanging in the sky, dripping shards of light. Beneath it, a dog and a wolf bayed upward, and a crayfish crawled from the water. In the middle ground two twin towers stood. "This is the 'when.' The Moon. The eternal feminine symbol, attached to the intuition that is so much its province, and that guides the High Priestess. You see the aquatic creature crawling out of the water; it creeps from the depths of the unconscious. The Moon teaches us that before we can be enlightened we must allow our most deeply buried feelings to emerge. They must be integrated into our conscious selves."

Daphne smiled almost dreamily. "This primitive creature challenges the rational mind—you see the twin towers—but what it symbolizes cannot be kept back. Once unleashed, the emotions demand recognition." Daphne's oddly mismatched eyes lent her the intense focus of a cat. Her face rose slightly to take in Fiona. "Certainly if you are to grow as a writer, as I believe you wish to do, you must examine your hidden nature. Perhaps that is what will release the chains you feel." She tapped one silver fingernail on The Devil card.

"Her profile looks almost stern," Fiona said, appraising the face of the Moon. Even as she said this, a small seed of fear lodged itself in the pit of her stomach. What might be buried in her unconscious and how would it be released?

"She does not judge, however. Remember that. Now, we reach the fifth card, the 'where.'" Daphne turned over the card, a divinely-illuminated hand reaching out of the clouds, bearing a wand. "And here we have the Ace of Wands. I told you last time the aces are gifts. This one imbues creativity and imagination. You see how the leaves fall off the branch on the left—creative potential literally drips from the staff. What has been given to you, you must use."

"If only I were more talented," Fiona mumbled.

Daphne shook her head and spoke sharply: "It shows false humility to complain that your gift is too small. Not to use your talents is an affront to God, the Divine Being, the Goddess, whatever you believe in. We were each put here to accomplish something. There is no time for self-negating thoughts."

False humility! Fiona heard the words as a stinging rebuke. Daphne obviously had no inkling of how difficult it was for Fiona to believe, or to trust, in her talents.

"It's not easy for any of us," Daphne continued firmly. "You must have courage."

She uncovered the sixth card. "The last card is the 'who.'" A dark but vibrant scene of flashing lightning flared up at Fiona. A gray tower emerged from a craggy mountain. The lightning sundered the large, gold crown from the top of the tower. In the foreground, two frightened figures, one wearing a much smaller crown or headdress, plummeted headfirst from the edifice.

Daphne paused. "The Tower. It indicates the most radical change, often a shift in your bedrock beliefs. This stage in the Fool's journey strips one of false values as well." Daphne once again gestured at The Devil, and then pointed to the falling couple in The Tower. "In this card, the man and the woman choose a very dramatic way of breaking their chains. Other, more gentle approaches exist. But sometimes, only an extreme method can blast people out of their complacency. The Tower purges outmoded ways in the crucible of change or crisis. It enables a purification by fire, if you will."

"It looks like the end of the world."

"Of one world perhaps. But The Tower signals greater understanding—you see the shards falling from the flames on the right. Ten shards, evoking the Tree of Life, the primordial seeds upon which mystical and philosophical laws are based."

"Have the two bodies fallen by accident or were they pushed? Or are they jumping to escape the fire?" Fiona asked, unnerved by the terror reflected in the faces of the plummeting figures.

"It doesn't matter. Their lives are changing whether they choose them to or not. The lightning symbolizes the violent flash of insight—they may be falling but they are heading toward greater self-knowledge." Daphne bequeathed Fiona a dazzling smile. "When people get this card, I always tell them"—her voice shifted into a passable Bette Davis imitation—"'fasten your seatbelts, it's going to be a rocky ride.'"

XVI: The Tower

The King is dead! Long live the King! Are those the twin poles of deception you've lived by? Face it, you're just a cog in a wheel; once you don't serve your function anymore, nobody gives a damn about you. So forget the hero bullshit. You're not the stuff of legend, so what? Buck up. You can still have a productive career. Save yourself—let some other sucker take the heat at the top.

—Richard Lester, pep-talk to Sigmund Froelich in the men's room

The next morning, as Fiona carted out the trash, Bettina appeared at her doorstep, wearing a purple sweat suit.

"Good heavens!" Fiona started.

Bettina slid her arm around Fiona and guided her back into the house. "I was jogging by and decided to drop in."

"Since when did you take up jogging?" Up the block, Fiona noted a red coupe identical to one Bettina drove.

"Listen, I have real news. I didn't want you to go into the office unprepared."

Inside, Bettina bustled around the kitchen. "You don't mind if I make some coffee, do you? You just sit down and relax. Gather your strength, you may need it." She hummed as she poured water into the coffee maker. "Have you talked to Darryl?"

"He just left about fifteen minutes ago."

Bettina eyed her friend with some exasperation. "I didn't ask if he had been here, I asked if you had talked to him?"

Equally exasperated, Fiona snapped. "Well, of course we talked. But I don't know what we should've talked about."

"Oh, never mind. Obviously, the two of you weren't focused on work." Bettina sat down opposite Fiona. She raised one hand and began to tick off her fingers. "Okay, here's the scoop: one, Kyle Cramer has dropped her suit against me. Two, she's decided to sue Sigmund for sexual harassment and for bribery or blackmail, I forget which. Three, it will be announced sometime this afternoon that Sigmund has been removed as chair." Bettina pushed up the sleeves of her sweatshirt and sat back, her freckled face flushed and pleased.

"Good Lord. Is the coffee ready yet?" Stunned, Fiona required an immediate infusion of caffeine.

Bettina complied and returned with two large mugs. "Pretty amazing reversal, huh?" She exuberantly spooned sugar into her cup, followed by a large dollop of cream. "Darryl's been good for you. You didn't used to keep any cream in the fridge," Bettina said approvingly.

Ignoring the reference to Darryl, Fiona said: "Reversal? It's a rout! My God, Sigmund has been chair of our department since I came here."

"He's been chair fifteen years," Bettina said. "And three months, if we were interested in those kinds of details."

"Which we most definitely *are*," Fiona said. "How did all of this happen?" Fiona cursed Darryl for withholding news of this magnitude from her, even though they'd had a very lovely evening of champagne followed by an equally effervescent time in bed.

"The videotape may have speeded things up some," Bettina said placidly, "but it would've happened anyway. Kyle came to her senses."

Noticing the gleam in her friend's eye, Fiona asked, "Bettina, what aren't you telling me?"

Bettina's eyes widened to a benevolent flare of green. "Whatever do you mean, Miss Scarlett?" She grinned.

"Did you show Kyle the tape yourself?"

"I wouldn't be in a room alone with her if my life depended on it. No, I sent it to her. And then Dennis talked with her in a very proper and professional office consultation."

"Dennis! But she once accused him of sexual harassment!"

Bettina shifted her generous torso in search of comfort. "He left his office door ajar. Believe me, no one takes any chances with that girl. Excuse me, that young woman. Of course, when she saw the tape, she saw how she had been used."

"But Sigmund looks like a victim on that tape as well."

"Fiona, please. Let me review the facts for you: which person on that tape is an adult, in a position of authority, paid to be a public servant of the university, and which one is young, subordinate, and paying tuition so that she may learn in a safe environment?"

Fiona nodded, but couldn't help but feel a flash of pity for Sigmund. "Poor Sig."

"'Poor Sig?' The bastard's finally getting what he deserves."

"I know it, B. But not only is his manhood—dubious to us, I know, but very precious to him—besmirched by this but he loses every bit of power he's so carefully built up. Along with losing face. It's a lot to take in."

Bettina flushed an angry deep pink. "Fiona Hardison, save your sympathy. Sigmund has dished out worse than this for years. With no remorse. He's been irresponsible and now he has to pay. What do you think would happen to one of us if we were fucking a twenty-year-old student—and wait, that's not the worst of it—if we promised to aid a student in a lawsuit against a faculty member in our own department in exchange for sexual favors?"

"We'd be in big trouble," Fiona admitted.

"No, we'd get our asses fired, that's what. We'd be dishonored. And pilloried in the press. And probably tarred and feathered and then burned as witches!"

"I see your point," Fiona conceded. "But wait, who is Darryl naming as the new chair?" Fiona stared at her friend, only to have Bettina uncharacteristically look away.

"Bettina, are you going to be the new chair?"

Bettina crossed one purple-encased leg over the other. "He has asked me. I haven't decided yet whether I will accept."

"Well, then, why are you looking so guilty?" Fiona demanded, now deeply disturbed that Darryl had mentioned none of these details to her. Even more puzzling, when had he and Bettina had time to discuss all of this? And where were they—and what were they doing—when they did it?

Bettina sighed. "I don't want to profit from Kyle Cramer's shenanigans."

"Do you mean you really don't, or you don't want to *appear* to profit?"

Bettina paused and looked out the window, her profile taking on a lapidary glaze. "Fiona, is something bothering you?"

Fiona's tongue felt swollen in her parched mouth. "I have to ask you something." She passed a cold, sweaty hand over her face. "This is very difficult for me."

"What is it?" Bettina's face now registered only concern.

"You've been sitting and telling me cataclysmic events for half an hour! But that isn't what I want to talk to you about."

"Oh. Well?" Bettina put her hands in her lap; her face focused on Fiona as she waited calmly.

Fiona took a deep breath. She experienced a rush of butterflies as if she were facing a huge audience. Or perhaps a firing squad. "What is the nature of your relationship to Darryl?" she finally whispered hoarsely.

Bettina looked blank for a moment. "Oh, you mean am I still sleeping with him? Fiona, if this has been bothering you, why on earth didn't you just ask me?"

Fiona gritted her teeth. "I'm asking you now. Are you?"

Bettina ran her fingers through her glorious auburn mane unconsciously. "Yes," she said. "But only very rarely."

Fiona closed her eyes; she felt a fog enveloping her, insulating her from the moment. Bettina's face appeared to recede a bit, and she said hollowly: "I thought you said you were involved with him a year ago."

"I was. Deeply involved. Now I'm not."

"You just have sex with him."

"Once or twice we've...fallen into bed, yes. That was the best part of our relationship, the only thing that worked really."

Fiona got up and walked into the living room, her limbs leaden. She sat down on the couch, her head cradled in her hands. "Please. I don't want to hear about it. I wish you had told me."

Bettina followed her and sat down next to her. She placed one hand firmly on Fiona's knee. "Honey, I know you're upset. But be fair. I had been seeing Darryl for a long time. When we stopped seeing each other, I wasn't possessive—I didn't make a fuss when you said you were going to go out with him. However," her voice turned a trifle cool, "I am not the one encroaching here."

Fiona felt confused, hurt, and angry by turns. "Are you saying I'm encroaching? Bettina, you're married."

"I know I'm married. And so is Darryl. But," Bettina's temper had reached a definite simmering point. "I don't want to be accused of sneaking around with your boyfriend, man friend, whatever. I have not changed my behavior toward Darryl."

"You just haven't shared it with me."

"My dear," Bettina said evenly. "There are some things I don't share, even with you. You are my best friend, but I don't feel that entitles you to every pathetic detail of my sex life." Fiona flinched and Bettina's coolness evaporated. "I did think Darryl was past tense. And he is, mostly. But sexual feelings aren't always as neat and tidy as we wish them to be."

Fiona edged away from Bettina. "Let's drop it. I feel that Darryl's just been toying with me. He doesn't really tell me anything. It's you he confides in. And that's fine. That's his privilege. I just don't know what he's playing at with me."

"Oh, Fiona..." Bettina touched Fiona's hair; her fingertips brushed her cheek. Fiona found the soft, gentle pressure relieved the tension she felt.

"Do you feel left out, sweetie?" Bettina asked. "I haven't meant to do anything to hurt you. What's between Darryl and me, well, I know it must look messy and complicated, but it's just old, unfinished stuff."

Bettina's voice, reassuring and intimate, heightened Fiona's confusion. She felt angry at everyone: Darryl, Bettina, herself. She didn't understand her own motives any better than she did theirs. She felt overwhelmed and foolish. She did what she always did when she found herself at the center of roiling emotions: she simply froze. She felt a part of herself retreat so that Bettina and her own feelings became muted in the distance. She heard herself speak as if in a fog: "I guess I do felt left out. How ridiculous."

The skin around Bettina's eyes crumpled in contrition. "I can't bear to think I've hurt you. You know it's you I love, Fiona," Bettina kissed Fiona's neck, her breath fanning her ear. "I'm so sorry," she said quietly. "Forgive me."

Fiona's stiff posture began to soften as Bettina put both arms around her and held her. She stroked Fiona's face again with those pliant fingers, and then began to knead her back, her strong hands melting the resistant muscles. "You're so tense," she murmured.

Bettina's hands moved hypnotically on her back. Aware of the other woman's firm, ample breasts against her, Fiona shivered slightly. "Bettina, I think I'd better get ready for work."

"Stay," Bettina said softly, her fingers threading through Fiona's hair. Bettina's eyes were half-closed, her face vulnerable and open, with no sign of her customary wit or poise. Fiona thought she might be seeing her friend truly naked for the first time. When Fiona hesitated, then drew away, even Bettina's voice seemed different as she asked: "It's Marvin, isn't it, and Darryl? Are they the reason why you can't be here with me now?"

Fiona looked into Bettina's face, at her smooth, flushed cheeks, the soft, shadowed skin under the muted green eyes. Bettina seemed so present, so sure. Fiona envied her. More than anything, she wished the woman beside her could grant her the same openness. I want you, Fiona thought, shocked by that simple truth, and the stark desire stirring from a deeply buried part of her. Her very skin thirsted for the touch of the woman beside her. Aloud, she said: "You make me feel very greedy."

Bettina sighed, her lips curving wide. "Then, what is it?"

Fiona said nothing. Bettina opened her eyes fully. She took one of Fiona's hands in both of hers. "I think I understand. You're afraid of what might happen if we let ourselves really love each other."

Fiona shook her head. She didn't think Bettina could understand her reluctance. "I'm not sure I could share you," she said simply.

After her graduate class, "American Moderns," Fiona sat in her office drinking a cup of coffee. It was five o'clock. The spirited discussion in her seminar about Gertrude Stein's need to identify with and yet distinguish herself from her male rivals had barely budged her mind from the morning. Fiona had embellished the seminar deliberations with a slide show of Stein and competing geniuses like James Joyce, Ernest Hemingway, and Pablo Picasso. Bettina's face superimposed itself easily over every other image, no matter how compelling: the famous 1906 Picasso portrait of Stein with its striking cubist planes; the two devastatingly handsome young men in Paris—Picasso in 1905, Hemingway in the 1920s; Joyce scowling at Sylvia Beach's Bookshop in Paris; the first typescript of *Ulysses*, the walls of 27, rue de Fleurus chock-a-block with modernist masterpieces.

Fiona paged through a large format book of Stein photos. Her students always found the woman with the twenty-first century mind and the nineteenth century tastes for comfort fascinating. Stein's private life, by current turn-of-the-millennia standards, played itself out simply: after she met Alice B. Toklas in 1907, they spent the next thirty-eight years together. Yet Stein had resisted Toklas when she first met her, criticizing her intellect and her sexual habits. Once again, thoughts of Bettina emerged as she compared her own messy personal situation to Stein's. Fiona had never experienced such reservations about Bettina, finding her always an ideal, stimulating, and insightful companion.

The morning's visit had ended on a further jarring note. As Bettina had risen to leave Fiona's house, a knock on the door preceded Darryl in the flesh. Bettina pressed her face warmly to Fiona's. "We'll talk later," she whispered.

Darryl watched their leave-taking appreciatively. "Sorry to interrupt, ladies. I forgot my briefcase."

Fiona, looking at her watch, wondered why he had waited a full hour to return for it. He picked it up from behind the kitchen counter and then hesitated in the doorway, looking from one woman to the other as if uncertain who to kiss on his way out. He looked handsome, yet very conventional in his three-piece suit and carefully-trimmed salt-and-pepper hair. He paled next to Bettina's exotic beauty.

"You haven't forgotten what day it is?" he said to the air in between them. Fiona thought he might finally tell her of Sigmund's fall from power. But when neither woman answered, he grinned, "All Hallows Eve. Time for transformation. It's the one day you can get away with being witches."

Bettina's eyes caught Fiona's along with the whisper of a smile. To Darryl she said: "I think witches have gone the way of apple-offering serpents and sorcerers. Women had to be witches if they wanted to be sexual. Now we can just be women."

She waved goodbye and strode out the door, leaving Darryl and

Fiona to stare at her retreating backside. The cheeks of her buttocks swung freely, enticingly, under the thin fabric of the purple sweatpants. Fiona felt certain she wasn't wearing any underwear. "Well?" She said to Darryl.

"Well, what?" He moved to the window to watch Bettina as she walked up the block and slipped into her car.

"Nothing," Fiona said, and headed to her bedroom to dress for work.

Standing in the kitchen with both of them, it was obvious that Darryl had eyes only for Bettina. Fiona's surprise had come in finding how true that was for herself as well. When Bettina had whispered, "It's you I love," an absurd happiness had surged through Fiona; the next moment uncertainty assailed her. Of course she had always loved Bettina. But where did that leave them?

And what about Darryl? Had Darryl manipulated Fiona in a time-honored but reprehensible practice, with the intent to deliberately make Bettina jealous? Uncomfortably, she turned her scrutiny back upon herself. She had thought her attraction to Darryl direct and uncomplicated, but in light of the morning any such "pure" or instinctual impulse seemed delusional.

In her office at the end of the day, she gulped coffee as if it could purge her of confusion. What a hopeless mess. She thought of her father, who had read her the adventures of the Argonauts as they navigated the perilous passage between Scylla and Charybdis. She wished she could talk to him about negotiating this harrowing romantic passage. Daphne Arbor's reading drifted into her consciousness: The Devil, The Tower. Perhaps the Greek myths applied after all, as those cards resonated with the journey to Hades, from where no soul emerged unscathed or untransformed.

Fiona had seen Sigmund twice since arriving at Helmsley Hall that afternoon, once emerging from the men's room and another time in the mail room. Both times she'd eluded notice. However, exiting the elevator before her class, she caught sight of the dapper figure of Richard Lester, the most senior professor in her department, standing in front of the department bulletin board, staring at the posted copy of "Ivory Power." Before she could escape, he turned and saw her. He nodded his head slightly in her direction. "Professor Hardison," he said.

"Professor Lester," she replied.

She turned to make her way down the corridor. "Ah—" he'd said.

"Yes?" she'd stopped, tensing her muscles. The usually serene Lester could suddenly strike with all the viciousness of a threatened swan.

"I knew Blake Burnois at Indiana," the dry, discreet voice announced.

"You too? I thought he'd taught there with Sigmund."

"He did. Professor Froelich and I go very far back." Lester smiled and elevated his chin, a characteristic gesture signaling he wished to occupy the moral high ground. "I don't think much of Burnois."

"You don't think he's intellectually up to par?" Fiona couldn't resist voicing his predictable denunciation before he could utter it himself.

"Oh, he's brilliant. But deeply flawed. Bad character. You can't trust him."

For a moment Fiona stared at him stupidly, amazed that Lester could recognize his own Achilles heel on someone else's foot. "He's a friend of mine," she said.

"I assumed so," Lester said, his hawklike nose pointed toward her. "Just remember, being sensational will not bring you the respect you desire."

Irked by his condescension, Fiona retorted: "Thank you for that word of advice. But it's odd, don't you think, how that very thing has helped so many in our department get ahead?"

Lester had snagged an endowed professorship on the strength of a few interviews on "Good Morning America." The invitation followed the publication of his book on celebrity that ironically awarded him his fifteen minutes of fame. "Solid scholarship sometimes attracts charges of sensationalism by the less successful," Lester countered.

"I couldn't have put it better myself," Fiona said and marched on toward her office.

She sighed now and put down her cup. It had truly been a day for the books. She decided to take herself out for a drink...or three. She hefted the stack of seminar papers turned in today and returned them to her desk. Better leave them here until tomorrow—they deserved better than her tired mind could give at the moment.

As she reached to switch off the lights, Anna Frayne, the administrative officer of the department, simultaneously knocked urgently on the door and pushed into the room, colliding with Fiona. She didn't appear to notice, but instead turned her blanched and stricken face on Fiona. "Thank God you're here," she managed, breathlessly.

"Anna—what? Are you all right?" Fiona grasped her firmly as Anna sagged forward and her arms dangled limply.

"No. Yes. Oh, my God." Anna grabbed the arms of a chair and half-fell into it. "I think Sigmund is dead. I just found him."

"Sigmund? You must be mistaken. I've seen him twice today. He seemed very well."

"Fiona, listen to me. I've just called 911. I think he's gone."

Sigmund, gone? It seemed impossible. Fiona was aware of the pulsing of a vein in her forehead. Her stomach cramped and she knew a hideous headache was coming on. Two months ago, she had wished this very thing. She had sat here and chanted misfortunes to befall Sigmund like a mantra: I hope publishers howl derisively in his face and burn his manuscripts, I hope his balls collapse the next time he looks at a woman, I hope he's deposed as chairman, I hope his hair falls out and takes his scalp with it—and most alarmingly given this new development—*I hope he drops dead.*

Anna sat crumpled in the chair, panting.

"Stay here," Fiona commanded. "I'll be right back."

"No!" Anna's face collapsed. "Please don't leave me!"

Fiona reached for Anna's hands and held them. "I'll only be gone a minute." She stepped out into the hall and rounded the corner just as a team of paramedics emerged from the elevator. She led them to the main office and hurried back to her own.

Anna sat rigidly, shivering. Fiona hurriedly poured her a cup of coffee and thrust it at her. It was old—stewed by now on the warmer—but Anna took it and held it close to her face, gratefully breathing in the rank, oily brew.

"What happened?" Fiona asked.

"I don't know. At five fifteen I brought him a cup of coffee. He was brooding over some papers on his desk—nothing unusual about that, of course. Then, well, I had just shut off the copy machine for the night and turned off the computers and I just thought—it was about ten to six—that I'd say goodbye. So I stuck my head in the doorway. You know how he keeps his door slightly ajar. Well, when I looked in he was slumped over. Collapsed. Papers all over the floor. I thought he might have fainted. But there was no pulse, no breathing, nothing."

Fiona gnawed on a fingernail. "Good God. Did you try CPR?"

"Oh, Lord. I never thought of it. His face was gray. I just knew it was too late. Oh, dear! My father died the same way. It's too terrible." Anna once again looked as if she might keel over.

Fiona had forgotten that Anna's father had suffered a fatal heart attack just two months before. The poor woman was still in shock from his death. "Oh how thoughtless of me," Fiona said hurriedly. "Of course you would know the right thing to do instinctively."

But Anna's anxiety rose to a fever pitch. "But you're right. I should have tried to save him. Oh, my God." She slapped down the coffee cup on the arm of her chair. Splotches of liquid sloshed over her beige blouse.

"Anna, stop, get hold of yourself." Fiona grasped the other woman's shoulders firmly and looked directly into her eyes. "Come on, let's go back to the office. People are there now taking care of everything. Can you stand up?"

Anna nodded, mute and miserable.

"Well, come on then. I'll help you. Just take it easy. Breathe. You did the absolute best that you could." Fiona hoisted Anna out of the chair, one arm around her shoulder, the other supporting and lifting her at the waist. "Can you help me just a little?" Fiona asked gently. "There, that's it."

Anna's fragile composure cracked further and she burst into tears. "I'm so sorry. I didn't mean to alarm you. And poor Professor Froelich. And after all these years we've worked together." She limped along with Fiona, her spine curving forward, her usual robust carriage discarded in her time of trauma. "I don't know what to do."

"Nothing. You don't have to do anything. Here, turn left. That's it. We're almost there." Fiona gently massaged Anna's right shoulder as they tottered together down the hall.

By the time they reached the main office, the hallway was cluttered with EMS workers and police officers. A young man in a green scrub suit addressed Anna. "Did you call 911?"

Anna shrank against Fiona and her tears gave way to sobs. She began to sputter in an incoherent mixture of sounds and hiccoughs: "Icouldntfimbhispulse...Imsosorrryyy...."

The attendant patted her back and said reassuringly: "I think he'll be all right."

"What?" Anna's mascara-stained face snapped forward. "But I saw him. He looked..."

"Dead?" The young man smiled. "Sometimes stroke victims look that way. He's responding well. He has a good chance for recovery. You must have called us immediately."

A gurney wheeled toward them. On it, Sigmund lay, wired by tubes and various pressure cuffs and monitors, drained of color. His features barely registered against the white blanket. His eyes lacked focus, direction, or recognition as he passed by.

Fiona suddenly felt very tired. Witnessing his current condition, it was hard to imagine that she had ever found Sigmund a threat. Sig didn't look powerful or evil, only used up and pathetic. A bit like she felt herself.

XVII: The Star

Virginia Woolf created out of the deep pool of her unconscious. Whatever the turmoil of her life, writing for her released the pressures of memory and imagination. Her novel To The Lighthouse, *which helped her to heal the pain and longing of her childhood, was an act of love. And an act of emancipation.*

—*Bettina Graf, class lecture for "Modern British Fiction"*

"Culture is made up of stories. The stories we tell reveal who we are, what we consider important, and what we want to pass on to others," Fiona addressed her undergraduate class. "The stories we tell in everyday life, like fairy tales, usually involve going from something old—a place, an awareness—and moving toward something new. Many novels and films follow this journey theme as well. It usually works like this: a person, usually fairly innocent, falls into a situation, goes somewhere (either psychologically or literally), faces trials, proves herself or himself, and is transformed. He or she is wiser and more worldly by the end of the journey. We see it in 'Rapunzel' as clearly as Huck Finn. It's the same old story—the hero's journey—with infinite variations."

The class was studying the film adaptation of Virginia Woolf's *Orlando*, in which the protagonist leapfrogs through several centuries, at times as a man, at others a woman. "Gender is both everything and nothing," Fiona began. "In a way, Orlando must determine what's inside regardless of her external trappings." The class decided that the next session they would each bring in a story to share, one that captured for each person the journey of discovery.

Driving home, Fiona remembered how, as a little girl, she had looked forward to special sessions with her father in his basement study. There, once or twice each week, the two of them gathered for storytime. The choice of book always fell to Fiona. She'd crouch in front of the bookcase, wanting them all. When her indecision reached a point of agony, she reached out with both hands, and lifted something from the shelf. No matter what its shape or condition, Fiona knew the volume in her hand could open to a world she had never imagined.

One day, when Bert Hardison had just finished reading, Fiona begged for another story, a new one, about a girl just like her. Her father smiled, and closed the book on his lap. "I think we should tell a story together. I'll choose the title: 'The Secret Pool.'"

Fiona protested that she didn't know any stories about pools. "Well," he said. "When you look at a smooth sheet of water that is very clear, what do you see?"

Fiona scrinched up her face, wondering if there was a trick answer. "Me," she finally said.

"Exactly. Then you do know this story. I probably don't have to tell it to you." He stretched his arms overhead and prepared to stand.

"No!" Fiona tugged at his shirt. "Please."

He lightly touched the top of her head and began: "High up in the mountains above the tallest trees, there once was a waterfall that tumbled into a secret pool. It was so remote that no one could find it."

"Why not?" Fiona asked, imagining a pool that was very deep and very cold.

"For one thing, it wasn't on any map. For another, you could only find it if you were lost. It was a pool you could only find when you had reached your limits."

"Hmm," Fiona said. "You mean when you had nowhere else to go?"

"Yes. One day a young girl wandered away from her village, made her way up onto the mountain, and got lost. She didn't care that she was lost, however, because she hated her life. Her parents had both died, first her mother from a terrible plague, and then her father in a war. The girl had a young brother whom she loved very much, but he was burning with fever and no longer knew her. No one expected him to survive. The young girl couldn't bear to lose her brother and so she went away, certain that everyone she had loved was leaving her."

"Oh." Fiona thought being left would be the worst thing in the world.

"What do you think she found when she was completely lost and desperate?"

"The pool," Fiona said. "Of course."

"I told you we would tell this together. And what do you think she would most want to find there?"

"A person," said Fiona. "Because if I thought everyone was leaving me, that's what I would most want to find."

"That's just what she found. The little girl came to a high wall that had a crack in it. She slipped inside and saw the waterfall. At the bottom was the pool and beside it knelt a woman with long, dark hair."

Fiona reached up and patted her own very short, blonde hair. "Did she offer the girl some water to drink? She must have been very thirsty by this time."

Bert Hardison nodded. "The woman gave her a drink from the jug that she had filled from the pool. The water was clear and fresh. It had a delicate taste of pine and flowers in it. It was the most delicious water the girl had ever tasted, and she drank for a very long time.

"'Now,' said the woman. 'Let me show you something.' She pointed to the waterfall and the stream of water that led to the pool. 'The waterfall, the stream, the pool, and the water pouring from these two pitchers represent the five senses that you have. By drinking the water from the pool you are reunited with the power that is within you. This water is very special, and it refreshes your spirit and your mind as well as your body.'" Bert turned to Fiona. "Can you feel it?"

"'This liquid contains the secret of health and knowledge,' the woman continued."

"What is the secret?" asked Fiona, her eyes wide and deep.

"Ah, I don't need to tell you the secret," her father said, "I think you know it already."

Fiona shook her head. "No, I don't know anything."

"That's what the little girl said, too," Bert continued. "The woman took her hand, led her to the edge of the pool, and then stepped back. What do you think the girl saw?"

"Herself."

"Yes, exactly. That's the secret."

"I don't understand," said Fiona. "How can seeing herself in the water help?"

"Here's what the woman said: 'When you are most weary and discouraged, you must look into the water. That is, look into the deepest part of yourself. All people are born with health and potential. But they get distracted. They look for others to take care of them, or for things like money or land or other riches. They forget they have the power to heal themselves.' The woman turned again toward the waterfall. 'The running water purifies everything. But in this pool, the water is calm. The stillness is the secret of health. When you are tired, you must rest. When you are disappointed, you must recover before you try again. When you are thirsty, you must drink and replenish your energies. After you allow yourself to fill up again, you will find you have new ideas on how to proceed.'

"The young girl looked up at the woman with the blue-green eyes and the dark hair. It was almost dusk, and the deepening light of the sky shadowed the woman's skin. The girl felt more peaceful than she ever had in her life. 'Can I stay here with you?' she asked.

"The woman regarded her seriously. 'You may,' she said. 'But you have a choice. You can either stay here with me and be apart from the world, except on those rare occasions when someone makes their way here, or you can take some water with you and give it to your brother to cure him. The two of you can then live your lives in the valley.'" Bert turned to Fiona. "What do you think she chose?"

Fiona sighed. "She didn't have a choice. She had to help him. She would have said: 'Please give me some water to take away with me.'"

"That's just what the girl said. Then the woman told her: 'Life is like that. We don't think we have a choice. We take the path we must take. The true path for us is often the only one we see. But it still is a choice that you have made, remember that.' She gave the girl a pitcher and stepped into the pool. She stared up out of the water at the girl. 'Dip the jug into the pool just once and whatever you have in the container will be enough.' The girl did as she was told. She looked deep into the water and for a moment, she saw her own face resting on top of the woman's and she knew she would live to grow up. She also knew she and the woman shared something very rare. 'Thank you,' she said. 'I will never forget you.'"

"Wait," Fiona interrupted. "Let me. And the woman told her that she would never forget her either. And then…then the girl went down the mountain and gave her little brother the water from the pool to drink. And he got better."

"Yes," her father said. "And when the girl grew up and got older, where do you think she went?"

Fiona yawned. "To the pool, of course. Down to the bottom."

"That's right. The girl returned and, after her mentor died, she took her place as the guardian of the water. And the legend spread over time that at the bottom of the secret pool lived a woman with long, blonde hair. You did know the little girl had blonde hair, didn't you?"

Fiona pulled into her drive. Even after all this time, she could still recall how real the taste of that water had seemed to her child self, so tantalizingly fresh, with its rich scent of pine and wild flowers.

She fussed about in her office for a short while. Her body went through the motions of clearing a space to work, but her mind focused on places like the secret pool, removed from ordinary time and space. In fables, those places offered a new way of looking at the world. She sat down at her desk and reviewed Edith's retreat from Paris after the War. Her punishing schedule, bouts of flu and three heart attacks, had seriously eroded her health.

After so many years tending for the ill and homeless, Edith left the city to finally care for herself. She bought an estate outside of Paris and one on the French Riviera. In the sunshine of her Mediterranean residence, Edith found peace and restoration. She told Bernard Berenson that in Paris she felt she had literally died, but in Hyères, she had come back to life "in some warm peaceful temperate heaven of the Greeks." She devoted herself to rest and restoring the houses and gardens of her new dwellings. She could not control the world, but she could construct a haven from it, substituting beauty and order for carnage and commotion.

Fiona reminded herself how in Edith Wharton's day, when a person of means was felled by exhaustion, or illness, or nerves, she or he decamped to one of the fashionable watering holes, like Salsomaggiore in Italy, that promised beautiful surroundings, the leading medical attention of the day, and relief from activity. Edith retreated to Salso often in her life, "dropping out" of her whirl of work and the cares of husband, friends, and household.

Fiona rose and ambled into the back yard. The late afternoon November sun felt mild on her skin, with temperatures that in her native Midwest heralded the time of year known as "Indian summer." In the electronic age, retreat proved more illusive. Fiona was tied to work and responsibilities and had limited time and income. A European hideaway felt out of reach. Fiona decided to visit a close-by retreat, Barton Springs Pool, a natural swimming hole, two football fields long, cut by the force of the rushing water into the surrounding lime-stone. The flowing spring maintained temperatures of a constant sixty-eight degrees.

After a ten-minute drive, Fiona sat on the grass under the trees on a steep bank and contemplated the water. By this time of year, the pool had emptied of all but the most faithful swimmers. Fiona pulled out *The Age of Innocence* from her pack, and propped herself up on her towel to read.

In a moment, she put the book down—she needed a respite from language and thinking. She wandered down the bank to the water's edge and sat, her feet dangling in the chill water. Her eyes scanned the outline of the pool and stopped on a shady area at one end. Two men sat together on the grass, their heads close together. Fiona flinched: it was Dennis Reagan and Blake Burnois. Had Blake flown back into Austin so soon, and without telling her? Surreptitiously, she glanced toward them again. They were standing now, poised to enter the wa-ter, and from their height and weight, she could no longer see any re-semblance to Dennis or Blake. She pushed her sunglasses more firmly onto her nose. Fiona, she admonished herself, you do need a retreat, from your own imagination if nothing else.

She took a deep breath and made the plunge off the pool's edge. Seconds later, she emerged gasping from the sudden chill. Swimming vigorously to warm herself, she crossed the long length of the pool and then lay back in the water, floating. Sycamore and pecan leaves drifted on the water alongside her. She narrowed her eyes until she could see only shifting patterns of light and shadow as the sunlight fil-tered through the trees. She felt unmoored, out of reach, alone.

After a while, she paddled back to the side of the bank where her towel and book still rested on the grass. As she pulled herself up the ladder, she heard voices and laughter. She observed a woman sitting on the grass halfway up the hill. Fiona took in the woman's auburn hair and full figure. She lifted her hand eagerly to wave to Bettina but then hesitated as a man flopped down on the blanket next to the woman. Instantly alert, she took in his muscular frame and dark hair. Was she seeing things again, this time Bettina and Darryl?

The man laughed and stood up. Darryl's voice came to her clearly and familiarly: "Come on, Bettina, I'll go in if you will." He took Bettina's hand and advanced toward the water.

Fiona retreated. Jealousy sliced through her as her body knifed back into the cold pool. She kicked powerfully, propelling herself deep under the surface, out of view. Beneath the water, for a few moments, she could neither hear nor see; she was alone. The air escaped from her lungs in a steady hiss. She opened her eyes and stared up through the murky water, a sea creature nestled in the liquid cradle of her lair.

XVIII: The Moon

*Academics overweight the power of their rational minds. When
confounded by life, they try to think their way out. Yet any child past the
age of five knows that when you don't know the answer, the best solution
is to just relax and go to sleep. Chances are, your dreams will do the
work for you.*

—*Darryl Hansen, notes for* In the Service of Narcissism, *his secret
history of the Department of Literature and Rhetoric*

Miriam called that evening. "You don't believe people get promoted
to their level of incompetence, do you?" Her voice wavered, revealing
an uncustomary uncertainty.

"Who are we referring to?" Fiona asked carefully.

"Me."

"You are the antithesis of incompetence," Fiona answered
promptly. "What have you been promoted to?"

"Chair," Miriam said. "Bettina has turned it down. She says she
wants to concentrate on her book."

Fiona suspected Bettina had other reasons for declining, not the
least that she didn't want to be beholden to Darryl, or suspected of
special privileges bestowed from his office, or—there were doubtless

others she could not even imagine. "I'm surprised you want to do it again."

"I am too, in a way," Miriam said thoughtfully. "But I couldn't think of anyone who had less to lose than I do. Therefore, that means my motives should be less partisan."

Fiona, genuinely puzzled, said: "What do you mean, less to lose? You have everything to lose. You have a great reputation as a scholar, an impeccable teaching record, and a habit of fairness."

"Exactly. I don't need anything particularly. And I don't feel dependent on other people's good opinion to get what I'm lacking. Ergo, I'm confident I can't be bribed, browbeaten, or debased. At least not easily."

"But you have everyone's good opinion." The intrusion into Fiona's consciousness of Lester, who found Miriam's lesbianism, cultural values, and personhood abhorrent, caused her to amend her statement: "Or mostly everyone's. I still don't understand how you have nothing to lose."

"Never mind," Miriam dismissed her airily. "I know what I mean and that's sufficient. My unwillingness to explain may be a drawback in my performance as Chair. As to why I want to do it, someone has to, and as I've been deriding the direction this department has gone for the past ten years, I have an obligation to take it on."

"Good luck. You're sure to be a vast improvement."

Miriam chuckled dryly. "I know what you think of the past occupant of the office, so that is a dubious compliment, but thank you anyway. My first order of business is to tell you that I found your letter of resignation in the Chair's desk drawer, eight weeks old. What would you like me to do with it?"

Fiona paused. "My God, I feel like a character in *The Odyssey*, on an endless journey of discovery and far, far from port. That letter was really dated only eight weeks ago?"

"Indeed."

Fiona experienced a moment of panic. She didn't know what she wanted Miriam to do with the letter. If she told her to pass it on, she'd have to get serious about another job. But what would it be? Fiona couldn't think straight. She needed more time—

"Fiona?" Miriam prodded patiently.

Incapable of making a decision, Fiona blurted: "Will you think me a coward if I recant on resigning?"

"Dear Fiona," Miriam said emphatically. "Worrying about finances and where one's next meal is coming from has never helped anyone become a better person, a better artist, or a better thinker. Of course I won't think you're a coward. Rather, I will applaud you for being sensible." Her voice rose to full throttle as she warmed to her theme: "And furthermore you're an excellent teacher and a scholar and so why should you let someone as unevolved as Sigmund Froelich drive you out of a distinguished career? Only a coward would allow that to happen! There, I'm through now."

"I would like you to rip it up," Fiona said humbly. "Would you like to know my thinking?"

"No. I accept your decision. Gladly."

Fiona heard the crinkling and tearing of paper. Miriam was a woman of swift action. Prompted by a twinge of guilt as well as curiosity, Fiona asked: "How is Sigmund? I've been out of touch today."

Miriam said promptly: "Lucky you. It's been mayhem around here. I've already fielded calls from the local press, the Provost's office, and a swarm of agitated faculty members. What's his name, Lester's new protegé, the one in comparative literature, was in here..."

"Alan Matthews? Or is it Carter Lambros?"

"We have two new Lesterites in comp. lit.? Which one has slicked-back hair and wears suspenders?"

"Matthews." Fiona suspected Lester had called in his acolytes to protest that their mentor hadn't been appointed Chair.

"Well, I've called a faculty meeting for Friday just to calm everyone down. Oh, and Sig's doing very well. His doctor says he's suffered a 'temporary paresis,' which I gather is a slight slurring of his speech.

He thinks it should clear up completely in the next few weeks. He's a very lucky man."

"I'm glad about Sigmund." Fiona hurried on: "Did you say a faculty meeting?" Faculty meetings occurred rarely in the Department of Literature and Rhetoric. The handful-and-a-half of full professors who made up the Executive Council decided everything behind doors closed to the faculty as a whole. Fiona couldn't remember when the full body of her colleagues last had met in the same room. "Does that mean we'll have to talk about Kyle Cramer and the videotape, with outcries about questionable scholarship a.k.a. 'Ivory Power'?"

Miriam's voice came through crisply: "Of course not. We'll mention Sigmund's ill health and the necessity of carrying on. You know, if we have regular meetings, people will have to admit they know what's going on around here. Wouldn't that be refreshing?"

Fiona sighed. "I don't know. It sounds like a lot of work."

"Fiona, you disappoint me. But I will let your cavalier attitude go this once, knowing you are under a great deal of stress." Miriam took a sip of something; Fiona heard the clink of ice cubes against crystal. "I'm changing the subject now. Would you like to come with me tomorrow to a seminar at Daphne's?"

Fiona looked listlessly at her calendar. "Why not? What is it?"

"Tomorrow's November 7th—it's the new moon. Daphne is giving a tutorial and a party. I'm not sure what it'll involve. But interesting people always come."

Fiona laughed. "That reminds me of Edith Wharton talking about the literary life of New York at the turn of the century. Or rather the lack of it. A friend invited her to a dinner party; Edith only accepted when the friend told her that the party 'will be very bohemian, I'm afraid.' She was desperate to meet other writers. But when she got there, she found out she was one of the literary, so-called bohemian guests she had come to meet."

"Are you saying that we'll be the only two interesting people there?" Miriam's wry voice crackled with amusement. "I don't know whether to call you narcissistic or jaded. But, in any case, I'll pick you up tomorrow night at 7:30."

Fiona returned her telephone to its cradle. She noticed she still wore the dusty shorts and top she had donned at Barton Springs after her swim. Dynamo streaked ahead of her into the bedroom and batted at her ankles while Fiona stripped for the shower. Happily, Dynamo dove into the discarded clothes and made a nest, her attention easily displaced from her mistress by the pleasures of a new hideaway.

When Fiona emerged, scrubbed and freshly clothed, she heard the solid clunk of a car door closing, and a moment later, a hurried knock.

Darryl stepped in as she opened her front door and stood awkwardly in front of her. His nose shone with a faint sunburn, she noticed with satisfaction. "Have a good swim?" she asked.

Startled, he shoved his hands into the pockets of his faded denim, pleated shorts. "Swim?"

"Barton Springs. I was there too this afternoon." Fiona sat down on the sofa and gestured for him to join her.

"Oh," he said. "I didn't see you."

"I was in the pool. Some of us go to Barton Springs to swim."

Darryl flushed slightly under his tan. He sat down at one end of the sofa and crossed his legs. "Fiona, we need to talk."

She leaned forward, both hands around one knee. "I agree. I'm glad you stopped by." Before he could say anything, she continued: "Darryl, I really enjoy your company. I do. But I'm just not comfortable with whatever's going on between you and Bettina. And since that's none of my business, you don't have to explain. But I need to withdraw."

Fiona looked out the window onto the darkening front lawn. Her neighbor, Carl, bent over his flower beds, mulching the soil with bark chips. A conscientious gardener, he was beginning his winter preparations. She turned back to observe Darryl's fine, regular features, the deep blue eyes murky with confusion and a shadow of something else she couldn't quite identify. She tried to keep her voice light: "I've realized I'm in over my head with you and Bettina. I'm about to get my feelings hurt very badly." She gnawed at her lips with her front teeth. "If I haven't already." She wasn't sure herself just who was hurting her feelings, Darryl or Bettina.

Darryl cleared his throat. "I don't suppose you have a beer, do you? Or a Scotch?"

She pointed toward the kitchen. "Help yourself."

He leapt to his feet and she could hear him rummaging among the bottles in the cupboard. "If you're making Scotch, I'll have one too," she said. "Ice and a hit of sparkling. I think there's some Ozarka in the fridge."

Darryl returned with two glasses. Handing Fiona hers, he gently clinked her glass with his before sitting back down. "Cheers," he said.

Fiona nodded and took a swig, enjoying the peaty taste on her tongue. Maybe they could skip all the explanations and counter-recriminations and just drink.

But Darryl obviously felt compelled. "So," he began doggedly, "you saw Bettina and me at Barton's today." He looked up and then down at the floor. He sighed heavily. "Things have gotten a little complicated with Bettina...again."

Fiona set down her glass on the oak coffee table with a thump. "Why not admit it—they've always been complicated."

"Yeah, well, you have a point." He straightened up and drained half his glass.

Fiona looked at him steadily. "I won't ask you why you wanted to have an affair with me when you're still obviously in love with Bettina. The big question is why did I respond knowing that you were?"

"I don't think you knew that," he said stiffly. "I didn't know it. I didn't think I was."

Fiona folded her arms across her chest and glared at him. "This is a ridiculous conversation. We're not in high school. It's okay, Darryl. I had a fine time. I hope you did too. There's nothing to say."

He passed his thick fingers through his hair. Darryl looked uncomfortable, like he'd just noticed the first allergic symptom to the thicket of poison ivy he'd waded into two days before. "I just want to say I feel like an idiot. I had more than a 'fine time.' You're a terrific woman, Fiona. The best. I hope you don't feel that I used—"

"Enough. Really, let's just stop here. I don't want to hear how terrific I am." Fiona blinked rapidly, infuriated by the prick of tears in her eyes. "Excuse me a minute. Can I get you some more Scotch on my way back?"

"Sure." He polished off the remaining drops in his glass and handed it to her.

Fiona went to the kitchen and ran cold water over her hands. It *was* like high school. Bettina was the prom queen every boy wanted, and Fiona felt crushed that she couldn't possibly compete. She dried her hands, turned around, and rested her back against the sink. No, that wasn't all of it. Bettina was her dear friend and she loved her and she couldn't imagine how any boy—no matter how good-looking—could be as attentive or loyal or loving as she, Fiona, was already.

Fiona supposed she didn't want Darryl any more than he wanted her: they liked each other; they both had been flattered; they both had set their sights somewhere else. Fiona pushed away from the sink. It couldn't be more simple: possessive of Bettina, jealous of Bettina's intimacy with Darryl and their obvious intrigue, Fiona felt just not charismatic enough or attractive enough to matter quite enough, to either of them. She felt twelve again, watching her parents, whom she'd loved excruciatingly, sharing a glance that proclaimed their love for each other so strongly that they couldn't see anyone else in the room. Their eyes said: you're mine; I'm yours; does anything else at this very moment matter?

So, Fiona, she asked herself, do you matter to anyone that much? Probably not. But you do matter to many people, quite a lot, and that's just going to have to be enough. For now. She straightened to her full height as she often had when she was young, telling herself: stand up, grow up, and keep your damn chin up.

The bottle of Scotch kept a lonely vigil beside her on the counter. Chin up, she grabbed it and marched back into the living room. She splashed a generous amount in Darryl's glass and then in her own. "Friends?" she asked, raising her glass.

"Friends," he said, smiling at her with grateful blue eyes. He looked young and vulnerable for a moment and Fiona thought: you must have been one cute guy in high school, Darryl Hansen.

They drank companionably for a few minutes. Then Darryl slouched against the sofa cushions. "It looks like Sigmund will recover," he said.

"It appears so."

He stared down at his drink. So," he said, "have you been playing any tennis lately?"

Perched on a huge electric blue pillow, Daphne held court in the center of a large, carpeted room. Candles at regular intervals and in assorted colors and sizes cast a mellow glow from every available surface. The only electric light in the room emanated in waves from two lava lamps. The lights illuminated the room and sparked highlights in Daphne's silver hair each time she turned her head. The space occupied a converted garage in the back of Daphne's house, a room Fiona had never been in before. Five people sat on the floor clustered around Daphne; others milled about munching canapés and drinking wine, or talked in scattered twosomes or threesomes throughout the room.

"Had it been a full moon tonight, we probably would have met on Mt. Bonnell," Miriam explained. Mt. Bonnell, a popular spot from which to view the city, Lake Austin, and the surrounding hills, also provided a natural, elevated gathering spot for those wishing to commune with the night sky.

Fiona whispered to Miriam. "I'm surprised she serves wine. I expected something more spartan."

Miriam snorted and said loudly: "Don't be silly—Daphne's a siren, not an ascetic. And why are you whispering?"

Fiona noticed Dennis hugging a corner by himself and went to join him. "I didn't know you went in for this sort of thing," she said to him.

Dennis winked at her. "I could say the same about you. But Carter's out of town and Miriam invited me." He stared at the eclectic group occupying the room with frank interest. "I'm surprised there are so many men here."

"Daphne has a large and varied clientele," Fiona said. "Dennis, can we have lunch in the next few days? I need some advice."

After they arranged a time, Fiona went in search of Miriam. Dennis made a bee-line for a very thin, very handsome blond man wearing jeans and a black denim shirt.

After an hour or so, the group settled down on the floor in a huge circle around Daphne. Buddha-like, she radiated a calm vigilance; Fiona had the sense that her eyes focused on each person with complete attention. In the background, as if from a great distance, Fiona heard the plaintive notes of a lone flute.

"The moon has three faces." Daphne began, her strange cat's eyes large and luminous in the shifting colors reflected from a nearby lava lamp. "The new moon, the virgin goddess, is symbolized by Artemis, The Huntress. Twin sister of Apollo, daughter of Zeus, she and her brother divided the sky between them: the day sky his and the night sky hers. The protector of the forest and of young creatures everywhere, Artemis was swift of foot and quick to anger. The new moon is young and beautiful like Artemis, full of promise, unspoiled. Meditate on it to recognize unfilled promise in your life.

"The second face is the full moon, and here Demeter the goddess of harvest wealth, the ripe and glorious fertile female, holds sway. The full moon makes lovers swoon, and souls everywhere feel the poetry of its luminosity, revealing the fullness of life. But like Demeter's happiness, which leaves her when she loses her daughter Persephone for part of each year, the full moon must wane. Life cannot stay at the peak of thrall very long. Meditate on the full moon to appreciate your deepest feeling.

"The third face, the dark face, is the most frightening. The goddess Hecate rules the darkness, the lower world. She is the witch, the hag, the dispenser of black magic. We instinctively fear what is hidden from us. Hecate rules our nightmares, our dread of what may come. Meditate on the dark face to acknowledge your fears."

The music grew louder and then faded once more. "Now," Daphne said. "Hold hands with those on either side of you and we shall begin a meditation." She waited a moment for everyone to comply. "Shut your eyes and take several complete breaths, through the abdomen, into the lungs, into your upper chest, and then slowly exhale. As I begin to count backwards from ten, let yourself relax completely.

"Ten. nine. eight. Begin to feel a quiet descend upon you. Breathe more slowly, more deeply.

"Seven. six. five. Imagine that you are beginning to walk down a long flight of stairs. The stairs are old and wooden, very narrow. They curve downward far into the earth—you cannot see the end of them.

"Four. three. two. one. You are at the bottom of the stairs now. You're blanketed in darkness. You see nothing, you hear nothing. You take two steps forward. Dimly, you see a door in front of you. Open it.

"As you open the door, a faint light glows in the doorway and grows slowly brighter, like the dawn. Walk through the door. What do you see? Say nothing, but imagine what is on the other side of that door. Take your time...

"Now, once you can see clearly where you are, you find that one path curves to the right and one to the left; another extends straight in front of you. Choose a path. It doesn't matter which one you take. There are no wrong turns. Choose your path and feel confident that it is the right one. For you. Now. As you walk on your path, you notice very tall grass on either side of you. If you extend your arms straight out, it's high enough to tickle you under your arms. This path extends for a time and then the grass gives way to woods. The light is soft in the trees, dappled from the thick canopies of leaves. Follow your path into the woods. On your right is a creek. The water rushes through it slowly. Sit down by the bank of the creek and listen to the spring burble. Dabble your fingers in the cool water if you like. Listen to your thoughts.

"As you listen, you will notice that, amidst the gentle sounds around you, you can discern a voice. Is that voice male or female or just a voice? You decide. Crane your head forward to hear the voice. It is speaking to you. Just now: it is telling you something. Remember it. Take a moment to inscribe those words in your memory."

Fiona listened to the voice. It was a female voice, she was quite sure. Her hands were damp, and they slipped on the fingers of the other hands she held to each side of her. She wanted to open her eyes, but just then, the voice said something very clearly, it said: "Don't wait. Ask. Ask for what you want." She listened again. "I am time," said the voice. "I do not last forever. Remember, dare to dream."

"The voice will subside," Daphne continued. "You may strain to hear more, but it has finished speaking. Rise from your seat at the creek and walk along the banks. Keep walking until you are out of the forest. Now, you are back in the grasslands. But, this time, flowers bloom all around you: their fragrance wafts over you. The earth is luscious and rolling, and the grass is a lush carpet of green. Birds sing all around you, and in front of you, a herd of deer races by. Choose a spot to sit and rest.

"As you rest, with the light on your face, warming you, bees and insects swarm about you harmlessly, humming, the songs of the birds thread through your consciousness. The world is full of riches and you are one of them. You feel something approach you. It might be a person, or an animal, or an unfamiliar being. Let it come. Open your arms to it. It will embrace you. It will give you a gift if you but accept it...

"You must surrender to receive. The gift may not be anything tangible or literal."

Fiona held her breath for a moment as she felt a rush of air on her face and a warm, smooth touch against her skin. She grew aware of her breathing slowing, her body relaxing. A male voice said. "I give you new eyes. You will see yourself differently." From the safety of his arms encircling her, Fiona looked out. She saw herself sitting in a pool of light, her expression radiant, complete. Was she looking at someone? Where was she?

Before she could determine a context for the image, Daphne's low, hoarse voice swept on, "Now, you are being released. Whatever has held you is letting go. You must let go also."

Fiona experienced a sharp loss when the being withdrew from her. She wanted that warm touch back and the voice to tell her more.

"That being is your guide. Even though you have withdrawn, he or she will be there for you whenever you wish. Begin to walk forward once more. This time, the path leads up a mountain. As you climb it, the light begins to fade into night. The path is smooth and safe, but it is steep. Keep rising steadily, up and up. The darkness becomes complete as you reach the top. There are rocks in a clearing, in a circle. Choose one and sit upon it. Turn your face up to the night sky. The night is cloudy, and there are no stars, and no moon. Reach your hand down and pick up what your fingertips encounter. Something is there. What is it?"

The room felt very warm, the breathing around her audible but slow. The hands on either side of her supported her. It was as if she floated on a sea of dreaming souls. Fiona reached down her right hand. She encountered nothing. She groped around the rock where she sat, but there was nothing. She felt a wave of anxiety wash over her.

Daphne's voice, barely a whisper, came to her: "Take your time. No one will rush you. Let yourself find your totem."

Tentatively, Fiona reached down with her other hand. Still nothing. She stretched her fingers out as far as they could reach; finally, she encountered something cool and smooth. Managing to slide it closer, she gripped it securely and picked it up. It was a book, bound in leather. Fiona recognized it; it was the wonderful blue book of fables she had dreamed about.

"Whatever you have found has great meaning for you," Daphne said firmly. "And it is yours, part of your magic. You will always have access to it. So let it fall from your hands, knowing it is within reach whenever you wish it to be.

"When you are ready, stand up from your rock, and look overhead. The sky is still black, still impenetrable. But there is new possibility in the air; you feel it. Take one step forward. In front of you, you will find a door; put out your hands so you can locate the latch. Open it and walk through. Yes, like that. You are now back at the bottom of the wooden stairs. Rest there for a moment, and then as I count to ten, you will retrace your steps and come back up.

"One. Two. Three. You have left your path behind and are coming back into consciousness. Keep breathing deeply.

"Four. Five. Six. Seven. You are beginning to get closer to the top. You see how the stairs are brightening gradually.

"Eight. Nine. Ten. You are back. You feel incredibly refreshed and relaxed. Now, open your eyes."

Fiona opened her eyes and let go of the hands she had been holding. The light, though it had seemed dim before, assaulted her eyes like a floodlight. All around her people sat, quietly, looking dazed. But she noticed the faces turned toward her appeared calm, with the new-minted smoothness of children awaking from a nap.

Gradually, voices and laughter erupted once again from the thirty or so people who filled the room, and the spell was broken. Fiona rose from the floor, as did the others. She had held one position for what felt like a long time, yet her body felt not cramped but surprisingly supple.

Dennis stood at her elbow, offering her a fresh glass of white wine. "What do you make of it?" he asked.

"I don't know. I do feel refreshed and alert. What about you?"

Dennis moved his lean body very close to her. "It worked as a kind of hypnosis for me. You know, I've been feeling very tense lately." He lowered his voice. "Blake has been calling a lot. And then, as we did this tonight, I just told myself to let all of that stuff go. I realize I like my life just the way it is."

"You meditated on the second face of the moon. And recognized the richness of the harvest," Fiona acknowledged, envying her friend his ability to immerse himself in the moment. "You rose to the spirit of the occasion. I'm afraid I found myself wishing it were this easy to go back in time."

Dennis regarded her with interest. Moods and thoughts flashed almost transparently across that receptive, mobile face; she imagined his students delighted in his open curiosity. "Well, you did move out of time tonight, in a way," he said. "When would you like to live?"

"Please, don't laugh. But I wish I could go back, for a day at least, into Edith Wharton's time."

Dennis spread one hand on the center of her back and pressed gently. It was an intimate, comforting gesture. "Well, then, you're lucky."

"Why is that?"

"You do that almost every day, don't you? With the new book? You re-create her every day." He sipped from his wine glass. "It's like acting, I imagine. You play the character; that means for however long, you are that person." His eyes, brown, empathic, looked into hers. "I can tell it's happened. You're changing. You look different."

The next morning, Fiona sat down to work on a particularly thorny part of her manuscript. After the War, Wharton had returned to the subject of her childhood, wrestling with a narrative she thought of as "Old New York." She dreamed of finally capturing the world she had known as a child. Since the War, that age had vanished so thoroughly, she feared the world might never know the small corner of it that had been her universe. The work plodded along. Yet, at some point she experienced a breakthrough, which allowed her to approach the subject in a new way. What had triggered the struggling work's transmogrification into *The Age of Innocence*, her masterpiece?

Inspired by her meditation the night before, Fiona considered that Edith's finding of the key to her manuscript might have been accidental. Given Wharton's immersion into the world of art and literature, perhaps she had stumbled onto an enabling metaphor in a referential way. Fiona stood and surveyed her own book shelves. Often she found herself scanning titles or beginning paragraphs or even illustrations for inspiration in her own work. Her fingers skimmed over a book of Ansel Adams' photographs, moved on to another of Picasso drawings. Her own library was haphazard in its organization. Fiona returned to her chair. The haphazard association was precisely the stimulus she was looking for. Fiona pictured Edith in bed, unable to write and so consoling herself with a book, perhaps James' *Portrait of a Lady*. After her own bitter experience, the disabling effects of marriage on James' heroine, Isabel Archer, affected her more strongly than ever:

As Edith mused on the melancholy Isabel staring out the window after Osmond has departed, another picture displaced it. Its title struck her first, "The Age of Innocence," as an image of a very young girl strayed into her mind. She frowned, trying to place it—of course, it was Reynolds' portrait in the National Gallery, a work that garnered much attention.

The girl dissolved in her mind into a swirl of bright fabric, the gleaming silver and china on dinner tables in her mother's time. A flash of evening wear entered the frame, old, before the turn of the century. The men still wore their silky, drooping moustaches. Edith blinked as if singed by her vision. That era hardly had seemed an age of innocence: for her it had been an age of trial, of denial, and of limitation.

Fiona imagined Edith pulling her writing board upon her lap, drawing out a fresh page, and scrawling across its top: "The Age of Innocence." The Joshua Reynolds' portrait not only provided a title, but gave her a way to make a gesture to Henry James. Edith's favorite James' novel was *The Portrait of a Lady*, it was the one she would name as among the special books of a lifetime's reading. Reynolds' portrait was the portrait of a lady, a very tiny lady to be sure, but Wharton knew that whenever her dear friend looked upon the earth, he would immediately recognize the connection. Possibly to delight her mentor's spirit further, Wharton created a counterpart to Isabel Archer—Newland Archer, a man, like James' character, with his whole life ahead of him, awaiting the imprint of irrevocable choices.

The conception of a novel as a frame to be filled intrigued Fiona. A brush of paint, a pen with ink, both were useless unless the artist's ideas wielded them surely, or at the very least with innovation. Perhaps all those years of listening to Bernard Berenson describe the great scope of European art had influenced Edith. Not that she needed influencing; she said herself she had a photographic memory of places and visual details.

No, Fiona reconsidered, Berenson hadn't spurred Edith to write by his soliloquies on masterpieces. It was the pressure—and the allure—of the blank page, the empty space. It begged to be filled, again and again. If one were a writer, or a visual artist, the challenge was irresistible. Fiona smiled; she knew that paradoxical pleasure well: the delight of making something new, the pain of imperfectly executing the imagination's bidding. She thought of the blank canvas in Edith's nocturnal vision, awaiting her imprint. Creating a work of art was just one form, a particularly intense one, of living one's life: the raw material was already there, the unoccupied space waiting to be filled. All one needed to do was start.

XIX: The Sun

There's no substitute for sunshine, especially with native plants. But this is central Texas. The light here is like a blast furnace—it provides energy, but too much too long will shrivel your landscape. What you want is moderation. You need enough light for growth but not so much that new life gets scorched.

—Marvin Graf, daily advice column on his gardening website

A purple-smudged autumn sky greeted Fiona as she turned right onto Avenue F from 45th Street. Austin had yet to record a serious freeze, and although the red oaks and tallow trees scattered crimson among the foliage, the pecans and live oaks sported sweeping, green canopies. Winter still seemed far away. Marvin, emerging from his greenhouse with a bougainvillea bristling with health, saluted her as she parked her car. Fiona clambered up on the porch and raised a fist to knock when she noticed Bettina, a cordless phone attached to her ear, pacing pensively in the dining room inside.

Fiona hesitated as Bettina's voice filtered through the wall. "...it isn't that, Darryl...no...how can you..."

Hurriedly, Fiona retraced her steps and poked her head into the greenhouse. "Can I bother you?"

Marvin tamped the soil around the bougainvillea, now nestled in a more generous pot, with short, expert strokes. "Sure," he said as she came nearer. He scratched his forehead with one glove and left a trail of mulch above one eyebrow.

"Here, let me," Fiona laughed and brushed the debris from his skin.

"I think Bettina's here," he said, checking the set of the plant in its pot with a frown.

"She seems to be on the phone."

"Mmm," Marvin said noncommittally, his usually ebullient manner not in evidence.

"What's up?" Fiona said. "Am I in the way?"

He removed one glove, probably once fawn-colored but now a darkly-mottled black-brown, and tucked it under an armpit. He ran the naked hand over his short blond hair. "Heavens, no. I'm just grumpy. Between calls from her attorney about the lawsuit, from Miriam about the department or with Sigmund's health status, and Darryl about god-knows-what, I don't think I've talked to my wife in weeks."

"Oh," Fiona said uncertainly. "And now an uninvited guest invades your sanctuary."

"That I can handle."

"Well, it has been...let's say *unusual* lately... at work." Fiona wondered which of the three callers was really upsetting Marvin.

"Isn't that always the story?" He sighed. "I'm starting a new website. It's time I made some money so Bettina can quit that madhouse."

"Cool idea. What's the name?"

Marvin grinned. "MarvinGardens dot com."

"It has a certain appeal," Fiona ventured.

He threw her a look of mock-exasperation. "Such enthusiasm. Remember Monopoly? Probably the most popular game in the history of board games?"

"Oh, right. Monopoly. I was wracking my brains—there's an obscure '70s movie with that in the title." She managed a self-mocking smile. "And I criticize the nit-pickers I work with. I've been in academia so long that I've lost the ability to take pleasure in the obvious."

Marvin placed the bougainvillea on the south side of the green-house. "I wouldn't worry too much if I were you. It's a reversible prob-lem. So," he said plunking down on a bench and motioning for her to join him, "Still seeing Darryl?"

Fiona sat down and stared at a smudge of grease on one tennis shoe. "No. I don't know what to call it, but we broke up, or broke off, or how about just stopped? A few days ago." Fiona sighed. "You were right. He was too nice, or too affable or whatever you said about him at my party. I shouldn't have trusted him."

Marvin studied her for a minute. He drummed his fingers on one knee. "Fiona, what is the deal with Darryl?"

Fiona's heart skidded. Had Bettina broken her cardinal rule of si-lence? Marvin was looking at her suspiciously. "What do you mean?" she asked carefully. "We just weren't a particularly good match."

"Well, that I could have told you two months ago. Aside from that, the man's a lady killer. A compulsive. I think he's after my wife." Marvin's chin jutted out aggressively.

"Uh-huh," Fiona said. "Well, that wouldn't surprise me too much I guess."

They looked at each other; Fiona found herself afraid to blink or look away.

"Look—" she began.

"Hey—" he said at the same time.

They both laughed uneasily. "I'll go first," Marvin began. "Fiona, I *know* Darryl's after my wife, so you don't have to panic."

Fiona noticed that Marvin placed whatever blame there was squarely on Darryl's shoulders. His vocabulary had no words with which to malign Bettina. "Whew," she breathed. "I mean, I'm not very good at...well, at not talking frankly with a good friend. So, what are you going to do?"

Marvin folded his arms across his chest, looking particularly mus-cular and obdurate. "I'm not going to do anything. It all depends on Bettina. I've never quite seen her like this." Marvin's eyes watered for a moment and he laughed shakily. "This kind of thing is something I always thought happened to other people's marriages, not ours."

Fiona threw an arm around Marvin and gave him a squeeze. "I'm so sorry, Marvin," she said and meant it. "You and Bettina are my role models in marriage. You've got to hang in there."

Marvin pulled a blue bandanna handkerchief from his jeans pocket—Fiona remembered her dad had always carried a red one just like it—and mopped his eyes and nose. "Yeah, well I'm pretty patient. But it takes two to hang in."

They sat glumly together in the greenhouse's dim light, as companionable in their solitary thoughts as two old salts brooding over the vagaries of their cruel mistress, the sea. Outside, dusk had given way to night.

A beguiling voice called out—"Hey, what are you two doing sitting out here in the dark?"—and Bettina, in a blue work shirt and navy tights, appeared in the doorway. "Have you started a club I don't know about?" Her voice sounded relieved, somehow, after the tight, quarrelsome tones Fiona had heard on the porch. Fiona stared at her appealing friend, struck by how Bettina's presence bestowed a note of delight wherever she went, but angry with her just the same.

"No girls allowed," Marvin said, and laughed. "Fiona's an exception. She's a woman."

Bettina beamed a not-totally-pleased smirk in his direction. "I'll have drinks for you two in five minutes. If you can bring yourselves to adjourn." Jauntily, and with a flash of shapely legs, she skipped out of the doorway.

Fiona turned to Marvin. "I just want you to know. Whatever happens. I'm your friend."

"Ditto," he said. "Do you think we need a club handshake? How about a decoder ring?"

Fiona smiled affectionately at him. "I'm going in. You coming?"

Marvin stretched his arms over his head wearily. "Just give me a few minutes. I have another couple of plants to repot."

When Fiona walked into the kitchen, Bettina was preparing martinis. She handed Fiona an ice tray. "Honey, you're mad at me, I can always tell."

Fiona shook her head and didn't answer.

"I heard you have called it quits with Darryl." Bettina hummed as she poured a few drops of vermouth in the pitcher. "That makes two of us."

The easy just-between-us-girls tone of Bettina's hit Fiona like a slap in the face. "Look, we don't have to pretend. I saw you at Barton Springs with Darryl last Friday afternoon. And he told me things were getting, well, his word was 'complicated'—again."

Bettina's forehead furrowed in perplexity; her green eyes opened wide. "Yes, I went swimming with Darryl. So what? That's what we did—we met at the pool after work and had a swim. I agreed to see him because after you and I...talked...the other day at your house, I wanted to tell him I was firmly out of his life."

Fiona blinked. "Bettina, that very evening he came to my house. And he assured me you were definitely in his life."

Eloquently putting her hands on her hips, her fiery hair standing up around her face, and looking every inch a queen, Bettina said: "Well, believe what and whom you want. I may be in his life but he isn't in mine. He just called and begged me to reconsider. I can't handle all of this, Fiona. You and Marvin and Darryl. My God. It's too much."

Startled, Fiona blurted: "Why are you lumping us all together?"

"Oh, for heaven's sake. I don't mean you're the same. I mean I'm feeling conflicted! I *love* Marvin—he's my husband. And I *love* you too—you're at the very least my best friend. Aside from my children, my loyalties are with Marvin and you. And Darryl? Well, he is a friend and an ex-lover, but I can't put his demands on the same level. To top it off, I'm sick of demands, period."

Fiona sat down at the kitchen table. She felt at a disadvantage, as though she had heard the tape with the twenty-two minute gap and

Bettina was operating from the unexpurgated version. "I don't think I've made any demands on you."

Bettina thrust both hands in her thick hair and held it straight out from her head. "I may scream!"

Accustomed to Bettina's dramatic outbursts, Fiona waited for her to continue.

Bettina strode across the room, waving her arms. "You haven't made any demands on me, exactly. But sometimes, like the other day, I'm very aware how much you mean to me. Fiona, it's hard for me to separate our friendship sometimes from..."

The door banged gently and Marvin came in. He leaned against the door jamb, gingerly, as if his mid-back pained him. Bettina softly touched his face. "Sweetheart, you look all in. The drinks are ready."

He smiled as if Bettina's touch were a rare, healing balm. "Let me just take a two-minute shower. I'll be right down."

"Poor Marvin," Bettina said. "Darryl called here the other day and said something to him, I'm not sure what, but I can imagine. The effrontery of the man!"

Fiona generously felt a moment's sympathy for Darryl, who had made two fatal errors. For one, "possession" did not belong to Bettina's categories of acceptable constructs. Her spirit clamored for freedom, which had been the appeal of Darryl in the first place. But if he assumed what was, in Bettina's view, the most dubious of the privileges of marriage—possessiveness—he'd lost his trump card—his carefree almost-single status—without playing it for all it was worth. As if his claiming Bettina weren't damaging enough, he'd broken another cardinal rule: Bettina could not abide anything that upset her home life. While a brilliant scholar and supportive colleague, and a flirt with occasional lapses, she took pride in reigning over her domestic sphere with calm and dignity. If Marvin was distraught, so was the carefully-nurtured retreat of home and hearth, and that could not be tolerated.

"And now Marvin is very upset," Bettina finished unhappily.

Fiona touched her friend's arm. "Bettina, Marvin is the very best man in the world. Don't ever lose him."

Bettina nodded, and rubbed her eyes roughly, distorting the entire upper portion of her face into a gargoyle mask. "Don't you think I know that? I can't bear to have him hurt. It's no one's fault but my own, I know." She straightened her shoulders and stared at Fiona. "I'm not doing this again. It's not worth it. And by God, Darryl Hansen isn't worth it. Don't worry. When I say this chapter of my life is closed, it's closed. No more other men." Bettina looked as fierce as a jungle cat warding off intruders from her young and their precious food.

"Well, good," Fiona said, taken aback. "I like the two of you together. I depend on the two of you together."

That was certainly true, but as she regarded Bettina, her friend's complexion heated by anger, her voice throbbing with the passion of her pledge, Fiona couldn't help remembering their long embrace those few short days ago. Bettina was simply a goddess, and goddesses by definition radiated allure. Others responded to their desirability, like star-gazers riveted to a supernova— it was one price of their rarefied position. Bettina might claim fidelity as her province, like a queen announcing her sovereign will. However, Fiona wasn't sure that dazzled subjects in the queen's realm would cooperate with the queen's dictum.

Back at home, Fiona sat down at her desk. Bettina's involvement with Darryl had a trajectory of its own, and she was relieved that its convolutions no longer ensnared her. She opened her book file, and scrolled through her last work session. Fiona intended to incorporate her draft into her class lecture on the film version of *The Age of Innocence*. She turned to her manuscript and to Edith's reconstruction of the Old New York of her childhood. From the remove of 1919, Wharton finally possessed the maturity and the artistry to interpret the world of her childhood as if it were any other fictional realm.

Reviewing her notes, Fiona more than ever was convinced that by creating this particular novel, Wharton was writing her way to freedom. As she gained distance, some of the pain and dislocation of the 1870's fell away and Wharton saw the nuances of Old New York more intricately. Its social codes no longer ruled her head or her heart. As Newland Archer struggles in the web of the traditions that ensnare him, slowly realizing that their limitations also provide the basis for a decent life, Wharton charts the fool's journey from innocence to worldly knowledge:

Once again, Edith constructed a central triangle around which the events of the novel revolved. Like its predecessors The Reef *and* Ethan Frome, *her book pitted two very different women seeking a conflicted, indecisive man. The central character of* The Age of Innocence, *Newland Archer, like Edith, grew up in the aristocratic, provincial world of Old New York and saw its provincialism as a limitation, and a source of suffocation. As the novel opens, Newland plans to be betrothed to May Welland, a thoroughly proper, unimaginative product of New York society. When May's cousin, the sophisticated Countess Ellen Olenska, enters the world of the novel, the opposing points of the triangle exert their pressure. Ellen, who has left an abusive husband abroad, has come home to seek the advice and solace of her Old New York family. While born to this society, she spent her youth in Europe. Now her European marriage and cosmopolitan tastes isolate her permanently as an outcast in New York. Newland almost immediately finds himself attracted to her: she represents the blend of old world and new, the quest for varied experience, the exoticism of foreign lands.*

The Age of Innocence *shares with* Summer *and* The Reef *an obsession with passion, with the question of how a life should best be lived. Newland Archer's life is one Wharton herself could have lived, and indeed, did live for the first twelve years of her marriage. Those years, filled with isolation and breakdowns, taught her well the costs of security and the blind adherence to convention. Wharton, through hard work and emotional risk-taking, did escape. Her liberation brought her success, yet it was hard-won.*

In her late fifties, Edith Wharton came to terms with a central truth: that one can never entirely escape the defining force of one's background. She accepted that each us is born into a world that defines us and provides us with standards of taste and rightness. Like the foods and water of a particular region, one's milieu adapts one to thrive in a particular geography, of spirit as well as place. After rejecting her own origins for so long, despising the inconsequential preoccupations of her leisured family, despairing of their shallowness and paucity of inner life, Edith Wharton accepted that these very things had shaped her irrevocably. They were the seeds of who she was able to become. Her struggle against these delineating characteristics, in a way, underscored the importance of their imprint.

Archer, unable to give up the structure of his marriage with May, strains to retain as well his fantasy of an ideal and unfettered life with Ellen Olenska. When he tells Ellen that he wants to live with her in a world where social distinctions and morality don't matter, to have a free life uncluttered by the demands of family and tradition, she responds sadly: "Oh, my dear—where is that country? Have you ever been there?" Ellen Olenska disappears, back to Europe, and lives a life filled with intellectual and artistic fervor, a life not beyond Newland's imagination, but beyond his capacities. Just as Edith Wharton found her destiny outside of the bounds of Old New York, Ellen lives her life off the pages of The Age of Innocence. *By the novel's end, Archer finally stops looking outside for the keys to psychological harmony. He finds peace with himself.*

Edith Wharton, too, chose her life. While it contained much richness, many brilliant achievements, and superb friends, it did not include a satisfying marriage or children. When she adopted France as her residence, she had to leave behind her family of origin and its support. In The Age of Innocence, *Edith makes peace with the costs of such a life; she salutes her hero for making the best of what the dictates of his personality will allow.*

Fiona nodded slowly as she wrote, convinced that through this key novel, Edith reconstituted the age of inconsequence of her childhood into one of very real personal consequence. In a way, the Gilded Age pushed her off the cliff. For while Edith came to peace with her own background, she still realized the necessity, for her, of choosing an alternate life from Old New York. Wharton stated that need succinctly in a diary entry from 1926: "Life is always either a tight-rope or a feather bed. Give me the tight-rope!"

Once again, Fiona admired the woman's capacity for risk, her courage in living from her heart and her mind. Fiona wondered if she herself could embrace such challenges with half Edith's courage.

The phone announced itself as Fiona mused. Absently, as if expecting an answer to her question, she picked it up.

"I'd like to speak to Fiona Hardison," a frank voice declared.

"Speaking."

"Ms. Hardison, or I should say Dr. Hardison, my name is Althea Richey. I'm with the Fleming-Cone literary agency."

Fiona held her breath. "Yes?"

"I understand you're working on a book about Edith Wharton, 'The Age of Inconsequence.' Frankly, it sounds like the kind of book I might like to represent. I'm wondering if you could send me some sample chapters?"

"Well...*yes*, I could. The book isn't quite finished. But I could easily send you, let's say, the first hundred pages. Would that do?"

"Nicely."

"I'm just curious," Fiona said, her head spinning in a pleasant but unfamiliar way. "Did you read about this book in *The Gazette of Higher Education?*"

Althea chuckled. "Yes, well, actually one of my associates did—she showed me 'Ivory Power.' Very funny. I once taught literature myself. At Smith. But it was the book on Wharton mentioned in Burnois' introduction which intrigued me."

Fiona sensed an interesting story behind the career switch, which predisposed her toward the woman. "Do you prefer being a literary agent to working as a professor?"

"Well, this profession has its downsides, as well. But I feel I have a bit more control over how I'm evaluated, and certainly more over my income."

"I can imagine," Fiona said. "All right, then, I'll send you the chapters tomorrow, along with a c.v. I don't have a formal proposal yet..."

"No problem. I can help you with that if I like the chapters. Which I expect to. Edith Wharton is one of my favorite writers." She laughed. "I almost said one of my favorite people."

"Oh, I know, when you read her extensively you feel a relationship," Fiona agreed.

"You find that too?" Althea said. "How nice. Well, I look forward to your pages. Thank you."

"Thank you," Fiona said. She asked for and made a note of the agency's address. When she put the phone down, she regarded it with some wonder. Thrilled by the call, she felt an urge similar to one Edith Wharton had experienced when she found out her first story would be published—she wanted to run up and down a long staircase to burn off some of the excitement. Unfortunately, Fiona's house was one-story.

The phone rang again and Fiona scooped it up—perhaps Ms. Richey had forgotten something.

"Dear one," Blake drawled. "Do I have news for you! Are you sitting down? I want you to be blown away, but not to topple to the ground and bash yourself senseless."

"Okay," Fiona said, mystified.

"I just received a call—about you, my little prodigal—from an agent at Fleming-Cone. Can you speak?"

"Althea Richey? I've already spoken to her," Fiona couldn't resist being the least bit smug.

"Drat. She got to you first. I did so want to surprise you. Never mind. But isn't it fabulous? She asked me for your home phone number. My dear, I told you 'Ivory Power' had legs."

That explained how Ms. Richey had found her. Fiona's phone was unlisted. "Thank you, Blake, for forwarding her to me," Fiona said sincerely. "And I'm sure you told her how wonderful the book is, even though you've read not a page!"

"Well," Blake drawled modestly, "I did of course embellish a bit. I didn't want the fish to wriggle away, after all. But, Fi dear, what luck—an agent, with a very respectable agency, and an old Wharton scholar at that. What could be better?!"

"Ah, she told me she was a fan, but not that she was a former scholar."

"Actually," Blake said, his voice barely containing his glee, "I taught with this woman, at Penn. And I wouldn't call her a 'former' scholar to her face, if I were you. She's quite erudite. Keeps up and still publishes, I think."

Fiona grimaced. "Ugh, you see how brainwashed I've become by the academic party-line? I can't believe I automatically assumed that anyone who quits higher education no longer pursues scholarship!"

"It is shocking," Blake said tartly.

"Blake..." A vague suspicion stirred in Fiona's brain.

"Yes, sweetums?"

"You didn't by any chance call this woman, this former colleague, and ask her as a favor to you to call me, did you?"

"Absolutely not!" he retorted vehemently. "Your merits won out. Truth to tell, I'd forgotten her name entirely, until she reminded me we'd taught together back in, oh, 1982 or '83, I think. After I left Indiana. Of course I was so shell-shocked then by the nightmare with Sigmund that who could blame me for having total amnesia?"

"Well, good. I just don't want to get my hopes up and then be disappointed."

"Honey, you're a good writer. Just undiscovered. Or you were undiscovered." He snickered. "Until 'Ivory Power' catapulted you into the public eye. Fi, darling, there's nothing we dear readers enjoy more than to laugh at those who take themselves too seriously. And, sad to say, no one is quite so stuffy and pretentious as academic pricks, if you'll pardon my slight bias."

Fiona gnawed a fingernail. "Well, that worries me a bit. I mean,

'The Age of Inconsequence' is serious and not satiric. It's not at all like 'Ivory Power.' Perhaps Richey will be disappointed."

"Don't even worry. Speaking of what worry can do, I've heard that your department finally did something right and replaced your chair. And with an excellent someone. Too bad about Sigmund's health," Blake added casually.

"Blake, don't crow. We're going to get older someday, too."

An offended growl drilled into Fiona's ear. "Hey, my feelings about Sigmund have nothing to do with his age."

"Still. He is suffering for his sins."

"Thank God for karma, or, as I prefer to call it, 'the law of compensation.'" Blake yawned. "Or in the case of a narcissist like Sigmund, As ye show off, so shall ye be shown up."

Fiona felt weary of Blake's obsession with Sigmund. "You really need to get beyond this. The man's had a stroke, so leave it alone."

To her surprise, Blake assented. "You're right. Well, dear one, keep writing. And congratulations on this latest bit of good news."

"Wait. Don't hang up yet. I'm wondering how much I should go into detail in the cover letter—"

"Oh, Fi, dearest," Blake chided. "How often do I have to tell you? When the sun shines, reach for the tanning oil, then just lie back and enjoy it."

XX: Judgment

Nothing is more true for actors than the old phrase, "Know Thyself."
And, I would add one other—write it down, memorize it, sleep with it
under your pillow—it will stand you in good stead in every aspect of
your life: "What other people think of you is none of your business."

—Dennis Reagan, studio class in Acting I

Outcomes in life often appear arbitrary, as if a capricious god had tossed a coin marked triumph on one side and failure on the other. Certainly Fiona felt that way when her carefully-prepared promotion file had been casually thrown aside and yet her quickly-penned barb at the process, "Ivory Power," had led to unexpected opportunities. So it must have seemed to Edith when her two books based on the Great War, *The Marne* and *A Son at the Front*, failed in spite of the topicality of their themes. Instead, a war-weary public embraced *The Age of Innocence*, the book she told Walter Berry might be of interest to only the two of them. The book mounted the best-seller lists. After the scant earnings of the War years, Wharton welcomed the financial success of the novel. The film rights sold for an additional large sum.

The Age of Innocence was a critical success as well. Not only did reviewers compare her to Conrad, James, and Jane Austen, but in 1921, the novel garnered the Pulitzer Prize, for the first time granted to a woman. While pleased, Edith only attached significance to the Pulitzer when she discovered that she was not the first choice of the committee. Apparently, Sinclair Lewis had garnered the majority of votes for his novel *Main Street*, which some members of the committee found depressing. When he learned that the majority decision had been reversed, Lewis, outraged, congratulated Edith but vowed that if he were ever awarded the prize, he would turn it down, which he did in 1926. Lewis' generous letter in the aftermath of the Pulitzer decision initiated a lasting friendship between the two writers.

Fiona contemplated the dilemma the contested Pulitzer Prize posed for Wharton. After decades of building her reputation book by book, she had finally received a major accolade. Fiona knew how infrequently writers received the critical stamp of success. Unlike athletics, where the finish line or the score made winners and losers obvious, the writer lived in the relativistic world of opinions. And for Wharton, who had finally outlived the damning praise of being a female—and lesser—Henry James, to be placed alongside James in the pantheon of authors must have proved intensely satisfying.

The image of a Wharton mature enough to take the politics over the Pulitzer in her stride inspired Fiona. She keyed to an "outtakes" file where she had begun storing sketches for a new book on Wharton, and wrote a scene dramatizing her subject's triumph:

During a two-week trip to England in September, Edith visited her friend Robert Norton at Lamb House, where, after the death of James, he lived as resident custodian. Her love of England was so confounded by her feelings for James that in her grief, she had feared she could never visit the country again. But the lure of those in her remaining inner circle drew her back. A few years younger than Edith, the slim, handsome Norton divided his energies among public service, travel, and painting.

"Our Henry would be proud of your success," Norton said, raising a glass of champagne to Edith. "I drink to seeing you and to your Pulitzer Prize. We are at an age, dear Edith, when we must celebrate life's favors to the fullest."

*Edith joined him in the toast; champagne was the only wine that she truly en-
joyed. "I must confess I knew little about the award prior to receiving it. To me, it
seemed simply a windfall to put towards the gardens at Ste. Claire! And, then, the
political reality of how it was conferred thrust its gorgon head in my face."*

*She paused, draping the soft woolen skirt of her smart, black suit more
smoothly around her legs. As she arranged her thoughts, she touched the strands
of pearls adorning her throat—she rarely felt completely dressed without them.
"Henry would have loved the irony of it. Can't you see it, Robert? He would pon-
der, and sigh, and then say something like this: 'A prize conferred upon you,
Edith, and when you least expected it, seemingly a stroke of pure fortune. You are
grateful. Then your pleasure is diluted. You discover that the Pulitzer was mys-
teriously snatched, no one knows how, from the hands of another writer, a writer
who truly coveted—and in many ways, deserved—the award (not that you did-
n't, of course, my dear). What, indeed, can that prize be worth? Through the puzzling intrigue of its dispersal alone, a great deal, I should imagine.'*

*"Oh, who knows what he would have said," Edith said, shaking her head, "but
I am sure we should all have laughed about it a great deal. I swear he took the
same delight in the flight of his thoughts as I do a motor-flight in a new automobile!"*

*She looked fondly at the familiar furniture of the sitting room, a site of so
many pleasant conversations. Each crease in a chair, every angle of a lamp possessed an attitude of its own, and contributed to the lingering presence of its absent master. "Why don't we just call it the Virtue Prize? Poor Lewis didn't get it
because they found his wonderful book too harsh, too real, not comforting enough
to readers about their precious America. When I found out that Joseph Pulitzer
established the thing to award novels that depict 'uplifting American morals' I
was stunned."*

*Norton frowned. "Henry, I hope you can hear this. That our Edith has been
accused of upholding American morals!"*

*The two friends broke into a gale of laughter. Robert poured more champagne,
the bubbles bursting merrily to the surface of their glasses. "I would feel foolish,"
Edith said, wiping her eyes with a plain linen handkerchief, "if it meant anything. But, of course, it doesn't. When our campaign failed to get Henry the No-*

bel, my faith in the rightness of how awards are bestowed reached its nadir, and has remained there. He was passed by, yet who was more the Master of literature than he?"

The memory of this travesty flattened their spirits a bit. "Well, it proves a point doesn't it?" Norton spoke slowly. "None of it matters, really. Only the work itself, and our own satisfaction with it. And the opinion of those we respect, of course," he added, inclining his distinguished head toward Edith.

The windows let in little light on this heavy November day. Edith studied the sombre overcast skies as if they contained a portent, and then turned to her friend, her face as pensive as the weather. "It is an enormous gratification to have the approbation of one's select peers, that is true. In the beginning, I was desperate for praise. And when I would receive it from someone I admired, like James or Paul Bourget or Vernon Lee, it sent me into the clouds." She looked critically at the backs of her hands. "But now I am getting old. And I know if I don't please myself, I will not be pleased."

Norton smiled. "Yes, I think I know what you mean. I've always painted to please myself. Which is a good thing, as my work has not particularly delighted anyone else!"

"But Robert," Edith threw back her head and raised her glass. "Reputation, the critics, the constant rating of it all—it all changes with winds of taste and whim. Or politics, as we've just found out. None of it means as much as a talk with a good friend." She drank deeply from the champagne flute. "Or even a good joke. That's how I want to be remembered, in fact. As a woman who loved her friends first, a good book second, and a great joke third. And I mustn't forget dogs, who are too important to rank." She paused, and sighed. "But it's so hard to order the necessities of life, isn't it? Perhaps we should put a good joke first?"

The day after Althea Richey called, as Fiona was preparing a package to send her, Darryl phoned her office. "Fiona? I just wanted to tell you that your promotion file is being reconsidered."

A sensation of alarm, and another of suspicion, crowded into Fiona's throat. At this stage of the semester, it would take nothing less than a papal dispensation to alter the measured path of the promotion machine at a university as entrenched in protocol as AU. "But this is very irregular, isn't it? The final decisions will be announced next month—I don't see how there can be time."

Darryl cleared his throat. "In light of the change of Chair...well, it's complicated. Let me just say that Miriam has reviewed the file, called a meeting of the Executive Council, and the committee has reversed its decision and sent it to me."

"I see." Fiona stared out her office window at a flurry of cedar elm leaves cascading onto the street below. The first cold front of the year, a "blue norther" as Austinites called it, huffed its way through the city, dropping temperatures thirty degrees in a mere twenty minutes. Shifts in the Executive Council point of view seemed as random and irregular as the capricious Texas weather. Fiona found the arbitrariness of the process—one that she had once seen as important and consequential—distasteful. "I think I'd like to wait until next year, and go through the regular channels."

"Really?" Darryl sounded very surprised.

Would Darryl understand her feelings that the decision-making in her case appeared, to her, hopelessly contaminated? Perhaps not. His involvement at this stage was minimal. Calling her as her Dean, he merely served as an emissary of the department. "I've thought a lot about that decision," Fiona said dispassionately. "Naturally. And I've decided my file really wasn't ready. Sigmund was right: I need the next book and I need it published and reviewed. By next fall, I believe it will be."

Her statement was greeted with silence. "Of course it's up to you," Darryl replied slowly. "I won't pretend it hasn't gotten harder to successfully defend the College's recommendations at The Tower level, so it's preferable to have an air-tight case. But your Executive Council obviously thinks your file is strong enough..."

"Yes, and that's just grand. But I don't think it's ready. Isn't it much easier, *pro forma* in fact, if my record is beyond reproach?"

"Well, of course. Another book will make your case indisputable."

"Good." Fiona thought a moment. "I want to earn my promotion, Darryl. Not have it just given to me."

"All right. I misunderstood, I guess. I was led to believe that you felt unfairly reviewed. And, looking into the matter, your record is very strong. Teaching and service are exemplary, research certainly acceptable."

Fiona doodled, drawing a crude labyrinth of twisting angles and intertwining circles. "I did feel judged unfairly," she said. "That's one issue. I'm trying to keep that separate from the file itself. I've come to see it all differently." She thought about explaining her decision in more detail, then said simply: "My own standards are what has changed."

"Of course I respect your decision," Darryl said briskly. "And I want you to know you'll have my support next year or whenever you choose to go up for promotion."

"Thank you," Fiona said.

"All right then," Darryl said. He paused, his tone changing slightly: "Fiona, having settled this matter, I wonder if we might talk...if we might get together. Say, for a drink after work tonight?"

Fiona stopped doodling. It had been about three days since Bettina had broken with Darryl, and ever since then, she'd been expecting him to call. "What's up?" she said, stalling.

"Oh, nothing really." His voice dropped listlessly. "I've just been missing you." He added quickly: "Something's come up and I really want to talk to you about it."

While she had promised herself she wouldn't ask, Fiona blurted: "Is it about us or about Bettina?"

Darryl paused and then admitted, somewhat sheepishly: "Bettina. But it concerns us, too, of course. Fiona, you're such an insightful friend. I feel that you understand me, well, better than I do myself in a way—"

Fiona sighed. "Darryl, I miss you too. But I don't think it's a good idea to see each other right now." While she really did feel the absence of Darryl in her life, she didn't relish an evening spent endlessly processing Bettina's motives, the state of her marriage, and Darryl's feelings of rejection. Fiona could easily imagine the conversation, which she strongly suspected would lead, after several hours, precisely nowhere, except to a huge energy drain and sense of futility, at least for her. It wasn't a prospect Fiona looked forward to. "The fact is, I'm working really hard on the book." She spoke earnestly. "I need peace in my life right now. Not distraction, or confusion. I'm really enjoying the writing and it's going well. Do you understand?"

Hoarsely, he said: "Yes....Of course I do." He said quickly: "I envy you your peace." Sounding boyish and almost shy, he added: "Maybe another time?"

"Sure." She hesitated, as she mastered, with effort, her habitual impulse to ask him what was wrong, and how could she help.... "Thanks for understanding. See you soon."

That evening, Fiona joined Bettina and Miriam for dinner. Miriam volunteered to cook, and so the three friends convened at her house in Hemphill Park. They gathered in the living room where a fire snapped in tribute to the sudden onset of winter. Bettina sprawled on a rug near the flames, playing with Miriam's notoriously shy cat, Alice, who had apparently allowed Bettina into her feline inner circle. She burrowed her little tiger-striped body into the neck of Bettina's sweater and promptly fell asleep.

"Vivian will join us for dessert," Miriam said, "If that suits everyone. I told her we would be talking intense shop and so she decided to have dinner with a friend. She loathes listening to me carp about Austin U. She says it's one step below psycho-babble." Miriam laughed. "She refers to it as psycho-drool."

Bettina's eyes rolled heavenward. "Sounds familiar. Marvin has almost forbidden the subject in our house."

"Unfair," Miriam announced. "He worked there for years, but now he's above it all. I remember the many times when he once joined in—with alacrity—to our complaint sessions. Now he expects us all to abstain along with him. The fanaticism of the recovering addict. It's true that most shop talk is drivel. Which doesn't mean that I don't enjoy it immensely." She removed her glasses and polished them. She held the lenses critically up to the light, frowned, placed them back on her face. "My contacts," she explained. "They were killing me today. Damnable wind."

"But, thank God, it's cold out," Bettina almost purred, rolling her shoulders as she luxuriated in her thick, green wool sweater. Alice woke instantly and pounced on the sudden movement, engaging in a fierce tug-of-war with a loose strand dangling from the sweater's rolled collar. "If I had to wear summer clothes one more day, I think I would have rebelled and gone to work nude."

Fiona giggled at the thought. "Think of the sexual harassment suits we'd have then!"

"Please, no. I haven't the stamina," Miriam said. "Let me get some wine. And let me just turn down the sauce. It's been reducing." She patted her stomach comfortably. "Better it, than me. We're having linguini with scallops. No one is allergic, I hope?" She headed into the kitchen with a flurry of short legs.

Fiona joined Bettina by the fire. "Has Darryl called?" Fiona asked Bettina in a low voice.

Bettina rubbed Alice between her shoulder blades. The cat squinted its green eyes at her love object, and fairly vibrated. "I wouldn't know," Bettina said, her own eyes almost the same shade as Alice's. "I'm screening all of my calls. I told him not to call my house again, so if he has, he's hung up."

"What about at work?"

"I'm afraid I haven't gone in these three days, or checked voice mail. You know, I have this delicious teaching schedule this semester—only seminars on Wednesday and Thursday—so I've been working at home. And, wonder of wonder, actually getting something done."

Fiona said: "Darryl called me today. At work," she hastily added. "I'm afraid he wanted to talk about you. I begged off. Bettina, do you think he and I have any chance of staying friends after all this? I—"

Miriam returned with a bottle of wine and three glasses on a plain, wooden tray. Typically, with her sharp hearing she had deciphered the mumblings a room away. Miriam reminded Fiona of her grade-school librarian, Miss Burkett, who could detect a whisper at a hundred yards. "Darryl told me the two of you talked today," Miriam said casually, and then raised her rather bushy gray eyebrows: "And that you don't want your promotion reconsidered this year."

"Here, let me." Bettina roused herself from the floor, took the tray, and poured Pinot Grigio into all three glasses. She sat down in a chair opposite Miriam, whereupon Alice leaped into her lap. Once the cat settled down, Bettina turned an alert expression on Fiona: "Why ever not?"

Fiona plunked herself down in the old black leather recliner next to Bettina's chair and extended her legs. The chair, huge and soft, enveloped her limbs in comfort. The subject under discussion, however, was anything but comfortable. "I was incredibly crushed in September, as you both know. I felt betrayed, overlooked, *skewered* by the Executive Council."

Miriam's face turned a mottled red-and-white. "There were three votes in your favor. That verdict was not unanimous, by any means."

Fiona regarded her friend's outraged face fondly. "Oh, I know the two of you supported me. I know how these things work, though. Most people are undecided or don't really care. All it takes is one powerful person to object strongly, and suddenly, those who didn't care rise up on their hind legs and vote in the name of rigorous *standards* that a few minutes before they didn't even have. I've been there—I've seen it happen. Sigmund, most likely joined by Lester and Harley, led the charge."

Frank Harley, an almost invisible senior professor, nonetheless carried enormous weight in decision-making. He was a specialist in Renaissance literature, widely published, and his concentration on the 15th Century misled the uninitiated.

Miriam addressed the source of confusion: "Just because Frank seems engrossed in an earlier century doesn't mean he's not incredibly savvy about the politics of this one. He has an uncanny ability to gauge the level of commitment people feel to a stated position. And an equally astounding capacity to influence a shift in someone's point of view, yet allow the person to think the change was his or her own idea."

"Frank was Dent in 'Ivory Power,' wasn't he? Rarely speaks, but somehow, miraculously, shapes all decisions." Bettina squinted like a student trying to decipher a row of mathematical formulae, aware that the solution is obvious if one understands the language of the hieroglyphics. "I wish I knew how he does it."

Miriam rasped: "There's no mystery about it. He and Lester and Sigmund talk together beforehand, exchanging chits and plotting outcomes. They've decided how matters will go before the rest of us even convene. They don't trust the slow process of consensus building—too uncertain—so they have their strategy well in hand while the rest of us are just dithering around waiting for the discussion to start. Think about it: they're a voting block, and each of them has several other professors in their pockets. When is the last time they diverged on a decision in the EC? I challenge you to remember one."

"But that gets me off the subject," Fiona said. "I don't really care about that, not now. What matters is that I was totally devastated. I had given that committee power to determine the worth of my career. When it evaluated me negatively, I fell apart. After I picked up the pieces, I was horrified that I had so little faith in my abilities."

Fiona poured more wine and drank, as if to soothe the sting from the memory. "You know, I almost quit graduate school because I realized I was too dependent on my professors for validation. I took two years off and when I returned, I promised myself that I would always have a strong sense of what my work was worth, and that I would be the final judge. Well, somewhere along the way, I lost that conviction."

"Honey, don't blame yourself." Bettina leaned forward earnestly. "How can you not care about external validation? Every year you're evaluated for merit pay, Sig writes you a letter about what you're doing and not doing—mostly focused on the negative, of course. Your own opinion of your work has no weight on what you're told or what you're paid. Gradually, you wait for those letters and the slim crumbs of approval that come your way. It's insidious."

"I don't blame myself. But I've had to realize all over again what I knew as a doctoral student—I can't live that way."

Miriam stabbed a chunk of cheese with a toothpick and popped it into her mouth. She chewed vigorously. "Are you saying evaluation is, or should be, meaningless?"

"Not to everyone," Fiona said. "Of course not. But let's face it, if we look at the record of promotion and tenure, there's a certain arbitrariness to the decision-making. Merit, which is all we have control over in our own records, doesn't always win out. And, as we know, research can be trendy. Yesterday's hot post-structuralist is passé today. The only control I have is to believe in my own work, then decide for myself whether promotion is important, and if I feel ready to undergo the gauntlet of scrutiny. Obviously, I wasn't ready this fall. I'm not sure I'll care to subject myself to that again. Not only have I lost faith in the process—I may have lost interest in the machinations of the system altogether."

"It's not completely arbitrary," Bettina said dryly, disengaging Alice from the armpit of her sweater. "Nationwide, the percentage of women who are lecturers at universities is about fifty percent. But when we get to the top rank of professor, women comprise only eight percent of the total. That can't be entirely a random fact."

Miriam put her hands on the table, as if it were her podium. "Let me tell you both a story. When I first came to this university twenty-five years ago, we were a small department, I think maybe fifteen faculty.

Hard to believe, I know. Frank Harley was here, and Lester. Sigmund hadn't even arrived yet. I remember there were two people, both men, up for tenure the second year I was here. One was a protegé of Lester's, one of his students in critical theory." Miriam paused to smile faintly. "Lester had managed to find a way around the rule of not hiring our own graduates. The other young man was a fairly traditional scholar, in American literature. He had been recruited several years earlier by Donald Court, whom neither of you knew. Court had been here a long time, very senior, very established, as was Lester. Well, Court and Lester were at odds. Bitterly."

Miriam leaned back, balancing her wine glass on one stout knee. "I remember thinking that both of these men were shoo-ins for tenure. Why not? Their records were both more than adequate, and each had a powerful ally. Lester was Chair of the department then." Miriam gave each of her listeners a pointed look. "And there was the crux of the matter."

Bettina and Fiona exchanged bemused glances.

"I say that because Lester wanted to stay Chair and Court had made it known he wished to succeed him. So you can imagine what happened."

Fiona, mystified, said: "Go on. Anything could happen at this point."

Miriam tapped a finger on her scalp above one ear. "Think," she said primly. "Not anything, just one thing. One of Lester's duties as Chair was to construct each case, including requesting the letters that supported each tenure file. As you know, those letters are crucially important. Well, it turned out that the man Court had recruited, Matthew Evans, had written a book, not yet published, that Lester sent out for review to one of his closest friends, no doubt with instructions." Miriam narrowed her eyes. "Lester's friend panned the book, writing a three-page, single-spaced, scathing critique. When another faculty member protested that the letter was so wildly negative that it should be discarded and replaced, Lester replied earnestly that it was against

AAUP directives to replace a letter in a tenure file. This is true. So the letter stood.

"The long and the short of it was this: The fight between Court and Lester resulted in a divided faculty vote for Matt's promotion; the unenthusiastic endorsement further weakened his case. With the damaging letter in his file, and a lukewarm recommendation from the faculty, Matt's file never made it past the College level. The Dean's committee did not pass it on to The Tower. Matt, badly shaken, left at the end of the year for another job. Lester accomplished two things in this move: one, he signaled to Court that he had the power in the department, and two, he removed a potentially persuasive advocate for Court before he could gain influence in the department. Three years later, Court, his power base eroded, his confidence destroyed, departed also."

Bettina shuddered in spite of the warmth in the room. She held out her glass. "Could I have some more wine?" While Fiona poured, Bettina went on: "So, undoubtedly, at least for a time, Matt Evans felt his career had been destroyed, and in a way, it had absolutely nothing to do with him."

"Indeed," Miriam agreed. "He had simply walked into a political maelstrom when he came to the department. Court had recruited him in good faith, and Matt had taken the job innocently, also in good faith, but as 'Court's boy' he was a target for anyone who had a grudge against Court."

Miriam lapsed into a fond reminiscence. "Matt and I became friends during that year. Quite good ones. You see, when I came, Lester had advised me pointedly to disregard him as a worthwhile colleague: 'He's inconsequential,' Lester told me. 'Stay away from him.' Well, those two statements were sufficiently paradoxical in their import that I was immediately intrigued with Matt. If Lester wanted me to avoid him, the man had to have some very charismatic qualities. And, as I found out, Matt Evans was very consequential—an intelligent man with a keen sense of humor. I keep in touch with him still."

"And, it goes without saying—but I have to ask—that Lester's ex-student was promoted and tenured?" Fiona replaced the wine bottle on the tray and sank back into her chair.

"Oh, yes. That ex-student was Darryl Hansen." Miriam looked at the empty wine bottle in Fiona's hand. "Let me get us some more wine."

"Ugh," Fiona and Bettina blurted in unison.

"Not 'ugh,'" Miriam remarked, pausing on her way to the kitchen for a refill. "Darryl benefited, yes, but that does not make him a bad person or an undeserving one. He couldn't help it that he was Lester's pawn any more than Matt could help it that he was ammunition against Court. We can call it the vagaries of institutional power, or 'the way of the world' as Congreve so memorably anointed it. Either way, one person benefits, another perishes, but neither necessarily *deserved* their fortune. Other forces surrounding them actually turned the wheel, not their individual selves or merits. And yes, Darryl eventually became Chair and now Dean—which shows he has support, that's all, and that he understands politics. He's also a very smart man. Matt is too. But Darryl was successful, at least in this instance, while Matt was not."

Fiona remarked to Bettina in a wondering tone: "So, having my promotion overturned in my favor is just as meaningless as getting turned down was earlier."

Bettina began, "Well, I don't know if meaninglessness is even relevant—"

Miriam returned and dispatched more wine into their glasses. "No, you mustn't ascribe to these decisions any meaning, at least of worth, or you will be permanently disheartened. You must decide whether or not you want to play the game, if it—the game—has meaning for you. For it is a game. One with rules as complicated as any sport. You decide how and whether to play. If you choose to engage in the scrimmage at all, it is because winning will provide you with something useful: make you a better teacher, or scholar, or advocate. Other-wise—" She lifted both hands eloquently.

Miriam resumed her seat on the sofa, her legs in sturdy, brown corduroy pants planted firmly apart. "You have tenure, Fiona. You can go up for this promotion. Or not. Or you can choose to leave academia and do something else. I hope you stay. But it is your choice, both what to do and how it affects you."

Bettina addressed Fiona, her green eyes concerned and serious. "It is depressing, sometimes. But it's the way these decisions are made. Corporations are inherently political. None of us can change that. But you mustn't worry. You've chosen sanity. You said it earlier: you want to choose whether and when you're ready for promotion. And I suspect that your energies are focused elsewhere anyway. You're already a step, or three, ahead."

"In the game?" Fiona smiled, and attempted to tame a curl of Bettina's hair that had sprawled across her friend's forehead. "I've decided I'm a storyteller, not a game-player. I think I'll just do my work and be happy with that."

"Quite right, too," Miriam said. "Now, shall we three meet again in the dining room, over some excellent food?"

XXI: The World

"Another year and the tired heart still beats as vehemently as ever. Ah, well—in summing it all up, let me say: Love and Beauty have poured such glowing cups for me that when the last drop of the last is drained I shall go away grateful—if not satisfied. Satisfied! What a beggarly state! Who would be satisfied with being satisfied?"

—*Edith Wharton,* diary, *1933*

In the beginning of December, Fiona drove to the Grafs' home in the early evening. Bettina was throwing a party in honor of Marvin's fiftieth birthday. Fiona too had much to celebrate, including a new contract with her agent, Althea Richey. Ms. Richey, enthusiastic about *The Age of Inconsequence*, expected a quick sale. Fiona didn't feel quite so sanguine about her book's prospects. Not that she wasn't tremendously excited to have Fleming-Cone marketing her book, but she tried, these days, to temper her expectations.

"And when we've sold this and you've completed it, I think a novel about Edith Wharton would be splendid," Althea had suggested. Fiona recalled Daphne's new moon party and her vision during the group meditation. Perhaps the book she had found during her meditation was a portent of a new creative turn in her work, a sign that dreams can become concrete when made flesh by the imagination.

Fiona smiled, thinking how Miriam would scoff at such an interpretation. She might even tell Fiona it smacked of psycho-drool or just plain drivel. For Miriam, if one wanted to do something, one just did it, portents be damned.

Snarled in traffic on her way to Bettina and Marvin's, Fiona pondered how she might approach a novel about Edith Wharton. Her mind gravitated toward the setting first. Houses had played such an integral role in the writer's life, particularly The Mount, the majestic stucco mansion set in the lush green of the Berkshire hills. If one could find the true spirit of The Mount, Fiona believed, one could find the essence of Edith Wharton.

Fiona hungered to encounter Edith's home as it had been when the novelist lived there. What she wouldn't give to be able to transcend time and space and walk, unobserved, amidst the past splendors of the mansion. Stopped in the downtown labyrinth of road construction, Fiona let her mind roam…

…and enter the heart of The Mount's main floor, the library. Paneled in oak, with elaborate scrollwork, the room's built-in book-shelves rise from floor to ceiling on three sides of the room. A striped dog bed rests on a fur rug in front of the great fireplace on the south wall. Fiona's hands linger along the green French marble mantle, the pads of her fingers tapping the moist stone as if in hope that it contains a residue of what had transpired in the room.

Pausing at Edith's desk, she touches the reassuring surfaces of Edith's blotter, pen-and-ink stand, and ashtray. She picks up a pen and tests its point on her fingertip: it still produces black ink. From somewhere else in the house, a clock chimes four. Tea-time. Yet no servant appears with a tray laden with pot and cups, and no guests sit in the chairs reading, or drowsing, or talking. On impulse, Fiona presses the call-bell near the doors that opens into the drawing room. A faint chime echoes somewhere in the empty house, and then fades away. Fiona remains as alone as before.

The broad bank of doors leading to the terrace beckons to her. The panes in the French doors glint beneath their layers of dust. Fiona grasps an oval knob, and the door swings inward toward her. Outside, a grand Berkshire vista of gardens and ponds and trees greets her. Layers of lawns and hedges lead down to Laurel Pond as she looks east, and everywhere heavy foliage soothes her eyes. Above her head stretches a striped awning.

Gliding alongside the white marble railings of the balustrade, Fiona walks until she reaches one of the obelisks that signals the Palladian staircase. She stands between it and its partner and begins her descent to the lime walk and the lower gardens. After fourteen steps, she comes to the lower landing with its inviting niche and fountain. She perches on the lip of the basin of the lion's-head fountain. A thin stream of water pours from its mouth onto the stained stone below it. Already badly cracked, the friable stone seems to settle further under her weight.

After a short while, Fiona stands and continues on the gravel lime walk, moving away from the staircase. She threads her way through the gardens until she comes to Laurel Pond. She stands, her heart throbbing in her throat, taking in the pastoral scene before her and its lone human inhabitant. For nearby, under a tree, stands a wooden bench, and on the bench a woman sits smoking, her dark hair shining in the sunlight.

Impossibly, the woman, so exquisitely merging with her surroundings, as tenuous in her perfect repose as an apparition, speaks to her: "Please join me," she says and turns toward Fiona, extending a small cigarette case.

Declining the cigarette, Fiona gratefully sits down beside the woman, whose prominent jaw and nose suggest distinction and a touch of hauteur. Hatless, she wears a simple, belted, brown linen dress which drapes neatly to mid-calf, silk stockings, and brown lace-up shoes of a beautiful, supple leather. Her feet and ankles are small and well-formed and belie the thickening waist of an older fig-ure.

"I hoped you'd come," Fiona says.

"I never did come back here again, you know," the woman replies. "I couldn't bear to see what had happened to it after I'd left." She plucks a crumb of tobacco from her lower lip and flicks it into the grass. "I loved it too much."

Fiona nods, thankful the woman hasn't lived to see the mansion taken over by the Foxhollow Girls' School, her lovely guest rooms transformed into dormitories. Or its later restoration that left it what she had never intended it to be—a museum, grounds trampled by the constant traffic of heedless, rushing feet.

"Houses hold great importance for you, I know," Fiona speaks hesi-tantly. "Especially this one. I admire its design very much. I read your story about the rooms of a house and a woman's psyche."

"'The Fullness of Life'? Oh dear, I'm afraid that in my early fiction I was simply shrieking at the top of my voice." The woman purses her lips judiciously. "But you were right to think there was still an inkling of truth in it, shrieks or no."

They sit companionably for a moment. Breathing in the scent of grass and the musky smell of the pond, Fiona says, "Have you ever no-ticed that the country smells so definitely green?"

"Oh, yes. And when you love the country, you must inhale that smell, deeply, from time to time." The woman draws the last dregs from her cigarette. In a practiced movement, she taps the burning stub on the bottom of one shoe and tamps it firmly into the ground.

"So, you never came back here?" Fiona asks, although she knows the answer.

"Oh, no." She smiles tightly at Fiona. "Nor to anywhere in America. Not after 1923."

"When you went to Yale," Fiona offers. "To walk in the procession for commencement."

The woman chuckles. "I marched in the procession at an old, established university, isn't that humorous? That I, who never spent a day at any formal school, was awarded an honorary doctorate of letters? The first, I understand, Yale ever accorded a woman. I wonder what my older brothers would have thought of that. Or my father." She cradles a hand around one soft cheek; the skin pleats slightly around her fingers. "My father would have been very proud, I think, that the degree was in letters." Her voice turns wistful: "He always wanted to write, you know. And I think he would have—oh, he scratched out some verse on the odd occasion—but I think he would have written seriously, if he hadn't lived with my mother."

The displeasure in her tone leads Fiona away from discussing the dour Lucretia further. "What did you think of Yale?"

"Yale? Impressive, controlled, restricted, grand." She compresses her lips wryly. "It reminded me of places where I spent my childhood. Positively medieval."

"Mrs. Wharton..." Fiona begins, delighting in the flavor of those four syllables on her tongue.

"Oh, please call me Edith." The thin lips stretch into a smile. "Mrs. Wharton sounds so old, and so matronly. Wharton is a perfectly good name, of course, a bit more distinctive than Jones, perhaps. Although my mother thought Jones quite the most distinguished name in the world, as long as one referred to The Joneses, that is, the particular branch of the family she had married into." Fiona wonders if the rumor she has heard was true, that it was Lucretia's conspicuous prosperity which fostered the expression "keeping up with the Joneses."

"Edith," Fiona breathes the name. It is such a proud name, short but strong, graceful and proper, like its owner. The word itself prompts associations: edict, edit, educate, Fiona recites to herself.

Edith regards her, a frank twinkle in her canny blue eyes. She looks at Fiona's unfamiliar attire, at her pleated trousers, her white t-shirt, her stockingless feet, clad in black clogs. Fiona notices the pearl necklace with its six strands, the "dog collar" Edith had prized, the one she'd had to have enlarged after the Great War because she'd put on weight. The warm, creamy jewels gleam softly in the sunlight.

"Well," Edith says, "We have a little time left. Is there anything you want to ask me?"

Thoughts crowd together and tumble over each other. But then Fiona's mind goes utterly blank. "Well, yes, but I'm not sure where to begin."

Edith taps one delicate finger against the silver cigarette case; then opens it and selects another cigarette. "Beginnings—they're difficult for most people. They weren't for me. Nor endings. No, for me it was middles. I remember when I was writing The Buccaneers," she sighs softly, "which I never finished. I suppose you know that?" She observes Fiona's nod. "Yes, well, I didn't have much choice about that, did I?"

Edith deftly removes a small gold lighter from a small bag on her lap. Of some cream-colored fabric, it bears an intricate design appliquéd in seed pearls. She lights the cigarette and drops the lighter into the bag. "In any case, I do remember writing in my diary at the time: 'What is writing a novel like? The beginning: a walk in a spring wood. The middle: the Gobi desert. The end: a night with a lover.' What I would have given for one more night with a lover instead of being left stranded in the Gobi desert." Edith narrows her eyes at Fiona as smoke wafts between them. "I suppose many people wish for that very thing. There's never enough in life of satisfying love or pleasurable work. We're all too fundamentally greedy." Edith lets the sun warm her face. "I know I've always been very greedy," she says softly.

"I love that comment you made about writing," Fiona says frankly. "I mean, I know that passage. I read it."

"You read my diary?" Edith seems momentarily shocked. A hand flies to the pearls at her throat.

"Well, it's in your archive now, at Yale. And, I found it in another place, in a critical book about your fiction."

"What is the book called?" Edith bends eagerly forward. Fiona imagines she was an apt pupil.

"*A Feast of Words.*"

"Oh, that's very good. That's perfect. Whoever wrote that understood something very important about my life. I did dine at that feast, almost every day that I lived." She sighs. "I was so very lucky."

Fiona, moved, says: "That's what I wanted to ask you. Were you happy? I've often wondered...and worried...that you weren't."

Edith's eyes half-close, and their hooded, veined lids make her face look sunken and old, as a cloud passing over the sun can swiftly drain a golden field of color. "Oh, my dear, you're still too young if you ask me that. Life can be full of many things, if we're fortunate, and some are so wonderful that every fibre of your being sings in unison, and others tear at your heart until you fear you won't hold together. And many, many others are something else, pleasant, let's say, or delightful, or boring, or dull, or just commonplace, or a mixture of two or three of those. The variation is simply endless."

Pausing to draw a breath, she continues slowly: "At the end of the day, it's the fullness that matters, the texture of your life, and that you've felt it. Who can measure happiness? Not even God. Because it's all in how we remember, isn't it? And each day, our memory shifts and slips and we envision it all differently."

"So you don't regret anything?" Fiona is doubtful.

"Oh, I didn't say that." A length of ash drops from Edith's cigarette. "*Une tristesse dans l'âme close...* Do you know French?"

"I'm afraid not very well." Fiona blushes her ignorance, she with a Ph.D. who can speak nothing but English.

"'A sadness in my shut-in soul...'" Edith translates dreamily.

"You regret feeling that way?" Fiona hopes she isn't pressing too hard.

"Oh no. That feeling nourished me through regrets, I should say. I loved being alone. It was an exquisite agony, sometimes, of course. I wouldn't give up my friends for anything. But to love your own company, well, I don't need to tell you the pleasures of that." She sweeps an arm in an arc, indicates the countryside. "To be here and alone. Or to be here with the one person you can share your aloneness with." She lapses into German: "*Unvergessliche Stunden.* Unforgettable hours."

Edith disposes of her cigarette, as she has before. She draws a small pocket watch from her bag and studies it. "I'm afraid I must go."

"Oh," Fiona says. "I've disturbed your solitude. I'm so very sorry."

"Are you?" Edith says sharply. The keen eyes soften. "It isn't time that takes me away. I have all the time in the world these days." Rising, her small cloth bag in her hand, she smoothes down her dress. She holds out her hand.

Fiona grasps it, the small bones of Edith's fingers feeling very fragile in her own larger hand. Almost wistfully, Fiona asks: "Do you know me?"

The novelist studies her critically. "Let's just say that I recognize you." Edith withdraws her hand. She begins to walk toward Laurel Lake.

Fiona watches the graceful, swaying figure float along the path for a moment. All the questions she has been too tongue-tied to utter clamor now for expression. "But you mustn't go," she calls after her. "I must ask you about Ellen Olenska. Was she you? And why did you make her live the rest of her life off the page?"

Edith turns and gives Fiona a ferocious grin. "Off the page? No, in the reader's imagination perhaps, and in Newland's, but that's rather on the page, don't you agree? I think it's quite clear what her life was like. You might read the book again if you're uncertain."

"But," Fiona feels almost desperate. "But, were you Ellen?"

Edith is still smiling. "You like Ellen Olenska, I see, you might even admire her. Her life strikes you as fascinating, her mind discerning, her will complete? And, perhaps you find her a marvelous blend of American and European, truly a cosmopolitan." Edith turns away and, with the wave of a slender hand, begins to walk once more. She calls out, a lilt in her voice: "She's a favorite of mine as well. But, my dear, haven't you noticed that the best lives exist in fiction?"

Fiona turned onto the Graf's street, regretful at the fading of her vision, aware also that the novel she wished to write had taken on a new urgency. Her reverie had sparked a strong desire to bring Edith back to life on the page for readers, but most of all, for herself...

Red and blue balloons lined Avenue F for three blocks above 45th Street. As the curb in front of the Grafs' was congested with cars, Fiona parked her ancient MGB a block distant from the house. She walked briskly up the street, cradling a dozen yellow roses in her arms to shield them from the chill air. After a few steps, she noticed a thin older man, his face strained and deeply lined, walking toward her slowly but erectly. As she drew opposite him, she was startled to recognize Sigmund Froelich. She couldn't imagine that Bettina had invited him to her party, but then she recalled that Sigmund, too, lived in this neighborhood.

"Fiona." Sigmund nodded to her and then stopped.

"Sig. Hi. I'm glad to see you up and about," she said genuinely. And then added, lying flagrantly, "You're looking very well."

"Thank you." He paused, working his mouth in a sideways fashion, as if the sight of Fiona caught in his craw, a strange-tasting mouthful which he hadn't yet decided whether to swallow or spit out.

She stepped back instinctively.

"Fiona," he repeated. "I heard the Dean wanted to overturn the Department's promotion decision and that you declined." Sigmund smiled wanly. Apparently he had decided to swallow after all.

Fiona returned his stare. "Yes. It seemed as capricious as the committee's ruling the first time." In her head, she heard Edith Wharton, referring to the Pulitzer Prize, anointing it "The Virtue Prize": to the least offensive go the spoils.

Sigmund's head hunched into his shoulders. He reminded Fiona of a buzzard, until he opened his mouth. Then, he turned reptilian: "You're a fool," he hissed.

Fiona smiled and pulled a long-stemmed rose from her bouquet. She thrust it at him. Stunned, he recoiled not by pushing the offering away, but by clutching his fingers convulsively around the stem.

"You could wear it," she said. "In your teeth is best."

She hurried past him down the street. Then, she charged up the walk and through Bettina's door without knocking, almost tackling Marvin, who had spied her approach and had stationed himself at the door to greet her. She deposited the flowers into his hands and kissed him. "Happy birthday, dear Marvin. I'm sorry but there are only eleven."

His face brightened. "Because I'm too young to warrant a full dozen?"

Fiona pinched his cheek. "That's it. How did you guess?"

Fiona accompanied Marvin to the kitchen, in search of flower food and water. There she encountered Dennis and Blake, grinning foolishly at one another.

"Surprise, Fi-Fi." Blake planted a big kiss on her lips. He looked resplendent in a soft blue cashmere blazer, a creamy, slinky shirt, and gray flannel slacks. His caramel-colored hair fell boyishly over his forehead. Although he was the same age as Fiona, she noticed, with an envious pang, that he didn't look a day over thirty.

"You sly thing," she said. "You didn't tell me you were coming!"

Blake draped a long arm around Dennis' slender waist. "We're eloping. There was no time for announcements, even to such a precious one as you."

"Eloping?" Fiona said. "But isn't Dennis already married?"

Carter came around the corner, looking dapper and studious, a new pair of horn-rim glasses framing his face. "Don't listen to him. He just never gives up." The three of them huddled together, their sleek heads almost in a line. Fiona thought they made a very handsome trio. She raised her eyebrows at Marvin.

"I'm on your wave-length," he said. "I think. It's unusual, but it just might work."

Blake shook his head. "Heterosexuals have the most perverse minds. I can't understand why the media doesn't pick that fact up."

"Unself-critical," Dennis replied. "Or not enough fags and dykes in the press corps. Or they're just too dull. Take your pick."

Blake placed his mouth near Fiona's ear. She felt a rush of warm air and then the feathery touch of slightly chapped lips. "Dear one, I spoke with Althea today. She's inspired by your book. 'It's just what the publishing world is waiting for,' were her very words. Think of it, Fi: the world is calling, and it's calling you!"

Blake straightened, paused for air. "Althea is *hot* for your manuscript." He drew back his hand sharply as if it had been stung. "The phone fairly sizzled in my hand. She seems to think you'll put the joie de vivre back into literary biography and perhaps reconstellate the sun, moon, and stars as well."

Fiona found herself, as was so often the case, reduced to helpless giggles at Blake's grandiosity. Afraid to take his flagrant exaggerations seriously, and yet not wishing to offend him by dismissing his statements out of hand, she simply laughed. "That's ridiculous. She hasn't found a publisher yet."

"Oh, well, I wouldn't be too sure about that. She is, of course, close-mouthed about her work, unlike others we know." Blake grinned. He gleamed with health, a satyr unashamed of his appetites. "Any day now, my love, I think you'll be very satisfied." His lips returned to her ear. "I recommend satisfaction. It so soothes the savage breast."

"You are a silly man. Delightful, but silly." Fiona pushed him playfully away and then looked into his clear blue eyes. "You're looking awfully well these days. Really. You're an absolute advertisement for clean living, something I know you don't even believe in. How do you do it?"

Blake fingered the lapel of his cashmere jacket with languid fingers.

"You're too kind. It must be my special brew: a dollop of intelligence, a litre of wit, and a soupçon of malice." He smiled down at her modestly.

"You're impossible," Fiona said. "I must find Bettina."

"Speaking of yummy good health, the goddess is looking spectacular tonight," Blake said. "Titania amidst her revelers. She's out back."

"I'll see you later then," Fiona said. "You're welcome to stay with me, although you seem well taken care of. Dennis and I are having lunch tomorrow. I presume you'll join us?"

He bowed. "Thank you. I may turn up at your doorstep later. I miss Dynamo. And your divine self too, of course."

Fiona picked up a glass of wine as she threaded her way through the house, greeting people she knew, smiling at those she didn't. Marvin's friends, many from the Botany Department, were out in force.

As Fiona headed for the backyard, Daphne Arbor appeared in the hallway in front of her. "Oh, hello," Fiona said, startled.

Daphne took Fiona's hand and squeezed it warmly. "Surprised to see me? Vivian has the flu. I'm Miriam's 'date' for the evening." She stepped closer to Fiona, her long deep purple dress appearing to float across the floor. "Actually, I'm scheduled to do a tarot reading for Marvin in honor of his fiftieth later on this evening."

Before Fiona could reply, Daphne fixed her disconcerting eyes upon her. "So, it has been an interesting journey of late?"

"Well, yes," Fiona replied. "Rather a lot has happened."

Daphne inclined her head. "Miriam tells me that your new book will soon be published."

"I hope so. It's looking that way," Fiona said. Daphne's utterance of the magic word "published" elevated her confidence a notch.

"Oh, I think you can count on it," Daphne said softly. She stood silent a moment regarding Fiona, her flowing silver hair sparkling in the soft hallway light, her hands poised in front of her.

"Well, wonderful to see you," Fiona said, a bit unnerved. "I'm going to get a glass of wine. Can I get you anything?"

As she turned to leave, Daphne said in her warm, hoarse voice: "If I were you, I'd tell Althea to accept the third publisher's bid. Neither of the first two houses are suitable."

At the mention of publishing houses, Fiona started. "What? But I haven't had an offer—"

But Daphne was already gliding down the hallway, fingers raised in farewell.

Outside, Marvin, Bettina and Miriam sat quietly on the back deck, enjoying the bright night sky. Bettina wore one of Marvin's yellow roses in her hair.

"It was so swell of you to bring Marvin flowers," Bettina said. "For some reason, because he grows them, no one ever gives him any."

Marvin winked at Fiona. "My pleasure in receiving your roses aside, do you think my wife is hinting that she wants me to supply the house, and her, with more roses?"

Bettina took Fiona's hand. "Ignore him. It's the ravings of a near-elderly man." She wrinkled her nose impishly at Marvin. "I have just two more years to gloat, dear." To Fiona she said: "Come with me a moment, I want to show you something."

They left the deck and walked down two steps to a lower patio. "Marvin found these small statues of Venus and Cupid. What do you think?"

Fiona inspected the four-foot high concrete figurines of the goddess of love and her son. "Well, they don't really seem to be Marvin's sort of thing at all."

Bettina laughed. "They're not. He's going to use them for display in a new greenhouse. He's rented a new space and plans to open for retail by Valentine's Day. He thinks they're kitschy but have you noticed that a lot of Austin gardeners like to go over the top?"

Fiona immediately thought of the yard full of flamingos on her block. "Yes, I think he's right. So, good for him for expanding. The new website is paying off, then?"

Bettina nodded, appearing distracted. She paused, licked her lips, and said almost timidly: "Fiona...I really just wanted to talk to you alone. I owe you several large favors."

"Me?" Fiona was fascinated. "Why?"

"You saved me in a way." In the glow from the landscape lights in the yard, Bettina's freckles stood out against the deepening flush of her skin. "By keeping your head, for one thing, and not letting me lead us into something neither of us was ready to handle. You know what I mean." She paused and gave Fiona a shy smile.

Fiona nodded, feeling shy herself. Was that true? Fiona knew she hadn't had time to think at all: she had simply stepped back out of her own confusion.

Bettina was still talking. "—and I realized I needed to pay attention to what I was doing. And to Marvin. I'm very grateful."

"I love you guys," Fiona said.

Bettina grasped Fiona's wrist lightly and held it. "And I love you."

Fiona leaned forward and kissed Bettina's cheek. The two women studied their wine glasses for a moment.

Up on the deck, a friend of Marvin's was placing onto a round table a large chocolate layer cake loaded with candles. "We should go back," Fiona said, taking Bettina's arm.

"Wait," Bettina said. The group from inside the house assembled around Marvin and the cake. Someone shut off the deck lights, and Miriam stood with a huge sparkler in her hand. A ragged rendition of "Happy Birthday" ensued. Marvin inhaled deeply and blew out all of the candles. The company applauded as Miriam stuck the sparkler in the center of the cake.

In the glow of the sputtering sparkler, Marvin's large fair face looked absurdly young and happy.

Bettina said softly to Fiona. "He's such a big, lovable thing."

"Yeah," Fiona said, squeezing her friend's hand. "That makes two of you."

The sparkler fizzled out at last, leaving the deck in the near-dark, lit only by the glow of the nearly full moon. Fiona looked up, half-expecting to see a falling star. She didn't, but it didn't matter. She made a wish anyway, thinking that it isn't only in fiction that a good life can be lived.

Sources

I gratefully acknowledge the following sources, without which I could not have written this novel:

On Edith Wharton:

Edith Wharton's stories and novels in general, and in particular *The Age of Innocence, Ethan Frome, The Reef,* and *The House of Mirth;* Wharton's memoir, *A Backward Glance;* and the following works about her: *A Feast of Words: The Triumph of Edith Wharton* by Cynthia Griffin Wolff; *No Gifts From Chance: A Biography of Edith Wharton* by Shari Benstock; *Edith Wharton: A Biography* by R. W. B. Lewis; *The Letters of Edith Wharton* ed. by R.W.B. Lewis and Nancy Lewis; *The Library Chronicle of the University of Texas at Austin* (number 31, 1985); and *The Mount: Home of Edith Wharton* by Scott Marshall.

On The Tarot and Myth:

The Complete Book of Tarot by Juliet Sharman-Burke; *A Feminist Tarot: A Guide to Intrapersonal Communication* by Sally Gearhart with a little help from Susan Rennie; *Voyager Tarot: Way of the Great Oracle* by James Wanless; *Tarot: The Royal Path To Wisdom* by Joseph D. D'Agostino; and *Mythology* by Edith Hamilton.